*W*indsong

Windsong

James D. Roaché

Northwest Publishing, Inc.
Salt Lake City, Utah

Windsong

This is a work of fiction.
All characters and events portrayed in this book are fictional,
and any resemblance to real people or incidents is purely coincidental.

For information address:
Northwest Publishing,
6906 South 300 West, Salt Lake City, Utah 84047
SP 12 28 93
Christopher

PRINTING HISTORY
First Printing 1994
ISBN: 1-56901-106-0

NPI books are published by Northwest Publishing Incorporated,
6906 South 300 West, Salt Lake City, Utah 84047.
The name "NPI" and the "NPI" logo are trademarks belonging to
Northwest Publishing Incorporated.

PRINTED IN THE UNITED STATES OF AMERICA.
10 9 8 7 6 5 4 3 2 1

This book is dedicated to my wife,
Mary Louise Peters Roaché

I
Huntington

The commuter train rumbled into the station hissing and squealing and belching fumes from the large diesel engine. Train smells filled the air with its arrival. Hot grease, over-heated rubber, stale air from the brake line and other unnameable and yet familiar scents drifted across the platform.

Walter Marshall stepped carefully, avoiding the ice. Salt crunched underfoot where it had been spread to melt the light snow from the night before. Small patches of sharp crust and frozen slush remained where the salt missed and a slip was assured for the unwary. He climbed aboard to take the same seat in the same commuter coach, or one identical, as he had for the past twenty-five years. The eight forty-seven was far less crowded than the earlier ones. There were few clerks or carpenters who could afford the luxury of beginning their business day at ten o'clock in the morning.

He took his overcoat and folded it, placing coat, hat, scarf and gloves in the overhead luggage compartment. He sat down in an aisle seat next to a man hidden by an open *Newsday*.

"Hello Bud," Walter said, placing his attaché case under his seat. Bud lowered his newspaper. Bud, like Walter, wore an expensive business suit, was graying at the temples, and wore gold-rimmed glasses. He radiated success, from manicured finger tips to polished, imported Italian shoes. A large diamond ring gleamed as he folded the newspaper and a Rolex watch peeked from beneath a gold-studded cuff. For years he and Walter had ridden on the same car into the city each morning. They knew much about each other but through all these years had never met socially. Bud lived in another township and three stops further east.

"Good morning, Walter. Looks like more snow." Bud glanced out the dirty window at gray skies filtering a dim light on the barren, ice-covered trees and soot-covered snow blanketed houses and lawns. By mid-March there was nothing enchanting about the winter scene. Too many months of short, cold days and dreary skies had been endured for suburban snowscapes to be appreciated.

"Yeah, a mess." Walter agreed.

The train gained momentum as it pulled away from the station only to break in two or three minutes to stop at the next station. Bud was reading his paper and Walter reached under the seat to retrieve some paperwork from the office to pass the time until the train reached Penn Station. He opened the case, thumbed through the few papers inside, and decided there was nothing worth bothering with. He looked across Bud's newspaper and out the window at the too familiar dreary morning and passing suburbia. Bud was flipping through his newspaper so Walter spoke, knowing that he wasn't interrupting.

"Haven't seen you around for awhile. Been on vacation?" Walter asked.

Bud folded his paper and stuffed it between the seat handle and the wall of the car, leaving it for any passenger who might want to read it later in the day.

"I wish," Bud said grimly. "Had a triple by-pass." He tapped his silk tie near his heart. "The old ticker was giving out. Fats and cholesterol and all that. The plumbing was getting all clogged up. They took a chunk of vein out of my leg and by-passed what was clogging." Bud made a face of disgust. "Quite an experience. I've never had a sick day in my life. Maybe a cold or two, but nothing serious. Then one day a little pain in my chest and a visit to the doctor, just to make sure everything is okay. And bang! The world's changed. Pain in the ass operation, a diet that doesn't let me eat anything I like, supposedly no cigars, exercises, and a lot of other rigmarole." He pursed his lips, shaking his head. "Things can happen kind of quick sometimes."

He glanced out of the train window for a few seconds and watched the passing vista and then back at Walter. He sighed. "I wish I could take a vacation. The Caribbean and some sun would be nice, but what with having to take time off for the operation and all, no way. I'm needed at the office now to clean up the pile of work that accumulated."

"Sorry to hear about it. How are you feeling now?" Walter asked.

"Better. Much better really. It just came as a bit of a shock. Heart trouble. Never thought it could happen to me. From what I've learned this is pretty common. Our diet and life-styles and such. When's the last time you had a physical?"

"It's been awhile," Walter admitted.

"Maybe you ought to have a check-up. They might catch something before it gets too far along. Maybe if I'd done that… But who could expect something like this? Like I said, I'd never been sick a day in my life."

"It happens," Walter said. Yes, it happens. It had happened to his wife Laura but she hadn't died suddenly. First it was finding a lump, and then two long years to waste away to skin and bones. And finally death. Two years of medical treatment and misery. He forced the thought out of his mind.

"I haven't seen Dave Meadows. He usually gets on with you." Bud looked around the car. Usually the same people rode the same train every day.

"Dead," was all Walter said.

"Jesus," Bud half whispered. "He was a young man. In his early sixties wasn't he?"

Walter nodded.

"How'd he die?"

Heart attack, was what Walter heard. But he wasn't going to tell Bud that. He wasn't sure anyway. No, it wouldn't make Bud's day any brighter. And Walter's morning wasn't starting very well either. "I'm not sure," he said. "It happened suddenly. I didn't hear about it until a week or so later."

"Boy." Bud stared off into space.

The rest of the morning did not help improve Walter's mood. There were the normal Friday morning meetings with clients, phone calls, and going over contracts and agreements, and then lunch. The elegant dining room at Wheel, Kedder and Matthews, Partners at Law was one of the perks Walter enjoyed as an Associate Partner. Junior Partners also dined there along with the five full Partners who reigned over the law firm. He joined the one hundred-twenty-year-old renowned New York law partnership soon after passing the bar and never regretted that decision. He worked his way toward the top and at fifty-nine he was sure he would become a full partner before his sixty-second birthday. All the signs were there for that great leap, both in financial rewards and prestige. His client list slowly changed so he dealt with only the biggest names and the corporations which paid the highest fees. The surer sign of his status and his continued rise in the firm was more subtle but perhaps a more accurate gauge of his position in the highly competitive atmosphere among the associate partners. Walter's efficient and dependable secretary for the past fifteen years usually had full time use of an assistant from the secretarial pool. Myra had reached almost equal status with the secretaries of the full partners.

Walter worked hard to reach the position he now held. Long hours, not so much now but a great deal in the earlier years, a gift for perceiving the nuances and accepted quirks in the law, and precise workmanship on contracts and opinions earned him the respect of the partners and clients. He was a likeable man, easygoing and considerate. All the ingredients were there to reach the top in his field of corporate law. And yet, lately something had been missing. The drive was gone. The goals, now so reachable, weren't as important as they had been. He was making more money than he needed and a great increase in income would make little difference. The prestige of reaching the pinnacle of achievement no longer glittered for him. Laura's lingering, painful death almost exhausted him.

Now, two years later, he had yet to recoup his motivation. Strangely, his loss of competitiveness didn't hurt him in the eyes of the Partners who would select him. He took more time now on each case and while dealing with a client. At this point in his career it was exactly what he should be doing. Walter was not only an excellent attorney but also a meticulous one.

He joined Bill Grady, also an Associate Partner. Walter didn't notice the floral center piece nor the crystal goblets and the finest of silverware and china. When he was promoted from one of the many staff lawyers and became a junior partner, some twenty years earlier, he had been in awe of this room. For him it represented the inner sanctum, not only a badge of success but the opportunity to touch history. Supreme Court Justices came here to lunch as guests. Ex-presidents, governors, cabinet members from both parties could be seen, met, and spoken to. Of course, not everyone with high office or great wealth was invited. They had to be conservative, preferably with old family ties, and in tune with traditionalist ideas of American society as those ideas were interpreted by the partners in order to qualify for an invitation. After Walter became a Junior Partner he used to go home and tell Laura who he saw and met that day and what they said and did and she would be impressed with his dealings with the "Great Powers" as she called them; it was another feather in his cap in her eyes.

Now, as he greeted Bill Grady and sat on a high-backed, hand-carved chair, he didn't take notice of who else might be in the room. The familiar had become commonplace. The waiter came and asked if Walter would like roast beef or swordfish and he chose the beef knowing it would be prepared the way he preferred it. Lunch had become Walter's main meal since he had become a widower. He didn't enjoy eating in restaurants and was only a fair cook. Washing dishes and pots, even with the automatic dishwasher, was a chore he did grudgingly and he refused to leave dirty dishes in the sink for the cleaning woman.

The meal was quickly served and as he reached for the salt shaker, as was his habit, he stopped in mid-motion. The meal was exactly what he expected and thought he wanted. Medium rare prime beef with mushrooms, baked potato with butter, broccoli covered with cheese sauce, and a garland of parsley. It was one of his favorite meals but now it made him think of Bud Hickson and their conversation on the train that morning. Cholesterol. The marbled meat had a slim margin of sweet fat, butter oozed on the sliced potato, and the thick golden sauce on the broccoli made him think of his arteries. He could smell the butter steaming from the mushrooms that covered his steak. He sliced the tender meat and bit into its juicy flavor. As he chewed he thought of the expression on Bud Hickson's face when Walter told him that Dave Meadows had died. Bud had been more annoyed than frightened about his heart problems up to that point. Now, as Walter thought about it, he knew what had flashed behind Bud's eyes. Fear. The realization that sudden death could strike without warning. As Walter swallowed the first bite, it didn't taste as good as it used to.

"What's the matter? Did you get a bad piece of meat?" Bill asked, taking a sip of the light wine that he always had with his lunch.

Walter shook his head with a grunt. "No, the meat is fine," he said, reaching for his salad, the meal no longer appetizing.

"By the look on your face it was like you had bit into an old shoe," Bill said.

"I was thinking of a friend. Heart trouble. And another who died recently."

"Pleasant thoughts for lunch." Bill leaned back, his ample belly a handy rest for folded hands, and appraised Walter. Bill was four years Walter's junior, in age, in length of service with the firm, and in approximate promotion dates. In many ways Walter had been his mentor and though they were both associate partners vying for extremely limited partnerships, they were friends. Bill owed a lot to Walter for much of his success. He wanted to be selected as a partner, but if Walter were selected before he was, well, he would be glad for him.

"Is anything wrong? Has your health been giving you trouble?" Bill asked, concerned.

"No, nothing like that. I'm fine. 'Fit as a fiddle' as the old saying goes. Just one of those days." Walter picked at his salad.

"Yeah, I get that feeling sometimes myself this time of year. Winter is too damn long. That's why I take a short vacation in February. Go to the Bahamas. It helps break up the winter. I get cabin fever. It's dark when I leave the house in the morning and dark when I return home in the evening. I sometimes wonder if I did the right thing buying that place in Connecticut. It's a long commute. But, you can't have everything. It's nice up there the rest of the year."

"Good afternoon, gentlemen," Tom Watson said as he allowed a waiter to seat him.

"Hello, Tom," Walter greeted.

"Good afternoon, Tom," Bill said, sitting up and becoming attentive. Tom Watson was seventy-six years old, had a mind as sharp as a razor, and was the first among equals of the five reigning partners. The young, and some not so young, staff lawyers gave him as much space as they could. They tried to stay invisible when he was around. Tom, Mr. Watson to them, could flip through a brief or scan a contract and spot any errors or omissions as though he knew they would be there before he looked. He would then go step by step through the document asking questions, sounding like a prosecutor during cross examination, and rattling any lawyer whose sloppy work he was inspecting. Thomas Watson was a tough taskmaster and many a grown man left his office near tears. His voice could cut like a knife and he gave compliments rarely. He expected excellence at all times, demanded it, but those few who did receive his notice for exemplary work sooner or later found their way to a junior partnership and a seat in this dining room. Not many made it.

"I don't understand it. The kids today," Tom said, without preamble, making a face as though he too had bitten into something sour as he picked at a bowl of sliced fresh fruit another waiter brought him as soon as he was seated. "Young people don't want to work, they don't want to earn what they get. They want it all now, not later after they've invested a little time and energy. I don't know if the country's going to survive with the kids coming out of colleges today. It's a shame, a real shame."

"What's up, Tom?" Walter asked, expecting to hear the story of Thomas Watson's youth again, perhaps for the hundredth time, about walking five miles to school in the snow and working his way through college and law school with honors and supporting his younger brothers and sisters, and pulling himself up by the boot straps, and on and on about the poor kid that struggled, worked hard, and succeeded in a tough world. The story contained everything except a log cabin. And it was true, every bit of it.

Walter and Bill exchanged glances trying not to smile. They had heard the story so many times that it was an inside joke.

"I have an intern working for me, a good kid and smart as a whip, and I asked him this morning if he were interested in joining the firm after graduation." Tom took another mouthful of fruit. Walter and Bill were both listening attentively. An offer from Tom Watson was an open invitation, and someone selected by him had a better than fair chance at advancement.

"Well, what do you think his reply was?" Tom asked, and went on, not expecting an answer. "He said he hadn't really studied our retirement plan. Can you believe that? Our retirement plan! Now here's a kid just starting out, got the world by the balls, and his first thought is about retiring. Jesus! He's at the beginning of his career, has his whole life ahead of him, and he's already concerned with sitting on his ass in some retirement village in Florida."

Tom finished his fruit and then tasted a cottage cheese salad. Walter and Bill looked at each other again. It was unusual for Tom Watson to get upset about an intern, or a staff lawyer for that matter. This intern must have been something special. No matter how bright and able he was, there no longer was any chance that he would be hired at Wheel, Kedder and Matthews. Walter and Bill had heard Tom slam the door.

"I wonder what I would do if I could do it all over again," Tom mused, absently stirring his cottage cheese with a fork. "They say youth is wasted on the young and I'm beginning to believe it. They squander their time. There's so much to do and a big, beautiful world out there. I'm not sure I would have changed anything I've done with my life but I sure would think long and hard about it." Tom looked up and grinned. "Listen to me. I must be getting old. I sound maudlin as hell."

"Bascomb doesn't think you're over the hill. You tore them up in court last week," Bill said. Bascomb Corporation had sued one of their clients and after negotiations and attempts at compromise failed they did what this law firm and most good law firms try not to do. They went to trial. No matter how strong a case nor how good a law firm, the outcome of a trial is never assured. Tom represented their client in court and won. Bascomb had sued but they lost and had to pay substantial penalties for bringing suit.

"Yes, that was fun." The pleasure of victory showed on Tom's face. "I wonder if I shouldn't have been a trial lawyer. There's no money in it of course, but I sure enjoy doing battle in court. It's a challenge every time. I think if I were Bryan, that's the intern I was telling you about, I would try it for a little while."

"It's good to see you still like to do battle." Walter was glad to see the twinkle in Tom's eye. Besides respecting Tom as a superb lawyer and a superior at the firm, Walter genuinely liked him. There was something in Walter's tone that caught Tom's ear and he looked at him, pondering his friend for a moment.

"How old are you? Not yet sixty are you?"

"Sixty in a couple of weeks. Why? Are you planning that retirement village in Florida for me?" Walter asked with a chuckle.

"Hmmm." Tom mused. "You're still a young man. I'm seventy-six. That's more than sixteen years. A lot can be accomplished in sixteen years."

Walter didn't know what to say and let it pass. They finished their lunch and left for their respective offices not noticing the concealed glances from the junior lawyers still at lunch.

Walter had a call coming in as he entered his secretary's outer office. "It's your daughter," Myra said questioningly, hand covering the telephone's mouthpiece.

"I'll take it," he said, extending his hand for the phone. "Hi, darling. What's up?"

"Oh, hi, Daddy. I didn't know if I was going to be able to catch you or not. I wanted to invite you to dinner Sunday, if you can make it," Lynda said, her voice still sounding like a young girl.

"What's the matter, somebody cancel and you need me as a fill-in?" Two months before Lynda had invited him to a dinner given for her husband's co-workers, fellow doctors, so that she could 'balance out' the seating arrangements. Walter had been 'balanced' with a newly-divorced psychiatrist who worked at the Veterans' Hospital with his son-in-law George, and Dr. Margaret Hatcher had been a handful. Margaret came on to him with all the subtlety of a tank in heated battle. Apparently being single was not Margaret's style and Walter was an eligible widower. By the strained looks Lynda gave him during the evening he knew he had not been setup for match-making and the next day Lynda had called him and apologized profusely. In a way it was flattering to be the recipient of so much attention by a much younger woman. But Walter wasn't looking for a mate, at least not one who managed to pry more personal financial information out of him than the Internal Revenue Service knew.

"Oh, Daddy. You're not still mad, are you?"

Walter smiled. "Mad? Why should I be mad? In fact I was thinking of getting the lady's phone number from you. She seemed rather interested."

"I'd say she was. Especially your bank book. You're not really interested in her are you?"

He could hear Lynda's protective concern. His daughter was trying to shield him from a prospective gold digger.

"What's wrong? Wouldn't she do as your step-mother?" He asked innocently.

"Oh Dad, please. I said I was sorry, didn't I?"

"Yes you did and I'm only pulling your leg. So, what's this dinner thing?"

"It's only us. You, me, George and the kids. I thought you might like to get out of the house for awhile. I'm making roast duck. That's if you don't have other plans."

"Plans? No, no other plans. Sure, darling, I'd love to come over. What time?" Walter's plans usually included a book or perhaps watching a little television if there was anything worth watching, which was rarely.

"Around two? Come early if you can. Georgie and Tracy would love to spend some time with you."

"I'll be there. Thanks for the invite, honey. Is there anything I can bring?"

"No. Everything's here. And please don't bring any more toys. I don't have space to put them."

"Okay. I'll see you Sunday. Bye-bye," Walter said, handing the phone back to Myra and thinking of which toys he might buy for his grandchildren.

II
Northport

Spring was officially a few days away but it felt like mid-May as Walter drove from his house on the north shore of Long Island to Northport, a distance of twenty miles. The road twisted and turned, passing through villages where once tall whaling ships sailed. Now the towns serviced different intermittent visitors, summer tourists, and the surrounding hills were becoming filled with middle-class commuters' homes half hidden by winter-barren trees. Snow still lingered on the north-facing slopes where the sun couldn't reach and in the shade of the few large evergreens which hadn't felt the bite of the developers' axe.

He drove with windows down and for a change not annoyed by the slow moving traffic. The breeze carried the smell of damp earth and pine and overhead a clear blue sky and a few puffy white clouds announced spring was near. He hummed along with the big Lincoln's radio, enjoying the freedom of fresh air and sunshine after months of dreary weather. He passed through the Village of Northport and for the first time noticed the Veteran's Hospital just beyond.

Leafless oak and maple trees allowed glimpses of massive brick buildings encircled by snow-patched hills. Walter's son-in-law, George, worked there caring for the insane. Dr. George Evans was a psychiatrist and fit the role perfectly. He had a full, short beard, smoked a pipe, had a penchant for smoking jackets with leather at the elbows, and spoke in a slow, assured manner as one who is fully in control. He appeared the archetypal Doctor Freud. George was nearly ten years older than Lynda and at times Walter could sense more of a father-daughter relationship than that of husband-wife. When he mentioned this to his wife Laura she laughed and told him it was his resentment toward George for taking his daughter from him. He had laughed and agreed but there was still something about George that could be unnerving. George never seemed to be able to stop being Dr. Evans. When Walter spoke to him, Walter had the feeling whatever he was saying was being deciphered and categorized for motivation and appropriate behavior. Laura hadn't seen George the same way and Lynda was happy in her marriage so he mentally shrugged and put it aside as his own personal quirk at having a psychiatrist as a son-in-law.

Lynda and the children were playing on the front lawn as Walter pulled into the driveway. The children screeched in delight on seeing him and came running to get hugged and badger him for the presents he usually brought.

"Hi, Dad," Lynda said, pulling the two squealing children free from tight grips around his neck.

"Hello, beautiful. How's my favorite daughter?" Walter asked as he accepted a quick kiss on the cheek. He teased Tracy and Georgie by shaking his car keys, a game he played when he had new toys in the trunk. They jumped to grab the keys as he jiggled them overhead. Tracy was two and was quickly bumped to the soggy ground by her bigger, four-year-old brother. Lynda groaned on seeing mud on Tracy's new dress worn especially for Granddaddy's visit.

"Look at you!" Lynda admonished. "Your favorite daughter is going to murder her two favorite children *and* their grandfather. I thought you said you weren't going to bring anymore toys. All the closets are packed. I'm tired of picking them up."

"No, *you* said I wasn't bringing any more toys. I never said that. I only said yes I was coming to dinner," Walter said with a wink, opening the trunk. They grabbed the boxes and immediately began tearing the packages apart. He had bought a talking doll for Tracy and a large fire truck for Georgie. Lynda rolled her eyes in a display of frustration but he knew that she enjoyed this ritual almost as much as the children did.

"Come on in everybody." Lynda picked up shreds of cartons off winter-scraggly grass. "Dinner's ready and I'm going to have to change clothes on these two."

George was in the living room with the television on, a book in one hand and a smoldering pipe in the other. Although it was Sunday, he was wearing a tie and one of his tweed jackets. Walter wondered if he ever truly relaxed. He rose to shake his father-in-law's hand, a pleasant smile his greeting.

"Hello, George. How's it been?" Walter plopped on an overstuffed, wing-backed chair and lit a cigarette. The furniture Lynda and George had furnished the house with reminded him of Victorian England. The windows were heavily draped, the furniture turn-of-the-century, and "collectibles" as Lynda called them crowding all available shelf space. His grandmother had a room like this.

As was his custom, George paused before answering. Even a "How are you?" seemed to require a certain amount of analysis.

"Fine. And yourself?" George asked, his voice modulating around his pipe.

"Good. It's a lovely day. It feels like spring."

George nodded sagely. "I hope it is an early spring. The

snow has been terrible this year. Getting back and forth to the hospital on these hills is a chore. Twice I was stuck there overnight. The roads were so bad there was no way to get in or out."

The children came bounding in and both had to sit on Walter's lap, each trying to get and keep his attention. It was a relief when Lynda came in and announced that dinner was ready. For some reason she had come to the conclusion that Long Island Duck was his favorite meal and she usually prepared it when he came over for dinner. He never tried to dissuade her but duck was never his first choice among meals. A thick steak was his preference but Lynda derived such pleasure in preparing everything just so for him he didn't have the heart to tell her that after six years of duck he would rather have a hot dog.

Lynda had been eight months pregnant with Tracy when her mother had died. She took it hard even though they all knew the end was near. Lynda was close to her mother even after her marriage to George. She would call daily and come visit with young Georgie at least twice a week while her husband and Walter were at work. Lynda felt a need to help fill the vacancy left by her mother's death. Even after Tracy's birth she tried to care for him while taking care of her own family. After a couple of months he hired a cleaning woman, told Lynda he preferred to prepare his own meals, and finally got her to stop hovering over him like a protective nanny.

With his son Harold it had been different. Harold left to go to Yale at eighteen and had been on his own ever since. They saw him for holidays and during the summers, less often while he was in law school. He moved to an apartment on the Upper East Side after graduation and his visits were rare. He was four years older than Lynda and married to a tall, thin, solemn-faced vegetarian whose main interest in life seemed to be saving the planet from mankind. They had a three-year-old son, Nathan, who Walter had seen a half dozen times. Harold had gone out on his own and stayed there.

His mother's death affected Harold the least. He visited her in the hospital, saw the suffering she was going through, and was relieved when it was all over. He attended the funeral, hugged his father and sister, and Walter hadn't seen him since. Winnifer, his wife, sent Walter birthday cards and holiday cards all with the theme of saving mother earth, and they kept to themselves. He didn't dwell on it, but he had been surprised by the seemly indifference of his son. Harold lived in his own world and once he no longer needed financial support he cut most of the ties to his family.

The conversation at the dinner table was light, most of the attention going to the children as they squirmed and played in the restrictive atmosphere of a long afternoon dinner. He always enjoyed these visits but this day he felt as the children did. It was too pretty a day to be in the confines of a stuffy house. Georgie and Tracy scampered to the fenced back yard as soon as allowed to leave the table. Walter told a little lie of having some work at home he needed to get to and after a brandy and good-byes he too escaped into the late afternoon sunshine. He hadn't intended on stopping but found he was out of cigarettes, so he turned down Main Street in Northport. During the summer this street would be bustling on a weekend afternoon but it was late winter and though the weather was fair the stores were closed and the streets were empty. He found a delicatessen near the end of the street and made his purchase. He lit a cigarette and looked across an empty parking lot to the docks and pier jutting into a protected harbor. The slanting sunshine softened colors of the picturesque scene and the southerly breeze tugged him in that direction. He strolled to the pier. Several fishing boats were tied at the dock. Nets hung from raised steel arms at midship, looking like wings waiting to be extended for flight. He remembered days spent fishing with his son, and then daughter as she grew, and watching trawlers slowly drag their nets across the Long Island Sound. Most of the boats needed painting and were scarred from the harsh use during the stormy winter. With the warm weather would come fresh paint and the boats would change from haggard workhorses to dainty butterflies with names like *Miss Ann* and *Lucky Lady II* and *Maria IV*.

At the end of the pier stood a large motor yacht freshly painted and sparkling in the softening light of the setting sun. The coolness of the water drifted up to him as soon as he stepped off land and onto the heavy planks of the dock. Small waves washed against the pilings but the yacht stood steady against her mooring lines. Small American flags flapped at both bow and transom, snapping as a rising wind veered to the west. Fresh varnish glistened on handrail and window casings and white paint glowed pink from reflected light. He slowly walked from the fantail to the pilothouse, the distance of the boat's deck from the pier diminishing to inches as he reached the pilothouse doorway. A "For Sale" sign was taped to the window of the pilothouse door, the handrail left lowered at this point so that anyone interested could step aboard. He hesitated. Curiosity, the perfect late afternoon setting, boredom and a dull evening looming, the beauty of *Windsong*, all drew him to step aboard and look around.

"Ahoy! Is anyone aboard?" he yelled, feeling conspicuous. His voice drifted across the protected cove. Two gulls took flight at the sudden intrusion. No movement or recognition came from his inquiry. Waves washed against pilings and hull and flags fluttered in the wind. He looked around at the empty pier and dock. He was sure the sign and lowered handrail were an open invitation and he would not be trespassing. He yelled one more loud "Ahoy" and stepped aboard.

The deck was steady under his feet. There was imperceptible movement of *Windsong*, but not the slightest of list by Walter's weight. She sure wasn't like the smaller boats he was used to. She was big, heavy and sturdy, much larger than anything he'd ever been on. Small waves from the bay washed against her hull but *Windsong* remained steady as a rock. He looked fore and aft along the hardwood deck. He guessed she was about eighty feet in length, and looking through open pilothouse doors, he estimated she had a beam of sixteen feet or so. She was massive, truly a house on water. A ladder gave access to the flybridge and upper deck. He thought of himself up there on the flybridge, wind in his face, bow cutting white spray through the sea, as he steered this powerful motor yacht to some enchanted island. He smiled to himself. It was an old dream he'd had a long, long time ago. He hadn't thought of it in years.

He went into the pilothouse, still feeling like an interloper, and called "Ahoy" one more time. He knew there would be no answer. The boat just felt empty, waiting. The large windows of the pilothouse gave a view of the long foredeck and the sloping hills to the harbor entrance. He could visualize dockside lines being cast off with yells of good-bye and smiling, waving well-wishers, powerful engines vibrating as he gained way, and the bow pulpit swinging to the center of the harbor entrance as he headed *Windsong* to sea. He chuckled. A boyhood dream and he wasn't a boy anymore. The chuckle stopped. No, he wasn't a boy any longer and he was beginning to feel like an old man. Was an old man, maybe. He let out a long sigh. The newly painted foredeck glistened, reflecting the setting sun's pale rays. The small waves in the harbor sparkled as they swept across his view. The deep harbor entrance created long ago by retreating glaciers beckoned the little boy seaman in him.

Walter grabbed the spokes of the steering wheel and rubbed the smooth, varnished wood surface. This wasn't like the new, stainless wheels they made today. Columbus or Nelson would have been comfortable holding this. A large compass stood in its binnacle. NNE it read. Sailing due north would take him cleanly out of the harbor, he judged. Two transceiver radios were attached to the bulkhead at eye level, the microphones on curled cords waiting for instant use. A depth sounder was off to the right. He hesitated, then turned it on, curiosity overcoming his normal shyness. A small, red light came on and in a few seconds, a nine appeared. Walter looked closely. The setting was in feet, not in fathoms. So, he had nine feet under the keel. Plenty deep no matter what the tide. He turned off the depth sounder and looked around the spacious pilothouse.

A companionway on the starboard side led to a lower deck and aft was a door leading into the greatroom at deck level. There was a galley to his right, electric stove, refrigerator/freezer, sink and horseshoe counter forming an alcove. He walked past and stood in the center of the greatroom. Wicker chairs gave the atmosphere of the 1920s and '30s when this room, it was just too big to be called a cabin, probably held thirty or forty guests to be served by white-jacketed stewards. It was eerie, like something taken from a time capsule.

Spiraling steps led to two bedrooms below and a full bath. Walter looked at the bath tub. That was something one didn't see very often on a boat. He went back on deck and walked the covered afterdeck, hand sliding along the newly varnished handrail, and looked over the side at the transom. The name *Windsong* was painted bright gold on dark mahogany with South Hampton in smaller lettering below as the ship's port of call. He watched the deep-green wavelets ripple past, eight feet separating the deck from the water. He moved along the curved handrail, the deck solid under his feet, a light breeze tugging at his jacket.

The ladder from the pilothouse led forward to a lounge that

grew narrower toward the bow. This was the one room where being on a boat was manifest. The boat shaped the room as it became narrower toward the bow. Two large portholes on each bulkhead and lapping waves against the bow brought with them the sensations of being confined in something afloat. Aft of the lounge was the stateroom, the largest of the bedrooms, another full bath, and beyond, the engine room. Two massive diesel engines sat silently, waiting for the turn of a switch and the push of a throttle to command them to propel *Windsong* to whatever destination the helmsman wished. Diesel and oil fumes filled the compartment. These big diesels were workhorses. They'd last forever if cared for. For some reason, he wanted to touch them, feel them, get a sense of their power, but a sheen of grease and oil held him back. Too messy.

He went up to the pilothouse and stood before the wheel one more time. The sun had set, pink streaks reaching to light and then dark blue sky. The air had turned cooler, the breeze cold on his neck and cheek, a reminder it was still winter and at these latitudes false spring could soon be followed by a wintery snow storm. He disembarked and stood on the pier. She was beautiful in the fading light. A millionaire's boat. Nothing he could afford, or at least used to not be able to afford. And she certainly wasn't new anymore. Not by a long shot. But maybe that's what made her so endearing. She had a history. She was a classic. On the spur of the moment he took out his wallet and copied the phone number printed on the For Sale sign. He doubted he would ever call, but he was curious. What would a boat like this cost?

He glanced back at *Windsong* before he got into his car. In the dwindling light from the west and the hooded lightposts of the pier, *Windsong* glowed white against the black water beyond. Dark hills fell to water's edge at the harbor's entrance where the Long Island Sound began and a doorway to all the lands the oceans of the world touched. *Windsong*, almost a pale ghost ship in the fading light, waited patiently for a captain to take her beyond that horizon to all those colorful ports.

Walter smiled as he slipped behind the wheel. He was being a silly old fool dreaming boys' dreams again. He started the engine and began driving up Northport's Main Street. He noticed most of the stores and shops had the air of old Northport with its heritage as a tallships' whaling center. For the tourist trade, of course.

The image of *Windsong* kept coming back as he drove through heavy traffic toward Huntington and home.

III
Windsong

It was two days before Walter called about the boat. On Monday he thought about *Windsong* several times, his mind drifting out of the office and to the water at Northport, but each time he stopped his daydreams and forced himself back to work. He had dreamed about *Windsong* the night before, or at least he may have dreamed of her. He awoke with a vague memory of sun and foaming sea, blue skies and puffy white clouds, wind and salt air. *Windsong* was not a clear part of the dream, if that was what it was, but he knew, or felt, she was part of what it was all about.

Perhaps it was the second night's dream that caused him to pick up the phone not long after arriving at work. It was a bad dream, one he had several times before, and he woke shaken and depressed. It was about his wife, Laura. She was a skeleton at the end, hardly recognizable except for her lovely, wavy black hair and pale green eyes. The pleading in those eyes when she looked at him during those last few weeks, and her request for him to find a way to end it, end the pain and suffering and lingering torture, would be with him to his grave. He held a mental picture of Laura lying in that hospital bed, sheet up to her chin, yellow skin taut against protruding bones and eyes pleading for help.

He called Tuesday morning and reached a boatyard in Northport and the man who answered said he would pass his inquiry to the owner. It was late afternoon before the owner, Mr. Dudley Shoemaker, returned his call. Dudley made a living in what some economists call the gray economy. He had no credit rating, neither good nor bad, since he lived in the world of cash and carry. He was diligent in filing an income tax form each year, having a not so paranoid fear of being called in for an IRS review. Each year he claimed just enough income so his income tax bill was zero. He showed sufficient income so that he could explain how he managed to buy groceries and pay for home utilities if called to do so.

At his father's death Dudley inherited a semi-dilapidated frame house near the water in Northport. The area had become prime property and the surrounding homes were owned by those from the city with newly acquired wealth. In the past few years Northport had become upper-income suburbia. Dudley's one concession to the changing neighborhood was to allow the trees, bushes and weeds in the front and sides of his rather large lot to become overgrown and hide his house from view. His driveway was a dark tunnel through overhanging tree limbs and crowding shrubbery. This was a good representation of how Dudley also made his living. Almost nothing could be seen from outside, whether by the IRS or anyone else.

Banks were anathema to him. Long forms, checks into his financial history, references, or having to explain to anyone how he earned a living, ran totally against the grain. He had no store, office, business phone or anything else that might give some clue as to what he did. He did have business cards, in fact several different cards giving various occupations depending on a given situation, and a post office box. His business dealings were done in person or through the mail. The number of his unlisted telephone at home was known by a very select few.

In the Town of Northport Dudley Shoemaker was considered the town character, a holdover from the historic town's past, and tolerated by old and new residents alike. He was a colorful character but one to be wary of in any business dealings. Dudley made his living trading, swapping, lending, borrowing, and using anything free, cheap or unattended. It was an old joke in town that you had to count your fingers after shaking hands with him. The thing was, he was good at what he did, and had never worked one day for another person. He lived by his wits and at times did very well. Walter Marshall was no match for him in the world of wheeling and dealing.

Walter's interoffice intercom buzzed. He pressed a button, "Yes, Myra?"

"There's a call from a Mr. Dudley Shoemaker. He says he's returning your call about a boat," Myra's tinny voice said out of the speaker.

A blinking light on the phone told him which button to push. "Walter Marshall here."

"Hello? This is Dudley Shoemaker. I got a message that you called about the boat?" Dudley asked, using his most professional sounding voice.

"Yes, Mr. Shoemaker. I did." Walter paused for a second, not sure where to begin. "I was out at Northport this past weekend and saw your boat at the pier. I looked around a little, I hope you don't mind, and I'm a little curious..." Walter's voice trailed off. Curious about what, Walter wasn't sure. The price? If he should buy a monster yacht, if he could afford it, and then sail the seven seas? What would he do with the boat if he owned it?

"Mind? Not at all!" Dudley said, heartily. "That's what she's there for. Glad you got a look at her. She's a beauty, isn't she?" Dudley asked, playing with a fish, jiggling the bait, seeing how much interest there was.

"Yes, she's a beauty all right."

Dudley's heart skipped a beat. A nibble! "I wish I had been there to show you around," Dudley told him, the sincerity real. He always did better selling in person rather than over the phone. "Yeah, she sure is a beauty. They don't make them like her anymore. The boats they build today, well, you just can't compare them. You know what I mean?" he asked, jiggling the bait again.

"I guess so. To tell you the truth I'm not too familiar with boats that size. And it's been awhile since I've owned one. We had a couple of boats when the kids were young, small ones more or less, for fishing and such." Walter felt he were talking to someone out of his league. An eighty-foot yacht!

"They're all the same, some just bigger than others." Dudley laughed, trying to keep the conversation light. He could hear, or sense, Walter's discomfort. "If you've ever owned a boat, then you'll just love *Windsong*," Dudley assured him. "She has everything you could ask for. And she's a classic. I'll bet there aren't a half dozen left in the world like her. No sir. They just don't make them like her anymore."

"Well, I was just curious..." Walter was shy about asking the price. For all he knew it could cost millions.

"That's the way boat buyers are supposed to be, curious. How else can you find anything out? I'll tell you, she's some boat. Especially for the price!" Dudley said, enthusiastically.

Walter was relieved. Dudley brought up the subject of price. "How much are you asking?"

Dudley had been calculating since dialing Walter's number. Dudley added it all up. Walter was a lawyer with an office in Manhattan, had to go through two secretaries to get to him. He had money, or at least made money. And he was older. His kids were grown. And he sounded interested and with some selling Dudley felt sure he could make him more interested. That was the positive. Now the negative. Walter Marshall wasn't a boat nut who *had to have* this particular boat. There were people out there like that. Dudley could ask for and maybe even get a quarter of a million dollars for *Windsong* if he were lucky enough to find one.

But someone like that would know about boats and anyone who knew boats, wood boats, would know what to look for and with *Windsong* one didn't have to look very far before the rot in the hull was discovered. Dudley estimated he had about forty-two-thousand dollars invested in *Windsong*. Everything above that was profit. He let his instinct take over the negotiation. It never failed him. "A hundred and twenty-five-thousand dollars is what I'm looking for. And a bargain at that. If I weren't a little short on cash I wouldn't be selling her at all. I could probably get more but, like I said, I got a couple of deals going and I could use some quick cash. That's why the price is so low." Dudley waited to see if his sales pitch would get a nibble. Come on, boy, take the bait!

"One-hundred-twenty-five-thousand," Walter repeated.

There was nothing in his tone that helped Dudley determine if his price was too high, low, or on the mark. "When can I show her to you?" he asked, approaching it as though Walter had accepted, or was at least considering, the price.

"Huh?" Walter was caught off guard.

"Tomorrow's a good day to take her out for a spin. We can take her for a ride, go to Connecticut if you like, short trip across the Sound, and you can get the feel of her. The weather forecast for the weekend ain't so good. Wind'll be getting up. Tomorrow's forecast is good. Light wind and sun. Not too cold either. It'll be a beautiful day to try her out. What time can I meet you?"

"Tomorrow's Wednesday. I doubt if I can just not come into work like that," Walter told him.

"Can't you check and see if you can break free? The

weather for tomorrow is just what the doctor ordered. It might be awhile before we get this again. Of course, *Windsong* could go out in almost any weather, but it might not be as much fun if we're bouncing around too much."

Dudley didn't relish the idea of going out on *Windsong* with high seas running. Her keel was nearly rotted through and quite a few ribs below the water line were in the same condition. They might go out in swells but chances were they wouldn't be coming back. *Windsong* was in no condition to take pounding waves.

"I don't know." Walter paused. He rarely took a day off even when he was sick. "I'm sure I'm needed here at the office."

"Can't you check? It would be a great day to go out." Dudley was near pleading.

"I'll see," Walter said, doubtfully. He pushed the intercom button, not bothering to put Dudley on hold.

Dudley listened intently.

"Myra?" Walter called into the intercom.

"Yes, Mr. Marshall?" Myra quickly answered.

"What's my schedule like tomorrow?" There was a pause and then Myra's voice, high-pitched from the little speaker.

"You've got a meeting with The Group tomorrow morning at eleven and then a conference at two-thirty with Mister Claymore on the Consolidated contract."

The Group was an informal bi-weekly meeting of junior and associate partners which usually amounted to little more than light chatter and gossip. It was held more for social communication and to prevent anyone from feeling or becoming isolated from the other members of the firm than having to do with important business. It was useful in its own way but could easily be missed. The meeting with John Claymore was of even less importance. They were supposed to be doing a preliminary review of one of Consolidated's contracts. John

Claymore was Consolidated's "in house" lawyer and took every opportunity to set up meetings, at a local bar if possible, and get away from his office. Consolidated's account was an important one but there was really no need to hold this meeting other than to keep Claymore happy. All it would amount to would be spending two hours of idle talk and watching Claymore gobble a half dozen or more double martinis. Claymore wouldn't mind rescheduling their meeting. He would probably take both afternoons off and charge his time to contract negotiations.

"That's it?" Walter asked, to make sure.

"That's all I have on your calendar."

"Call John Claymore and reschedule our meeting for any day that's convenient for him and not in conflict with anything I've got, would you please. Also, I won't be coming in tomorrow."

It was a few seconds before Myra responded. Her boss never took a day off like this. "Call Mister Claymore and reschedule your meeting," a slight pause, "and you won't be in tomorrow."

"Right."

With handset pressed hard against his ear, Dudley had been listening with interest. On hearing Walter's last comment Dudley was ecstatic. He had taken the bait, hook, line, and sinker. Now all Dudley had to do was play him, feed him some line, work him a little. A hundred and twenty-five-thousand dollars! He tried to keep his excitement under control. He thought he'd never get rid of this lemon.

Walter came back on the phone. "Mister Shoemaker?"

"Yeah, Mister Marshall, I'm here," Dudley responded, playing his cards close to his vest, not letting Walter know he had been listening in.

"Hmm," Walter cleared his throat. "It seems that I will be able to get free tomorrow after all. What time can I meet you?"

Dudley calculated swiftly. He needed time to get some fuel aboard. There probably wasn't five gallons of diesel in *Windsong*'s tanks and she was a guzzler; man, was she a guzzler! He also had better get a charge on the batteries. *Windsong* had been riding at anchor most of the winter. It would be a hell of a situation if he lost this sale because he couldn't get the engines turning over. It couldn't be too late though. The afternoon winds would be picking up and with it the seas and Dudley didn't want to be on *Windsong* in no seas.

"How about ten o'clock?" Dudley asked.

"Ten o'clock would be fine."

"Good. I'll meet you at the dock, okay?"

"Fine. I'll meet you there."

"I'll have the boat all ready to go. I'm sure you're going to love her." Dudley worked the line, working this fish, starting the process of landing this one-hundred-twenty-five thousand dollar prize.

"I'm looking forward to it. Good-bye, Mister Shoemaker."

"Good-bye, Mister Marshall." It was cold in the phone booth at the boatyard. A damp, late afternoon breeze blew in off the water but Dudley's palms were sweating. Little beads of perspiration formed on his upper lip and forehead. He had a deal going. Oh, how he loved deals! He rubbed his sweaty hands together walking toward his car with excitement and determination. He had to get the boat ready. He had a fish on the line, a big fish, and he had to land him. Dudley couldn't believe his luck. A big, dumb, rich fish was going to jump right into his boat.

Walter leaned back in his leather chair and thought about what he had just done. In thirty-five years he had never just taken a day off like that. Playing hooky was the phrase that came to mind. It was like a kid playing hooky from school. He smiled to himself, bemused by his belated immaturity. He was chasing a kid's dream so why not think in kid's terms? The odd thing was, he felt no guilt about taking the day off. The office would run without him for a day. He certainly had time coming to him. He hadn't taken a vacation—my God—since before Laura died. That summer before she died. It hadn't been much of a vacation, either. Laura was becoming very sick by then and spending every day at home with her, watching death make his conquest little by little, had drained Walter. It was a relief to go back to work.

He swung the large swivel chair and looked out the office windows. He had a corner office, a sign of high status at Wheel, Kedder and Matthews, and two windows were considered a perk. He looked from one to the other. The tall buildings of Lower Manhattan filled both. He walked to the corner to see if he had a view of water. Manhattan Island was surrounded by water, the Hudson River on one side, the East River on the other, and New York Bay to the south of Battery Park. No matter how he stretched, buildings obstructed his view. No water could be seen. Odd, he had never thought of that before. His building was not as tall as many of the surrounding structures. No matter how high he climbed in the firm's hierarchy, and with advancement his office would move up a floor or two, he would never be able to see any. The building just didn't go high enough. He went back to his desk and returned to what he was doing before being interrupted by Dudley's phone call. The water would have to wait until tomorrow.

At one time *Windsong* was well cared for as attested to by her age. The original owner loved her as a most prized possession. He took great care of her even when he reached an age when he rarely, and towards the end, never, went out so he could enjoy the summer weather on the water. At his death, *Windsong* was sold to a real estate broker who used her mainly to impress potential customers and she stayed tied up to the dock. Little use was made of her engines, she consumed fuel at an alarming rate, and the absolute minimum of maintenance was done. *Windsong* only need look good above the waterline.

During an economic down-turn the real estate broker found it expensive to keep up with the cost and for two years no care was given the boat. With few customers to bring aboard he eventually sold her to two partners who had wanted to use *Windsong* as a charter boat.

This never did work out. The need of licenses, insurance, cost of maintenance and slip fees and other expenses they hadn't expected was greater than the amount of money that came in from the few charters they received. Then, for two seasons, the partners tried charter fishing, taking groups out on one- to three-day trips. This also was not a financial success and during this time the interior of the boat really took a beating. Beds, couches, rugs, and most of the furniture were eventually wrecked by drunken fisherman who couldn't care less.

Finally, *Windsong* was sold to Dudley Shoemaker for what she was worth for salvage, thirty-two-thousand dollars. The two diesel engines were worth this much. They were over twenty years old, having been replaced by the original owner before he died, but had relatively few running hours on them. Plus there was a generator, a great deal of brass fittings, ground tackle and other useful items still aboard.

But the hull was rotted. Wood boats need constant care or it isn't long before they find their way to the bottom. *Windsong* hadn't had that care for a long time, but Dudley had no intention of scrapping her. He hired two high school boys who hung around the boatyard and had them do what superficial repairs they could. He gathered some used furniture to replace what had been damaged, painted and polished where it would impress the most, and hoped to snag an unwary landlubber for a buyer. It was a gamble. Dudley invested an additional ten thousand dollars in cosmetic repairs, but it was the kind of gamble he liked to take. He never once considered the likelihood that people might drown going out on an unseaworthy boat. That was their problem. His was a "buyer beware" world. Ethics were for theologians.

The next morning Walter parked his car in the mostly empty parking lot at Northport. Winter still held Long Island and these few spring-like days were forecast to end the next day when rain mixed with snow was to shower the coast. A lone fisherman casted from the pier near *Windsong*, flipping his lure with relaxed grace, the plug arching high into the calm air and striking a placid sea. Empty floats stood anchored in the protected bay waiting for warmer weather and the arrival of summer pleasure craft. The commercial fishing boats were gone, nets, crab traps, and various gear piled on the vacant dock. At the end of the public pier *Windsong* waited.

He walked slowly along the rough, wooden planks toward *Windsong*, his eyes following her smooth lines from bow pulpit to stern, enjoying her beauty. Her architect knew what he was doing. She was perfectly proportioned.

Dudley was right. They don't make them like this anymore. Her fresh, white paint shined in the hazy sun and her heavily varnished wood sparkled. She was riding higher than on Sunday. The tide was in and her deck was two feet above the pier. Dudley was no where to be seen. Walter stopped at the lowered handrail and called into the open doorway.

"Ahoy, there!" he yelled, feeling a little ridiculous playing at being a seaman.

"Come aboard!" came a muffled voice from somewhere below decks.

He stepped up on deck and entered the pilothouse. Dudley's head appeared at the foreward companionway. He came up the steps smiling and wiping oil off his hands with a greasy rag.

"Just checking the engines. They're fine." Dudley had

added several quarts of oil to the engines. He finished wiping his hands with a flourish and stuck his hand out to Walter. They shook. "Mister Marshall, I presume?" Dudley said, giving Walter his most hearty handshake.

Walter nodded. "Mister Shoemaker?" Walter asked, completing the formalities.

"Himself. I'm sure glad you could make it. It looks like we're gonna have us a pretty day. She's all fueled and ready to go," Dudley said with enthusiasm. "Like me to show you around before we cast off?"

"I looked a little bit last Sunday, but, yes, I'd like a tour if you have time."

"Time? I've got all the time in the world!" Dudley said happily. And he did. He'd spend all the time needed to land this fish. Whatever it would take Dudley was willing to give. Mr. Walter Marshall's happiness was his only concern at the moment. "This here boat's one of the finest I've ever seen," Dudley said, spreading his arms out to encompass *Windsong*. He spoke in his most cultured "Down East" twang, the disappearing dialect of New England seamen. His "This here boat" sounding like "This har boat."

Dudley struck the large brass bell near the wheel. He had polished it that morning. *Windsong* was etched boldly across the bell, 1926, the year she was built, below. It rang dully from the knuckle strike. "She's a beauty all right. Like I said, they don't make them like her anymore. You never see a bell like this on a new boat. No, sir! That's a collector's item all by itself. Nowadays they're all fiberglass, stainless steel, and mirrors. Why in most of them you'd be afraid to go to sea. They're built to just look pretty. Not this one. Oh, she's pretty all right. Beautiful. But she was also built to go places! Yes, sir. They knew how to build them back then."

Thus began a twenty minute tour of *Windsong* as Dudley raved about the old-fashioned quality of workmanship, gave a fictitious history of *Windsong*'s many long trips, and steered Walter wide of any part of the boat he didn't want him to see. Walter followed along saying little, listening with great interest, feeling more and more comfortable with being aboard. Somehow Dudley's extravagant claims struck a chord. It was just what he wanted to hear. If there were any defects, Walter didn't see them. By the time Dudley started the engines and they were ready to cast off, he'd fallen in love. To his eyes *Windsong* was one of the most beautiful boats ever built. Of course she would have some defects, any boat this old would, but she was something special. He felt it deep in his gut. He wanted to own this boat. He wanted to go places with her. The boyhood dream came alive.

Dudley cast off and quickly returned to the pilothouse and took the wheel, slowly adding power to *Windsong*'s twin engines. They eased away from the pier and headed toward the harbor mouth, the powerful engines below vibrating the deck under their feet.

"Here, take her," Dudley offered, stepping away from the wheel.

"Are you sure?" Walter grabbed a spoke to keep *Windsong* from swinging off course. He was nervous but the thought of steering this big, beautiful boat filled him with pride.

"Of course! She's the easiest thing in the world to handle. She answers the helm real nice once you get to know her a little," Dudley told him. This may or may not have been true since the only times Dudley had piloted *Windsong* was a short distance from place to place within the harbor for repairs.

"Thanks," Walter said, a grin starting as he stepped before the wheel. They motored along at little more than idle speed and Walter spun the wheel a little to the right to see how *Windsong* responded. It seemed like a long moment before the bow began to slowly turn toward starboard. He spun the wheel to the left to catch the turn and again it took awhile before she stopped her swing and began to turn toward port. He tried to judge *Windsong*'s turning momentum and turned the wheel right long before they were pointed toward the harbor mouth. When *Windsong* stopped her swing they were nearly on course. He corrected with a slight turn of the wheel.

"You're catching on quick," Dudley said.

"It's been awhile. And I've never owned anything as big as this." Walter almost added "before" at the end of the sentence. Emotions were running through him at cross currents. He was enjoying this, loving it, but tugging at his conscience was the question "why?" Why was he doing this? What was behind this flight from his normal world of quiet reality? Was he trying to live a fantasy, a boy's dream? What would he do with *Windsong* if he did own her? He wasn't the type of man to be doing these things. He was quiet and conservative. More than that lately. For the past two years he had become more and more a recluse. His life was simple, unadorned.

Dudley reached over and pushed the throttles forward. Instantly the big, powerful diesels roared. *Windsong* slowly gained speed as twin propellers raced to move her massive weight. The whole boat vibrated as they gained momentum, *Windsong* cutting through the small swells coming into the harbor. Walter could feel her trembling through the wheel. He felt attached, part of her. A buoy marking the channel to the harbor entrance grew larger and soon they were past, their wake rocking the buoy, causing its bell to gong as it swayed.

During his lifetime Walter had owned a day-sailer, a sixteen-foot sail boat, and a twenty-one-foot inboard-outboard power boat that he and his family used for fishing trips during summer. That ended when his son, Harold, went off to college. He had sold the boat right after that, neither his wife nor daughter very interested in being on a rocking boat, getting sunburned, and catching fish they had little interest in eating.

Now, steering *Windsong*, he felt as though he were driving an apartment house through the water at high speed.

"She's big, isn't she?" Walter asked, as *Windsong* cut through low, rolling swells. The wind was light. *Windsong* neither rocked nor rolled in such small waves. The wind blowing in through the doorway was caused by their own speed. The white spray of the bow wake flew off each side.

"Yeah, she's big." Dudley agreed. "Seventy-eight-foot and she has a sixteen-foot beam. But she's sure got some speed for a boat this size."

Dudley was impressed. He had never opened the throttles before. He hadn't taken *Windsong* out of the harbor. He hoped the strain of the engines at full throttle didn't break something loose. "Hull design," he told Walter. "Like I said, they don't make 'em like this no more. She was made to travel."

Walter tapped the glass face of one of the gauges. "The fuel gauge reads empty."

"Yeah, well, I only took on fifty gallons of fuel. Didn't think we'd need any more. Maybe it just ain't registering. She holds nine hundred gallons."

"The speed indicator isn't working." Walter tapped a finger on this instrument also. He glanced across at the other gauges. Neither of the two tachometers to the engines registered any RPMs, water temperature was zero, voltage indicator showed nothing.

"It might just be clogged. The water intake. She ain't been used much lately. It wouldn't take much to get her right."

"Nothing seems to be working," Walter told him. "Maybe a fuse is blown or something."

"Yeah, maybe that's it," Dudley readily agreed. He knew there was nothing wrong with the fuses. He'd had the instruments checked. The wiring to them, as most of the wiring on the boat, was old and frayed and needed to be replaced. This would've been expensive and Dudley had let it pass. He wasn't going to put any more money into the boat than he absolutely had to. "I'll check out those fuses after we get back. Can't be too big a deal."

Dudley didn't know if the gauges would work or not. The instruments below deck also may or may not have been working. Again, there was no way of knowing. Most things needed to be replaced. The boat was old and worn out. Doing any of that would have been pointless in any case. Until the hull was made sound most of the other things were of little consequence. Except, perhaps, the water temperature gauges to the engines. If one of the water intakes were to clog or something else go wrong, those engines could burn up in a minute. All Dudley could do was hope for the best. He wasn't going to put any more money into the boat. It was too big a gamble. It would be up to the buyer, hopefully Mr. Walter Marshall, to deal with these problems. Dudley knew he had to get the conversation off of the negative.

"She handles beautifully, doesn't she?" There was a trawler ahead dragging its nets, barely making way, and Walter turned the wheel to the right. *Windsong* slowly turned in that direction.

"Yeah, nice." He looked over at Dudley, grinning. He couldn't help himself. He was enjoying this. Maybe he was just a kid with a new toy. He didn't care anymore. He was doing something he liked and it didn't matter if it made a lot of sense. He could treat himself. It was along time since he did something for the simple pleasure of it.

Dudley could see the pure joy on Walter's face. He grinned wide too, equally happy. He was going to land this fish. He knew it. He could feel it.

"Boy, would I like to take a trip down to the islands with this," he told Walter. "If I didn't have so much going on I wouldn't sell her. I'd take her to the Caribbean and live the good life for awhile. Did you ever want to do something like that?" Dudley prodded.

"Yes, I have."

"Do you have any family? The boat's certainly big enough."

Walter nodded. "A son and a daughter, both grown. Some grandchildren too."

Dudley decided not to ask about a wife. "They could all go with you. There's more than enough room. I'll bet they would enjoy it."

"Maybe," Walter said, thinking. "But if I did take a trip it would be alone, I think. They've got too much going on to take an extended vacation. I guess I would need a mate to help though. *Windsong*'s a little too big for one person to handle, with docking and all."

"Mates are easy to find," Dudley assured him. "There's always one or two guys hanging around the docks and boatyards looking for a ride. Most of them experienced sailors. I'll bet I could hook you up with someone in a flash. You might even find a female mate," Dudley chuckled, "to go with you."

Walter laughed. "No, thanks. I think I'd have enough of a headache just handling the boat. I don't think I need a woman along."

"Might make it interesting."

"No, I was married too long. Almost thirty-five years. My wife died two years ago. I'm too set in my ways to be making any changes now."

"Sorry about your wife."

"Thank you." Walter eased the throttle back and they slowed. The engines were less noticeable as they cruised along at half speed. Dudley was grateful that Walter had lowered the power. At full throttle *Windsong* would consume fifty gallons of fuel in no time.

The high overcast was thickening, a forerunner to the changing weather that was to come that evening. The sea was dark green and had an oily gloss. Scattered trawlers dragged nets, their speed so slow they appeared to be standing still in the expanse of the Long Island Sound. No small pleasure boats were out. The water temperature was not much above freezing and it was Wednesday. A few determined fishermen might venture out on a weekend if the wind were calm, but not today. Walter turned *Windsong* back toward Northport. It was impossible to distinguish the harbor entrance along the distant coastline. He had steered mostly north as he left port so he put *Windsong* on a southerly course and scanned the coastline waiting to pick out a familiar landmark. Dudley watched and said nothing. He would let Walter pilot the boat in. He sat on a chair in the corner of the pilothouse. He became a passenger until they neared the pier. Walter was now the pilot and master of the boat. Dudley hoped he could make that a permanent situation.

IV
Plans

It was Friday morning when Dudley called. All day Thursday he waited for Walter to phone, even giving his very private home number, but nothing had happened. Dudley knew it was dangerous to allow too much time to pass. He'd been in this business too long not to know he had to strike while the iron was hot. And the iron seemed hot enough two days before. Walter wanted the boat. It didn't take a sharp salesman to see that. But Walter said he needed a little time to think about it and would give Dudley a call. Time was Dudley's enemy in this situation. Anything could happen to sour a deal if enough time were allowed to pass.

"Walter Marshall here."

"Hello, Mister Marshall. It's Dudley Shoemaker. How are you this morning?"

"Fine, Mister Shoemaker, just fine. I want to thank you again for the trip on Wednesday. I enjoyed it very much."

"My pleasure. I was just wondering if there was anything else I could do. I mean, would you like to go out again or can we get together and talk. I'm a reasonable man. I'm sure we can work out a deal."

There was a pause before Walter responded. "I'm not sure.

Oh, I love the boat. *Windsong*'s a beauty. It's just that, well, I don't know what I would do with her. She's too big to use as a weekender and..." Walter didn't continue. He was thinking he would soon be sixty years old and too late in life to begin living boyhood dreams. Sure, he wanted to buy *Windsong* and sail off to some beautiful island and enjoy a carefree life for awhile. Who wouldn't? But that wasn't him. It was a childish fantasy. A wonderful, lovely, exciting fantasy, but not something he, Walter Marshall, attorney-at-law, soon to be sixty years old, could possibly do.

Dudley knew he had to do something quickly. His fish was wiggling hard and if he didn't start playing him just right this fish was going to slip off the hook. "She's really not that big. Of course you could use her as a weekender. Why, that's the beauty of owning a good-sized boat. It gives you range. You can easily run up to Cape Cod for a weekend or most anywhere else. That's something you can't do with a smaller boat. And you can still take a long cruise if you want to. *Windsong*'s good for whatever you'd like to do."

"I don't know. I'm really not sure it's for me. I'm going to need a little more time to think about it. I don't want to tie you down or anything. If you find another buyer interested, don't feel obligated to me."

Dudley's heart sank. The deal was going down the drain. He had to get the ball rolling again. "I was thinking, Walter, about those gauges and all. Not working I mean. I had intended on getting everything fixed and shipshape but like I said, I'm working on a couple of deals and been kind of busy so, how about I drop the price ten thousand. That'd be more than enough to cover the cost of any repairs you might want to make. We'll drop it down to a hundred-fifteen-thousand. How's that sound?"

It was a moment before Walter responded. Odd, but he hadn't thought about the price of the boat very much. One-hundred-twenty-five-thousand dollars was a lot of money.

One-hundred-fifteen-thousand dollars was still a lot of money, but money had not been foremost on his mind. *Windsong* touched something deep inside him. Long forgotten dreams and a part of himself that were suppressed many years before had resurfaced. It was like a young boy was living in an old man's body. He was both and yet felt as though he were neither. The boy, the young man, had survived within him all these years.

The face he saw every morning when he shaved reminded him he wasn't a kid anymore. He was getting old. His life was behind him. But something inside kept telling him it wasn't true. There was more. There had to be more. He didn't like getting old. He was already tired of being old. Money had nothing to do with whether or not he would buy *Windsong*. He was sure he could afford her if he really wanted her. What he wasn't sure of was what he was supposed to do, who he was supposed to be, or maybe who he really was.

"That sounds very generous. I wish I could give you an answer right now, but I can't. I'm going to have to think about it a little longer. I don't mean to hold you up or anything but..."

"You're not holding me up. No, sir. It's just that, like I said, I got this deal going and a little cash would be handy right now but if you need some time, of course, I'll wait. I'm not trying to rush you or anything."

"Thank you. I'll call you if I decide anything."

"Good. Good. Er, you wouldn't mind if I give you a call, say the beginning of next week or so? Just to stay in touch?"

"No, give me a call if you like. I don't know if and when I'll know for sure. It's kind of up in the air."

"That's all right. Fine. We'll just stay in touch."

After their good-byes Myra came in and placed the inter-office mail on his desk. He opened the manila envelope and flipped through the memorandums, stopping at a page with names and dates partially filled in. It was the office vacation schedule. With his rank and seniority his name was near the top. He stared at the paper lost in thought. Besides work and the daily routine of taking care of himself, what would he do with his time this year?

As an associate partner, he was expected to take six weeks vacation. Sometimes his co-workers took a little more, sometimes less, and each individual was expected to fit his free time in with his work load. They were liberal with vacation time, or any time taken off for that matter when it came to the senior attorneys. As long as the job was getting done and the clients satisfied, no one would be questioned about his comings and goings. He thought back on how much vacation he'd taken lately. The year before he took one week off and spent it puttering around the house. The year before that had been much the same. It was as though he felt obliged to fill in something after his name each year and so entered a date and took a week off. It was not something he looked forward to. There was work to be done at the office and little to do at home. Three years prior, he spent those two long weeks with his ailing wife. That had been a vacation of torture. As he thought back he realized it had been five or six years since he had taken all of the vacation allotted him.

He flipped through a Rolodex file and dialed a number. "Cramer," came quickly, as the call was answered on the first ring.

"Hello, John, it's Walter Marshall."

"Walter! How are you?" came a friendly reply. John Cramer had been his broker for over twenty years and during that time they had become friends in a professional way. Walter was not a speculator in the stock market but over the years he steadily purchased shares in mostly blue chip corporations and had a fairly large portfolio by now.

"I'm fine. How have you been doing lately?" Walter leaned back and looked out the window at rows of other office windows in the building across the street.

"Same as always. Have my ups, downs, and sideways."
John Cramer chuckled at his own little joke. "Long time no
see. What can I do for you?"

"I'm thinking of buying a boat and I was wondering how
much cash I had around."

"A boat, eh? That sounds nice. How much cash were you
looking for?"

"One-hundred-twenty-five—no, one-hundred-fifteen-
thousand dollars."

John let out a whistle. "Wow, that must be some boat."

"To tell you the truth I'm not sure I'm going to buy it. I was
just wondering. I've kind of lost track of what my account
looks like with you. I have some money in the bank, savings
and such, but nothing like that amount."

"Well, you do have... Let me see." Walter could visualize
John punching in information on the computer, pulling Walter's
file out of an electronic memory. "Let's see... You've got
about fifteen-thousand in cash, and that's about it. I wouldn't
recommend selling at this time. I got a feeling the market's on
a rise. In fact, I didn't realize how much cash you did have. I
would recommend getting in with one or two good prospects
that have just come up."

"Hmm. No, I'm not looking to buy right now. I was
thinking, maybe I could sell off something that hasn't been
doing much lately."

John was friendly with Walter, in fact he tried to be
friendly with all his clients, but he was also a businessman and
he certainly didn't want to see Walter pull one-hundred-
fifteen-thousand dollars out of his account. "You're not thinking of buying this thing cash, are you? Wouldn't you be better
off with a bank loan rather than liquidating some very good
investments?"

"I'm not sure. It's been such awhile since I've checked on
my financial status that I figured I'd give you a call."

"Your financial status is pretty good, at least at this end but... Let me see. Here's something. You've got a CD maturing in a couple of months."

"A CD?" Walter didn't recall holding a certificate of deposit.

"Yep." Walter could here the clicks of a calculator in the background as John totalled figures. "It ought to be worth about seventy-eight-thousand dollars with the interest compounded."

"Seventy-eight thousand dollars?" Walter was incredulous.

"Yeah, don't you remember? It was, er, some of the, er, insurance money left over after your wife's death." John knew, or sensed, how hard Walter had been hit by the loss of his wife.

"Laura's money? My God, I'd forgotten all about it." As his spouse, Laura had been insured by Wheel, Kedder and Matthews for one-hundred-thousand dollars. He paid the funeral director and bought a family plot for Laura, a space for himself, and four more vacant plots for their children's use. The remainder of the money he sent to John Cramer. At the time, Walter was in no mental condition to be making rational stock market decisions, so a large portion of the money was put in a one year certificate of deposit that would "roll over," be re-invested, if the money were not withdrawn. Walter buried his wife, paid the bills, and put everything he could about the ordeal out of his mind. It was as though the life insurance policy had never existed.

John's voice pulled his thoughts out of the past. "If you do decide to buy a boat and use cash instead of a bank loan my suggestion is you cash in the CD rather than sell off any of your holdings. Interest rates are down and I believe you have a higher potential for better earnings by staying in the market."

"Thanks, John. I'll let you know."

"Say, what kind of boat were you thinking of buying?"

Walter knew John liked to sail and probably, no, definitely, knew more about boats than he did. In one way he was afraid of sounding foolish but he was also interested in what John might think of *Windsong*. "She's an older boat. Built in 1926. Wood construction, of course. She's seventy-eight feet long and kind of... pretty."

"I'd guess so! Wow! Seventy-eight feet did you say? She must be something!" John owned a thirty-foot sloop that cost him over fifty-thousand dollars. The thought of owning a seventy-eight-foot boat, of any kind, impressed him.

"Yeah, she's unusual. And big, for me at least. They don't make them like her anymore."

"What are you planning on doing, taking a trip?"

"I'm not sure. I guess I had been thinking of taking a cruise down to the Bahamas or something like that."

"That sounds like one hell of a trip. I wish I were going with you. My wife and I keep talking about a cruise. We both love to sail. But each year we put it off. Something always seems to come up. We never seem to have the time."

"I'm still not sure I'm going to do it. I'll give you a call about that CD if I decide I need it."

"Right. You do that. In any case, you ought to get your money out of CDs. The rates are down and I think you'd be better off in the market."

"Maybe. We'll see."

"Oh, Walter?"

"Yes?"

"You did say it was a wood boat?"

"Yeah, all wood. They didn't have fiberglass or anything like that back then."

"Have you had the boat surveyed?"

"Surveyed?" The only kind of survey Walter could think of was for land and property boundaries.

"Yes, surveyed. Get a specialist who really knows boats to take a look at her. It doesn't cost much and you'll know what kind of condition she's in. Wood boats can be tricky. There can be hidden rot and it can cause all kinds of trouble. A surveyor would spot something like that. It might save you a lot of heartaches down the road."

"No, I haven't done that, but thanks for the info."

"You bet. Good luck with the a... What's the name of the boat?"

"*Windsong.*"

"*Windsong.* Good luck with her and I'll be talking with you."

Walter thought about John Cramer and his wanting to take a long cruise with his sailboat. Each year he and his wife put it off and the probability was they never would go on that trip. He remembered all the times he and Laura had hopes or made plans to do things together and then something would come up and it would be canceled, put off for another time. And another time never came. It was much the same with the children. He spent time with them. They did things together. He enjoyed being with his family. But when he thought about it now, he hadn't spent half, maybe not one tenth, the time with them that he would if he had to do it over again. The years had just slipped past and then they were gone. All of them, and he couldn't go back and do it right the second time. You only get one shot at it and right, wrong, or indifferent, and when it's over it's over.

He shook his head as if to shake these thoughts from his mind. Every time he got involved with *Windsong* or something about *Windsong* it was as if floodgates opened. Memories and feelings came rushing at him, awkward and uncomfortable, issues he thought he had dealt with long ago. Somehow *Windsong* broke his routine, shattered his peace, brought him out of his comfortable world. Before *Windsong* he thought he lived a quiet, simple, and yet productive life. Now he was wondering if he was living simply or if he had just turned the world off and stopped seeing and feeling. He was starting to question whether there was any purpose to what he was doing. Or was the question he was really asking was there really any purpose to life? That was silly. It was kind of late in the day to start pondering philosophical questions along those lines.

A lawyer spends a good deal of his professional life helping others plan for their future. He may draw up a contract, make a will, a deed to property, even a divorce, would all contain elements for a clearly defined course of action in the future. For over three decades Walter Marshall had been doing these things for others. He was good at it, very good. But when he looked at himself, and more and more what it looked like in the future, he saw a blank contract. There was his life with the firm. There would probably be a full partnership in the not too distant future and greater wealth and prestige, but the excitement at that prospect was gone. Would it really matter to him? He would continue to have some contact with his daughter and those two sweet children of hers but he was only on the periphery of a family. That family existed on its own. He would just pop in and out for a short visit now and then and it would have no effect as they continued on with their lives. His son had drifted away and they had almost no contact anymore. He barely knew his grandson, Nathan. Harold was living his life his way and that was the way it was supposed to be.

He stared at the papers on his desk, unseeing. His life had become dull. More than dull, pointless. He was comfortable, or at least accustomed to, "the simple life" as he called it. But when he truly looked at how he was living, his daily and weekly routine wasn't "simple," it was meaningless. It was repetition without end. Without end, that is, until the Grim Reaper came and then it would be all over and none of it would matter in any case. And sometime since Laura's death he had stopped being a man alone and had become a lonely man. He realized that now. He was lonely and he didn't know what he was supposed to do about it. He took a deep breath and slowly let it out. He pressed the intercom button and Myra's voice came on.

"Yes, Mister Marshall?"

"Do we have any coffee out there?" Walter wondered if he really wanted a cup of coffee or just wanted to have another person nearby for a few moments. All he needed to do was ask Myra a question or two and she would fill him in on the newest gossip in the firm.

"Sure do," Myra called back. "We've got some good doughnuts here, too. Fresh." Myra hoped he would take some. He needed something. He hadn't been looking well lately and he had become even more quiet than usual.

"No, thanks. Just the coffee will be fine."

"Be right there," Myra said, a little disappointed.

V

Birthday Gift

Saturday morning was damp, cold, and overcast but Walter was working on his lawn, heavily dressed against the chill. There were patches at his trouser knees where he knelt on the soft earth. He weeded and fertilized the lawn and shrubs, making ready for the spring season. It was something he enjoyed. His continuous and meticulous care of the land-scaped property showed in a lush lawn, blossoming bushes and shrubs, and a neatness that was eye catching to any who passed. The house was also spotless. On most weekends he could be found scrapping, sanding, and painting either inside or outside of his comfortable home.

After Laura died Walter found he had little to do with his time. In the evenings he would come home, prepare a simple dinner, and then read or watch television until bed. The weekends were harder for him. Two long days and evenings with little to do and no desire to go anywhere alone. He needed to do something to fill the time. He stopped the lawn service and began taking care of it himself. Then he began to paint and learned how to do repairs around the house. He bought books, asked a friendly hardware salesman hundreds of questions, bought a basement full of tools, and slowly became proficient at carpentry and painting. It felt good to stay busy and to see the results of his labor. A side benefit was the exercise he received. With mowing and puttering and patching and painting he worked his way into good physical condition.

As he dug into the dark, cold soil and pulled each weed out by its roots, his mind kept drifting to sandy white beaches and warm sun and surf. The scene kept coming back to him. Palm trees swayed in the breeze, shapely women, tanned and healthy, strolled at the water's edge in skimpy bathing suits, possible companionship and laughter beckoned him. The summer's vacation schedule still waited on his desk, his dates yet to be filled in, and he was wavering between making a commitment and buying *Windsong* or just shrugging it off as a flight of fancy by an old fool who just didn't want to accept things as they really were. He could always take a week or two and fly down to the Bahamas or Hawaii or anywhere else for that matter and not make such a big deal out of it.

He rose from his knees and brushed the dirt off his hands. He looked around at the surrounding homes, many of which were now visible because of the barren trees. Some had boats covered with canvas for the winter in driveways or backyards, pools also covered, doors and windows closed tight against the cold, and no one to be seen. It was not the kind of morning when many people would be outdoors. He went to his front door, carefully wiping his feet before going in, went to the telephone and dialed his daughter's number.

"Hello?" his daughter answered, still his little girl.

"Hi, Lynda. How are you?"

"Dad! Hi?" Lynda said, then with concern, "Is everything all right?" It wasn't often that her father initiated telephone calls.

"Fine. I was just thinking about you and thought I'd give you a call and find out how you all were doing."

"How nice!" she said, happily. "It's good to hear from you. We're fine more or less."

"Oh? What's up?"

"The kids as usual. One has an ear ache and the other a sore throat. They take turns. They get over one and get the other. They'll be okay. I took them to the pediatrician and they both got medicine. Same old stuff. They've had it before and they'll have it again. The only thing is they're driving me crazy. They're both so cranky." Walter could hear the exasperation in his daughter's voice at being stuck in the house with two sick children.

"Isn't George at home?" Lynda's husband was often off on weekends.

"No, the stinker. The good doctor was called into the hospital early this morning. Some kind of emergency I guess. You know, for a doctor he's not real good about being around sick kids. I think if it were up to him he'd give them a shot or something and put them out for a day or two until they were feeling better. Maybe that's why he went into psychiatry. Sick people make him nervous." Lynda chuckled.

"As I recall, you and Harold used to have the same problems. Ear infections and such I mean."

"Yeah, I remember. You know, I never appreciated how much trouble a parent goes through until I became one. You and Mom had your share with us."

"It's all part of growing up."

"Yep, I guess so. Say, Dad, I was going to call you. Can you come to dinner tomorrow?"

"I was just there last week."

"I know, but to tell you the truth, your birthday is next week and I almost forgot about it. I wanted to throw you a little party or something. Maybe I can get Harold and Winnifer to come out."

By the way Lynda said it he knew that she hadn't called her brother yet to see if he would come for his father's birthday party. This was short notice and probably Harold wouldn't take the long trip from Manhattan. "Don't bother, honey. With the kids sick and all it would probably be better to skip it."

"But it's your birthday. You're going to be sixty. That's a big event, sixty. We ought to do something."

"Thanks, but no thanks. I don't think being reminded all day by everyone that I'm getting old is the most enjoyable way to spend a day. Thank you for the thought, though."

"Well, I do have a present for you. If you don't come and pick it up I'll bring it over to you as soon as the kids are better."

"Thank you, honey. You didn't have to do that."

"It isn't much. Just a little something." There was a slight pause. "Are you doing anything special for your birthday?"

"No, I hadn't thought about it. I had been thinking about buying a boat though."

"Really?"

"I haven't made up my mind yet. I was just thinking about it."

"Good for you. I think it's a great idea. You need something to keep you busy. When we were kids you used to have a boat. You used to like to be out on the water fishing and all. I never liked it. Still don't. That much water around me makes me nervous. And there's never anywhere to go to the bathroom."

"There's a place to go on this one. There are two bathrooms as a matter of fact."

"Two bathrooms? How big is this boat?"

"She's seventy-eight feet."

"Are you kidding?"

"No. She's a big boat," Walter said, smiling at his daughter's reaction.

"I'd say! Seventy-eight feet! That's not a boat. That's a… battleship!"

"She's not really that big."

"I'd like to see it. Maybe I wouldn't mind being on it. It

would be like being on a cruise ship or something. I thought you were talking about a fishing boat like we used to have or maybe a small cabin cruiser."

"I think you'd like *Windsong*. She's big enough so we could all go out on her. There are three bedrooms, four if you wanted to use the forward lounge as one, and plenty of space. The children would love it." Walter didn't know why but he felt as though he were trying to sell the idea of buying *Windsong* to his daughter.

"I'll bet they would. We'd have to keep them in life jackets and tie a rope on them. They'd probably be overboard as soon as you turned your head."

"It was just an idea," Walter said meekly. It hadn't taken much of an objection for him to quickly back away from the idea.

Lynda heard her father become deflated. She was sorry she mentioned anything about the danger to the children. He needed something to pull him out of the depression he was sinking into. The last thing she wanted to do was to talk him out of doing something he would enjoy.

"I didn't mean it wasn't a good idea. It's a great idea! We'll figure out something with the kids. They'll be okay. You need to do something for yourself for a change. I don't know how long it's been since you've treated yourself. Why don't you? Why not get yourself a birthday gift?"

"A birthday gift?"

"Sure, why not? Treat yourself special. You've always worried about taking care of everyone else. Why not think of yourself for once?"

"I hadn't thought about it that way. It was just an idea. Thanks, though."

"You bet. I want to see it as soon as you buy it."

"Maybe. There are a few details that have to be taken care of first."

"Good. Let me know. And Dad?"

"Yes, Honey?"

"I'm sorry about the party."

"There's no need to be sorry. You know I don't like parties that much anyway."

"What I mean is, I'm sorry I almost forgot about your birthday."

"Don't worry about it. You've got more to worry about than my birthday. That family of yours is more than enough to keep anybody busy full-time."

"That they are." Walter could hear one of the children crying in the background. "There they go again. For sick kids they sure do like to beat up on each other. I'll call you back later. Let me see if I can keep these two from killing each other."

"Okay. 'Bye, Honey."

He spent the rest of the day outdoors, his thoughts wandering from captaining *Windsong* to unfamiliar places, to tanned young women and warm, white beaches. On occasion he'd stop and inwardly laugh at himself, feeling both foolish and guilty about desiring women so young, but then he would allow his daydream free again and be on a warm beach with a beautiful woman at his side. He worked steadily, digging and raking at the roots of trees and shrubs, adding compost and fertilizer, pulling weeds and turning soil. The physical labor felt good. He'd be tired by evening and sleep would come. He needed to expend this energy, wear himself out, or the nights would be long and sleep little more than drifting in and out of bad dreams.

On Sunday morning he had his usual breakfast of toast and coffee. He stared out the window where light rain fell from low clouds. Another dreary day. He thought of *Windsong* and lush, tropical islands again. He was restless. He dressed and began the drive to the store for a Sunday newspaper. When he reached the intersection where he would have turned left he turned right instead. He didn't want to be in the house reading about what other people were doing nor did he want to spend a day reading a novel about people living exciting, fascinating lives while he sat on his easy chair and became another piece of unmoving furniture. He needed to do something, get out, be alive.

He took the Long Island Expressway east toward Northport. He hoped *Windsong* was still at the pier. He had to look at her one more time. He needed to make up his mind one way or another. He couldn't go on this way. He felt trapped, trapped in the life he was living, trapped in getting old, trapped even in his own self. He didn't know what had happened or why it had happened but he had reached a point where he could no longer go on. Something had to change. Something had to be different or he felt as though he were going to burst. There was a knot, no, more like a cylinder of pressure about to explode, pushing against the inside of his chest. He drove well above the speed limit on the slippery road and didn't care. He wasn't sure if he were running toward something or from something and it didn't really matter. At least he was doing something and not idle, dormant, waiting on age and death.

He drove down Main Street in Northport and it was a ghost town on this chilly Sunday morning. The rain stopped but a steady wind blew from the east, a harbinger of a cold front moving down from the north. The parking lot at the public pier was empty and Walter parked facing *Windsong*, relieved. She sat at the end of the pier waiting as she had the week before, tied snug against sturdy pilings, her cheery colors a bright spot in gloomy surroundings. He walked down the pier, wind tugging at his clothing, salty sea-spray striking his cheeks, and he felt good being free of the confines of the house. He took deep breaths as he strode determinedly toward the boat, enjoying the invigorating cold air. He was alive, strength surging through his limbs.

Windsong stood steady against the pilings, spring lines holding her. As before, the For Sale sign was taped to the pilothouse window and the handrail lowered for easy access to board. Walter stepped on without hesitation.

The smooth, freshly painted deck was slick from rain and spray. He made a mental note to refinish portions of the deck with skid preventing paint or some other material. He wouldn't want to work on a slippery surface in heavy weather while at sea. He walked around the exterior of *Windsong* inspecting her more carefully this time. He now noticed the sloppy painting done by the high school boys and the rough patching. His learning to become his own handyman would be extremely useful now. He could do better work than this.

He went below and inspected each of the cabins, again finding slipshod work and the use of cheap materials. Initially it annoyed him to see how uncaringly the work was done, but after considering it, it made sense. Dudley Shoemaker wanted to sell the boat. He was putting in as little time and money as he could get by with on *Windsong* to prepare her for market. It's not the way Walter would do the work, but in the real world people usually approach selling things this way. It was strange, but he felt better after seeing some of *Windsong*'s imperfections. He knew he wanted to buy her, had wanted to own her since seeing the For Sale sign in the window. She'd looked beautiful. Now he knew he could make her more beautiful.

As he stepped out on deck he noticed a couple standing on the pier admiring *Windsong*. The woman noticed him and smiled.

"Hi," she said, pleasantly.

"Hi," he returned her smile and nodded at her companion. They were young, probably in their early twenties.

"It's a nice boat," the man said, looking at *Windsong* with approval. Walter said nothing. Apparently they assumed he owned *Windsong* and for some reason he didn't want to tell them he wasn't her captain.

"It's big. I'll bet we could put our apartment in it ten times," the woman said. The man stiffened.

"Come on, honey. Our place isn't that small," he said, defensively.

"Oh, you know what I mean." She placed her hand on his arm to pacify him. "It's just that I've never seen a boat this big, at least up close."

The husband or boyfriend seemed placated and once again looked at *Windsong* with interest. Walter could detect a Brooklyn brogue as they spoke. He looked to the parking lot and next to his Lincoln was parked a battered Toyota. He guessed they were a couple of city kids out for a Sunday drive. The weather was lousy but that hadn't deterred Walter either. He had to get out of the house and guessed they felt the same way, bad weather or not. A mist began to fall and the woman put her hands into her coat pockets and hunched her shoulders.

"Would you like to come aboard?" Walter offered.

"We're not looking to buy it," the woman said. "We couldn't afford something like this. We were just looking."

"Why don't you come aboard anyway. At least you'll get out of the rain." Walter stepped clear of the opening in the railing so they would be able to pass. For some reason he wanted to share *Windsong* with this couple, two others who were suffering from cabin fever and had to get out of their apartment and go somewhere and do something.

"Could we?" the woman asked her companion.

He shrugged. "Sure. Why not?"

The woman walked to the opening at the handrail and stood looking down at the water between the two foot opening separating the pier from *Windsong's* deck. The man came and took her elbow. "Let me help you, Honey."

Walter noticed a slight bulge beneath the woman's long, heavy coat. Because of the dark, loose-fitting garment he hadn't noticed she was pregnant. He held out his hand to help her aboard and a simple wedding band told him that they were a young, married couple. She stepped aboard and stood there for a second, making sure of her footing. The husband followed and they went into the pilothouse.

"Boy! Look at all of this," she said, eyes wandering from radios to compass and depth sounder and engine gauges.

"Yeah, it sure ain't like the rowboats in Central Park," the husband agreed, glancing around. He went to the door leading to the large cabin. "Hey, look at this," he called over his shoulder.

His wife came and peered into the single room that covered most of the deck. "It's got a kitchen and everything!"

"Why don't you go on in and look around?" Walter said, enjoying playing host. He followed them into the greatroom.

"It has everything. The kitchen is even bigger than ours." The wife looked from place to place in the galley. Walter noticed each time she mentioned their small apartment and compared it with *Windsong* her husband became annoyed. His voice was tight when he spoke again.

"We'll be getting a bigger apartment, with the baby coming. I told you that."

"I know," she said, walking to the center of the large room and putting her arms out as a ballet dancer would. She took several small steps and twirled, coat flaring as she spun. "It's like a ballroom. We could dance the night away in here."

"Maybe someday we'll own something like this. You could invite your family out from Brooklyn. They'd love it. Your Uncle Tony would have a crap game going in that corner over there," her husband responded.

His wife laughed, cheeks pink from being outdoors and eyes shining. She had that look of health that some women get while pregnant. "He would," she agreed. "And Momma would have a big pot of spaghetti sloshing all over the stove and the kids would be hanging off everything in the place. It'd be a wreck in fifteen minutes." She laughed again.

Walter watched them, enjoying their dreams with them. He guessed they were working-class people with little chance of ever owning a boat such as this. But they could dream and as long as their dreams didn't turn them bitter because others had and they didn't they could share moments of escape from that little apartment in Brooklyn and live in their fantasy. He had been doing much the same lately. The difference was he didn't have a lovely, dancing, pregnant wife to share the dream with. But at least he could afford the boat. He might not be able to buy their youth, but he could buy a piece of their dream.

"Would you like to see below?" Walter asked, walking to the steps leading to the cabins beneath. They followed and began a tour of *Windsong*. The wife "oohhed" and "aahhed," darting from place to place discovering and pointing out *Windsong's* charms. She was like a child with a new toy. She asked dozens of questions and he answered them as authoritatively as he could. Her husband followed behind enjoying her pleasure but at the same time uncomfortable in surroundings well beyond his financial reach. He tried to play her game of "Wouldn't this be wonderful?" and "We could do this and that and go here and there," but his heart wasn't really in it. He knew the realities of low pay, a baby on the way, and paydays already stretched to the limit. Walter watched and listened to what was said and even more importantly what was left unsaid as the young couple scrambled about the boat. In an odd way they were much like him. A dream had come alive and yet the practical self was there constantly raising objections. He watched the young wife, radiant with health and pregnancy, animated and alive with hopes for the future. The husband followed along, not objecting to her world of fantasy, but ever present with his world of practical reality. He had always been much like this young husband, but watching the wife happily enjoying her afternoon he knew he had become infected by the same virus for living, even if it were only within a fantasy, that she had.

By the time they finished Walter knew he was going to buy *Windsong*. He also knew he wasn't going to buy her just to take her out a few weekends during the summer. He was going on a trip. He wasn't sure where or how but he knew that was what he would do. He wanted some of the life that radiated from this lovely woman. He hoped *Windsong* could show him how to find it. Most of his past died with his wife, and his present had become tedious boredom. He needed a dream, a future.

They were standing on the deck ready to leave *Windsong* when the wife, Vickie, asked him, "Can I ask you a question?"

"Sure," Walter said.

"I know it's presumptuous, but why are you selling it?"

"Selling it?"

"Yeah. How come you're selling the boat?"

Walter laughed self-consciously. He had been caught in his act of ownership. "I'm not selling it. I'm buying it."

"Ohhh." Vickie grinned. "That's nice. I hope you have good luck and a lot of fun with it."

"Thank you. I hope so too."

"Come on, Joseph," Vickie jumped lightly onto the pier. "It's getting late and it's a long drive home. I'll bet you're starving."

The husband took her arm. They both turned and waved good-bye. He returned their wave and watched them walk to their old car. The husband held his wife around the waist, hugging her to him, as they walked. The car pulled out of the parking lot and onto Main Street and disappeared as they headed back to Brooklyn.

VI
Wheel, Kedder
and Matthews

This Monday morning was different from previous Mondays. Walter slept well and woke feeling excited about the prospects for the coming day. The train trip to the office passed quickly while he read the newspaper's classified section searching for marine equipment, and flipped through the paper looking at vacation advertisements, stopping and considering those islands in the Caribbean that might be within *Windsong's* range. He was beginning a mental list of additional equipment he would need for navigation and ship's safety. *Windsong* wasn't ready for an ocean voyage and much needed to be installed before he could begin his trip. A durable life raft was first on the list. Next would be a location finder, satellite weather receiver, and a long-range radio. With satellites in the sky and modern receivers, a craft could be equipped to sail anywhere in the world. He would install whatever electronics needed so he could go wherever he chose. It excited him to think about leaving Northport and be able to go to any port in the world, the only restriction being the amount of fuel he could carry. Dudley Shoemaker had been vague about *Windsong's* range when Walter asked. He was going to have to verify fuel consumption before he began any long-range ocean sailing.

These thoughts occupied him all the way to the office. Once there Myra handed him his schedule for the day and he was grateful to see he had time this morning to begin the process of buying *Windsong*. Myra noticed a change in him and hesitated before leaving. "Did you have a nice weekend, Mister Marshall?" she asked.

"Quiet, really."

He looked at Myra, a little surprised. They had worked together for years but always kept a rather formal, professional relationship. He knew very little about her other than she was divorced and had two grown children and lived in Queens. They rarely spoke about their life outside of the office. Her asking about his weekend was unusual.

"You seem to be in an exceptionally good mood this morning," she said, tidying his already neat desk. For months she had watched Walter become more and more withdrawn and had worried in silence. What could have brought about such a change?

He grinned. It was a happy face. Spending all day outdoors Saturday, even though the sky had been overcast, put color to his flesh. His eyes were clear and sharp. Something happened to snap him out of his depressed state. "I guess I am." He stopped and thought for a moment. He did feel good. "I was thinking about taking a vacation."

"I should hope so. It's been years since you took a real vacation. Are you doing something special?"

"Maybe. I've been thinking of buying a boat. Maybe taking a trip."

"That sounds wonderful. You deserve it," Myra said, emphatically. "I brought the vacation sheet in Friday. Did you see it?"

"Yes, I have it. Speaking of which, would you call Tom

Watson and see if I can meet with him for a couple of minutes this morning? It's about the vacation schedule."

"Right. I'll call his office now."

"Thanks, Myra."

"Do you want some coffee? We have coffee cake too."

"Hmm, that sounds pretty good. Sure. I'll have some."

"Right. I'll be right back." She left quickly, happy to see her boss in such a good mood for a change and glad he was going to eat. His suits were beginning to hang on him, he'd lost so much weight during the past winter. She hummed as she prepared his coffee and snack in the outer office.

He dialed Dudley's phone number. After several rings. "Northport Marina."

"Is Dudley Shoemaker there?" Walter wondered what connection Dudley might have with Northport Marina.

"He's not here right now. He might be in later, might not."

"Is this his office number?" Walter asked.

"Naw, he ain't got no office. He just gets his calls here sometimes. Is this about the boat?"

"Yes, I'm interested in buying it."

Bee Williamson, the owner of Northport Marina, was an honest man and he knew more about *Windsong* than he wanted to know. He was also a distant cousin of Dudley Shoemaker and Dudley was a fairly good customer in his own way. Bee Williamson paused before he spoke again. He felt he needed to say at least something about *Windsong*'s poor condition.

"Are you planning on using her?" Williamson asked, hoping that whoever was calling was buying *Windsong* for salvage.

"Of course. What else?" Walter asked, perplexed.

"You know she needs some work," Williamson said. It was the least he could do as a warning to a potential buyer that there were things wrong a new paint job wouldn't fix. He'd caulked and sealed some of the major leaks below the water line but that wouldn't do anything to help with the wood rot.

Walter assumed the man was trying to get some work for Northport Marina. "Yes, I've been out on her. I know there are a few things that need to be done. I'll probably be taking her over to you to have some navigational equipment installed. And I'm sure I'll find a few other things I'll want done."

"She needs a lot of work," Williamson said again. To anyone who knew anything about boats, especially wooden boats, this comment would be a red flag signalling danger. But Walter didn't hear this. What he thought he heard was a man looking for business.

"I know," Walter said, dismissing Bee Williamson's unheard warning as a sales pitch. "And we'll get around to doing what needs to be done. Soon, I hope."

Williamson said all he was going to say about *Windsong*. If Dudley found someone foolish enough to buy a boat that might be beyond repair, Williamson would have to let nature take its course. "If you'll leave your number I'll have him call you as soon as he comes by," he said, with an internal sigh. It was a tough world out there. The big fish were always eating the little fish and it sounded as though Dudley Shoemaker found another fish to munch on.

Walter thought for a second. He had Dudley's home phone number. He would try that first. "I have another number. If I can't get him there, I'll call you back."

"Okay. Good luck."

"Thanks." Walter dialed Dudley's home.

"Hello?" Dudley answered.

"May I speak with Mister Shoemaker?"

"This is him."

"Good morning. It's Walter Marshall."

Dudley's voice brightened. "Good morning. It's good to hear from you!"

"I went back and took another look at *Windsong* yesterday."

"You did? Good. Good. I'm sorry you didn't call. I would have met you in case you had any questions or anything. We could've taken her out if you wanted."

"No, I just wanted to have another look. I'm interested in buying her."

"You are? Well, good!" Dudley said, gleefully. "I'm sure you'll be happy with her."

"I think I am already, in a way," Walter smiled into the phone. In less than twenty-four hours he had changed. He was thinking of the future now, planning, making arrangements. It was as though a switch had been turned on and he was alive again.

"Wonderful! When can we get together so I can sign her over to you?"

"I'll have to get the financial arrangements made first. While I'm doing that, I'd like to get *Windsong* surveyed."

Dudley was stunned. This would torpedo the whole deal. A surveyor would find the hull damage and put it in his report with the probable recommendation not to buy. It would be devastating. Dudley thought fast, as was his forté. "Well, Mister Marshall, I was hoping we could move along on this. Getting a surveyor out here will take a few days, maybe even a couple of weeks. Like I was telling you, I got this business deal going and the reason I'm selling the boat is to get some cash, quick. It's not something I can wait on. So, if it's all right with you, I'll make you a deal." Dudley spoke rapidly, the words flowing. "I'll drop the price again. I'd like to close this as quickly as I can."

Walter had no idea how long it would take a surveyor to inspect *Windsong*. He also wasn't sure how he was going to purchase *Windsong*, whether by trying to gather enough cash or possibly taking out a loan. He hadn't expected Dudley to be pushing so hard to sell.

"I'll get things going as quickly as I can," he told Dudley.

"Yes, yes, I'm sure you will, but how about I drop the price to ninety-five-thousand? Could we get everything done in the next couple of days then?"

"Ninety-five-thousand?" Walter would have been willing to pay the asking price of one-hundred-fifteen-thousand, or the original price of one-hundred-twenty-five-thousand dollars. He was not much at bargaining over prices with a salesman.

"That's a good price, Mister Marshall. I've dropped the price thirty-thousand dollars. You couldn't ask me to do more than that, could you? "

"Why, no. It's just that I can't see how I can come up with ninety-five-thousand dollars in just a couple of days." Ninety-five-thousand dollars! Who had cash like that lying around?

Dudley began to panic. He had to find a way to close this deal. He might never find another buyer and eventually he would have to sell *Windsong* for salvage and take a ten-thousand dollar loss. That was if he could get thirty-two-thousand dollars for salvage. "I'll tell you what," Dudley said, sounding as if he were surrendering. "Like I've been saying, I've got this big deal cooking and I want to strike while the iron's hot. I'll be in on the ground floor. Since you've caught me short I'll make you an offer you can't refuse. We'll make it seventy-five-thousand. It's the best I can do. It's much less than I paid for her but I'm willing to take the loss. I'll make it up on the deal I'm getting into. The boat's worth a lot more, but, what the heck. It's only money, right?" Dudley tried to laugh and it came out as a cackle. His mouth and throat were dry, nerves tingling. He was in the midst of a deal, the one true love in his life.

Walter didn't know what to say. He hadn't been haggling. Dudley's dropping the price by fifty thousand dollars caught him by complete surprise. That was a big savings. And *Windsong* had become more than just a boat. She was his escape, his safety valve releasing the internal pressure he felt.

"Can I call you back," Walter needed time to think about this new development. "Will you be home for awhile?"

"I'll be here. Will you be calling soon?"

"I think so. I just need to check and see what I can do. That's still a lot of money to come up with so quickly."

Dudley felt he was close, very close, to making this thing work. "I'll be waiting on your call. I can only hold this price for a short while, just so's I can get into the other deal. If we can't work this out in the next couple of days then I'm afraid I'll have to back out. It's only that I need the cash right now."

"I understand. I'll get back to you as soon as I can."

During the phone conversation Myra had brought in coffee and a piece of coffee cake. She left as quietly as she came. He barely noticed her. Absently, he sipped the luke-warm coffee and took a bite of cake thinking about the money. He could pay cash for *Windsong* if he decided to. The money was there. Laura's money. No, not Laura's money, he corrected himself. It was his money. He was the beneficiary. That was what an insurance policy was for, to ease the pain of loss. It wasn't a trade of *Windsong* for Laura. Laura was gone. *Windsong* was there. He needed to start to live again.

The inter-office buzzer sounded and Myra's voice said, "I have your appointment with Mister Watson this morning."

"What time?"

"He's available all morning. Just go on up whenever you're ready."

"Thanks, Myra."

"Right."

So that was set. Walter felt confident he could ask for as much time as he needed to... to what? To get his head straight? To get his life together? To have some fun in the sun and maybe even find the woman of his daydreams? He didn't know. All he knew was he had to do something, anything, to break out of the stifling rut he was in. Should he take two months, three months, maybe more, time off? He knew Tom was a cautious man. He would talk with him and not make a final decision at this meeting. Tom would have Walter's time log sent for, probably going back to the first day he went to work for Wheel, Kedder and Matthews, and check to see how much time off Walter had taken over the years. He would discover Walter took little vacation in recent years and even in the early years had rarely taken the full six weeks allotted. Over the course of all those years it would add up to many, many months, perhaps a year or two of vacation Walter never used. He would then send a pleasant note telling him to take whatever time he wanted so long as it wasn't too disruptive with his client load. He knew how it would work out even before going to see him.

He dialed John Cramer's number.

"Cramer here."

"Hello, John. It's Walter Marshall."

"Hello, Walter. What can I do for you? Have you decided to buy a few of those stocks that look good?"

"No, I've decided to buy the boat."

"Oh? Have you had it surveyed and everything already?"

"Not yet," Walter decided he wasn't going to tell John that he was going to skip the survey. As a lawyer he knew it was best to seek expert advice when venturing into something unfamiliar. That's how he made his living. But in this he wasn't being a lawyer. He was a man seeking escape. "But I'm sure everything's going to work out. So, I want to sell whatever Certificates of Deposit I have."

"Let me see." Once again he could hear the clicking of a keyboard as John pulled his file out of the computer. "As I think I said last time, you have a substantial amount in CDs maturing in May."

"I'd like to cash them in."

"Okay. They'll be available on May seventeenth."

"No, I want to cash them in now, today."

"Today? But you'll lose all that interest!" John Cramer sounded truly distressed. For him this was the same as burning money. "And there will also be a penalty. Can't you put off payment until May or at least get a short-term loan? Why give it to the banks?"

"It's no big deal. Don't worry about it. Cash them in."

"If you're sure this is what you want to do," John said, not liking to see this much money come out of Walter's account.

"Can you get it all done today?"

"Of course. It's all done electronically."

"Could you have a courier bring the check to my office?"

"No problem. It'll be there this afternoon. I just wish you weren't doing it this way. Maybe it would be better for you to get out of your less active stocks."

"No, sell the CD's." The Certificates of Deposit were the last tie Walter had with Laura's death. He was sure now that he wanted to get rid of them.

"Okay, Walter. If that's what you want. The check will be in your office this afternoon."

"Thanks, John."

After he hung up he felt better. It was as though a weight was lifted off his shoulders. It was done. He was on his way. He wasn't sure where or how but he was going to start living again. He dialed Dudley's number. It was time to begin.

VII

Departures

By mid-June Northport had changed considerably. Pleasure boats rode at anchor in a small, protected bay, each freshly scrubbed or painted, swaying in unison to wind and current, a colorful herd of small craft waiting to be sailed or driven beyond the breakwater and out into the Long Island Sound. The surrounding hills were no longer earth-brown and dreary, but alive with shades from near-yellow to deep green and splashes of red maple here and there catching the eye. The color of the sea had changed also. An early morning haze and a pale blue sky reflected off shiny, light green wavelets drifting into the harbor. Winter was past and the heightened activities of the summer season were about to begin at the old whaling Town of Northport. Summer residents were already on park benches and strolling along the water's edge.

Walter was below decks tracing an electrical line that was blowing fuses. The electrical system had been re-worked several times in the past and no one had bothered to take out the old wiring. The result was a tangled mess. Tracing any particular line was a nightmare. He cursed softly under his breath, a habit he recently acquired as he became involved with working on *Windsong*. He had learned, and continued to learn, more and more about the problems with the boat. He crawled on hands and knees in the narrow space in the bilge, tugging at wires as he tried to locate the short or grounded wire that was causing the fuse to blow to the forward cabin. He slammed the back of his head into a cross brace and cursed again, louder this time, and began a reverse crawl out of the claustrophobic confines. It was useless to try to make repairs now. It would take hours to trace the faulty wire, if it could be done, and this morning was not the time for it. They would be leaving soon.

He went on deck and checked his watch. It was nearing eight o'clock and Fred was supposed to be there at eight. Fred Calone was his mate, helper and companion for the trip to the Bahamas. Fred was eighteen and had just graduated high school. He took his final exams early and was going to miss graduation ceremonies so that he could take this trip. He planned on starting college in September and a summer of traveling, sightseeing, and living on a boat and being paid for it was a dream come true. Dudley introduced him to Walter soon after he bought the boat. He was one of the young men who hung around the boatyard and worked when work was available and went fishing when there was no work to do. He was a willing worker and had become fairly knowledgeable about boat repair. Walter felt fortunate in having him as a Mate.

It was past eight o'clock and he was getting worried. Fred was always punctual and of all days this was not the day to be late. They needed to give themselves as much time for traveling during daylight as they could. Unforeseen problems could come up with *Windsong* and he didn't want to be stuck with a breakdown in the shipping lanes of New York Harbor at night. He and Fred did everything they could to make*Windsong* ready for the cruise but anything could happen once underway. Breakdowns happen when least expected, and he was beginning to believe this was especially true of *Windsong*. The run from Northport to the New Jersey coast might be the most dangerous part of the trip.

An automatic bilge pump came on and a small stream of water flowed out of *Windsong*. He had been only slightly conscious of how often the pumps operated until the previous night. He slept aboard for the first time and each time a pump would come on he would wake with a start and lie awake until it stopped. There were four pumps in the lowest part of the boat and they seemed to take turns. The night of continuously interrupted sleep didn't help his nerves for beginning the trip. The fact that water was constantly seeping through cracks and seams of *Windsong*'s hull didn't do much to help his confidence either. All wooden boats leaked a little. He learned that through speaking with other boat owners and from the extensive reading he had been doing. But something told him that *Windsong* leaked more than normal, even for a boat her age and size. He had added this to the ever growing list of things to check and repair. The list had become pages long, most of which were minor, but would keep him and Fred busy during the trip.

Finally a car pulled into the parking lot and Fred got out and took a duffel bag from the back seat. His girlfriend, Ginger, came from the driver's side and opened the trunk. Fred took out a large valise and put it beside the duffel bag. He and Ginger spoke for a moment and then kissed. They held their embrace so long that Walter wanted to call out but said nothing. He turned and went into the pilothouse instead.

A small diesel generator hummed quietly in the engine room. He checked the gauges on the new instrument panel he'd installed. Everything looked normal. The fuel tanks were full, batteries held their maximum charge, and all else that he could think of was done. He started the two large engines that were to drive *Windsong* toward their destination. They quickly caught and he lowered the rpm to idling speed as the deck vibrated. He turned off the generator. The main engines would supply their power needs while under way. He turned on the new radar and in a few seconds the screen came to life and a cluttered bay and surrounding hills flashed back as the beam swept across the harbor. He turned on both radios and lowered the volume until the sound of the engines drowned out the static. Once again he glanced at the instrument panel. All was normal. They were as ready as they were ever going to be.

He was studying the charts for Long Island Sound and New York Harbor for the hundredth time when Fred entered the pilothouse. He squeezed through the narrow door, duffel bag on his shoulder and bulging suitcase in hand. He wore a knitted cap, matching dark blue knitted pullover shirt, faded dungarees, and sneakers. He truly looked the part of a seaman about to go to sea. Walter smiled.

"Glad you could make it," Walter said lightly. There was no point in berating him for being late. What good would it do? He knew Fred wanted to go on this trip almost as much as he did.

Fred dropped his duffel bag and suitcase on the deck and wiped his brow. He was too heavily dressed for the warm June morning. "I'm sorry I'm late, Walt. Something came up. I, er, didn't expect it to happen."

"No problem. It should only take us six or eight hours and we'll be at Barnegat Inlet. If we run late we can always use the radar when it gets dark," Walter said with a confidence he really didn't feel.

Fred picked up his luggage. "Where should I put my stuff?"

"Either of the cabins aft," Walter told him.

"Either of them?"

"Whatever makes you happy."

"Can I use the big one in the back?"

"Sure. What's the difference? They're both empty."

"I'll take that one," Fred said happily, dragging his baggage toward the stern. The aft cabin was the large one with a king size bed. Walter chose the cabin directly below the pilothouse. It was also one of the larger cabins but that was not why he planned on sleeping there. It was next to the engine room and closest to the pilothouse. It was close to being in the center of the boat and if anything went wrong he wanted to be able to get to the engine room or the pilothouse, with all it's controls, as quickly as possible.

Fred was back quickly. "Are we ready to get underway?" He had taken off his seaman's cap and pull-over.

"As ready as we're ever going to be."

Fred grinned. With his fair complexion and ruddy cheeks he made Walter think of the old tale, *Billy Budd.*

"I'll get the lines." Fred trotted over and began making the lines ready to shove off.

They had become a good team. Each weekend for the past two months they either worked on *Windsong* at the marina or took her into the Long Island Sound so they could both become familiar with how she handled. They practiced docking many times, Walter at the controls and Fred handling the lines, and both felt fairly sure they could handle the boat with at least some finesse. The last weekend Fred touched up the paint on the hull where they had brushed against dock or pilings as they landed. *Windsong* was a big boat and hard to handle in confined spaces when the wind was up or when Walter made a slight error in judging speed or distance. They practiced as much as time would allow and both knew they would have to be careful as they sailed into unfamiliar ports.

Walter walked to the pilothouse door and looked to the stern. Fred finished preparing the line to cast off. "Ready?" Walter asked. Fred grinned and nodded, the excitement of the prospects the summer might hold shining in his eyes.

"Let's go to the Bahamas," Fred yelled back loud enough so everyone on the pier would hear. He was proud of *Windsong*, proud of his seamanship, and proud to be sailing to the Caribbean.

"Let go the stern line," Walter called, and with a flick of the wrist Fred snapped the line free of the piling and trotted to the cleated forward line. He looked back and Walter nodded. Once again with a practiced snap he freed the forward line. Walter stepped back inside and stood at the wheel.

He didn't put the engines in gear immediately. There was a slight breeze blowing from the south and he allowed the wind to slowly push *Windsong* from the pier. He was learning how to use both wind and current to help control *Windsong*. The tall, broad side of the boat acted like a sail and she drifted first a foot and then it was five feet from the North Shore of Long Island. He eased on power and steered toward the harbor mouth. Fred called and waved as he stood at the stern, his girlfriend onshore calling and waving in return. Walter pushed the throttles forward and *Windsong* gained cruising speed. He listened to the engines, eyes sweeping across the gauges, and felt the vibrations beneath his feet and coming through the highly polished steering wheel. There were times when he felt he and *Windsong* meld, becoming one, *Windsong* a living thing and Walter both Master and slave to her.

As soon as they cleared the harbor mouth he pushed the throttles to full speed and steered west toward New York City. There was a barely noticeable roll as *Windsong* cut smartly through the waves, white spray flying from her bow, engines humming below decks. The wind whistled through the open doorway and the sun glistened off the white deck. He felt free, glad all the preparations were over and the journey beginning. Unconsciously, he hummed an old tune that had been popular when he was in college.

"Want some coffee?" Fred asked. He had been standing

quietly on the other side of the pilothouse watching the shore recede as Northport became smaller and then disappeared behind a point of land.

"Sounds good." Walter picked up a chart and checked their position.

"If it stays calm like this I'll be able to cook us some lunch," Fred called from the galley.

"I made some sandwiches," he called back. "They're in the fridge."

"The coffee'll be ready in a minute. Want something to eat now?"

"No, maybe later." Walter's nervous stomach didn't want food this morning.

The Long Island Sound narrowed as they headed west. Throgs Point and Throgs Neck Bridge loomed ahead, the first of the seven bridges they would sail under before they were in the Lower Bay of New York harbor and in the open waters of the Atlantic. They would be beginning the trickiest part of their trip soon. The western end of the Long Island Sound became a narrow channel where fierce currents wrecked many a boat. A receding tide became noticeable as they neared the bridge, the water rippling and twirling past concrete bridge supports. For the next five miles they would be running against the currents as the sea emptied from the channel and coves and bays. He glanced up at the heavy traffic on the bridge. Hundreds of cars looking like miniature toys crept along in both directions. Hundreds, perhaps thousands, of people passed overhead in the time it took *Windsong* to travel beneath. Each human being in those cars was part of the complex system that made possible the existence of a great metropolitan area. Each person was doing what he or she was doing for his or her own reasons and yet the total effect would allow an extremely complex social and economic system to work.

Walter smiled. His life had become simple since leaving the pier. All he had to do was to keep from wrecking *Windsong* on the rocks and hidden shoals which dotted the passage to the East River while subsurface rivers of water twisted and pulled at her hull. His hands were never idle, constantly swinging the wheel a little to the left and then the right as he tried to hold the boat in the center of the channel.

Fred turned on the radio and soft music came from the galley. He and Fred had reached a compromise on which station they would listen to, Fred liking the harsh sounds of modern rock and Walter usually selecting classical music. Each had to compromise and the station they selected played contemporary songs that were easy to listen to. Fred called it, "Elevator Music."

"Rikers Island," Fred said, after they passed under the Bronx White Stone Bridge and the prison island came into view.

"Uh huh." Walter looked at the island covered with low, dreary buildings where tens of thousands of prisoners were held for New York City.

"That's one bad place to be, that Rikers," Fred said, having heard stories of the rapes and beatings and murders that were common for the inmates.

"I'll try not to run aground there."

"If you do we'll get in the life raft and paddle back to Northport. I don't even want to be shipwrecked there."

"I'm not worried about Rikers," Walter said, glancing at the chart that lay in front of him. "What concerns me is Hell Gate."

"Hell Gate. That's a funny name." Fred came and looked at the chart.

"Want to know how it got its name?" Walter asked.

"Sure."

Walter thought back to what he had read about Hell Gate and the many other navigational hazards they would be traveling by on their trip south. His cabin held a small library on navigation, weather, small boat handling, boat and engine repair, and volumes on local histories of places where they would be stopping. He had been reading and studying since the day he decided to buy *Windsong*.

"Back in the old days before the invention of steamboats or any kind of power, the only way to go was under sail. Seamen and their ships were at the mercy of wind and tide and current. Look at the current," Walter said, pointing. "It's about six-knots coming through here. It gets worse at Hell Gate; at least that's what I've read, and the currents seem to come from all directions where the East River meets the Long Island Sound. If you were in it and the wind died down or changed direction or anything else went wrong, you could be dragged onto these rocky shores, over the centuries hundreds of boats were lost."

Fred glanced at the chart and then at the rock-filled shore. "If we lost power, would we end up like that?"

"We have two engines," Walter reminded him.

"Yeah, but if there were fuel contamination or something like that, we could lose them both."

"Nice talk, Fred. Now's not the time to be coming up with a suggestion like that."

"Just thinking," Fred said, his easy smile returning. "That would be a hell of a thing, wouldn't it? Get shipwrecked on the first day out and right here in New York City."

"Why don't you check the engines?" Walter said, ending the conversation.

Fred had verbalized exactly what he'd been thinking and hearing it wasn't helping his churning stomach. He was feeling less and less sure of being able to pilot *Windsong* in these treacherous waters. He had set a course and destination as if he were driving a car on a cross-country trip. He should have checked the tide schedule and timed their departure accordingly. It was obvious they were going to run this nasty stretch of water under some of the worst possible conditions.

He thought he'd planned everything before they left. He hadn't considered the effects of the tides in these waters even though he'd read about it. He wondered what else he might not have thought of.

Fred came up the forward ladder wiping oil off his hands. "Everything looks okay down there," he said, shoving the oily rag into his back pocket.

"We'll be in the East River in about ten minutes." Walter spun the wheel harder now, fighting the ripping cross-currents as he steered *Windsong* through the channel. They were making the same speed through the water as when they started, the speedometer indicating twenty-eight knots, but the slower movement of the shoreline told him that they were in a current that must have been exceeding eight knots and, therefore, slowing their forward progress by that much. Eddies and whirlpools spun along the shoreline and there were noticeable changes of color as one current struck another. *Windsong* cut through all of it with relative ease, Walter usually overcorrecting as a current would tug at bow or stern, wheel spinning as he held *Windsong* in the channel.

"It's kind of like people," Fred said, staring out over the bow.

"What?"

"The water. You think you know what's there but beneath the surface all kinds of things are going on."

"That's pretty heavy. I didn't know you were a philosopher." He glanced at Fred and noticed how serious he had become.

Fred shrugged and gave him a halfhearted grin. "I'm not. It's just that, well, Ginger and I, I mean Ginger is..." He became silent, whatever it was he was going to say about his girlfriend Ginger was left unsaid. He could tell Fred wanted to talk about something and probably needed to talk about it. Since it was only he and Fred aboard Walter sensed that he should pursue the conversation and let him say whatever he needed to say, but Hell Gate was just ahead.

"There's a lot of truth in what you say, but right now we'd better concern ourselves with what we're doing. Once we get by Ward Island we've got it made."

Water from the upper reaches of New York State contributed to their departure. Streams and rivers hundreds of miles away fed into the Hudson River and began the journey to the open sea. The last Ice Age had formed the Hudson Valley and created its deep river bed. An ice pack miles high slowly melted and receded leaving a north-south scar in the earth. Manhattan Island stood at the southern end of the great river with the East River branching off the Hudson and encircling the eastern portion of the island. After the spring rains the water level was high and millions of gallons per minute poured south toward sea level. The East River and Hell Gate were at the lower end of this funnel where fresh water mixed with the sea.

Walter steered *Windsong* to the left, following the channel as it swung south around Ward Island. The Triborough Bridge passed overhead and in what seemed like seconds they were in the East River and racing past the massive buildings of Manhattan. A swift following current pushed *Windsong*'s ground speed over thirty knots. There had been no dramatic challenges or troublesome cross-currents once *Windsong* had entered Hell Gate. The transition from wrestling with turbulent water to being carried along with the smooth flow of the out-going river and tide happened so quickly and with so little event that it took Walter a moment or two to realize it was all over. An oncoming harbor tug blew one deep-throated blast at *Windsong*. He answered with a single honk from the horns on the upper deck. They passed port to port, each taking the right-hand side of the channel.

"Boy, look at that tug struggle up river." Fred watched the snub-nosed tug push a large white wake before it. It was moving against the tide and barely making forward progress as *Windsong* raced by.

Walter nodded. "They're slow but those engines can push a small mountain."

Fred walked from one side of the pilothouse to the other. "The City sure looks different from here, doesn't it?"

"Yeah, most people don't get to see this view."

"We're past Hell Gate, aren't we?"

"Yes, that's all over."

"It wasn't so bad. Not like I expected after hearing you talk. I didn't even notice anything."

Walter laughed. "I'm sorry it didn't meet your expectations. Maybe we should go back and try it again. Maybe I can find a rock or something to run into."

"You know what I mean. Those currents before we got there were pretty bad and after hearing your story about those shipwrecks and all, I expected at least *something* to happen."

"To tell you the truth, I did too. Thank God it didn't. I had all I could handle in those currents."

They swept past Newtown Creek and Greenpoint on the northern tip of Brooklyn. A large, modern cargo ship was being unloaded on one of the old piers. Dilapidated warehouses and rotted docks lined the shoreline, grimy tenements and a decaying neighborhood extending beyond. The clean, modern cargo ship flying a foreign flag stood in sharp contrast to a dying part of the city. America had matured, and in some places had reached a point beyond maturity, and many ports in the New World could now match any of the worst of the decadent ports around the world. He felt for those people living in poverty in those dirty buildings. It was like having miniature third-world countries right in their midst. New York City was a crazy place with rich and poor and everyone in the middle all mixed together.

"Funny," Fred said, staring out over the bow, no longer

enjoying the unique view as much of the skyline passed by.

"What's funny?"

"I wonder if it isn't always like that."

Walter steered with one hand and held a chart of the Upper Bay in his other, glancing down occasionally as he kept track of *Windsong*'s position as they passed through the crowded and unfamiliar waters. Luckily, water traffic was light. He put down the chart and rested both hands on the wheel.

"What are you talking about, Fred?"

"I was just thinking. I was wondering if that's not always the way things are. We worry about the worst of things that could happen and then it doesn't turn out that way after all."

Fred looked at him and gave a sheepish grin. "Like the water back there. We were worrying about the worst that was yet to come and by the time we got there the worst had been while we were doing all of the worrying. You know what I mean?"

"I think so, about the water anyway. What's up? Is something wrong at home?" Fred never spoke like this. It was usually light chatter and playfulness. Something was truly bothering him.

Fred looked away and his lightly flushed cheeks turned a deeper red. "I don't know. What I mean is, there's a lot going on back there."

"Want to talk about it?" Walter was resigned to hearing him out whether the time was opportune or not. Whatever was bothering him might affect the whole trip and it was better to get his mind back on the boat and not have him drift away as he had been doing all morning.

"I'm not sure." Fred looked over at him and cast his eyes down. "I trust you, Walt, but I think I have to do some thinking first."

"Whatever you say. I'm here. If you feel like talking, I'm ready to listen."

"Thanks. Maybe later."

"Okay, but in the mean time, you want to check the engine

room again? And check the fuse box. There's a short some-where. I tried checking it but there wasn't time this morning. Maybe we can trace it this evening if we get in early enough."

"Sure. You want a fresh cup of coffee first?"

He thought about his stomach. The nervousness was gone. Maybe Fred was right. The worrying could be worse than the doing. "Why not?"

With a quick step Fred was in the galley and the radio turned up and he was singing. It was as though his mood turned on and off like hot and cold water. "You want one of these sandwiches?" he called.

"Sounds good. Check that refrigerator while you're at it. I'm not sure but I think that thing is acting up. It didn't feel too cold this morning."

The door to the refrigerator slammed. "Seems okay now."

They were nearing Downtown and he could see the green of Battery Park on the shore of the southern tip of Manhattan. The Wall Street area was abeam and he looked at the tall buildings that surrounded the one where he had worked for so many years. He couldn't see his building. It wasn't as tall as the others. He ate a tuna fish sandwich and drank a large mug of coffee as Manhattan fell to the stern. The Statue of Liberty gave them a silent good-bye as they passed under the Verazanno Narrows Bridge and out into the Atlantic Ocean. Walter checked his watch. Barring mishaps, he was sure they would make Barnegat Inlet before sundown. *Windsong* began a gentle rising and falling as she rode the incoming swells of the Atlantic, spray flying from her bow, engines humming under his feet. He ate a second sandwich. It tasted delicious.

VIII
Chesapeake

By evening of the third day, Walter and Fred had established a daily routine. Walter would be the first awake and after a quick walk-through of the boat, checking for leaks or anything else unusual, he prepared a breakfast of scrambled eggs, toast, and coffee. He then woke Fred and they ate together in the greatroom on the main deck and discussed plans for the coming day. Then it was starting engines, casting off, and an eight to ten hour run to their next stop-over for the night. Fred would make a light lunch while they were underway, and they would take turns driving *Windsong* as one relieved the other throughout the day. The evenings were spent doing minor repairs on *Windsong* until dark, and then, after a discussion of the merits of preparing various meals, Walter would put frozen dinners into the microwave. Both were content not having to cook or wash dishes.

Walter brought enough food to last them for weeks. But, by the look of things, it wouldn't be long before they would have to replenish their supply of prepared microwave dinners.

Windsong was at anchor off of Point Lookout in the

Potomac River. A cool breeze blew off the Chesapeake Bay east of the point of land that protected their anchorage. This would be the first night they would not dock. Twilight was dwindling and a three-quarter moon rose, the sky clear and more and more stars becoming visible. The sound of the generator was just audible from the engine room and the lights from the interior of *Windsong* created a cone of light in the darkening waters surrounding them. They were on the afterdeck looking at sky and stars and the twinkling lights coming from shore, both savoring these quiet moments. Small waves lapped at *Windsong*'s hull and this only added to the stillness around them. It was as though they were in their own little world, dark waters separating them from the other world and its demands.

"Want to hear some music?" Fred asked.

"I don't much care either way," Walter replied, and stirred.

He relit the pipe that had grown cold in his hand, the flare of the lighter on the dark afterdeck revealing his tanning face. "To tell you the truth, I was enjoying the quiet. It's peaceful out here."

"Yeah." Fred was silent for a moment and then said, "It makes things seem a million miles away. I mean, being out here away from everything and everybody, things seem a little different. You know what I mean?"

"Yes. I guess that's why men go fishing when there aren't any fish or they don't even like fish, or they sail, or just go out riding. Once you leave shore you leave everything behind, at least for awhile. It gives you a different perspective. I'd almost forgotten how much I enjoy it."

Fred stood and walked to the handrail. He flicked his cigarette in a high arch and they both watched the glowing ember streak through the dark and then disappear into the black water. "Look at all of those lights," he said, looking at the Maryland shore across the Potomac. "I was wondering.

What do all of those people do? How do they all live?"

Walter was silent for a moment as his eyes traced the shoreline and clusters of vari-colored lights. "They all manage, I guess. Most of us are born somewhere, grow up there, find a way to make a living. I guess most people die not that many miles from where they were born. People *find* a way to manage, to survive." Walter tried to chuckle but it came out as a "humph." Then he said, "There aren't too many options."

They were silent again. The flag at the transom snapped in the breeze. Small waves curled and splashed along the hull and a cable that had worked loose flapped rhythmically against the radar mast. Their view changed as the wind shifted and *Windsong* swung her bow to the new point of the wind. Fred lit a cigarette and inhaled deeply. "I've been thinking a lot lately."

Walter waited but after the pause continued to lengthen he said, "I've noticed you've seemed somewhat preoccupied these last few days. You're usually not so quiet."

"There's been a lot to think about. You know I was going to start college this fall?"

"You told me."

"And Ginger was too. She wants to be a nurse."

"You mentioned that, too."

"Well, maybe we'll have to put things off for awhile. Maybe I'll get a job and start earning some money."

"Why would you do that? I thought you were already accepted at Southampton College?"

"I am. I even got a scholarship. I was thinking of majoring in engineering."

"So why don't you go to school and get your degree? It's hard to make a living these days without an education."

"I know," Fred agreed, a touch of sadness in his voice.

Once again Walter waited for him to speak. There was something wrong and Fred was holding back, keeping it in.

Walter knew how much he'd been looking forward to starting college in the fall and how proud he was of the academic scholarship he received from Southampton. He talked about it quite a bit as they had worked together during the weekends before they sailed. Walter wondered if it might be money that was concerning him. If need be, he would help. A couple of thousand dollars shouldn't stop a young man from having a career.

"Is there any way that I can help?" Walter asked.

"I don't think so, Walt. Not in this. It's kind of personal." Fred thought for just a moment. "It's just that... I'm not sure where to begin."

"My father used to tell me if you can't begin in the beginning, begin in the middle. Wherever you begin it's the beginning."

"Begin in the middle. I guess the middle would be... Ginger's pregnant."

"Ohhh," Walter said, the sound long and drawn out. Much of what Fred had been saying and how he'd been acting lately made sense now. He was an eighteen-year-old with a girl-friend who was pregnant. That would cause a sensitive young man to do some thinking. He thought about Fred and Ginger's long good-bye hug and kiss on the pier before they sailed. Was now a good time for them to be separated? Should Fred be on this trip with him? Was he running away? How would he handle the boat if Fred decided to leave? Suddenly, he and *Windsong* were drawn into Fred's personal life.

"Yeah. Ginger didn't tell me until the night before we left. She'd just found out for sure a couple of days before. She's not that far along. She has time to... to do whatever it is she decides to do. Or rather, what we decide to do."

"You two haven't had much time to talk about this then." Walter said this as both a question and a statement.

"No. We figured maybe it was better this way. Being apart,

we could each decide what we thought best. She knows I want to go to college. I know she wants to become a nurse. She took all of the courses she needed in high school so she could go right into nursing school. We had our plans all figured out. Now this. We sure hadn't figured on this."

Walter was tempted to ask why they hadn't taken precautions to prevent this, but held the question back. What difference did it make now? Ginger was pregnant and discussing the whys and wherefores wouldn't change that one iota. They were both too young for marriage, but Fred was certainly not too young to be a father nor Ginger a mother. Society put great demands on young people. They were expected to stay in school, hold back their adulthood, for many years after puberty. Perhaps it was too much to expect from them, to curtail their natural instincts and desires. He and Laura had waited until after they were married until they had sex, but they might have been an exception even in their generation. He didn't know. There was a generation gap between him and Fred. Times change, values change, and he wasn't sure what was acceptable in society any longer.

"How do you feel about it, Ginger being pregnant, I mean?" Walter asked.

"I don't know. I love Ginger. At least I think I do. We've been going together for over a year and a half. We were probably going to get engaged sooner or later. We never talked about it but I think we both knew that. But with just starting college and everything we weren't making any long-term plans or commitments."

"What about Ginger? What did she say?"

"She said she could get an abortion if that's what I want."

"And do you?"

"I don't know." Fred slumped in a chair and lit another cigarette. "No, I don't want her to have an abortion. That's my child she's carrying. But I don't know what else we can do.

What happens if we get married? How am I supposed to support her and a baby? Where am I going to find a job that pays anything and where are we going to live? And what about college? When will we ever be able to go to school? I don't want to be stocking shelves or sweeping floors the rest of my life. I'd have to give up my scholarship and it would be years before Ginger could get into nursing. Maybe neither of us would ever go to college. Isn't that too high a price to pay?"

Walter was at a loss. How could he give this young, tormented man counsel? Fred should be able to go to college and have a career and hopefully earn a decent living. Ginger should too. But what about the baby? Didn't it have the right to be born and to live a life?

"What about your parents?" Walter asked, avoiding giving advice and hoping Fred could find his own answers if he were allowed to talk his way through the problems.

"Her parents or mine?"

"Both, I guess."

"My mother would have a heart attack if I didn't go to college. It's all she's talked about ever since I can remember. Neither she or Dad did. She works in a bowling alley taking care of the counter and books and such. My father drives a truck. He's union so he makes a pretty good living but it's not what they planned for me. For the longest time Momma wanted me to be a doctor. When I finally convinced her I didn't want to go into medicine she was willing to accept my becoming an engineer. I like to make things and build things."

Fred stopped for a minute, puffing on his cigarette. The last of the evening twilight was gone and *Windsong* was surrounded by black water that extended to an invisible shore. The breeze died and *Windsong* swung in a lazy arch.

"And Ginger's parents," Fred began. "They're something else. Her father would kill her and me if he knew she was pregnant. They're old-fashioned Italian. She's the oldest of three daughters and she's supposed to have a big wedding and all the family is supposed to come and all that stuff. Even if we decided to get married they would want to kill us. There's no time to set up a wedding and reception. It would kill them not to be able to throw a big bash and have their beautiful *virgin* daughter come down the aisle with the whole family present. It would be a family disgrace for their daughter to get pregnant before she was married. Ginger's afraid of her father and to tell you the truth I am too. He'd go crazy. There's no telling what he'd do."

"Sounds like quite a mess."

"Yeah, quite a mess," Fred said softly.

"Have you made any decisions now that you've had time to think about it?"

"No. I wish I could. The more I think about it the more complicated it gets. Even if we do what's right nobody's going to be happy."

"Do what's right? And what's that?"

"Get married. Have the baby. Try to set up an apartment for ourselves. It'll mean neither of us going to college and no big wedding. Everybody'll be mad at us and I don't know if we can even make it. Good paying jobs are hard to find and I don't have any experience at anything except working on boats a little. There's no money in that and the only time there's work is in the spring and summer. I guess we'd get some money from the wedding gifts and such, but what would we do after that?"

"You haven't spoken to Ginger since we left Northport?" They had spent the first night at a marina at Barnegat Inlet in New Jersey and the second night at Port Penn on the Delaware River. Walter couldn't recall seeing Fred use a public phone at either place but he might have.

"No. We agreed to wait a few days and think this thing through. I was thinking of giving her a call when we stop tomorrow night. We'll be in Virginia, right?"

Walter nodded in the dark. "Portsmouth."

"I'll call her from there."

"Do you have any idea what you're going to say?"

"Not yet. All I know is I'm beginning to feel like a rat, like I'm running out on her. And that's not what I want to do. She's not alone in this. We're both involved."

"Do you need to call her at any particular time? We can stop almost anywhere. There are plenty of marinas down the Chesapeake."

"No. I'll call from Portsmouth. She'll be in school all day anyway. I'll catch her at home in the evening."

They sat silently for awhile, Fred chain smoking nervously, Walter thinking about Fred and Ginger and being eighteen years old and still in high school and having to make decisions that might profoundly effect them for the rest of their lives. He bought *Windsong* and went on this trip because he felt his life had become a void. There was little happening and little meaning in what he had been doing day after day. Fred and Ginger's lives *had meaning* and there was certainly plenty happening. Pain and difficult decisions waited. Love and companionship and happiness might be there also. It was all part of the package. Living could be a messy business.

The wind became light and variable as the last of the day's heat dissipated from the land. *Windsong* swung, pointing north and the black, jagged hills of Virginia defined the heavens to the south. A country road followed the shoreline and an occasional car's headlights would sweep around curves and hills and weak beams of light would swing across the black water. Streetlights wound up one hill and lights in clusters dotted a backdrop of obscure forest.

"You know," Fred said suddenly, his voice loud in the stillness. "I've got a sister. She'll be thirteen soon. There's just the two of us and I've had to kind of look after her ever since she was little. She was sickly when she was a baby and they gave her some medicine that, well, reacted bad on her. It slowed her mental development I think is the way they put it. It's not that she's dumb or anything like that. It's just that she doesn't learn as quickly as most other kids in school. She's a nice kid really.

"Anyway, I've always had to take care of her, look after her, when my parents weren't home. It was my responsibility to see that she was okay. You know what I mean? Anyway, what I'm getting at is I've always been brought up to be responsible. I couldn't just think of myself. I wanted to be on the baseball team but my Mom had to work some evenings and Dad had to take long hauls with the trucking outfit he works for so there were times when I couldn't go to practice after school. I ended up quitting the team that first year. I was pretty good. I may have gotten an athletic scholarship if I'd been able to play but it was more important that somebody be home and look after Sis. It was my responsibility and I did it. That's the way I was brought up."

"But now I don't know who I'm supposed to be responsible to. Am I supposed to be responsible to myself and getting an education and maybe making something of myself? Am I responsible to my parents and how hard they've worked so I could go on to college and be something? Am I responsible for Ginger? She was the one who was willing to go on the pill. I don't know what happened, what went wrong. And what about a baby? I don't even know how I can support a kid. And I don't even want to think about Ginger's parents. Whatever I do I won't make them happy. Unless, of course, Ginger doesn't have the baby and they never know anything. I don't know. I just don't know."

Fred took a deep breath and collapsed back onto the recliner. He took out a pack of cigarettes, found it was empty, crumpled it and threw it over the railing. "I'm sorry to bend your ear like this, Walt. It's just that I feel that I can trust you, and I had to talk to *somebody*."

"I'm glad you did. I only wish I could come up with some

good advice. I really don't know what to say, how to be helpful."

"Naw, there's no way anybody can give advice on something like this, I don't guess. It's something I'll have to decide myself. You're just listening is helpful. It's one of those times when you have to pick the lesser of two evils, if that's the way to put it. No, not evil. That's not a word that I could apply to any of this, especially not to Ginger. I love that girl. It's just something that happened. But now I have to try to figure out what I'm supposed to do."

Walter thought about Ginger. She was small and pretty, with dark wavy hair and large brown eyes and long eyelashes. She looked tiny when she was near Fred, with him big and muscular and she small and slim. He remembered how she had clung to Fred during their final kiss there on the pier. Fred had been late that morning. He said something had come up. He certainly hadn't been exaggerating.

Fred stretched and yawned mightily. "It's getting late. I guess I'll turn in. I can't think anymore. My mind's gone dead." He went to the doorway and looked back. "Thanks for listening. I'm sorry I dumped all this on you."

"That's okay. I'm glad we talked." Walter wished there was more he could say.

"Good night." Fred entered the greatroom and walked toward the stairs leading to his cabin.

"Good night," Walter called over his shoulder.

The wind was calm. He shivered in the cool night air. He walked toward his cabin, stopping to turn the light out in the galley. He flicked it off and then back on. The amount of electricity one bulb would draw would mean nothing to the generator. He left the light on so *Windsong* could more easily be seen by any vessel that might approach during the night. He went below wondering how long the sound of the generator in the next compartment would keep him awake. Maybe he hadn't chosen the best cabin.

IX

Intercoastal

Walter was on the upper deck of *Windsong* trying to keep his balance as he stood on a shaky deck chair and taped a cable to the mast. Fred approached from the marina office, head down and eyes on the ground, muscular body swaying with each slow step. They had reached Portsmouth early that afternoon, the trip down the Chesapeake Bay having passed smoothly and quickly in a calm sea. They spoke little during the day, each anticipating the results of the phone call Fred just made. Walter finished taping the cable just as the arm of the deck chair gave way with a snap and he tumbled onto the deck with a thump and a yell.

"Are you all right?" Fred called, looking to the upper deck where the sound came from but seeing no one.

Walter stood brushing his knees, "I'm all right," he said, and picked up the broken deck chair lifting it high enough so Fred could see it. It was a tangled mess of canvas and broken wood.

"I guess it wasn't built to be used as a ladder," he said, sheepishly.

"You're not hurt?"

"No, I'm okay. I'll meet you on the afterdeck. I'm going to throw this in the dumpster and I'll be right back."

Fred went to the covered afterdeck and lit a cigarette. Walter returned after discarding the broken chair ashore, stopping first and getting two cups of coffee from the galley. He handed a cup to Fred and sat on the other lounge chair. He took a sip and rubbed an elbow bruised during his fall.

"I got a hold of Ginger," Fred took a gulp of coffee and then a drag on his cigarette.

"And how did it go?"

Fred looked down at the deck. "Okay, I guess."

"What did she say?"

"Not much. She just wants to know what I want to do. She's still leaving it all up to me. And she misses me," he added softly. He looked out over the water of the bay. "She sounded kind of scared, I think."

Walter waited but after a moment passed he asked, "Have you decided what you want to do yet?"

"No, I haven't. I'm still not sure what I should do. I do know what I *don't* want to do. I don't want to run away and leave Ginger with all the problems. And I don't want to do anything that I'll hate myself for the rest of my life." Fred thought for a moment. "I guess we ought to get married. That would solve at least one problem. It still won't make Ginger's family very happy. They've been planning on her having a big wedding and there's no way we can set anything like that up."

Walter thought for awhile before he spoke. It seemed a decision on marriage had been made. "You're both Catholic."

"Yeah," Fred nodded. "But we don't go to church much."

"By the sound of it, I think Ginger's family want a church wedding."

"Oh sure. My family would too."

"What if you were already married, say, by a Justice of the Peace?"

Fred looked at him. This was leading somewhere. Walter sounded very much like a lawyer as he asked these questions. "I'm pretty sure they would still expect us to get married in the Church. Catholics are funny about that. If you're married by a Justice of the Peace, I guess you're married but it's not the same. You're expected to be married by a priest. That makes it official, or something."

"So if you were married by a Justice of the Peace you would still be expected to be married again by a priest in a church, right?"

"Sure we would."

"What if you and Ginger had been married secretly for two or three months and then Ginger finds out that she's pregnant. She would have to tell her family then, wouldn't she?"

"I guess so. You can't hide that too long."

"Her family might be disappointed and maybe even a little angry but what's done is done, right?"

"I guess so."

"So then they would set up a church wedding as quickly as possible, wouldn't they?"

"Her mother and father would have fits but I'm sure that's what they would want."

"After the wedding you could have a reception. It might not be quite what her family would have wanted but I'm sure something could be arranged, don't you think?"

"Yeah, my father knows a lot of people. I'm sure we could get a hall. Have a band and that sort of thing. Her folks wanted a big sit down dinner and everything top shelf. It would break them financially, but that's the way they would want to do it. Like this it would save everybody a lot of money." Fred was getting enthusiastic.

"So if you were married by a Justice of the Peace first, this is pretty much how things would go, isn't it? Once the shock wore off, your families would accept what had happened, you two running off and getting married on the sneak and all, and they would do the best they could to make things work out, wouldn't they?"

"Yeah, they'd be pretty pissed off but there isn't much they could do."

"If you were married quickly by a Justice of the Peace and then told everyone you'd been married for awhile, perhaps things won't go as badly as you'd been projecting."

"But what about the date on the Marriage Certificate?"

"How many Marriage Certificates have you seen?"

"None."

"I've seen one. My own on the day I was married. It's been in a safe deposit box ever since."

"What about the priest? He might ask to see it."

"Do you think there would be a problem if you told him the whole story? The truth?"

"Naw, not with Father Fagan. I've known him all my life. I was altar boy for almost three years. In some things he's really tough, but if we tell him the truth I'm sure it'll be okay. He'd marry us."

"Do you think this is something Ginger might want to do?"

"I'm sure this is what she'd want to do. She wants to get married. I know it. I feel it. She hasn't insisted on anything. She's left it all up to me but I think deep down I've known all along she wanted to get married and have the baby. I do too, in a way. The only thing making it so hard is college. I still ain't figured out how we'll manage that. Maybe there's a way. I got a full tuition scholarship but I can still take out student loans. If I hadn't gotten this scholarship that's what I would've had to do anyway." Fred grinned. "We can say the scholarship is for the baby and the loans are for me."

"Why don't you call her back and ask her what she thinks?"

"What about you?"

"Me?" Walter asked, surprised.

"I can't just leave you here. You can't handle the boat alone. Maybe I should stay until we reach the Bahamas. Then I can fly back to New York."

"No. I'll be fine. I'll manage. Maybe I'll pick up some-body along the way. You go make your call. It's important. *Windsong* and I will get along just fine if we have to."

Fred walked to the handrail and stopped. He was blushing beneath his growing tan. When he spoke his eyes were once again downcast. "Er, there's another thing. I didn't bring much money with me. I don't have enough to buy a ticket home."

"Don't worry about that. You have some pay coming to you. You'll have more than enough."

Fred was still hesitant. "I don't want to leave you stuck. This... this whole thing. I didn't know about anything, Ginger's pregnancy and all, until the night before we left."

"I know. Go make your call. If you're going to get married, it's probably best to get things started."

"Okay. I'll tell her to get a safe deposit box."

"A safe deposit box?"

"Yeah. Like you said, for the Marriage Certificate. We'll put it in there and what's in there is nobody's business but ours. Whatever date is on it is between me, Ginger, and God," Fred said forcefully, as he turned and left.

In less than as hour he was gone. He'd returned from his second phone conversation grinning from ear to ear. He was getting married! Ginger loved all his ideas and cried and wanted him home as quickly as possible. Fred called the Greyhound bus station and there was a bus leaving for Wash-ington at six and from there he could catch the New York-Washington shuttle. Walter paid him two weeks wages in cash although they had been underway only four days. He also gave Fred a sealed envelope with instructions to open it on their wedding day. Walter had written a check for five hundred dollars made out to Mr. and Mrs. Fred and Ginger Calone as a wedding gift. Fred had tears in his eyes as he said good-bye and then dashed to the waiting taxi.

Walter watched the taxi pull away and tried to imagine what it was like to be eighteen years old and rushing off to get married and start a family. He was a good, honest, hard-working kid. He'd manage. Then a bilge pump clicked on and Walter listened as a small stream of water poured over the side. While at a marina *Windsong* was connected to shore power and there was no need for the generator. Windsong was quiet except for the gurgling splash near her stern. He went below to try and find what was wrong with the wiring to the forward cabin lights.

Early the following morning Walter reviewed the charts for the Carolinas. There was good anchorage just north of Moorehead City, North Carolina. He would stay in the Intercoastal Waterway through Albemarle and Pamlico Sounds, as he remained inside the barrier islands and away from the treacherous reefs off Cape Hatteras. Once beyond Moorehead City he could go into the Atlantic and sail along the coast. He could make better time in open water. There were no lift bridges to contend with and he wouldn't have to be concerned about other boat traffic in a channel. He had been topping off the fuel tanks at each stop and had a good idea of *Windsong*'s fuel consumption by now. He cast off and headed south. The wind was calm and he had little trouble maneuvering *Windsong* out of the tight confines of the marina. He forgot about making coffee or breakfast and didn't think about Fred Calone other than he was no longer aboard. Whatever needed to be done Walter would have to do by himself. All his thoughts were on *Windsong*, the weather, shallow water and running aground, and the lift bridges he had to contend with until he reached open water.

Traveling alone proved to be less difficult than he had

anticipated. As he reached stretches of open water he used the autopilot he'd installed. This freed him to make coffee and sandwiches, make quick trips below to use the bathroom or check the engines, or stand on deck outside the pilothouse, leaning against the railing in the breeze and watch the passing shore. He turned on the radio and found a station that played many of his favorite old songs and turned the volume high enough so he could hear the music while on deck, coffee cup in hand, cloudless blue sky and warm sun driving winter's discontent from him. He was both passenger and commander aboard *Windsong*. The autopilot steered, the engines throbbed, scenery passed, and he became more and more distant from his life on Long Island and New York City. He felt detached, no longer part of the goings on ashore. His world had become *Windsong*. It surprised him to discover that he was glad to be alone. Fred was helpful but also a distraction. Alone he was free of any ties with New York. It was just him and *Windsong*.

He dropped anchor off of Harkers Island in late afternoon. Moorehead City was several miles to the west and he could see the few tall downtown buildings on the horizon. Cape Lookout was to the south and barrier islands protected *Windsong* from the open sea. The depth sounder read twenty-two feet of water under the keel. It was good anchorage. Land surrounded him in all directions and no swells could build even if the wind rose. During the afternoon cirrus clouds drifted from the southwest and the sky became hazy silver. The NOAA weather broadcast called for a low front to move in overnight with rising winds and rain squalls.

He ate supper on the afterdeck—the paper plate held a nearly cold chicken dinner in his lap—watching tiny cars and vans travel down the single road that ran along the barrier island and the beaches that faced the ocean. The temperature was still in the eighties as the cloud-obscured sun settled toward the horizon. Each day became a little warmer as

Windsong sailed south. It would be two days before summer officially began but here in North Carolina, and even more so as he continued south, summer had already begun. He finished eating the last of the now cold chicken and leaned back and closed his eyes. He dozed, not fully asleep and not fully awake, thoughts almost forming and then dissolving as he allowed his body to relax.

A strong odor brought him out of a light slumber. He sat up and looked around and listened. It was a moment before it caught his eye. A small puff of black smoke drifted past the port handrail, dissipating as it was carried by the wind. He ran to the railing. The exhaust from the generator spewed a steady stream of black smoke from its exhaust outlet one foot above the water line. Something was wrong, terribly wrong. The steady hum of the generator was little different than normal but there was no doubt that oil was being burned in at least one of the cylinders. He ran to the pilothouse and down the ladder and into the engine room. The generator was running smoothly, nothing giving him a clue as to what was making it burn oil. He pressed the emergency stop button and the generator became silent. There was barely enough light coming through the portholes for him to check the oil level. It was low. He knew it was well up in the safe range when he started it an hour or two before. A ring on one of the pistons must have cracked allowing oil to be sucked into a combustion chamber. This would be a major repair and in the meantime he would have to do without auxiliary power.

The room was becoming dark. He went to his cabin and got the large, heavy-duty flashlight he kept by his bed. He returned and put all but the navigation switch in the off position. He didn't want anything that wasn't absolutely necessary to be drawing on the batteries.

It was a long, hot, restless night. Heat from the engines running during the day not only made the engine room as hot as a sauna but also raised the temperature in his adjoining state room. He tried to force himself to sleep but the heat and a nagging feeling that he had forgotten something kept him twisting and turning on soggy sheets. It was well past midnight when it came to him with a jolt. He grabbed the flashlight and ran to the engine room and opened the electrical box. He had turned off the bilge pumps. He threw the switch and immediately all four pumps went on. He lay in bed listening as one by one the pumps turned themselves off once they had lowered the water in the hull. Each time a pump would come on or a larger wave splashed against the hull or the wind shifted and the anchor line creaked, he was fully awake. Then he would close his eyes and wait for sleep. Images came, his wife when she was young and then the haggard, living corpse just before her death, his children young and playful, a gaping hole in the hull of *Windsong* with foaming water pouring through, all came in a repeating pattern as he tried to will his body to relax and his mind to sleep.

It was raining lightly when morning finally came. He started the engines and turned all electrical switches back on. The refrigerator and freezer could only be off for so long. He needed refrigeration if he were going to save the fresh and frozen food he had packed in both. He winched the anchor up and headed for Moorehead City. The wind was from the south at about fifteen knots and dark, low clouds spilled a steady rain against the pilothouse windshield. He took *Windsong* at slow speed back into the Waterway channel and headed to the one marina at Moorehead City that could handle a seventy-eight-foot boat.

Kelly's Marina had its own private channel leading off of the Intercoastal Waterway and he steered *Windsong* slowly up this narrow, deep-water path. Large power boats and sloops filled all available docking space except for the fueling station directly in front of the marina office. *Windsong* filled the narrow channel. Walter had *Windsong* moving as slowly as possible and still have steering ability. He adjusted *Windsong*'s slight drift due to the wind and aimed to come alongside the dock. He cut the engines and ran forward so he could heave the bow line to a teenage boy waiting. *Windsong*'s momentum kept her moving at a steady three knots. Boats were tied to pilings and wooden walkways in all directions. If he missed at this attempt there would be no second chance. *Windsong*'s momentum would carry her into the boats tied directly ahead. He held the line until he was sure he could heave it and reach the young man waiting and watching. He cast the line; it was quickly grabbed and the boy walked along with *Windsong* keeping pace so he could tie the bow line to the far end of the dock. Walter raced to the stern to prepare to throw the stern line ashore.

Windsong moved slowly and relentlessly forward. He had misjudged only slightly but his slight error quickly became evident. Ten feet from the bow *Windsong*'s hull struck a piling. There was a groan that was almost human as both piling and hull absorbed the impact. *Windsong* continued to move forward, her forty tons giving her impetuous. There was a grinding sound as *Windsong* brushed along the pilings. The boy looped the bow line and ran to catch the stern line from Walter. By the time he tied it *Windsong* had stopped.

The boy stepped back and wiped wet hair from his forehead. "Wow, that was some landing!" From near the bow to just short of the transom there was a three foot wide skid mark.

Walter climbed over the handrail and jumped onto the dock. "Damn!" He rubbed the unsightly black streak. His rubbing did no good. No amount of scrubbing would get this off. This portion of the hull would have to be repainted.

"Why didn't you put it in reverse?" the boy asked.

"I couldn't be at the controls and be ready to cast you a line both," Walter snapped, annoyed with himself and the boy with such a silly question.

The boy looked from Walter to *Windsong*. He wanted to ask why Walter hadn't just stayed at the controls while he steered the boat to a stop and *then* cast a line ashore, but he said nothing. This older man didn't seem to be in the mood for polite conversation. Instead he said, "Wow," again. "I've never seen it done *that* way before."

Walter looked at the boy, jaw muscles tight. "Is there anyone in the office?"

"Yes, sir." The boy pointed to the building near the dock. "The boss is in there."

"Thank you. And thanks for the help," Walter said, trying to regain his composure.

"You're welcome." The boy looked back at *Windsong*, shaking his head. That was an awfully big and expensive boat to be treated in such a way.

X
Adrift

The taxi splashed through puddles in the rutted drive and stopped in front of the marina office. He stepped out and his foot sank ankle deep in red mud. He cursed and pulled his foot from the sucking ooze. The driver looked back and saw what happened. "Sorry about that," the driver said. "I'll pull up a little. The way it's been raining lately the ground can't take no more."

Walter held his mud-encased shoe off the floorboard as he drove a few feet to where the ground was higher. He stepped out and stamped his foot, trying to shake the sticky mud free. It stopped raining and the sky was beginning to clear but throughout the day there had been thunderstorms. The weather front had passed and the forecast for the next two days was for clear skies and light winds. He looked at *Windsong* tied to the dock where he left her that morning, the ugly black streak along her white hull a clear reminder of his inadequacy as a pilot.

"Want me to help ya take this stuff on the boat?" the driver asked in the slow drawl of the Carolina shore.

"No thank you," Walter said, impressed. It's the last thing in the world a New York cabbie would do. "We can leave it here and I'll load it later."

"If'n I didn't know you were a sailor, I'd a sworn you were goin' campin'." The driver untied a strap holding the boxes on the luggage rack on top of the taxi. "You gonna stop out on some island and camp out or something?"

"Maybe," Walter replied, not wanting to take the time to explain why he would be needing all the equipment. "In any case, it'll be handy to have aboard."

The driver looked over at *Windsong*. Now there was an expensive boat. All these rich Yankees. Buying hundreds, maybe thousands of dollars of camping equipment and maybe he wouldn't even be using it. The driver thought of the old camper on the back of his pickup. He glanced at the price on one of the boxes as he unloaded it. This one thing cost almost as much as he'd paid for a used camper. Rich Yankees! They had all the money and he couldn't figure out how they did it.

"She's all fueled," said the pimply-face boy who helped with the lines earlier that morning. "She didn't take much."

"Thanks." Walter told the boy. "No, I didn't use much. I just wanted to top off. I don't want to pull into too many marinas if I can help it."

"That might not be a bad idea," the boy agreed, looking at *Windsong* and the mark on her side. Walter followed his gaze and gritted his teeth.

"I'll be leaving early tomorrow so if you'll figure up my bill I'll pay you now. If I did any damage to the dock I'll take care of that too."

"No damage to the dock. It sure didn't do much good for your boat though." The boy started to leave, a coiled hose slung over his shoulder. "The boss has your bill all made up in the office," he called back as he stomped through muddy puddles, pants tucked into knee-high rubber boots.

Walter took the last of the bags out of the trunk and put it by the others. He paid the driver and the taxi pulled away leaving him standing beside a waist-high pile of boxes and bags. He bought all he might need for the rest of the trip, at least as far as Fort Lauderdale. He looked up at the sky again. There were fewer clouds than before. He left the packages on the ground and went to the marina office.

A very round, middle-aged man was behind the counter. He looked up when Walter entered. "I called all around locally and there ain't nobody got parts for your generator. The only place would be from the manufacturer," Kelly said, wiping his balding head with a handkerchief.

"Thanks for checking. I don't want to wait for ten days to two weeks for parts. I'll go on down to Fort Lauderdale and see what they can do there."

"Suit yourself."

"The boy said you had my bill?"

"Sure do. Is there anything else you need?"

"No, I don't think so. I bought a bunch of stuff in town. Lamps and things like that. I'll manage without a generator for awhile."

"I could get you a gas generator if you're interested. I could have it here by tomorrow," Kelly hoped to make a sale.

"No thanks. I think I'll stick with diesels."

He paid the bill and loaded *Windsong*. While tied up at the marina, *Windsong* was connected to shore power. The electric stove was working so there was no need for the portable gas stove he bought along with kerosene lanterns, extra flashlight and batteries, canned food, cot and netting, and a dozen other things he thought might be handy if he were to be away from shore for several days or weeks. From now on he was going to travel *very* easy. He would stay in the Intercoastal Waterway all the way to Fort Lauderdale and have the generator repaired or replaced there. He would go to the Bahama Islands if he could find someone, an experienced seaman if at all possible, to go with him. Bumping into the dock only caused cosmetic damage to *Windsong* but it jarred him back to reality. He wasn't a seaman and no matter how good or how big a boat may be, what it all came down to was how good the man at the helm was. He didn't have enough experience and he knew it. He would stay in the Intercoastal Waterway and hopefully out of trouble.

The following morning he was up and preparing to get underway before dawn. He ate a light breakfast, boiled some eggs for later use, topped off *Windsong's* water tanks, and when the sky lightened in the east, disconnected the power line from shore. After yesterday's debacle he wasn't going to attempt to maneuver *Windsong* in the packed marina under power. He tied a long line to a cleat on the bow and tied the other end to a piling near the entrance of the marina. It took him several minutes to do this. He had to climb aboard many of the other boats to get around masts and taller cabins, pilings and other obstacles. Once he secured the new bow line he started engines and released the lines securing *Windsong* to the fuel dock. He went to the bow and slowly, inch by inch, pulled *Windsong* about. It took all his strength and nearly twenty minutes before he hauled the massive boat around. The sun was just peaking over the horizon as he untied the line from the piling and powered *Windsong* up the channel.

He would anchor at Charleston Harbor that evening. It was an easy run at moderate power. He could anchor in the wide, deep harbor out of shipping lanes in water deep enough to be sure *Windsong* wouldn't go aground at low tide. He listened to music, changing stations as he traveled down the coast. He no longer turned on the short-wave radios. The sudden interruption of captains calling had become intrusions. He preferred the isolation of just him and *Windsong* and open water. He turned on the autopilot whenever channel traffic allowed, went back on deck and leaned against the railing and absorbed the sun's warm rays and *Windsong*'s self-made breeze. He felt free. He was self-sufficient now. Whatever he needed was aboard *Windsong*. Much had changed when Fred Calone left him at Portsmouth. The trip was no longer a search to fulfill some unspoken youthful fantasy of beautiful islands filled with lovely women and adventure. He was alone now, truly alone, separated from all that was routine and familiar. He needed time to think, time to be away from whom or what he had become, time to re-establish who he was and what he wanted to do and why. It was as though he had been living the two years since Laura's death under the momentum of a previous life. The momentum had dwindled until he, his life and what it was all supposed to be about, had come to a standstill.

He dropped anchor within sight of Fort Sumter in Charleston Harbor. It was late afternoon and he made preparations for living aboard without electricity. He had battery power for lights if need be, but he'd use the batteries as little as possible. He needed to be sure there was enough juice in them to start the engines in the morning. He unpacked the kerosene lanterns and filled them. In the galley he hooked up a portable propane stove. Next he unpacked a cot and mosquito netting and put it on the open afterdeck where he could sleep in the cool breeze. The sun was setting by the time he was done and he sat on the afterdeck eating a sandwich and drinking a cup of tea as he watched a clear sky change from blue to red and pink and then the darker heavens creep from east to west. Lights came on ashore and he lit one lantern and set it on the deck beside the chair. The burning wick made a warm circle of amber light around him.

A light on-shore breeze blew and the tide was coming in. *Windsong*'s bow pointed east, facing wind and incoming tide. A light chop washed by, water black and silent except for an occasional ripple against the hull. He felt totally alone, almost invisible, as he watched Charleston come alive for the evening. Fred Calone had looked at lights such as these and asked him what all these people did, how did they all make a living? His answer had been quick and sure. They all managed. They found a way to make a living, have families, do the things that people seemed to do. Fred had asked him, Walter the Wise, and he had given him the best answer he could. People did seem to manage somehow, but it wasn't the question that had begun to gnaw at Walter lately. His question had become why. Why was everyone doing whatever it was that they were doing? What was the purpose of it all? He was no longer sure. Something was missing. Purpose perhaps, or maybe hope. It was as though he, his life, had been one of those lights on shore then someone or something had pulled the plug. He lived in a place of darkness now, and he didn't know why or how it happened.

The days and nights became a blur as he and *Windsong* slowly continued south. He was no longer thinking of a destination nor the fact that sooner or later this long vacation would end and he would have to retrace his course and return to New York. He anchored the next night in the Savannah River and then on to Cumberland Island in Southern Georgia. The weather held and it was bright days, hot and sticky, and nights at anchor when it would become cool with a steady seabreeze.

The following evening he anchored near Ponce De Leon Inlet north of New Smyrna Beach. The weather report was for one more day of fair weather and then a low front moving in from the west and thunderstorms for the next day or two. He studied the charts of Florida's east coast. Cape Canaveral was less than fifty miles south. He checked the cruising guide book, *Sailing Directions,* and found there were several marinas at Port Canaveral where major boat repairs could be done.

He had planned on continuing to sail south until he reached Fort Lauderdale but the thought of being in a big, crowded marina no longer appealed to him. He'd stop at Port Canaveral and see if he could get *Windsong's* generator repaired there.

This last night at anchor was not a good one. Perhaps it was the strong current tugging at *Windsong* as the tide rushed in and then out of Ponce De Leon Inlet, anchor line straining first in one direction and then the other. Maybe it was because there was a waning moon and he had anchored far from any lights. The stars were there, cold and indifferent, as they had before mankind. They added little light to his solitary world. He noticed the bilge pumps each time they came on. He thought he had become accustomed to them but now their clicking on and off kept sleep from him. He had been absolutely alone for several days and maybe that was it. Whatever the cause, his thoughts became as dark as the night encircling *Windsong*.

He had never felt so alone nor lonely as he listened to the water trickling past, an occasional splash of a fish jumping, a bilge pump turn on and then off. He wondered if taking this vacation and trip hadn't been a mistake. He left home and work seeking to break free of the growing depression that clung to him day after day. Instead, the suppressed fears that lurked deep within were surfacing. He had no defenses now. He couldn't go to his office and find distraction nor find some new project to piddle with around the house. Here it was only he and *Windsong* and the black water that surrounded them, finding its way into her. He could empathize with *Windsong*. She was old too. Without her pumps to keep her dry, the sea would claim her. Kill her. His pumps had been his work, his routine, his practiced ability to keep from thinking about himself too much. Now these pumps were turned off and the black water of his fears and loneliness were filling his hull and he felt himself sinking ever deeper into total despair.

Death didn't frighten him. Not really. In fact it might come as a blessing. He had been feeling so useless, everything he did and everything around him so purposeless, that an end to it might be an easy and simple answer. Death was not an enemy to be fought off at all costs. It was a natural thing, less to be feared than a continued life without purpose, adrift, without destination or purpose.

He felt as a displaced person might feel after a great war. Whatever his nation had been it no longer existed, at least not as he knew it. Slowly his world had changed, and except for Laura's death, almost without notice. Suddenly he was an old man all alone with a future filled with emptiness. He had no home. He had a house, but he had no home. There was only a silent, empty building waiting for him in Huntington. He was nearing the peak in his career at Wheel, Kedder and Matthews. He worked toward this for years and now it didn't matter anymore. He had no one to share it with, no one to impress. No one.

These thoughts in many variations kept him company through the night. At daybreak he hoisted anchor and slowly motored out of Ponce De Leon Inlet and headed south toward Cape Canaveral.

XI
Port Canaveral

The heat was oppressive. At mid-morning the onshore sea-breeze had yet to begin. The still air pressed against him, the humidity so high that sweat formed in droplets on all skin surfaces and pooled where it could, catching at his collar, waistband, and running down his calves into soiled sneakers without socks. Walter sat on the dilapidated bench in front of the bait/tackle/boat supply store tapping his foot, glancing at his wristwatch every few minutes, wondering how late it would be before Jerry finally arrived and opened for business. It was already forty-five minutes past opening. Jerry usually arrived smiling and a little hung-over, offering no excuses about his lateness. Schedules, time in general, had little meaning to Jerry and Walter wondered how he could stay in business with his door more often shut than open. But Jerry was helpful and knowledgeable, always free with his time and advice with Walter as well as all others who came to him with their problems.

Scallop boats were unloading nearby, tethered side by side, a crane with large scooping jaws digging into the massive piles on the afterdeck of the boat nearest the dock. A conveyer whistled and groaned as the crane's jaws opened and spilled hundreds of pounds of shellfish onto the slowly moving belt. The sea-reeking scallops were swallowed by a black hole in the building where they would be shelled, cut, washed and packaged.

The mounds of scallops on the deck were huge for the size of the boats. The harvest was good this year. After two years when few, if any, scallop beds could be found, each captain and crew sought to gather as large a haul as possible on every trip. A few days before one of the boats was found capsized, one body trapped in the hull, two crew members missing, and the general consensus being their load shifted and the boat capsized. It must have happened quickly, too quick for a radio signal to tell anyone they were in trouble, and it was over silently and with finality. The Coast Guard was still searching for the two missing crew, but there was little hope held by those who knew the sea that anyone would be found alive. And yet the boats still loaded as heavily as ever, swaying on the swells as they entered port, on the brink of capsizing with each list, the men gambling they could bring back an overloaded boat each time.

Jerry pulled into the graveled parking lot in his battered red pickup, white dust thrown up by skidding wheels, a slowly drifting cloud of pulverized scallop shells announcing his arrival. He emerged from the dust cloud wiping his eyes and coughing, spitting airborne grit. He strolled easily toward Walter, smiling broadly on seeing him. His long red hair protruded from beneath a soiled baseball cap and large ears forced their way through hair that hadn't felt a scissor in six months. Jerry was a big man, big in every way. He was well over six feet tall, carried an extra forty pounds of muscle and fat, was loud of voice, free with his money, and always willing to spend as much time as needed helping a customer or friend.

Walter liked him though there were times when waiting on his late arrivals or being caught by his early departures was frustrating.

"Morning, Walter," Jerry said, taking a large key ring and unlocking the door.

Walter followed him into the coolness of the air-conditioned store. It was a relief to be out of the heat and humidity. "How are you?"

"All right, I guess. Hot as hell, though." Jerry chuckled, his laugh becoming a hacking cough. "Smoke too much," he said, lifting his baseball cap and scratching his unruly hair and smiling ruefully. "And drink too much, and run around with women too much. Sometimes I wonder... if there isn't an easier way to live." He filled a coffee urn with water and coffee, the pot available for him and free to the steady traffic that would be in throughout the day.

"Too much partying?" Walter asked. He had been coming in at least once a day for a week and had seen the results of Jerry's late night parties. There were mornings when he was little more than a walking hangover.

"Yeah, I guess so. But what the hell. There isn't much else to do."

Normally Walter spoke little, being taciturn by nature, but Jerry's friendly, easy-going way was infectious and he found himself talking with this gruff, bear of a man as he would with few other people. Rarely would he think of asking about someone's personal life but to Jerry he said, "Did you ever think of settling down? Get married, maybe, and stop living the wild life?"

"Tried it." Jerry shook his head. "It was worse than it is now. That crazy broad I was married to made my life even more miserable. If that's what married life is all about, and I'm not saying that it's true for everybody, then you can have it. That woman was a crazy son-of-a-bitch and she made me a crazy son-of-a bitch. Thank God she moved to California. It's a shame about the kids, though. I'll bet she's got them as crazy as she is, or will be by the time they grow up."

"You have children?"

"Yeah, two. A boy and a girl. I haven't seen them for, oh, a couple of years now. After the divorce the ex met up with some religious nut and *she* got religion and they moved to California. Now she's a Bible-thumping, lying, screaming no good bitch. It was bad enough when I just had to put up with her. Now she says she's got *God* on her side and I have to listen to her holy-roly bullshit every time I call and try to talk to the kids." Jerry sighed. "Nope. Married life is not for me. I'll be paying child support for the rest of my life because of my one attempt at that business and I'll be damned if I'll get myself in a situation like that again." Jerry lit a cigarette and inhaled deeply. "You married?"

"No, I'm a widower. My wife passed away two years ago."

"Sorry to hear that. I guess you were married a long time."

"Almost thirty-five years."

"Wow, that is a long time. I guess you were one of the lucky ones."

Walter nodded. "I guess so."

They were silent for a moment, the coffee urn percolating and the aroma of freshly brewed coffee sweet in the air. Jerry set out two large mugs, chipped and stained, in preparation of his morning eye-opener.

"By the way," Jerry said, scratching at something that had dried to the lip of one of the cups. "I called that supplier up in Jacksonville yesterday. The parts for your generator will be in tomorrow or the next day."

"Thanks, Jerry. And thanks for all the help you've been giving me. I'll pay for the long-distance calls you've had to make."

"No problem. As I said, my ex-wife keeps trying to get

every penny I have anyway. There's no point in trying to get rich. She'd find some way of getting whatever I have and buy a second Cadillac to drive to church and show her friends how much God loves her and how good he treats her. With my money, of course."

"She sounds like quite a lady."

"Lady is not a word that I've ever applied to that woman. Even when I thought I was in love with her I wouldn't have been able to think of her as a lady. Bitch has always been more appropriate."

As harsh as Jerry's words were he didn't seem angry. At least not anymore. It was more like disgusted resignation.

Walter brushed at a bare knee smeared with soot. He cursed silently. Everywhere he touched or brushed against something on *Windsong* he picked up soot. Two nights before, the latest of the continuing series of mishaps occurred. Fire on the boat! He probably would have been killed by smoke inhalation if he'd been sleeping in the stateroom. But, as had become his habit since the generator went out, he was sleeping on the afterdeck on a cot under mosquito netting where a cool sea-breeze blew. Below decks it was impossibly hot. Summer was now upon Florida and he had yet to get used to the heat and humidity, if ever he could.

The fire started in the engine room near the battery compartment. A frayed electrical wire arced and ignited a small pile of dust and dirt that accumulated over the years. The smoldering fire crept upward between the hull and paneling to the engine room overhead and then stateroom, up the bulkhead to the upper deck and the smoke exited at the seam where the deck and pilothouse met. It hadn't been a fire of heat and flames, just smoldering wood and paneling amidship and below deck.

Thick, black smoke filled every corner of the boat. Eventually the acrid smell of his burning boat had awakened him from a deep sleep.

Putting the fire out was a nightmare. He woke with a start, jumped out of the cot, getting snared in the mosquito netting, and ran into the greatroom and black smoke. He could see nothing and within seconds he was hacking from the smoke and fumes. He felt his way into the pilothouse and freed the bottled fire extinguisher and flashlight. He went back out on the deck to catch his breath, his throat and lungs burning. It was three o'clock in the morning and not a soul was in sight on the poorly lighted dock. He took a deep breath and dove back into the pilothouse, down the ladder, and peering through the cone of light from his flashlight through the black smoke, found his way to the engine room.

He knew the fire had to be in the engine room or at least have started there. He quickly emptied the fire extinguisher, aiming the nozzle in all directions, no tell-tale flames to guide him to the smoke's source. Smoke slowly billowed from seams on deck but he had seen no flames. There was a fire somewhere below but *Windsong* was not a burning inferno nor, he hoped, in danger of exploding. The nearest public phone was almost a mile away and the time it would take to run there, if he could run that far, and call the fire department and then try to run back and wait on the fire trucks would only allow more time for the fire to spread and probably start to burn. He looked around the dimly lit dockside once again. No one to help or go call for help. He noticed a small water hose on the dock and made up his mind. If he was going to save *Windsong* he was going to have to do it himself.

He jumped onto the dock and turned on the water. A lazy stream poured out. There was no nozzle. He dragged the hose on board, and taking a deep breath, once again entered the pilothouse. He'd heard or learned somewhere that you should never open windows in a burning building. Well, if he were going to fight *this* fire he was going to have to get rid of some of the smoke. He opened the starboard side door and pilothouse windows, went below to the master stateroom and opened the large portholes there, and unable to hold his breath any longer, returned on deck to catch his breath. The end of the water hose lay on the deck of the pilothouse, its meager stream spilling uselessly down the companionway. He still had no idea where the fire was.

On the next trip down he dragged the garden hose behind. While tugging on the hose and feeling his way in the blackness below, he pressed his hand against the bulkhead. Heat radiated through the wood. He now knew where some of the fire was. He punched his fist through the overhead tile and shoved the hose into the hole. He left it there and came back on deck where he could breathe again. All through the night he continued his silent battle with the fire this way. He punched dozens of holes in the soft overhead, eventually tearing most of it down, and kept soaking one area after another. With his bare hands he tore paneling free from the bulkhead and shoved in the hose. Eventually he worked his way to the engine room and the fire's source, tearing at tile and paneling as he went. Again and again he ran on deck, caught his breath, held it, and returned below, but slowly the smoke became less and, eventually, the fire was out.

As the soft glow of dawn grew brighter on the horizon, the early morning fishermen found a soot-black Walter Marshall dragging soggy and singed tile, insulation, and paneling from *Windsong*'s belowdecks. He was a sight to behold: covered with black soot, water streaked, eyes red from smoke and exhaustion, hair standing in all directions, stiff from dirt and soot. He determinedly made trip after trip into *Windsong* and carried out another arm load of debris that he piled onto the dock. He had put the fire out. Alone. And now he was determined to make whatever repairs were necessary to put *Windsong* back into shape. With grim determination he spent most of the morning gutting a large part of *Windsong*'s interior. He would either fix this boat or she was going to kill him trying. One or the other was going to happen. He was now taking *Windsong*'s defects personally.

His memory of the night of the fire, the frustration of more and more repairs needed on *Windsong*, and his determination to personally make the repairs where he was able, all passed through Walter's mind as he sipped coffee and watched semi-transparent shrimp swim at the bottom of the bait tank. Jerry hummed tunelessly and stocked shelves.

"Say, Walter," Jerry called.

"Huh?" He turned and looked up at Jerry on a ladder placing boxes on an upper shelf.

"You still need a way of carrying materials to repair your boat, don't you?" Jerry asked.

"Sure do."

"Has the insurance adjuster been out to take a look at *Windsong* yet?" Jerry came down the ladder and leaned on the counter.

"In a day or two he said." Walter was still trying to get used to dealing with people in the South. Everything seemed to take three times as long as it should. On buying Windsong he bought an insurance policy with extensive coverage and he had called an agent whose office was located just a few miles from the port. He called the same day as the fire, two days ago. He was still waiting for the man to come and give him a damage appraisal.

"You're going to need a truck, aren't you?" Jerry asked, taking a sip of coffee and scratching at his navel, his expanding belly growing over a slack belt.

"I guess so. It's going to take quite a bit of material to get the damage repaired."

"You sure you want to fix *Windsong*? She's got a lot of problems, you know. Might be more expensive to fix her than to replace her."

"I know. But I want to try. I'd hate to see her go to the wrecking yard."

Jerry nodded. He understood. Some people become attached to their boat as though it were a child. They spoke as though they were living things with personalities. Jerry had seen hundreds of owners who would purchase something for their boats before they would buy something needed for their home or even their children. "I've got that red pickup I don't need anymore. Just bought a new one. Well, not new, used, but in pretty good shape. Got a top for the back too. Be better when I'm hauling stuff. Everything won't get wet every time we get a shower."

"I could use it. How much do you want?" He had noticed Jerry's old pickup. It was a wreck, dented, blowing black smoke each time Jerry started it, muffler almost gone, engine going clackity-clack. But it did run and might hold together long enough for a few short trips.

Jerry reached into his pocket and tossed a key ring to him. Instinctively he reached out and caught it with his free hand. With the sudden motion, coffee spilled on his shirt and shorts.

"You can have it. I couldn't take any money. It may break down as soon as you get in, though I doubt it. That old truck just won't quit. But I got this other one now and I won't be needing it. You keep it. It's either that or I sell it to a junk yard for a couple of bucks." Jerry shrugged. "It's no big deal. If, I give it to you and it breaks down I don't have to feel I screwed you or something."

Walter looked at the keys in his hands. He wasn't sure what to say.

"Come on, let me show you a few things about 'Ole Red Eye' as I call her." He put the keys in his pocket and followed Jerry out.

"We'll get the paperwork straightened out tomorrow," Jerry said as he led the way across the gravel lot to the truck.

"I don't know where the hell I put the ownership to this thing. I'll have to dig around at home. I know I got it somewhere. The tags are good for a couple of months and the insurance is all paid up so it'll be OK for awhile."

"Shouldn't we get it changed into my name and change the tags and insurance and everything?" Walter asked, wondering about his liability while driving this wreck.

"If you want to. To tell you the truth, I wouldn't fool with it if you're only going to use it for a couple of weeks. Why bother? You can leave it here when you're done and I'll get it over to a junk yard." Jerry patted a lose fender lovingly. "This old baby sure has gotten me around."

Walter walked around the old pickup. There was rust everywhere, the salt air eating away at every edge and scratch. The exhaust pipe dangled near the ground, held by a wire. The windshield wipers hung at a strange angle, with frayed rubber about to shed, fenders loose and shaky to the touch, and a window missing on the driver's door. Holes big enough for a foot to fit through pocketed the bed. A white film of dust covered everything including the interior. Walter doubted if it was safe to drive this thing.

"Before I forget," Jerry said, as he rummaged through a glove compartment filled with trash, "it can only hold a couple of gallons of gas. There's a hole in the tank. I checked it. There's no danger. It's just if you put in more than a couple of bucks it leaks. It's a pain in the ass, but for the short trips you're going to be making it won't matter. I intended on fixing it but never got around to it."

"You're sure it won't leak on the exhaust pipe and cause a fire?" Walter asked, becoming more and more doubtful about using this pickup.

"Naw. I've been using it for months. It's safe. It's just a pain in the ass having to stop all the time to get gas. It's been kind of shortening my range, if you know what I mean."

He was about to say he didn't think the pickup would meet his needs and he would rent one instead. Before he could speak a car pulled into the parking lot, a cloud of white dust enveloping them, then drifting away. A woman got out and smiled at Jerry. Walter guessed she was in her twenties, pretty, no, beautiful was a better adjective. Her eyes were dark brown and sparkled. Brown, wavy hair reached bare shoulders and a halter restrained round, firm breasts. She was wearing shorts and tanned, shapely legs supported her, round hips curving into slim waist above form-fitting shorts. She glowed with health and energy. He found it hard to take his eyes off her.

"I brought you something," she said to Jerry, reaching into the car and taking out a cake. "It's your favorite, German Chocolate."

"What's this for?"

"It's only a little something, to say thank you for all of your help with the roof."

"You didn't have to do this," Jerry told her, happily eyeing the cake.

"It's the least I could do. You guys worked a whole day. I still don't know how much I owe you for the materials you bought."

"Don't worry about that," Jerry said, dismissing it with a wave of his hand. "Is everything okay? Did the roof stop leaking?"

"Dry as a bone. We had that heavy shower yesterday and not a drop came through. Thanks, Jerry. I don't know how I would have gotten it done without you."

"No problem. Glad I could help." Jerry looked over at Walter. "This here's Walter. Walter, Nancy," he said, introducing them.

"Hi," Nancy said with a smile, white teeth gleaming.

Walter returned the greeting and began to blush beneath his tan. He realized how he must look. His clothes were smeared with soot. He hadn't shaved in two days and needed a haircut. He looked down, trying to hide his embarrassment and his eye caught sight of a big toe working its way through the top of a canvas sneaker. He felt like a scruffy old man in front of this lovely young woman.

"Come on in the store before this cake melts," Jerry said, carrying the cake in both hands like a gift to an altar.

"I can only stay a minute," Nancy said, following him. "I've got the kids at home."

Walter followed behind trying not to stare as she gracefully walked through the heat, back wide and strong, the string of her halter tied in a bow just off center. Her narrow waist went to hips and round buttocks moving beneath, muscles in thighs and calves rippling with each step. He followed, drawn, pulled along in her wake.

"The coffee's fresh. Have a cup," Jerry offered as he pushed soda cans aside to make room for the cake in a large refrigerator.

"I can't stay. I left the kids next door and I don't want to be away too long. I just wanted to stop by and say thank you." Nancy hugged herself with a shiver. "Brrr, this place is cold. How come you keep the temperature so low?"

Jerry chuckled, a smile and a laugh coming easily to him. "I don't know. Just getting old I guess. Can't take the heat anymore."

At the word old Walter averted his eyes. He had been watching Nancy, and as she wrapped her arms across her chest, the soft flesh of her breasts threatened to break free of the skimpy halter. He felt like a dirty old man gaping at this lovely young woman, but he couldn't help himself. It had been a long, long time since he had been with a woman. His wife had been pretty when they were young and became elegant as she grew older, but she never was sexually attractive as Nancy. He looked at the ceiling, the walls, the shelves, anything to keep his gaze off her. He wanted to leave, to get away from being in her presence. This wasn't doing him any good. He felt a growing knot in the pit of his stomach.

"We're having a cookout Friday night. You're coming, aren't you?" Nancy asked Jerry.

"Sure. I wouldn't miss it for the world."

"And bring Pokey," Nancy said, turning and walking toward the door. Walter stood just inside the entrance and stepped aside to allow her to pass. She smiled a thank you.

"Of course. I couldn't go anywhere without my little Indian," Jerry called as she left with a good-bye wave.

The tiny brass bell on the closing door signaled her departure and suddenly Walter also felt the cold chill of the air-conditioning. He went to the counter and filled a mug with steaming coffee. A part of him was glad she was gone. Her presence brought too many suppressed or, perhaps, even forgotten instincts. It had been a very long time since a woman affected him like this. He felt like an awkward, gangling teenager. That was crazy. He was sixty years old.

The tingle of the bell announced someone had entered. Nancy stood looking helpless and frustrated.

"My car won't start," she said to Jerry.

"Huh?" Jerry looked up from an inventory list.

"My car won't start. The starter's finally given out completely."

"Are you sure it's the starter?" Jerry asked, coming from behind the counter.

"Yeah, I'm sure. It's been giving me trouble for awhile. I was going to get it fixed but," she paused, "I was trying to get a few extra dollars together."

"I'll take a look."

"There's not much point. I know what it is. I need to replace the starter."

The door closed and he was left alone not sure what he should do. He wasn't a mechanic and wouldn't be very helpful. He probably couldn't find the starter on her car, he knew so little about automobiles. But that's not why he would go and he knew it. He put the mug down and left the store feeling like a lecherous old man and a clumsy teenager all rolled into one. Hot, humid air struck him as soon as he stepped out the door.

XII
Nancy

There was a grinding as Jerry tried to start Nancy's car. It was an older model station wagon also beginning to rust. One of the fenders was a mis-match, a replacement no one bothered to paint. Heat waves shimmered from the car's hood and top. Nancy stood by watching as Jerry quickly turned the key on and off. Each time stripped gears ground in protest.

"I guess you're right." Jerry slammed the door. "You need another starter. I hope the flywheel isn't too chewed up. It's a pain in the ass replacing one."

"Darn. How am I going to get home? I promised the kids I wouldn't be gone too long. And what am I going to do with this thing?" Nancy frowned as she looked at the station wagon.

"Leave it," Jerry said. "I've got a buddy dropping off my new pickup. He's a mechanic and can take a look and see what needs to be done. He can either fix it here or tow it to the shop. I'll call you later on and let you know what's going on."

"I guess I'd better call a cab," Nancy said, disappointment in her voice. She was thinking of the repair bill and maybe a towing charge plus an unexpected taxi fare.

"No need. Walter can take you home."

He stepped forward. "I'd be glad to." Forgotten was his objections to driving Jerry's dilapidated truck. If that wreck was a hazard on the road, so be it. He would have driven a tricycle if it had two seats and he could carry Nancy with him.

"Oh, thanks, Walter. I hate to bother you." She looked at him with those deep brown, sparkling eyes.

The knot returned to the pit of his stomach. "It's no bother. I didn't have that much to do anyway."

"Thanks again, Jerry. Give me a call when you know something, okay? It's not much of a car but it's all I got," Nancy climbed into the old pickup and slammed the door. Fenders rattled from the impact. He got in and after several attempts and a final hard tug, managed to get the door on the driver's side to close. He put the key in the ignition and stopped. There was a stick shift on the floor, the worn knob giving no clue as to where the different gears might be. It had been years, decades, since he drove a standard shift. He put his foot down on the clutch and started the engine. The truck belched a puff of black smoke and then roared to life, leaking muffler making it sound like a motorcycle. Tentatively, he moved the stick until it felt as though he had it in gear. He eased his foot off the clutch and raced the engine. The pickup began to creep forward. He put his foot back down on the clutch.

"Reverse is over here," Nancy placed her hand over his and pulled it to her and down. Her hand was soft and yet firm. He could feel the strength of her grip.

"Are you okay with this? I'll drive if you like."

"No, I'll be okay. It's just that it's been awhile since I've driven a standard shift," he said, feeling foolish.

He raced the engine and eased out the clutch. The truck began to roll back and then with a double jerk, stalled. He felt his cheeks getting red. More and more he was feeling like a clumsy old fool. He restarted the engine, and giving more gas this time, backed the truck around. Jerry stood off to the side, arms folded across his broad chest, grinning. He was enjoying the show as Walter struggled with Ole Red Eye.

"First is to you and up," Nancy told Walter, then looked at Jerry with a scowl. This guy couldn't even drive! Jerry grinned back at her.

He raced the engine and put the shift into first gear. A blue-black cloud drifted from beneath the cab. He was pulling away when he heard Jerry yell something. He stepped on the brake and almost stalled again. He and Nancy were being bounced back and forth in the cab as he inexpertly handled the pedals.

"What?" he yelled. His face was red and Jerry's grin widened.

"I said, don't forget about the gas. It's probably getting pretty close to empty."

Automatically, he looked at the fuel gauge. The pointer rested below empty. The truck would only hold two dollars worth of gas. Of course it would read empty.

"Yeah, I'll get some," he yelled back, and began the process of getting rolling again. Nancy said nothing and he wouldn't look at her. He couldn't help feeling like a ten-year-old who had fallen off his bicycle in front of his girl. He clenched his jaw and worked his way through the gears and headed the truck toward Cocoa Beach.

"You do live in this direction?" he asked, not taking his eyes off the road.

"Yes, about five miles. I'll let you know when we get close," she said over the noise of the muffler. "There's a gas station a block or two on the right if you want to get some." He nodded and drove even slower as the pickup rattled along in the right lane, cars flashing by as they passed him. He pulled into a convenience store with gas pumps in the front, shock absorbers squeaking and groaning as he drove over a small bump at the curb. He pumped two dollars worth of gas and went into the store to pay.

Nancy had been watching him. His shirt and shorts were not very clean, soot making them gray and dingy. His low-cut canvas sneakers were nearly worn through and he needed a shave and a haircut. He looked like many of the men, most of them down on their luck, who hung around the port looking for work on the fishing boats or maybe to pick up a day's pay at one of the marinas. Jerry said something about Walter living on his boat. He was probably one of those boat-bums, as some people called them, who traveled from port to port working a little here and there and then moving on. Her heart went out to these men. They looked so lost and lonely. They drifted from place to place with no family or friends.

He came back and climbed into the cab, slamming the door. Nancy took two dollars from her purse and held it toward him. She couldn't see him spending his money on gas to take her home. Half the men hanging around the docks didn't have two dollars.

"Here," she said, offering him the money. "At least let me pay for the gas."

He looked at the two dollars she held almost under his nose. It took a second or two for what she was saying to register.

"No, no. That's all right," he stuttered, his cheeks beginning to flush again. Now he knew he looked like a hobo. She didn't think he could afford two dollars for gas.

"Take it," she insisted. "It's only right."

"No, thank you," he said, starting the engine. "I can afford it." He made this last statement more forcefully than he meant to. He was angry with himself, with this embarrassing situation, and with feeling so out of place. The whole thing was ridiculous.

She shoved the two singles into his shirt pocket and leaned against the rattling door. He left it there, not knowing what else to do. He was conscious of her sitting beside him, conscious of his yearnings, and frustrated that he was acting like an immature idiot. They drove in traffic along the beach road for a few moments before Nancy spoke.

"Make a right at the next light." He turned, and after another instructed turn, stopped in front of the small house where she lived. "Thanks, Walter. I appreciate the lift." She got out and held the door open.

"You're welcome." He noticed a breeze brush some loose hair against her cheek. Each time he looked at her he felt he should look away. His hunger had to be obvious.

"I hope you'll be able to come to the cookout this Friday. It's nothing special. Just some friends and neighbors coming by. It'll start around nine o'clock. Try to come if you can," she invited earnestly.

"I, er, I," he stammered. "Sure, if I can."

"Good," Nancy said with a smile and then slammed the door. Dust particles drifted inside the cab as he watched her walk into the house. He turned around and headed back to the port. He was getting used to driving a standard shift once again and this time it went smoothly.

He drove along A1A through Cocoa Beach trying to become familiar with the area. He would be buying quite a bit of materials as he repaired *Windsong*'s damage. There were several small malls and he spotted a hardware store where he might find some things he knew he needed. It was late June and school was out, and the summer tourists had arrived. Everywhere he looked there would be at least one woman, and usually many, wearing skimpy bathing suits and most of them shapely, young and healthy. He couldn't help noticing.

"Jesus," he said, aloud. He didn't understand what was happening. It was as though he'd just reached puberty and his hormones hadn't stabilized yet. He'd always considered himself a man with normal sex drives, albeit after Laura's illness progressed and since her death he managed to put his sexual thoughts on hold. In fact, he believed he had reached an age where it really didn't matter anymore. Somehow meeting Nancy re-opened that door. No, the door hadn't been re-opened. It had been blown off of its hinges with a searing blast.

Nancy was married. She had to be. She had children didn't she? What was he thinking? He wasn't thinking and that was the problem. It was totally out of character for him to behave this way. He felt, and acted, like a puppy trying to be noticed and played with. He was a grown man! Mature. Hell, he was way beyond mature. He was over the hill and he knew it. Why was he so drawn to this woman—this married woman!—and unable to control his emotions? For two, no, three years he managed to live without sex. He had put it out of his mind, refused to think about it. Sex was for other people, younger people. He'd had his life and now it was other people's turn. He accepted that. Right up to this morning he had accepted that. Now he wasn't so sure. He wasn't so sure at all.

Jerry was sitting on a stool behind the counter. He looked up, and on seeing Walter, grinned.

"I see you made it." Jerry folded a newspaper and put it down.

"Yeah, once I got used to it. It's been a long time since I've driven a standard shift."

Jerry went to the coffee urn and filled a mug. "Want a cup?"

"Sure."

"Milk and sugar?"

"That'll be fine."

"That Nancy's some nice lady, isn't she?" Jerry asked.

"Lady? I thought you didn't use that word with women anymore."

"I don't. Not very often. But Nancy's different. The same way my ex-wife could never be anything except a bitch, Nancy could never be anything but a lady. It's the way they're made I guess."

Walter had to force himself to speak. He couldn't let this opportunity pass. Normally he was a quiet man. Never would he pry or gossip.

"What makes Nancy different?"

Jerry had walked around the counter and sat on his bar stool. He looked at Walter, frowned, then looked to the ceiling, scratched his head, tugged at an ear, scratched at his protruding belly.

"I don't know. It's just that she's so... nice. I don't know how to explain it." Jerry thought for a moment before going on. "All I know is she's sure bailed me out when I needed her." He looked at Walter and grinned. "Literally. She's always there when you need her. She's like that with everybody. She's always so... helpful." Jerry shrugged his massive shoulders and took a gulp of coffee.

"What's her husband like?" Walter asked, trying to sound nonchalant.

Jerry looked at Walter who was studiously sipping his coffee, eyes averted. He liked this man. For the past week or so Walter had been coming in and he was always pleasant. Even when things were going lousy for him, like the fire on the boat, he was calm and considerate. A gentleman. Funny, Nancy was a lady and this guy was a gentleman. Jerry smiled to himself. He was a little old for her, but, why not? There were no rules, and if there were, everybody kept breaking them anyway. They would make a cute couple. Yeah, he would see what he could do to get them together. It might be fun to watch.

It had been so long since Walter had asked the question. He looked to see if Jerry had heard. Jerry grinned. "Interested?"

Walter blushed. Jerry chuckled at his embarrassment but didn't tease him anymore. He was too sensitive and too nice a guy.

"Divorced. And unattached as far as I know." Walter was

once again sipping his coffee, looking off to the side. Jerry prodded. "She'd be a catch for some guy. She sure is pretty."

"Yes, she's pretty." He whispered into his cup, eyes blank.

"She has some shape. You wouldn't believe she had three kids," Jerry offered, watching for Walter's reaction.

"Three children?"

"Yep. She's got a houseful. The oldest one's in school I think."

"What happened to the husband?" Walter asked, not knowing why he was pursuing this but knowing that he had to.

"Ran off," Jerry told him. There was more to it than that, but it was all pretty complicated and he didn't want to get into details. He had known Nancy for a long time, since she was married. In fact, he met her through her husband. She was a good friend and a nice lady. If her life was a little complicated, well, then it was a little complicated. That's the way things worked out sometimes.

"I can't believe a man would leave a woman like that," Walter said, still gazing at the far wall, thoughts far away.

"Her husband was a goofball. I knew him before he married her, How he got her to marry him, I'll never know. She's a sweet kid. He was a real asshole."

Walter put down his coffee mug and shook his head. "Kid is right. She's young enough to be my daughter."

Jerry laughed. "Don't let that bother you. I'm going with a broad who's young enough to be *my* daughter. It's okay. It's allowed as long as they're not so young as to be jail bait."

Walter appraised him. He looked to be in his mid-thirties, too young for his statement to be true. "You're kidding."

"Wait until you meet Pokey. You'll see. She's eighteen and looks about twelve." Jerry chuckled, enjoying the incredulous look on Walter's face.

"What do you do with a girl that young?" he asked, still not sure if he believed Jerry or not. Jerry was always pulling everybody's leg if he could get away with it.

"The same thing you do with a thirty-eight-year-old but more!" Jerry laughed and slapped his thigh. "You'll meet her. You're coming to the party Friday night, aren't you?"

"Party?"

"Yeah. The cookout at Nancy's. The fellers here at the port usually bring tons of fish and one of her neighbors owns a bar and he brings kegs of beer. There'll be plenty to eat and drink. There's music and dancing. It's always a good time."

It was a while before Walter responded. He knew he wanted to see Nancy again, but he also knew he must have made a terrible first impression. He looked like a bum, had acted like a clumsy imbecile, and felt like a dirty old man. His emotions were completely out of control. Maybe it would be better never to see her again, get his boat fixed, and get the hell out of here. He was too old to be going through this kind of turmoil.

"I don't think so," he told Jerry. "She invited me but I think I'd better pass. I wouldn't know anyone there."

Jerry took his refusal as a challenge. He had been hoping to play Cupid and now Walter didn't want to play the game.

"But you've gotta come!" Jerry insisted. "She's invited you. Of course you don't know anybody. You're always on your boat. How are you going to get to know people unless you go out and meet them?"

Walter took his empty coffee mug to the rear counter and rinsed it and set it on the soiled towel near the urn. "I'm not sure," he told Jerry, and that was the truth. He wasn't sure of anything. "Maybe I'll come."

"Good. You need to get off that boat for awhile. You're on vacation. You can't spend it sitting here at the port."

"You're right about that. It certainly hasn't been much of a vacation."

"You know the way to Nancy's house, or do you want me to come by and pick you up?" Jerry persisted.

"I know the way. I can get there by myself. That is, if the truck doesn't come apart."

The memory of Walter and Nancy bouncing and stalling made Jerry chuckle. Ole Red Eye and Walter made quite a sight. "She'll be okay. She's got plenty of miles left in her."

Walter walked toward the door. "I guess I'll get back to the boat."

"Damn," Jerry said, stopping him. "I completely forgot. The insurance feller came by right after you left. He's out there now, checking the boat."

"It's about time. Maybe I can get to work on her now and not have to live in such a mess. Thanks, Jerry. I'll see you later."

Windsong was tied to the dock at the far end of the port. There were four marinas at Port Canaveral but none had space available for a boat her size. This meant *Windsong* couldn't be hooked up to shore power and he continued to use kerosene lanterns and portable gas stove. The food in the refrigerator and freezer had spoiled and he cleaned them out shortly after arriving at the port. He still had plenty of canned food he could prepare but was mostly making do with sandwiches, milk, soda and snacks he purchased at Jerry's place. He worked from first light until dark each day, especially after the fire, and cooking and housekeeping were far from his thoughts. The days were filled with work, the nights on the cot on the afterdeck long and lonely. His main focus each day was to get *Windsong* repaired as quickly as possible so he could once again get underway.

He felt stuck here in Port Canaveral, not knowing why he was putting himself through all this. He could be home in Huntington in a comfortable house and not working fourteen hours a day on a boat that seemed to get into progressively worse shape no matter how much work he put into her. But he knew what was waiting for him in Huntington. Loneliness. There was loneliness here too, but at least he had *Windsong* to focus on. He could put all of his energies into repairing her. Until today. Until he met Nancy. Now his feelings, his longings, his loneliness, forced their way to the surface. He couldn't suppress them any longer. The pressure, or knot, or whatever it was, was building deep within his chest again. He felt trapped, trapped within himself, within *Windsong*, within Port Canaveral, within an aging body that still contained an active mind with hopes and desires that could find no outlet.

He tried to push his bleak mood aside. It made him ill-tempered and he didn't like himself when he was unpleasant. He stepped aboard *Windsong* looking for Jim Blackman, the insurance agent. There was no one to be seen on the upper deck.

"Mister Blackman?" Walter called down the companionway to the forward compartments.

"Hello," came a hollow reply from the lower part of the boat. "I'm in the engine room."

Walter went below and passed through the forward compartment and his gutted bedroom, electrical wires dangling from torn ceiling, studs and scorched ribs where walls had been, and the smell of a recent fire thick in the air. He entered the engine room where the fire began. Here the overhead and the port bulkhead had also been ripped out, slightly charred ribs and hull planks showing the path of the fire. The insurance agent stuck out his hand as soon as Walter entered the engine room.

"Hello," he said pleasantly. "I'm Jim Blackman."

"Walter Marshall." They shook.

"This is much worse than I thought," Blackman said, spreading his arms to encompass the damaged engine room. "When you called and said you had a fire that you'd put out yourself, I didn't think the damage was this extensive." Blackman tried to brush a streak of soot off the sleeve of his white shirt, but rather than helping, the black grime spread on the white linen. He had specks and streaks of soot and oil all over his shirt and pants and the tip of his tie looked as though it had been dipped into black ink. There was no doubt that he had given *Windsong* more than a cursory inspection.

"Sorry about the mess," Walter said. Jim Blackman's clothes were ruined. No amount of cleaning would ever get the stains out. "I've been trying to get it cleaned up."

"It looks like you've been pretty busy. This was some fire. Why didn't you call the fire department?" Blackman asked. He doubted the fire had been deliberately set, there were enough fire hazards throughout the boat that sooner or later something like this was bound to happen, but it never hurt to ask a few questions. One never knew when a fraudulent claim might be made.

"No phone," Walter said with disgust. "If I'd taken the time to run to the nearest telephone the whole boat would have gone."

"Makes sense. Did you put it out all by yourself?"

"It started about three o'clock in the morning. There was no one else around."

"It must have been quite a night."

"Indeed it was," Walter said, emphatically. "I hope to God I never have to go through anything like that again."

Jim Blackman was satisfied. The fire hadn't been deliberately set. The boat was insured for seventy-five thousand dollars. Far more than it was worth. If Walter Marshall wanted to get his money out of the boat he could have let it burn to the waterline. "How long have you owned the boat, Mister Marshall?"

He thought for a second. In a way, it felt as though he had been aboard *Windsong* for a long, long time. It had only been two weeks since he left Northport. "I bought the boat in March so that's about three, three-and-a-half-months."

"Not very long," Blackman observed. "So this is the first time you've taken it very far?"

"Yes," Walter answered, wondering why Blackman was asking so many questions unrelated to the fire. "Why do you ask?"

"Well, while I was checking the fire damage I noticed there was quite a bit of damage below the waterline." Then Blackman added quickly, "Not related to the fire of course."

"Damage?" Walter's eyebrows shot up. "What kind of damage?"

"You've never owned a wood boat before, have you Mister Marshall?"

"No, I haven't."

"I've owned a few and I insure a bunch of them." But not one like this, Blackman was thinking. This one is as close to a watery grave as any he had seen in a long time. "Would you like me to show you something?"

"Sure."

The door to the crawlspace in the bilges was open and Blackman bent over and entered the pitch black opening. There was a splash as his foot struck water. He took a small pen-like flashlight out of his shirt pocket and clicked it on. A small, narrow beam lit their way aft. "Water's getting a little deep down here," Blackman said, his voice echoing in the cramped space.

"I turn the engines over a few times a day and run the pumps until she's dry." Usually he ran the engines every few hours, even during the night, and kept the bilges relatively dry. But this morning he had been busy with Jerry and Nancy and time had passed unnoticed.

"She's leaking pretty bad and let me show you what's part of the problem," Blackman said, standing bent over between the propeller shafts. "Here's the keel beam," he put his hand into the oily, black water. "Feel it?"

He put his hand near Blackman's. He could feel the smooth wood under his finger tips. It was the twelve-inch wide oak beam that ran the length of the boat.

"Here," Blackman offered Walter a screwdriver. "I borrowed this from your toolbox. Push it into the wood."

He put the tip of the screwdriver near his hand underwater and pushed. There was some resistance but the screwdriver sank into the softened wood up to the handle.

"Rot," Blackman said.

Walter pulled the screwdriver out of the soft keel. "Rot? The whole boat?"

"No. Just a third, maybe half the way up to the bow. It's where water's been on and off for some time. It's the same with the ribs. Toward the bottom where they're often in water there's a lot of rot. They're yellow pine. The hull planks are oak. They may still be okay. I don't know." Blackman grunted. "Let's get out of here. If I stay bent over like this much more I'll never be able to straighten up again."

Walter led the way to the bright square of the door to the engine room. Once able to stand, they both stretched. Blackman was about fifty years old, with thinning hair and round in the middle. Sweat dripped off the tip of his nose and his clothes clung to him. It was hot and humid in the still air below decks. He took out a handkerchief and wiped his face and neck.

"Let's go up and get some air," he said, panting a little.

Walter followed him up on deck. They stood in the shade of the pilothouse, the breeze coming in from the ocean feeling cool even though the temperature was above ninety degrees. After being below, it was refreshing.

"What does it mean?" Walter asked. "Can it be repaired?"

Blackman didn't answer immediately. He wiped his face and pudgy neck with a damp handkerchief and then held it to flutter and dry in the wind. "Anything can be repaired. It all depends on whether you want to sink that much money into it.

I wouldn't, I don't think. You'd have to find a boat yard that could work on a boat like this, get it hauled, and have them tear out the keel and a bunch of those ribs and replace them. It would be expensive."

"But could it be done?"

Blackman looked at him, soot smeared, soaked in sweat, but sounding determined to fix the boat. Now Blackman was absolutely sure this owner hadn't set fire to his boat. He honestly hadn't known how poor the condition of his boat was. Blackman felt sorry for him. He was sure he had been taken in when he bought it just three months earlier. "Sure it can be repaired. But like I said, it would certainly be expensive. I'm not sure it would be wise to invest that much money in it."

"What else could I do? Sell it?"

"Mister Marshall, let me be candid. This boat is dangerous. I don't know who sold it to you or how you bought it in the condition it's in without knowing, but this boat is in no shape to be used as it is. If you were to take it out in the ocean, there's no telling what might happen. If any bad weather came and big waves, she might break her back. She'd sink in minutes. You might not even have time to get a radio call off. If you sold it to someone without telling them about the condition the boat's in, you'd be doing that person a great disservice. As I believe has been done to you."

Blackman hadn't intended on making a speech but he was angry. He loved the water and boats. That was a major reason he moved to Florida. He spent a great deal of his free time fishing and sailing. He knew the ocean and, therefore, respected it. Anyone who would sell a boat in danger of breaking up and not tell the buyer was beneath contempt. Lives could be lost, children included.

"I see," was all Walter said.

They were silent for a moment, each trying to get relief in the relative coolness of the breeze. Jim Blackman still wasn't sure how to approach this claim. The total damage might be more than the boat was worth, but the value of an old boat like this was flexible. It was worth what someone was willing to pay. There was no "book value" that could be argued in court.

"You are going to fix the boat?" Blackman asked.

"What else can I do? I can't sell it and I'm certainly not going to just walk away from it. I guess I'll have to fix her up. Besides, I intended on doing more work on her anyway. It'll cost more than I expected. I'll have to accept that and just get it done."

Blackman nodded. "Okay. I can't give you a figure on the fire damage right now. I'll have to go back to the office and do some figuring. Also, while I'm at it, I'll make some calls to a couple of boat yards. There are two that might be able to do the kind of work you need done. On the keel and hull I mean. I'd hate to see you try to take this too far."

"I appreciate your help."

"No need to thank me. Seaman's is still your insurer. I'd hate to have to pay a claim for the rest of the boat if she went to the bottom."

Blackman started to leave and then stopped before stepping onto the dock. "By the way, I'll have to include the rot damage in my report to the insurer. I doubt if they'll reinsure next year unless you've repaired the hull and get a surveyor's report. I just thought I'd let you know."

"I understand. And thank you for your help with the boat yards."

"You bet. I'll call Jerry's later today or tomorrow morning with my estimate on the fire damage and where you can get your boat repaired close by."

"Thanks again, Mister Blackman."

"Yes sir, and good luck," Blackman said, stepping onto the dock and beginning the long stroll back to the parking lot.

Walter went into the pilothouse and started the starboard

engine and turned on the bilge pumps. He went below to shower and shave. It was early afternoon. He had time to find a barber and get a haircut. He promised himself that from now on he would take care of his own needs first and then look after *Windsong*. The boat needed so much work there was no point in trying to rush it.

XIII
Cocoa Beach

For three days, and more so during lonely evenings, Walter struggled with the question as to whether he would go to Nancy's party on Friday. Each day Jerry prodded him to go, insisting he needed to get away from *Windsong* and get out and meet people, and finally he capitulated and agreed to go. He made it sound as though he were going to Nancy's only to appease Jerry. Though he and Jerry were different in so many ways, in age, education, life experiences, each saw something in the other that brought respect. Throughout the day he would find some reason to walk over to the store to purchase something or to ask a question or just to chat. Jerry's free-wheeling life-style was the complete opposite of the way Walter approached things. Jerry lived for today and said to hell with tomorrow and seemed to be enjoying his life.

Walter had always been conservative. He planned for the future. Slowly but surely his position and income at Wheel, Kedder and Matthews had climbed. He put his two children through college. He saved and invested a portion of his earnings since the first day he went to work. He had money in the bank, stocks and bonds, homes, a secure income at his law firm, most of the things success should bring. He also was totally miserable. He had reached his future and felt hollow. So he went to the party Friday night. What the hell did he have to lose?

He parked the pickup half on the grass and half on the road at the end of the street where she lived. Cars, vans, and pickups lined both sides of the road on Nancy's block, her guests using every available parking space. As he drove by he saw people milling at the front door, shadowy figures at lighted windows, and music blaring from inside. The other houses in the neighborhood were dark and quiet. He wondered if the neighbors were at the party or if they had secluded themselves behind darkened doors. He walked the half block toward the growing sound of music feeling nervous about trying to mix in with a crowd of strangers. It was nearly ten o'clock and the party had been going for about an hour. He had planned on being late, hoping Jerry would already be here and there would be at least one person he knew. One person besides Nancy.

He took care in how he dressed this evening. He knew he must have looked like a street bum the first time she saw him and he was hoping to appear more respectable this time. He selected a light-weight blue blazer jacket, light gray trousers, polished imported Italian loafers, and knitted white shirt open at the collar. He shaved for a second time that day and a haircut made a great difference with his unruly hair. Unconsciously, he tugged at his jacket as he approached the front door. The jacket and trousers had become loose on him since the last time he wore them at an informal Country Club affair in Huntington. He had lost weight during the long winter.

Any concerns he might have had about being properly dressed for the backyard cook-out were quickly put to rest. On the lawn outside the open front door were several people talking and laughing. One man was dressed in business suit and tie and alongside him stood a bearded biker with a bare chest and leather vest. The biker's arm was draped across the shoulder of a young woman in a very skimpy bikini with a black leather motorcycle jacket draped over her shoulders. With them was a woman wearing a long, print dress and alongside her was an auto mechanic still in greasy coveralls with "Texaco" and his name, "Bugsie," embroidered on his chest. No one noticed him in the semi-darkness as he went past.

The small house was packed with people. The volume of the stereo was far too loud for anyone to have a normal conversation. People were yelling to be heard over the music and occasional laughter was overpowered by drums, guitars, and roaring horns. He edged his way to a doorway that led to the kitchen.

Here, too, it was crowded, people standing or sitting at the table eating off of paper plates, bowls of salads and platters of cold cuts and chicken on the kitchen table and counter. A keg of beer was on the floor near the door and a steady stream of party-goers nudged their way to refill plastic cups. He saw neither Jerry nor Nancy among the crowd. A thickening cloud of cigarette smoke filled both rooms and his eyes were beginning to water. He smoked, but this was more than he could take. He maneuvered his way back to the front door. Once outside he filled his lungs with fresh air. Besides the smoke, it must have been twenty degrees warmer inside the house. That many bodies crushed together created its own heat.

He stood on the front lawn unsure what to do. He felt more alone here, more a stranger, than ever. He didn't belong here. Perhaps after all of the years of being married and having a limited social life he had lost whatever social skills he may have possessed. That, and the fact that he had always been shy.

Perhaps it was the fear of appearing as foolish as he felt he was. He didn't know. What he did know was that he had made a mistake in coming. He was a stranger trying to fit in.

He began walking back to the pickup when a light caught his eye. A fire was burning in Nancy's backyard and he could see faces glowing in the warm light. Two men were stroking guitars and singing, one of them Jerry. Walter stopped. He couldn't hear their voices nor the guitars, the blaring music coming from inside of the house drowning them out. Then Nancy came into view, her white blouse, radiant face and light brown hair shining in the flickering firelight. He stood in the dark front yard, apart and alone. The feeling of being so separated came to him again, deep in the pit of his stomach. He thought of *Windsong*, dark and silent, tied to the dock at the port. There was little waiting for him there. Only more loneliness. Slowly he began walking toward the backyard, an invisible moth drawn by the light of the fire.

As he neared the circle of people ringing the crackling fire he could hear Jerry and the others singing. It was a song he didn't know but most of those here knew it and were singing along. Nancy's eyes were closed as she sang with the others about lost love and broken hearts. Her deep voice was lost among the others. Jerry led the group, his strong baritone surprisingly mellow. At song's end Nancy opened her eyes and glanced around at the encircled group. On seeing Walter's faint image beyond the light of the fire she stopped and stared, perplexed. He was familiar but it took her a moment to recognize him. Once she did she smiled and began walking to him. He watched her come, afraid of what might happen next but glad that he wasn't driving back to *Windsong*. He returned her smile as she approached.

"Hi," Nancy said, beautiful in the soft firelight. He could smell the faint aroma of perfume

"Hi," he responded, wanting to touch her. He couldn't

help himself. He felt like an overgrown oaf wanting to reach out and grab a beautiful butterfly.

"I almost didn't recognize you. You look so... different."

"I was a little dirty when we first met. I was working on the boat."

"Oh, I didn't mean that," she said, embarrassed. But she did.

He was quite different from the dirty, unkempt man who had driven her home three days before. Walter was graying at the temples but the rest of his hair was thick and rich brown. His deep blue eyes followed her every move, handsome face so serious. She could sense a strength in him, somehow comforting to be near.

"It must be the light. Last time I hung out Christmas lights. It was pretty, and a little brighter, but an electrical storm came and I felt like we had a lightening rod back here for all of Cocoa Beach."

"It's a nice party. Big crowd."

Jerry and his partner were singing another love song. The people in the back yard were subdued, speaking in hushed voices or singing or humming along with the music. There were really two parties going on, the loud crush in the house and this quieter group in the back.

She looked to the small gathering around the fire and then to the house where a thump, thump, thump of a bass could be felt as well as heard. "Yes. Too big. You can't even breath in the house." She shrugged and smiled. "I only do this twice a year. They're all good friends. It's my way of trying to say thank you for the help a lot of them give me."

"It's nice back here," Walter said, nodding toward the fire.

"Yeah, I don't know how anybody can stay in the house. It's like an oven." Then, noticing that Walter didn't have anything to eat or drink offered, "Would you like something to drink. Soda? Beer?"

"A beer would be good."

"Here, hold this." She handed him her partially filled plastic cup. "I'll get you some." She went into the darkness, bound for a lantern hanging from a tree limb near the water where the yard ended. A wide canal reached from this yard to houses on the other shore. Lighted windows and porches from the opposite side reflected off the black water of the canal, palm trees silhouetted twice, in backyards and inverted on rippling canal. Now that his eyes had become accustomed to the darkness he could see more objects and people. There was a keg on the table under the lantern where Nancy was pouring him a beer. Next to the table were two or three dark figures cooking over a grill, the strong odor of fish drifting to him with a shift of the wind. Jerry saw him and gave him a big grin and an exaggerated wink as he continued to play and sing. He waved back.

Nancy returned and handed him a cup, taking back her own. "I'm sorry, it's mostly foam. These characters drink the stuff so fast that the keg never gets a chance to settle down."

He looked at the opaque plastic cup filled to overflowing, the upper half all foam. "This is fine."

"I'm afraid it's not very cold either," she said. She was holding her cup in front of her and Walter touched his cup to hers.

"Cheers," he said, and drank. The tip of his nose went into the foam and he had a mustache across his upper lip when he brought the cup down. He wiped his nose and lip with a handkerchief.

Nancy took a sip of beer, watching him over the rim. Her eyes were black and piercing in the dim light. He had to look away, feeling as though she could see right through him. Firelight danced in eyes that always seemed to sparkle.

"Who's this?" a voice asked from near his elbow. Unnoticed, a young girl had joined them and was standing at his side.

"This is," Nancy had to stop and think for a second to remember his name, "Walter."

The girl, about eight years old, Walter judged, held out her hand palm down, as though waiting for a formal kiss from a courtier. She was wearing an evening dress that reached to the grass. "How do you do? I'm Helen," she announced.

He bowed slightly and shook her hand. "How do you do?"

Helen stared intently at him. There was no doubt that this was Nancy's daughter. Helen had the same wavy hair, though a bit more sun-bleached, and the same dark eyes and slim nose over full lips. Nancy must have looked just like her at Helen's age.

"I think I saw you before," Helen said to him.

"Walter was kind enough to take me home when the car broke down at the port," Nancy told her daughter.

"Oh, now I remember. You were driving Jerry's old pickup truck."

"The same." Walter nodded.

Helen was still staring at him in the dim light. "You look different," she said, repeating her mother's phrase.

"As they say, clothes make the man," Walter said, unhappy to be back on this topic.

She looked to her mother. "He's pretty ain't he, Momma?"

"Isn't he," Nancy corrected.

Helen stamped her foot in a fit of anger. She was annoyed at being corrected in public especially now when she considered herself co-hostess for the party. "Isn't he pretty then!" she said at the top of her voice.

Several heads in the group near the fire turned to see what the screaming was all about. He felt his face flush, embarrassed at being the center of attention.

"Yes, he's pretty," Nancy agreed, trying to soothe her. And sensitive, Nancy thought, noticing his deep blush. "How's work going on the boat?" she asked, hoping to make him feel more comfortable.

"Slowly. Getting parts and materials is proving to be difficult." He was still waiting on the parts for the generator and the lumber yard had to order the materials he needed.

"That's usually the way it goes," Nancy said with sympathy.

She noticed that he spoke differently from most of the boat people who hung around the port. He sounded educated and was probably another of those professionals who for some reason or another decided to drop out of society and join those living on the margin. She assumed the reason he was having trouble getting parts and materials was because he had no job and no money. Many of Jerry's friends lived in a world of marginal existence.

"Nancy, we're out of soda," a woman called, from near the house.

"I have more," Nancy called back. "Excuse me," she said to Walter, and walked off into the darkness towards the house.

"Do you want to sit by the fire?" Helen asked.

"Sure."

He followed her small, slim figure in a light pink dress. They walked to an empty place in the circle and sat cross-legged on the damp grass. Jerry and his partner were playing a rapid instrumental and many in the crowd clapped in rhythm. The fire crackled and popped as sparks drifted overhead in the heated air. Jerry ended his strumming with a flourish and there was applause and hoops from the crowd.

"Did you have something to eat?" Helen asked.

"No. I'm really not that hungry."

"You ought to eat. There's plenty of fish. Have another beer, too." Helen was trying so hard to be the perfect hostess that he couldn't refuse. He drained his cup. "Thank you. I guess I will try some fish. Not too much, please."

Helen smiled happily and left to get him some food. His empty stomach grumbled with the onslaught of beer. He couldn't remember if he had eaten that day or not. He realized he was hungry but had been so nervous about coming to a party full of strangers and also seeing Nancy that he hadn't thought about eating.

"Howdy stranger," a booming voice said from above and behind him. Walter turned to see Jerry and his girlfriend.

"Hello, Jerry."

"I want you to meet Pokey. Pokey, this here feller's the one I've been telling you about. Pokey, meet Walter," Jerry introduced them, his words a little slurred. He was holding a pitcher of beer in one hand and had his other arm draped over Pokey's slight shoulders. He drank from the pitcher and burped. There was no doubt that he'd been drinking his share of beer.

"Hi," Pokey said, smiling at Walter. She was dressed the way Hollywood envisions Indian maidens in films about the Old West. She wore moccasins, hide-colored dress with tassels at the fringes, brightly colored bracelets and necklace, topped by a band around her forehead. Fair skinned arms and face, blond hair in a pony tail and wide blue eyes belied any possibility she had a drop of Indian blood in her veins. She was slim, petite, and very young. Jerry held her tightly to his side with his huge hand and she seemed smothered by his massive bulk.

"I told you I was old enough to be her father, didn't I?" Jerry patted Pokey lovingly on the head. "But you love me, don't you?" He grinned happily, eyes a little out of focus.

"Yeah, you big jerk," Pokey pulled Jerry and sat down next to Walter.

Jerry thought that was funny and laughed, slapping his thigh. "Ain't she something?" He hugged Pokey and she rolled her eyes in feigned disgust but snuggled up tight. "This here's my little Indian girl, Pocahontas. Ain't ya, honey? And I'm Captain John Smith. And one of these days she's gonna save me from getting my head chopped off. Ain't ya, Pokey?"

"It'll probably be tonight if you don't let me drive. You're in no condition to get behind the wheel."

"You bet," Jerry said, reaching into his pocket and handing her his keys. "You drive. I'm just along for the ride."

Helen returned balancing a paper plate piled high with fish from the grill. She handed Walter his beer and then carefully placed the overflowing plate at his knee on the grass. "I told them you only wanted a little but he gave me all this anyway. He said we had too much and somebody had to eat it."

"Thank you, Helen."

"I have to go now. I have to take care of the other guests."

"You've been very kind."

Helen smiled at the compliment and then turned and walked hurriedly toward the house. He eyed the mound of fish wondering if there was any way he could possibly eat it.

"If we're going to the club and do any dancing we'd better get a move on. If we hang around here any longer you'll be too loaded to walk much less dance," Pokey said to Jerry.

"Okay." Jerry drained the last of the beer in the pitcher. "Let's go dancing." He rolled on all four and then stood, rocking slightly.

"It's been nice meeting you, Walter," Pokey said, as she rose.

"Come, my princess," Jerry said, in his booming voice. "There's places to go and things to see."

The other guitarist was playing and singing softly as he sat near the fire, a woman beside him with her head on his shoulder, eyes closed. The others around the diminishing fire were either silently watching the embers or speaking in subdued voices. It seemed as though the world had become a much quieter place once Jerry left. He looked at the plate of fish in front of him. A growling stomach told him he was more than ready to eat. Helen hadn't given him a fork or spoon or napkin. He broke off a piece of fish with his fingers. It was a thick fillet covered with some type of spicy sauce, delicious, moist and fresh. There were no bones and he picked at the food as he watched the glowing logs hiss and sputter while the guitarist strummed. The pile of fish slowly disappeared as his eyes and mind watched the fire, thoughts at a standstill.

"How was the fish," Nancy asked, as she sat next to him. She had come so quietly he hadn't noticed her.

He looked at the empty plate. "Good. I can't believe I ate it all," he said to himself as much as her.

"The fishing's been good lately. The guys sure brought plenty."

They were quiet for awhile, Nancy staring into the fire. He was happy to have her beside him but he didn't know what he should do next. He looked out of the corner of his eye, unable not to look at her. She was in profile, the firelight enhancing the rich color of her tanned skin and sun-bleached hair. Her forehead was unwrinkled, nose upturned a little toward the tip, mouth full and relaxed, strong chin sloping to neck, shoulders, and round, full breasts. She was immobile as dark eyes reflected the flickering fire, breasts slowly rising and falling with each breath, loose-fitting blouse unable to hide the shapely figure beneath. He drank in the sight wanting to imprint her features indelibly in his memory. Whatever it was about this woman that ignited his manhood, it intensified each time he was near her.

He tried to think of something to say, some way to start a conversation. He had an almost painful physical attraction he felt for her, and also felt like an awkward little boy. She seemed not to have taken any special notice of him. But he wanted her to notice him. He wanted to know that she cared that he existed. What he really wanted was for her to feel for him what he was feeling for her. That's what he really wanted.

"How's your car?" Walter asked.

"Jerry got it fixed. It was the starter like I thought. His

friend fixed it that afternoon and brought it here. He's something. He won't even tell me how much it cost. He said everything's taken care of. The guy owed him a favor."

"He's a nice guy."

"Yeah. I only hope he doesn't kill himself when he's out partying one of these days. He can really be wild sometimes. Thank God he met Pokey. She seems to be able to control him, at least a little."

He didn't want to bring the subject up but couldn't help himself. "How old is Pokey?"

"Eighteen or nineteen, I guess." She looked at him and smiled a little, the flickering flames making her more beautiful than ever. "Kind of young, huh?"

"A lot younger than Jerry."

"Oh, I don't know. In a lot of ways, mentally, emotionally, plain common sense, I'd say she was about ten years older than he is. He's a wonderful guy but sometimes he doesn't seem to care what he does to himself. It's almost as though he's trying to self-destruct. He's been a lot better since he met Pokey."

They were quiet for a moment and then he asked, "Does she always dress like an Indian?"

Nancy chuckled. "No. Only when she's around Jerry. He likes her to dress that way. I guess he's a little kinky. She works at a bank. He's the one who's a little crazy, not her."

There was a pause again, Walter unable to keep the conversation going. He wanted Nancy to stay and these moments to continue. When she was near he didn't think about loneliness. The guitarist continued to play softly, singing on occasion, the others circling the fire quiet, the crackling fire their mutual conversation. He was part of a group, strangers though they were, and the darkness and Nancy's presence let him fit in. He belonged. He knew when he returned to Huntington, and the drudgery that awaited him there, this night around a campfire with Nancy at his side would probably be the highlight of the trip. He tried to absorb each minute, make it part of him, so he could take at least this much back. There was no hope this beautiful woman sitting beside him would ever feel toward him as he was feeling about her. He could understand that. He was an old man with little or no future. She was young and beautiful. He could accept it. There was little else he could do. Nancy barely knew he existed. She was friendly and no more. It was the way it was supposed to be.

"Gee, I wonder what time it's getting to be," Nancy asked, breaking his thoughts.

Walter held his wristwatch to see the dial by the light of the dying fire. "Twenty to twelve."

She jumped up. "I'd better get everybody moving. I have to shut this thing down at twelve. My neighbors go along with me having these parties but midnight's the limit. This crew would stay all night otherwise."

Walter also stood. "I guess I'd better be going."

"Oh, you don't have to leave right this minute. As long as I get that music turned off and most everybody out of here the neighbors won't complain. It's more the noise than anything else," she said, and turned to go to the house. She was scarcely visible when she waved to him, in case he were leaving. He returned her wave with a weak shake of his hand and she was gone.

Others around the fire were getting up and saying their good-nights. One of the men brought a garden hose and doused the fire, hissing steam billowing into the night air. The party was over. The signal had been given. The thump, thump, thump of the bass coming from the house also stopped. The group he had been sitting with broke up and individuals and small groups walked in darkness to their vehicles. He followed. Nancy's invitation to stay a little longer had been no more than a courtesy. He went to the pickup and started the engine. It was satisfyingly quiet. He had the exhaust system replaced that morning. At least he wouldn't be disturbing Nancy's neighbors.

XIV
The Break

The next morning Walter was working on the overhead in what was his stateroom before the fire. Jim Blackman, the insurance agent and adjuster, had been good for his word and Walter had received a check for over eighteen-thousand dollars. Eighteen-thousand dollars seemed more than a fair amount especially since he planned to do much of the repair work himself. The weekends spent in Huntington learning how to do simple home repairs were bearing fruit. He felt confident that much that needed to be done, at least by the fire, he could fix. Blackman also gave him the name and phone number of a boatyard in Titusville that could haul *Windsong* and do the major repairs needed on the hull. It would be two weeks before there would be space in the boatyard for *Windsong* and he was determined to get as much work completed as he could before making the twenty mile run to Titusville and turning *Windsong* over to the yard workers. They could repair the hull, something he couldn't possibly do, but he could do the rest.

The check from the insurance company caused a problem, or at least made him do something he hadn't planned. All his banking accounts were in New York and transferring funds through the mail would take time. He opened a checking account at a bank in Cocoa Beach, depositing the insurance check and much of the cash he had hidden on *Windsong*, and now had a new mailing address of General Delivery, Cocoa Beach, Florida. There would be many bills to pay and drawing on a local bank would make things easier.

The interior of the cabin was crowded with materials he'd purchased early that morning. The deck was stacked with lumber, ceiling tiles, rolls of electrical wires, boxes of nails and screws, and other equipment. He was standing on a crate tugging on an old electrical line, soot, dirt and dust showering him as he yanked on the wire trying to free it from a snag at the bulkhead. He leaned out to get a better grip and felt the crate begin to slip. He let go of the wire and tried to regain his balance but it was too late. In an instant he was in a free fall. One second he was standing on the crate and the next he was grasping at air. The pain that surged through him as he hit the oaken deck was unbearable. He let out a gasp and then the air in his lungs was trapped by a constricted throat. He twisted in slow, contorted movements, gasping, contracted throat making strange animal sounds as he tried to escape the pain surging up his right side.

He'd left a crowbar lying across some lumber on the deck and this caught his full weight when he fell. The thigh bone broke with a loud snap the instant that his upper body hit the deck. He lay there groaning, his breath coming a little easier now, and held his right thigh with both hands. There was no blood so he knew he hadn't been punctured or cut. He lay there a few moments, the pain subsiding to a throbbing, piercing ache in his right leg. He tried to move and a bolt of agony froze him. He was soaked in sweat, the hot cabin adding to the burning torture that pulsed from his side with each heart beat. He lay there for awhile waiting for the pain to lessen while he tried to figure out what he should do next.

He was alone on the boat and it was rare for fishermen to fish from the dock in this part of the port. With little hope that he would be heard he yelled "Help!" several times. No one responded. He slowly rolled himself onto his left side, piercing pain coming each time he made a movement. He was panting and sweating, but he made himself move. Holding his right thigh he dragged himself toward the steps to the forward compartment. He pulled himself up one step at a time, stopping at each step to catch his breath and allow the pain to subside. He then inched along the carpeted deck to the steps leading to the pilothouse.

When he reached the pilothouse he stopped and lay there letting the breeze blowing through the open doorways cool him. He looked at the radios above the steering wheel. If he could stand he could call for help. He pulled himself to the wheel, still on his left side, right hand holding his leg trying to keep it immobile. The less he moved it the less it hurt. He grabbed the steering wheel and tried to force himself erect. Pain shot through him and fell back to the deck. There was no way he could get to the radios. He would have to get help from someone on the dock. He worked his way out of the pilothouse and onto the open deck. There was no one in sight. He looked at the eighteen inch space separating *Windsong* from land and knew he could never cross that wide space. He would have to wait until someone came to get help.

It was twenty minutes before a fisherman came strolling along. Walter called and waved to the man a number of times before he was close enough to hear. He stopped, looked in disbelief at Walter lying on the deck yelling and waving, and then trotted over and jumped aboard. He dropped his fishing pole and tackle box and knelt over Walter. "Jesus Christ, what the hell happened?"

"I think I broke my leg."

"Holy shit! How'd you do that?"

Walter waved the question off. "I've been lying here for

awhile. Do you think you could call an ambulance for me?"

The man looked back at the empty dock and then in the direction of the distant buildings close to the mouth of the port where there were public telephones. He looked back at Walter's sweat-stained face and eyes that showed the pain he was in. "Are you going to be all right until I get back?"

He tried to sit up a little straighter and grunted when pain forced him not to move. "I'll be okay. Just hurry, please."

"Damn right! I'll be back as soon as I can. I'll call an ambulance and then come right back," he said, rising and sprinting off *Windsong* and running at a rapid trot back in the direction of the parking lots and port buildings.

He was gone before Walter could say thank you, jogging at a steady pace in the heat and bright sun. He watched the shrinking figure and then closed his eyes and lay his head on the deck. The worst was over. Help was on its way.

Jerry was working on a crossword puzzle, sipping black coffee, hoping the three aspirins he'd taken would help his pounding head. He was hung over as usual and flinched each time the bell on the door rang and a customer came in. He hated Saturdays. It was his busiest day, and therefore the day he made the most money, but he hated it anyway. He always went out Friday night, and Saturdays, especially the mornings, could be torture. The sound of a siren became louder and he cursed under his breath. He expected the noise to diminish as the emergency vehicle took one of the port roads away from his store, but instead the nerve-shattering siren came right alongside his building and onto the sidewalk and then down the side of the port. He closed the newspaper and went outside to take a look.

About the only time an ambulance came this close was when they pulled another body out of the water. It was usually a murder victim, a crew member from one of the fishing boats or a transient who happened to be at the wrong place at the wrong time. It happened once or twice a year and Jerry had known some of the victims and some of the men who had stabbed or shot them.

The sky was deep blue and Florida's July sun beat down on his throbbing head. He shaded his eyes with his hand and could see the flashing lights of the ambulance stopped at the far end of the port. He was about to go back to the healing air-conditioning when he noticed Walter's boat tied near where the ambulance had stopped. He was undecided what to do. Walking in this heat and sun with the hangover he had was suicide but that ambulance was close to Walter's boat. Very close from what he could make out from this distance. He moaned inwardly and began walking.

His pace quickened when he got close enough to see that the ambulance was parked alongside *Windsong* and then he was running when he saw two attendants carrying someone on a stretcher off the boat. He reached the ambulance just as one of the attendants closed the rear door. Jerry was huffing and puffing from the exertion of the run and the heat when he spoke to the driver.

"Who got hurt?" Jerry asked, between gulps of air.

"I dunno," the driver said, trying to step around Jerry so that he could get into the cab of the ambulance.

"I think I know who it is. Open the door so I can speak to him."

"I can't do that," the driver said. "I gotta get him to the hospital."

Jerry stepped in front of the driver, blocking his way to the cab. "I said open the door!" He was breathing hard, eyes bloodshot and bulging, rivulets of sweat running down his face. He was about a foot taller and one hundred pounds heavier than the driver. The man looked at him and thought better of any further argument.

"The whole fucking world's crazy. Did you know that? You're all fucking crazy," the driver said, backing away and opening the door with a frustrated jerk. He'd been at this for almost sixteen hours, having been forced to work a second shift when a co-worker called in sick, and a weekend night of broken bodies in car wrecks, a bloody knife fight in a bar, and one gunshot victim with his brains blown out had worn him out. He needed to go home and get some sleep.

Jerry stepped up on the bumper and peered into the dark interior. "That you, Walter?"

The emergency medical technician glanced over at Jerry but continued to listen intently as he held a stethoscope to the chest of the figure on the stretcher. There was a grunt and then Walter spoke. "Yeah, it's me Jerry."

"What the hell happened?"

"I think I broke my leg."

"Goddamn!"

The EMT clipped a stethescope around his neck. "We need to get this man to the hospital. Do you mind?" he asked, annoyed at the interruption and the open door allowing all the hot air into the air-conditioned interior.

"Are you okay?" Jerry asked, ignoring the EMT.

"I'll be fine."

"I'll meet you at the hospital."

"Thanks, Jerry. I'll see you there."

Jerry stepped down and slammed the door shut. "What hospital are you taking him to?" he asked the driver.

"Cape Canaveral."

"Get going. And get him there fast."

The driver shook his head in disgust and walked to the cab mumbling, "Crazy, crazy, crazy." He started the ambulance and turned on the siren. There were only two other spectators who had come to watch and certainly no traffic here on the broad, empty dock, but the driver kept the siren screaming anyway. He was angry and tired and the least he could do was make a little noise and let his frustration out.

Jerry walked back to his store to lock up and get his pickup. There was a man standing at the door when Jerry arrived and took out his keys.

"Are you closing now?" the man asked, surprised.

"Yeah. I got something I gotta do," Jerry said, pulling the door shut and turning the lock.

"But I got bait on the counter. I was waiting for somebody to pay," the man complained.

Jerry gritted his teeth and unlocked the door and flung it open. "Get your bait," he said, jaws tight. This was not turning out to be a very good morning.

The man darted in and returned with a frozen package of bait. He held a twenty dollar bill out to Jerry. "Pay me tomorrow," he said, relocking the door.

"But I have to work tomorrow."

"Next time then. Whenever. I don't care," Jerry said, walking away leaving a befuddled customer standing with bait in one hand and a twenty dollar bill in the other.

There were a dozen people waiting inside the emergency entrance. Most were sitting silently, staring at nothing, waiting. A few were at the door, smoking. No one spoke. Jerry walked up to the glass-enclosed reception desk. The woman sitting behind the thick security glass was speaking on the telephone and studiously avoided his presence. He waited while she talked on and on and on. Finally, she hung up and immediately began filling in forms. He had to speak through a small hole cut in the center of the security glass.

"I'm looking for Walter Marshall. They brought him in an ambulance."

The woman looked up, tired eyes that had seen it all, dull and indifferent. "Who did you say?"

"Walter Marshall. They just brought him in an ambulance."

"They have him in the back," she said, and continued filling in forms piled in front of her.

"What the hell does that mean, 'he's in the back.'" Jerry demanded, voice rising.

The woman looked at him, a huge man with strange looking eyes, and her hand moved close to the security alert button. "A man was brought in a couple of minutes ago. They brought him directly to one of the examination rooms."

"How is he?"

"Are you a family member?"

"No. I'm a friend."

"I'm sorry, but only a member of the family can be with the patient in the examination rooms."

"Lady, he ain't got no family. I'm it. And all I want to know is how the guy's doing, that's all." Jerry's frustration level rose. He hated petty bureaucrats, bureaucracy, and petty bullshit. He tried to hold his temper while his head pounded and the taste in his mouth was dry cow manure.

The woman hesitated for a second and then moved her hand away from the emergency security alert button. "I'll go see what I can find out," she said, getting up and disappearing behind a partition.

Jerry spotted a water fountain on a far wall. He drank the sour tasting, cold water until his stomach began to hurt and his mouth still felt dry. Two policemen escorted a man in. The man under arrest had drying and coagulating blood caked on his head, running down his face and neck, and splattered on shirt and pants. He was handcuffed. He shuffled, head down, between the two policemen. They held him at arms length, holding his shirt daintily by their fingertips, as they guided him along trying not to get any of his blood or filth on their clean, tailored uniforms. When they reached the door leading into the emergency room one of the officers turned the knob and found it locked. They stood there patiently, each holding a piece of the prisoner's shirt with a thumb and forefinger like a dirty rag about to be thrown away.

The receptionist returned and on seeing the policemen pressed a buzzer. An officer turned the knob and opened the door, and with a tug, the prisoner leaned forward and began following with a stupefied shuffle. The door clicked and locked behind them.

Jerry went to the reception window and bent down so that he could hear through the hole cut in the glass. "They've taken him to X-ray. It'll be awhile. The doctor says he's pretty sure your friend has a fractured femur but otherwise he thinks he'll be okay."

Jerry felt relieved. At least Walter was going to be okay. "Thank you." And then, "What's a femur?"

"Thigh bone," she said, and picked up a pen and returned to the stack of forms on her desk.

Jerry looked around the waiting room. What was he supposed to do now? He was about to ask the receptionist how long it would be but then thought better of it. She said, "It'll be awhile," and that was probably all the information he was going to get. He thought of going back to the store and re-opening but that would leave Walter stranded here. There was no way of telling when he might be released. He scratched his head and tried to think. There was a public telephone near the door and he dialed Pokey's number. He let the phone ring for a long while and hung up. He tried to think of someone else he might call and dialed another number.

"Hello?" Nancy answered in her husky voice.

"It's Jerry. I'm at the hospital."

"The hospital? What's wrong?" Her voice expressed concern.

"It's Walter. They came and got him off his boat a little while ago."

"My God! What happened?"

"They think he broke his leg. He's in X-ray now."

"How did it happen? Is he going to be all right?"

"I don't know what happened. I wasn't there. I only followed the ambulance over to the hospital."

"What can I do? Do you need help? Do you want me to come? I'll have to bring the kids with me."

Jerry wanted company but the thought of three noisy kids wasn't appealing. "No. No need for you to come. There's nothing to do here. I guess I'll just wait and see what happens, whether they're going to keep him or release him or what. I just thought I should call someone. His family's all up in New York and I have no idea what their phone numbers are."

"Well, let me know if I can help."

"Okay. I'll give you a report later if I ever find out what's going on myself. I'll talk to you later."

It was almost four hours before they wheeled Walter out on a gurney. He smiled as soon as he saw Jerry, the painkilling drugs working well. "Hi, Jerry," he said, sounding fine. "Sorry about all of this."

"No problem," Jerry said, and with a wave of his hand erased four hours of total boredom. "The question is, how are you doing?"

"I'm okay, although I sure have found a way to screw up a vacation. The doctor says I'll have to stay in this thing for six weeks. A sheet covered Walter to his chest, a bend in the right knee making a small tent there. He pulled the sheet back from his right side to reveal a cast from his right foot to midway up his chest. He was in a partial body cast to prevent any movement of his upper right leg.

"That's quite a contraption." Jerry touched the hard, bulky cast and made a face. "How are you feeling other than that? Did you hurt anything else?"

"No, just the leg. It was my own fault. I meant to buy a ladder but forgot. I was standing on something and it slipped and that was it. Hurt like hell when it happened, but I'm okay now. They gave me a shot for the pain and some pills to take when it hurts."

The male nurse at the head of the gurney asked, "Are you parked near the door?"

Jerry looked at Walter lying flat on his back, a cast half enclosing his right foot and going to his chest. "Is it all right for him to ride in a pickup?"

The nurse shrugged indifferently. "If that's what you've got, that's what he'll ride in. I'll help you load him if you'll bring your truck by the ramp."

Jerry brought his truck to the base of the sloping walkway at the emergency entrance door. They covered Walter's naked crotch with his shirt and shredded shorts that had been cut off him. Walter watched groggily, the pain medication making him sleepy and uncaring. They wedged him into the cab of the pickup, the stiff cast preventing him from sitting, buttocks barely touching the front seat.

Jerry started the engine. "Where we going," he asked, wondering what he was supposed to do with a naked man who looked like he belonged in a hospital bed.

"Back to the boat. I've got to keep the bilge pumps running, keep her dry."

"The boat? Bilge pumps?" Jerry was shocked. Walter needed to be in a bed with someone looking after him, not on a boat. "Maybe I should take you to a motel or something."

"No. To the boat," Walter insisted. "I can't just leave her. She's leaking too bad."

"How about just for one night? There's a motel real close to the port."

"No. The boat," Walter insisted again. His eyes were little more than slits as he tried to keep them open, the pain medication working extremely well.

Jerry drove slowly and carefully back to the port, occasionally glancing at Walter as he nodded in and out of a light sleep. His shoulders were jammed against the back of the seat and his head was forced forward with chin on chest. He looked perfectly relaxed with his hands folded over the small pile of clothes in his lap and his left leg, butt, and the rest of his body naked. The wide strip of plaster of Paris across his chest bit into his flesh.

They parked alongside *Windsong* and Walter opened his eyes. "That damn boat's liable to kill me one of these days," he said, more to himself than to Jerry.

"I think you're crazy," Jerry said, not getting out, hoping that Walter would change his mind. "You can't stay on a boat in the shape you're in. How are you going to get around? How're you going to walk and all? Why don't you let me take you to a motel, at least for tonight?"

"You don't understand. I have to be aboard. *Windsong's* leaking and I have to keep those pumps going. In a couple of weeks I'll be able to put her in dry-dock and they'll fix all that. Until then I have to take care of her. The doctor said I'll be able to walk with crutches. It'll only take a little practice. I hate to bother you but do you think you can get me a pair of crutches? There must be a place you can buy a pair or rent them."

Jerry got out and slammed the door. "You know Walter, I thought you were the one sane person around here. But you know something? You're as screwy as the rest of them. And me." He opened the door on Walter's side. "Where am I supposed to put you?"

"I can stay on the afterdeck. I have a cot set up. I usually sleep there anyway."

Jerry reached in and put one arm under the cast circling Walter's chest and the other under the leg. Lifting, he swung his legs out first and then eased him completely out, cradling him in his arms. Jerry was big and strong and even with the additional weight of the cast he lifted Walter without much trouble. He carried him to the afterdeck and put him on a lounge chair. A mosquito netting covered the cot. He lifted this out of the way and with a grunt lifted Walter again and laid him on the cot. He pulled the sheet over Walter's lower half and dropped the netting. He stepped back and looked at his handiwork.

"If this isn't the damnedest thing," he said, shaking his head.

The pain-killing injection they had given Walter was beginning to wear off and he was becoming more alert. "I'm dying for a cigarette. Could you get me some? I have a carton in the galley."

Jerry got him a pack and gave him one. Jerry reached in his pocket and took out his cigarette lighter and lit it and placed both on a small table where he could reach it and an ashtray. Walter took his wallet out of his cut-up shorts and handed Jerry a piece of paper and a one hundred dollar bill.

"I hate to keep bothering you, and after this I promise not to be anymore trouble, but could you get this prescription filled for me? It's for pain medicine. And maybe they'll have crutches at the pharmacy. As soon as I have those I'll be able to take care of myself."

"Sure you will," Jerry said, sarcastically. "Like shit you will. Sure, I'll get the prescription filled and get you a pair of crutches if I can find some. But I still think you're making a big mistake. You shouldn't be here. You need to be someplace where you can be more comfortable and someone can look after you. Why don't you let me call your family and let them know what's going on?"

"No, I don't want to bother them. I'll work this thing out myself. I thought about it, but there's really nothing they can do. They're busy with their own lives. They don't need to be worrying about me. *And I don't want to go back like this.*"

Walter said the last sentence through clenched teeth. There was no doubt how determined he was.

"Okay. If you insist. I'll be back as soon as I can. Don't go anywhere," he said, grinning.

"Thanks, Jerry." Walter waved languidly and brushed the mosquito netting, knocking the ash off his cigarette. The burning tip landed on his bare chest and he brushed and beat at it, wiggling as he was held in place by the rigid cast.

Jerry rolled his eyes and said, "Jesus." He shook his head and left.

Walter reached out and got Jerry's lighter and re-lit the cigarette. He was fully awake now and wondered how long it would be before the pain medicine they had given him wore off and he would be needing the pills Jerry was getting.

XV
Dixie

Jerry dialed Nancy's number as soon as he got in the store. Maybe she would have some ideas as to what he might do about Walter. It rang several times before she picked it up.

"Hello?"

"Nancy, it's Jerry. I got Walter out of the hospital."

"How is he?"

"Okay, I think. He's a little drugged from the pain medicine right now. He broke his leg and they put him in a monster cast. Other than that, nothing else is broken."

"Good. I'm glad he's going to be all right."

"That's the point," Jerry said, his voice rising. He was getting angry with himself for once again getting involved with people and situations that were ongoing headaches. "I brought him back to his boat. He insisted. The jackass is in a cast up to his chest and can't even move and I don't know how he can possibly take care of himself. I'm on my way to get a prescription filled and see if I can find some crutches for him."

"Won't he be able to walk, at least enough to get around, once he has crutches?" Nancy asked, calmly. She was used to

174

Jerry getting agitated and blowing things out of proportion.

"That's what he says, the jerk. But you've got to see this guy. He's wrapped like a mummy. At least half a mummy. The guy needs somebody to take care of him, for a few days anyway. And I don't want to be the dumb son-of-a-bitch stuck with the job. I got other things to do."

"Why don't you take him to a motel, some place with room service?" she asked, and added, "or maybe he can't afford it."

"He can afford it. He's got plenty of money. He's a lawyer for Chrissake. It's not that. He's just being thick-headed. He's more concerned about his boat than he is about himself. They fixed his leg but they should have done a little work on his brain. He can't even go and take a piss. The bathrooms are below deck and there's no way he can go up and down those narrow steps wrapped up like he is. Those passageways are too narrow."

"What can I do, Jerry? I hardly know the man."

"I don't know. Maybe if you talked to him. Maybe he'll listen to you."

"How about his family? Couldn't you call them?"

"They're all up in New York, and I don't know who they are or their phone numbers. His wife's dead but he has a couple of kids, but he won't let me call them. What am I supposed to do? I don't want to be this guy's nursemaid."

Nancy was silent for a moment. She really didn't want to get involved with another of Jerry's crises if she could help it. But he had more than he could handle, again, and he was a good friend. "I'll come over if you think it'll help. I'll have to see if I can find someone to mind the kids."

Jerry let out a sigh of relief. "Thanks, Nancy. I don't know what I'd do without you. In the meantime, I'll go to the drug store and get the medicine. I'll meet you back here at the store. Okay?"

"Okay, Jerry," Nancy agreed, resigned to being party to another of his fiascoes.

He hung up and took a six-pack of beer out of the refrigerator, locked the door to the store, and went to his pickup. He opened a can of beer and drank it in one long swallow. Sweat began to run off him from the heat in the cab. He popped another can of beer open and started the truck.

Nancy was waiting for him when he returned with the pills and a pair of crutches. She stood in the shade of the building and came out to the parking lot as soon as she saw the pickup approaching. Jerry was holding a small bag along with the crutches.

"I got 'em," Jerry said proudly, holding the crutches out like a prize. After drinking the six-pack of beer and stopping at a local pub and having a couple of shots of bourbon, his good humor had returned. "I had to search around, but I found a place that sold them."

"I see you stopped at a couple of other places besides," she said, noticing the liquor on his breath.

"Aw, don't start. It's been a long day."

"It's your life. You're going to do what you want to anyway. What about Walter? What are we supposed to do?" They began walking toward *Windsong*.

"Maybe you can talk some sense into him. You'll see when we get there. There's no way he'll be able to manage on the boat."

"I don't know why I should make a difference. You know him a lot better than I do. I've only met him twice. Why should he listen to me?"

"I don't know. You seem to have a way with people. You can usually get someone to do what you want them to."

"That's a joke," Nancy said seriously. "I only wish it were true."

Jerry said no more. He needed help and he certainly didn't want to provoke her. They approached *Windsong* and she was impressed. It didn't fit image she'd formed about Walter.

There was no doubt that the boat was expensive, not a decrepit wreck a semi-vagrant would live on. Walter was lying on the cot, sheet pulled up to his waist, smoking a cigarette. He looked up, stunned at seeing Nancy with Jerry.

"I got your stuff for you," Jerry said, putting the bag on the table and slipping the crutches under the cot. "I brought Nancy along. Maybe you'll listen to her."

"Hi," Walter said to Nancy, and tried to smile. The pain medication was wearing off and a dull ache had started in his leg and grew more painful with each passing moment. The pain showed in his eyes and the shakiness of his voice. A nurse in the emergency room had wiped most of the dirt from his face but some soot was left around his eyes and they appeared dark and haunted. He pulled the sheet a little higher on his chest, conscious of being naked underneath.

"Hi, yourself," Nancy said lightly, in her best sick-room voice. "I hear you've been making a nuisance of yourself."

He looked at Jerry and frowned. "I'm sorry I've been so much trouble to you Jerry. I'll try not to bother you anymore," he said apologetically.

Before Jerry could respond Nancy answered. "That's not what we're talking about. Jerry doesn't mind being helpful nor do I. What we're talking about is you staying on this boat. It's not a good place for you. You can't take care of yourself here."

"I'll be okay. I have to stay aboard to look after the boat. Now that I've got these crutches," he looked over at Jerry, "and thanks for getting them for me, I'll be able to get around and do what I have to do."

"That's bullshit," Jerry said loudly.

Nancy stepped forward and picked up the bag holding the medication. She opened it and took out the small container. "You look like you're hurting." She handed Walter the vial.

"Thank you," he said gratefully. He read the label. The instructions were to take one or two capsules for pain every four hours. He unscrewed the cap and shook out one. He held it in his palm. He didn't have any water to chase it with. He was about to pop it into his mouth when Nancy restrained him with the touch of her fingers on his wrist.

"I'll get you some water," she said, and went into the main cabin. She returned a moment later with a glass of water and a gallon jug of distilled drinking water she found in the galley. She handed him the glass and put the jug on the table next to the cot. Walter raised himself on one elbow so that he could drink. He swallowed the pill and emptied the glass. Silently, Nancy took the glass and re-filled it and handed it to him. He said thank you with his eyes, where Nancy could also see his discomfort and embarrassment. He was ashamed to have her see him like this, helpless, sweaty, and probably smelling bad. If he had any hopes of her ever wanting anything to do with him, those hopes were now gone. He felt like a helpless, useless old man. He turned his head and closed his eyes. He couldn't look at this beautiful young woman anymore. It hurt too much. The pain in his leg was getting worse. He prayed that the pain medication would go to work soon.

"Mind if I look around your boat?" Nancy asked.

"No, go right ahead," he said, not turning his head.

She looked over at Jerry who was sitting on the handrail watching them. Jerry made no move to come with her. He had stopped being a participant and had become an observer. It was in her hands now. She frowned at him and Jerry grinned back. Somehow the problem of Walter had shifted to her. She made an angry face and he grinned even wider. She sighed resignedly and went inside *Windsong*.

She walked through the great room and galley and into the pilothouse, went below to the forward lounge and stopped on the steps leading into the stripped cabin where Walter had been working. She went back to the upper deck and down the aft stairwell to the cabins and the bathroom there. There was no way he could negotiate the spiraling stairwell nor could he possibly get down two flights of stairs forward and then have to climb over building material in that cabin to get to the bathroom there. She went back to the afterdeck resolved to get him off this boat somehow. He was sick. He was hurt. And Jerry was right, the jerk didn't know what he was saying as he insisted on staying aboard.

Walter's head was still turned away when she returned. She looked at Jerry and grimaced. He spread his arms and shrugged expressively.

"It's a very pretty boat," she said to Walter.

"Thank you," he said, not turning his head. The pain was still there. It had stopped getting worse but it hadn't lessened yet. He was waiting for the medicine to work, and he didn't want her to see him like this. There was nothing else he could do but lie there, head turned, eyes closed, and try to become invisible.

Nancy stood, hands on hips, trying to think of something to say or do that might get this hurt, semi-drugged man off this boat and somewhere more appropriate, where he could heal. Jerry avoided eye contact with her. He was doing all he could to dump the problem.

"Walter," she called. He didn't respond. She said, "Walter" again, louder this time. He turned and looked at her, his dark blue eyes glazed with pain and the drug now entering his system. "Walter, you can't stay here," she said, softly.

"You don't understand. I'm needed to take care of the boat. I have to keep the pumps running. I can't just leave her. I appreciate your coming and caring but I'll manage some-how. I have to."

Nancy didn't answer right away. She was trying to under-stand why a man would jeopardize his health and maybe even his life for a boat, even an expensive boat. It didn't make any sense. She tried one more time to change his mind.

"We'll take care of the boat. Jerry or I can run the pumps if that's all it's going to take. Right, Jerry?" She looked over at Jerry and he shrugged his shoulders, neither a yes or no. She pursed her lips. He wasn't being helpful at all. "The thing is, you can't take care of yourself here. How are you going to cook? How are you going to eat? You can't even go to the bathroom?"

Walter blushed deeply at the mention of using the bathroom. He'd needed to urinate for some time and it was getting worse. He knew he couldn't negotiate the steps even with crutches, but he could urinate in a pot or bowl and pour it down the sink. All he had to do was to be able to make it to the galley and he would be okay. Defecating was something else. He didn't have to do that now and would worry about it when the time came. He wanted them to leave so that he could try the crutches and get to the galley. He would let his bladder burst before he would stand naked and on crutches in front of her.

"I'll be okay, Nancy. Really," he told her, hoping they would leave soon. She still stood, arms akimbo, dark eyes looking into his soul. But he had a defense against those eyes at the moment. Pain and the mind-dulling pain-killer helped him resist her plea.

"There's nothing I can say or do that'll change your mind?" she asked.

"I'm fine. Thank you for coming," he said, unconvincingly.

Nancy nodded, as though accepting this, turned and started to leave. "Come on, Jerry," she said as she passed, leaving without saying good-bye.

Suddenly they were gone and he was alone. He waited a couple of minutes to be sure and then the pressure from his bladder forced him to move. The pain pill was helping some and he found that he could move even with the steady throbbing ache coming from his leg. He reached under the cot and got the crutches and propped them against the cot. He carefully eased his right leg over the edge and allowed the weight of the cast help him lift his upper body off the cot. He grabbed the crutches, and with jerking motions inched his way erect. He tottered for a second, but managed to stay erect.

He worked his way slowly into the main cabin one foot length at a time, the bent knee in the cast keeping it off the deck. He strained to hold his water and managed to make it to the galley and found a bowl and relieved himself. The pain in his bladder had become worse than the ache in his leg. There was a towel on the rack near the sink and he wrapped it around his waist. With slow, cautious steps he wobbled his way back to the afterdeck and cot, sweat dripping from the effort. He made it. Somehow everything was going to be all right. In a little while he would try it again and start the engines and get the pumps working and the hull dry.

Fifteen minutes after Nancy called, Billy Tillman roared into the port. He didn't stop in the parking lot but jumped the curb and parked the great Harley-Davidson motorcycle illegally on the sidewalk beside Jerry's building. It was late afternoon but the sun was still high and the seat of the motorcycle would be blazing hot in minutes if left in the sun. He always parked in the shade, legal or not. Billy had just completed working on the carburetor when his mother called him in from the backyard to take Nancy's call. He had pulled on a black leather vest to cover his bare chest, jumped on the bike, and wheelied out of the yard in a cloud of flying dirt. He didn't mind coming to see what Nancy needed him for. He had to check out the carburetor adjustment anyway.

Nancy and Jerry were waiting for him when he entered the store. Jerry stood by an open refrigerator and threw one, two, and then a third can of beer to Billy who expertly caught them and plopped one in the stretched pockets on each side of his vest and popped the top on the third and sucked it down in seconds. Nancy watched the ritual and waited until they completed their childish game before she spoke.

"Thanks for coming, Billy," she said.

"Sure, kid. What's up?" He retrieved a can from his vest and opened it.

"Do you remember a fellow who came to the party last night? He's in his late fifties I guess, tall, graying at the temples."

Billy thought for a moment, sipping the beer. "Naw, it don't ring no bells. I spent most of the night trying to play with Pattie's tits. She's got some pair but kind of sensitive about them. You know what I mean?" Billy beamed as he remembered Pattie's half-hearted attempts to keep him from fondling her.

"Anyway," Nancy continued, ignoring his remarks, "he broke his leg this morning and he's in a cast. He's on his boat tied up down at Port's End. It's not where he should be. He can't take care of himself there."

"So?" Billy asked, looking over at Jerry. Jerry kept his face blank. The ball was in Nancy's court and he was going to leave it there.

"So, for some reason he won't listen to anyone. He insists on staying on the boat even though he shouldn't be there. He needs help. He can't do for himself."

"Nancy, you're always picking up stray critters hurt along side of the road and that kind of stuff. When you gonna grow up? If the guy wants to stay on his boat, why not let him? It's his life. You can't help every sick puppy, you know."

"He's not a puppy, he's a man," Nancy said defensively. "And if it were a hurt puppy I would try to help. I couldn't leave a dog, much less a man, hurting when I know I could help."

Billy shrugged, burped, scratched his hairy chest and belly, and opened the third can of beer. He was a giant of a man, taller, heavier, and more muscular than Jerry. Tattoos covered his arms and chest, unruly black beard beginning to streak with gray, dark and dirty hair reaching to his shoulders. He looked like a wild man and usually was, but not when it came to Nancy. She could control him when no one else could. Though he looked at least ten years older, they were the same age and had been lifelong friends.

"What do you want to do?" Billy asked.

"Take him to my place. At least for a day or two. Maybe the pain drugs they're giving him have his mind foggy. He seemed like a very intelligent man last night. I don't think he's thinking straight."

"Your place?" Billy's bushy eyebrows shot up. "What are you gonna do with him? You can't put him out in the backyard like you do your cats and dogs."

"I'll think of something. Let's get him over there first. Maybe once he's off the boat he'll listen to us. We'll use Jerry's truck. You brought him home okay, didn't you?" she asked Jerry.

He nodded. "He fits."

"Come on. Don't take no for an answer," she said, leading two of the biggest and strongest men on Cocoa Beach to fetch Walter.

Nancy was the first to arrive on the afterdeck, Jerry and Billy following behind whispering and snickering. Walter was laying on the cot, naked except for the towel covering his mid-section. "We're going to take you to my place," Nancy announced as she approached him.

"What?" Walter asked in confusion, first checking that the towel was in place and then trying to rise on his elbows.

Jerry put Walter's vial of pills and cigarettes alongside him on the cot and grabbed the side poles at his head.

"Ready?" he asked Billy, who had come to the foot of the cot.

Billy gave a conspiratorial wink. "Let's go." They lifted Walter and cot without effort.

"Wait! Wait!" Walter yelled, first at Nancy, then twisting to speak to Jerry. Walter had no idea who the monstrous giant was holding the foot of the cot. "You can't do this!"

"Nancy says you're going to her place, so you're going to her place." Jerry informed him as they began carrying him off *Windsong*.

"Easy, Walter," Jerry said gently to him as he wiggled helplessly, not sure what was happening. "Don't knock yourself off and get yourself hurt worse. Easy."

"But you can't do this! This is kidnapping!" Walter yelled.

"You're too old to be a kid," Billy said, grinning at Jerry. He was enjoying this. "If Nancy says you go, you go."

"But, but..." Walter sputtered, still wiggling.

Nancy put her hand on his forearm. "Shh, you'll see. It'll be better this way. Let us help you. Shhh." She spoke softly, stroking his forearm as she walked beside him to the back of the pickup, much the way she would try to calm an injured animal who was snapping at the hands trying to help it.

They put Walter and the cot in the open bed of the pickup. Jerry hadn't gotten around to putting the cap on the back. This is what they planned as they followed Nancy aboard *Windsong* whispering. It was quick and easy. Walter and cot both came at once. Billy climbed into the back of the truck and sat on the edge as Jerry drove to the parking lot. Billy jumped off and mounted his motorcycle and Nancy went to her station wagon. Walter called after her trying to get all this stopped. He was confused, angry, embarrassed, and frustrated at his helplessness.

"But... you... can't... do... this!" he screamed. She ignored him, acting as if she hadn't heard a word.

They caravaned down A1A, the main road through Cape Canaveral and Cocoa Beach, Nancy following the pickup and Billy behind her on his bellowing motorcycle. The wind whipped at the mosquito netting held by a crossbar above the cot, net flapping straight out in the wind. Walter pulled the sheet over himself and had to hold the bottom of the sheet with his good left leg and the top with both hands to keep it from being torn away in the wind. They had to stop at traffic lights as they passed through tourist-crowded Cape Canaveral and the adjoining City of Cocoa Beach and drivers and passengers in the other lanes looked with great curiosity at him laying in his tangled net-covered cot. He had never been so mortified. He felt like a freak on display. Eventually, he pulled the sheet over his face and hid in the flapping cloth. He couldn't believe this was happening.

Once at her house, Nancy led the procession as Billy and Jerry followed carrying Walter. A group of children playing in the next yard stopped their game and lined up along the walkway to watch as Walter passed. A neighbor across the street also looked on, guessing that he was a casualty from the party the night before. Walter watched all this as if in slow motion.

Nancy moved a coffee table from the center of the living room and they put him there. Jerry patted his shoulder.

"There, that wasn't so bad, was it?" Jerry said.

Billy couldn't hide a smirk and had to turn away to keep from laughing. It had been quite a sight seeing Walter driven down the main drag in the back of the pickup, sheet and netting flying, Walter wrestling with the sheet, trying to keep himself covered.

Walter was at a loss for words. The past fifteen minutes were beyond anything he'd ever experienced. It had all been so ludicrous, so absurd it was outside of anything he could have conceived in his worst nightmare. He was a shy man, quiet and conservative, and being driven down a busy street naked and being seen by hundreds, maybe thousands of people was more than his mind could accept. He looked around his new environment and tried to regain his composure. What the hell just happened?

"He's going to need some clothes," Nancy said.

"Anything else you need, Walter?" Jerry asked him.

Walter looked from Nancy to Jerry, mouth agape. "Are you all right, Walter?" Jerry asked him, truly concerned. Walter looked very pale even with his tan.

Nancy came to him and put her hand on his forehead, checking to see if he were feverish. Her cool hand helped bring him back to reality. The shock of being driven down A1A had been greater than breaking his leg. But now that it was over the pain in the leg returned, the bumpy ride and all the twisting and turning not having helped matters. He looked up at her standing above and behind him, her hand to his forehand. He had an upside-down view of her: bare belly to halter and shapely breasts, face bent down, wavy hair framing her face, concern in her eyes as they searched his. He felt himself relax under her cool hand and caring gaze.

"Nancy," he said, "I didn't want to bother anybody."

"You're no bother. We all need help now and then."

Jerry picked up Walter's cigarettes from the cot. Amazingly, they hadn't blown away during the trip. He lit a cigarette and put it between Walter's lips.

"You're a lucky son-of-a-bitch, you know that? I'd break my leg if I thought Nancy'd take care of me," he said, with a leering grin.

"I'm liable to break it for you if you don't watch yourself," Nancy retorted.

"Right-o," Billy said, as he came from the kitchen and handed Jerry a pitcher of beer. "There's about a third left in each keg," he informed Jerry. They each drank from a pitcher.

"Don't even think about it," Nancy said quickly. "You guys aren't going to sit here all night getting drunk. I haven't got the place cleaned up from last night."

"No problem," Jerry said, and drank.

"Jerry'll get you some clothes if you tell him where they are," Nancy said to Walter.

He looked down at the cast on his leg. "I don't think I have anything that'll fit over this thing."

Nancy inspected the cast. "I can fix it so you can get shorts over it, I think."

"Where do you keep your stuff? I'll bring you something," Jerry offered.

"In the aft cabin."

At the thought of *Windsong*, Walter frowned. "Seriously, Jerry, I can't leave the boat like this. The pumps have to be run and I have to use the engines to do that. I'm not hooked up to shore power. The batteries will be dead in no time if left on automatic."

"I'll run 'em while I'm out there and get the bilges dry," Jerry assured him.

"But what about tomorrow and tomorrow night. You can't keep running there day and night. It's too much."

When Jerry didn't answer, Nancy spoke. "Why not bring the boat here? You can tie it at my dock out back if you can get it in here. There's an electrical outlet that'll work."

Jerry thought for a minute. "It'll fit. That's a wide canal you got back there." Jerry turned to Billy. "Want to take a ride tonight? We'll bring the boat over. Old Walt will have all his stuff then."

"Can we take the beer with us?" Billy asked.

"Take the damn beer," Nancy said heatedly. "But don't you guys get loaded and wreck the damn boat."

Walter listened to the exchange as the discussion went on above him. His future was being decided, at least his immediate future, and no one bothered to ask his opinion. He looked up at Nancy. She was as beautiful upside-down as she was right-side up. Being here might not be the worst thing that could happen to him. He said nothing.

"Sounds good to me," Billy said. "Let's get the beer loaded and I'll bring my bike to my mother's. I'll ride with you." Billy didn't like to leave his Harley out on the street. It was the one and only possession he cared about.

They guzzled the last of the beer in their pitchers and left to get the two kegs left over from the party. Nancy watched, shaking her head. They were like nitric acid and glycerin. Put the two together and anything could happen, especially with alcohol added to the mixture.

"Will you be all right for awhile?" Nancy asked Walter. "I left Little John with a friend and she has to go to work soon."

"I'm okay," he told her, although he wasn't sure. The pain in his leg had been growing steadily worse by the minute. He felt around and found the vial containing the pain pills.

Nancy was at the door when she said, "I'll be right back."

The front door opened again and a little girl came in. She stood looking at Walter, the cot, and the cast. She had dark eyes like Nancy's, and her gaze was steady and unflinching. Her skin was cream colored, not only from the sun but a natural tone, and her short hair was black and curly. She stood there, unmoving, black eyes locked on him. It was unnerving.

"Hi," he said, trying to smile, the pain preventing it. "What's your name? I'm Walter."

"Dixie," she said, in a quiet little voice.

He tapped two tablets from the vial and replaced the cap. She watched each of his movements and then quickly disappeared into the kitchen. He heard water running and she was back carrying a large glass, walking carefully so as not to spill any. When she reached his side she held it out to him. He threw the pills in his mouth and drank the whole glass of water and handed it back to her. "Thank you, Dixie. How old are you?"

"Four."

"You're very bright for four," he complimented.

"I know," she said, placing the glass on the coffee table and sitting on a chair facing him. Once again she stared at him steadily. He turned away and closed his eyes. The pain was getting worse, throbbing, aching. He took a deep breath and waited for the pills to take effect.

XVI
Moored

He was sitting on a lounge chair that Jerry had taken off of *Windsong*. The back legs were propped up by two-by-fours and numerous pillows supported his back. It was comfortable here in the back yard in the evenings with a cool breeze blowing in from the sea, the children quiet and being entertained by the television in his room while munching on cookies and getting crumbs all over the bed. Walter was puffing on a pipe that he was slowly learning to like more than cigarettes. Nancy had once mentioned she liked the aroma of his pipe tobacco and he had been smoking it more since then. His switching to a pipe was but one of the many changes that had taken place in the last six weeks.

Lightning illuminated thunderheads just above the western horizon, heated air rising from still warm land feeding moisture to local storm cells. Tomorrow the weather would be different from Florida's normal summer weather of hot and humid days with afternoon and evening thunderstorms. Most of the east coast was under a hurricane watch, although the tropical storm out in the Atlantic south-east of Florida was expected to stay off-shore and move north. It was also possible Tropical Storm Edward wouldn't become a hurricane and it might swing north-east and never threaten land. The weather predictors couldn't be sure. They never really were with hurricanes and Tropical Storm Edward had formed early in the hurricane season and was especially hard to predict. What they were sure of was in less than twenty-four hours the Cocoa Beach area would have rising winds and rain squalls.

Walter looked at *Windsong* tied to the small dock extending from Nancy's backyard. She was moored snug and secure to the little wooden dock but he knew he would have to do much more if the wind really got up. After tomorrow morning he would be able to do that. He had an appointment at the doctor's office and the cast would come off. It would be like being released from prison, but as sometimes happens with men who had been held in the security of a prison for a long time, he was as frightened at the prospect of being released as he was happy to be finally free. In the dim light he could just make out the old, wooden ladder leaning against *Windsong*'s tall hull and gave access from the low dock. The ladder could just as well have been a fifty-foot wall to him. It had kept him off of *Windsong* while he hopped about in confining cast and crutches. A weak light from a small bulb in *Windsong*'s galley was left on continually to help any boater who might come into the narrow canal at night. The dock and her wide beam filled much of the waterway. An extension cord ran from an outlet on the dock through a porthole to *Windsong*'s pumps and the small light. As far as Walter could tell the leak or leaks in the hull were no worse now than they had been six weeks earlier. The pumps came on and off with a steady regularity and he could detect no change. He called the boatyard in Titusville and *Windsong* was now scheduled to be hauled for repairs in four days.

Tomorrow morning the cast would come off and he could

get aboard *Windsong,* but he doubted he would be moving her. Trying to steer in high winds through the narrow canal and then the limited space of the Banana River would be nearly impossible. In all likelihood *Windsong* would be staying where she was tomorrow night. He would fasten more lines to the dock and trees in the backyard if "Eddie," the nickname the newscasters had given Tropical Storm Edward, was to come nearby. He would know more tomorrow.

He more or less knew what he would be doing with *Windsong* in the coming days and weeks, but about his own immediate future he had no idea. He said nothing to Nancy or anyone else, made no plans, and had no thoughts beyond the moment when the cast would come off and it was time for him to leave this house and this family. He said nothing and Nancy said nothing but he knew that once he was no longer an invalid he would have to leave. It wouldn't be right for him to stay and he couldn't even if she had asked him, which he knew she never would. It had been difficult enough with him in a cast, but once out and fully a man again, it would be impossible to live under the same roof with her and keep the same relationship they'd had for the last six weeks. He would go insane. There were times in the past weeks when he felt that he *was* going insane. Nancy being so close and yet so distant had been daily torture. He couldn't take it anymore and yet the thought of not having her near was more unbearable. Perhaps that was why he had made no plans beyond getting the cast off. When he reached the point where he would have to leave Nancy and the children, his mind would turn off. He could see nothing after that. There was nothing after that.

The hinges on the rear screen door squeaked and it banged shut. He didn't have to look and see who it was. The sweet scent of the soap Nancy used when she showered filled the air with her presence. He heard her sit on a beach chair a few feet away. This was a microcosm of the past month and a half.

They spoke little to each other and yet each knew where the other was and what he or she was doing at any particular moment of the day. It was part of the insanity of their relationship. He was afraid to express his true feelings for her, afraid of rejection, afraid of being asked to leave even though it was such torture to stay, afraid of losing her or at least the part of her that he had. Sometimes he was even afraid to look at her. He knew she had to be able to see what he was feeling. It would show in his eyes, his face, his whole body. There were times when she would come near and he could feel her warmth, real or not, and smell her scent, and see her lovely face and shapely figure and he would have to turn away, trembling. He would go to his room or crutch-hop out of the house and take deep breaths trying to clear his mind of her.

He was more an emotional cripple than a physical one. He was so frightened she would reject him if he spoke of his love for her, that the thought would make him break out in a sweat. What if she said no? What if she told him he was a foolish old man and she was only trying to be kind? What if she asked him to leave? He would die if she said that. His body might keep on living but emotionally he would die. Without Nancy and her wonderful children he had grown to love he would be nothing. The thought of returning to Huntington and an empty house and loneliness was a sentence of solitary confinement. He couldn't think about it.

He breathed in her scent, closed his eyes, and leaned back on the lounge chair. One more night and it would be over. He didn't know what he could or should do, but as so many times before, he wouldn't take the gamble tonight. Tomorrow he would be forced to do something. What he would do he didn't know, but for tonight he would take what painful pleasure there was and accept it. Surreptitiously, he turned his head and peeked over at her. She was drinking iced tea, lips caressing the tall, slim glass, the light from the rear window behind putting her in white profile against the dark. She had her wet hair wrapped in a towel, a white turban crowning the face that flashed into his mind at unexpected moments throughout the day, skin so unblemished it appeared translucent in this light. A damp, stray curl escaped and shivered in the soft breeze, brushing against a small, perfectly shaped ear and down to the smooth skin of her neck.

She was wearing a thin bathrobe, belt tight around a slim waist, calf and knee showing in the slit caused by crossed ankles. Her breasts pressed against the light cloth, nipples clearly defined, chest moving slightly with each breath. Her eyes scanned the horizon as she watched the distant lightning. He pulled his eyelids closed, shutting out her image. But her fragrance was still there and her vision filled his mind and soul.

Nancy could feel Walter's eyes on her. She didn't know how, but she knew when he was looking at her full of yearning and desire and, she had to admit, love. She was used to men staring, many of them with hunger and lust. Working at a diner near the beach, she was in contact with men all day or evening, depending on which shift she worked. Almost daily she was offered a date and often much more and had become hardened to the sly and sometimes off-colored remarks she had to put up with if she were to continue to work at the restaurant. It was a good job for her, with her limited education and experience. The hours were flexible and that made it easier to find babysitters for the children, and the restaurant was close by. The tips were always good, her good looks and friendly smile great assets. And she had learned how to handle the occasional groping hand or remark that went too far, usually without losing a customer or a good tip. She found a way to deal with men, but Walter was different.

Nancy had grown accustomed to living a life without a man in it. She had been working since leaving high school with only breaks in between when the children were born. She owned this house free and clear and managed to keep up with the bills one way or another. She didn't have much but what she had she earned and she had grown to enjoy her independence. The experiences she'd had with each of the fathers of her children caused her to believe she was far better off without getting involved with another man. She had been hurt and she swore to herself that she would never leave herself open to that again. She had many men friends and she was going to keep it that way. They would be friends but never, ever, lovers or another husband. This held true until Walter had literally been dropped into the middle of her life.

She had no idea what she was thinking when she insisted that he be brought to her house. She guessed she thought he would only be there for a day or two and then other arrangements would be made. She really hadn't been thinking at all, only going with her instincts when she saw someone hurt and needing help, and she did what she had thought was right. But once Walter was here he stayed and the odd thing about it was that one part of her was glad he stayed. The other part of her was annoyed at him and herself. For awhile she was angry with him for not leaving when it became obvious that he could take care of himself and really didn't need to be there anymore. She had been mistaken about his being broke. Money didn't seem to be a concern in the least to him. He could have gone to a motel or anywhere else he wished if he had wanted to. But he hadn't. Not only was he well enough to take care of himself but eventually he became the full-time babysitter, cook, and in general, househusband. It happened slowly over the weeks and each step along the way seemed natural.

As each day passed and she got to know him better she began to care for him a little more. It was probably the way he got along with the children that affected her most at first. It took just a few days and the children were clinging to him. He even managed to break through prissy Helen's hard shell and they could spend hours reading, talking, and sharing time together. That was something she could rarely do with her eldest daughter. Nancy didn't understand why but she and Helen had never become friends, at least they had never become as close as she would have liked. But Helen was comfortable with Walter and they could talk together as mother and daughter never could.

Two-year-old Little John followed Walter around like a puppy. Wherever Walter was, there Little John would be. Her son discovered all he had to do to get Walter's full attention was to grab one of his crutches and hang on. Walter was stuck until Little John got his way. Walter didn't mind the constant demands for attention. In fact, he enjoyed being with the children. They were together from morning until night and he didn't tire of it. She had never met a man like him.

Dixie had been the greatest surprise of all. She was extremely shy and quiet, much as Walter was, but together they would talk and he found a way to get beneath Dixie's serious demeanor and could usually get her to laugh in that high-pitched giggle Nancy loved so much. Maybe she hadn't said anything to him about leaving because of the children. Each had become close to him, in his or her own way, and it was good that they could have a "father figure" to relate to.

She hated to admit it but she also had grown to care for this man. She resisted as much as she could, refusing to let herself be attracted to him. She spoke to him only when absolutely necessary and gave him as much space as she could as they shared this little house together. But his kindness, his gentleness, his constant attempts to please her, kept washing against the walls she tried to build around herself. He was a caring, loving man and no matter how tightly she tried to insulate herself against him, his presence would seep through her defenses.

She recognized her growing affection for him and that

recognition made her more determined to have as little personal dealings with him as she could. This caused her to speak to him in a way that she had never spoken to anyone in her life. She was more than short with him, she was curt. One afternoon she came home from work and found him hanging laundry on the line alongside the house. He was balancing himself on one leg as he pinned her wet brassieres and panties to the clothesline. His doing her laundry, her very personal laundry, as well as the kids clothes made her very uncomfortable. For some reason his handling her undergarments embarrassed her. When he came into the house after finishing this chore, Little John and Dixie trailing behind, Nancy spoke to him. The words and the way she said them were a result of her turmoil.

"I don't want you doing my laundry anymore," she said, sharply and forcefully, very different from her normal self.

Walter stopped and rocked on his crutches as if he were struck. He looked at her in total surprise, jolted more by the tone than the words. A blush started at his neck and crept up his cheeks and soon his face was crimson. He looked down at the floor and when he spoke it was softly and with great effort.

"I'm sorry," he said. It was almost a croak. "I won't do it again."

Dixie looked, mouth open and eyes wide, from her mother to Walter and back again, trying to understand what just happened. Little John, not understanding all the words but sensing the tension, hugged Walter's good leg and looked to his mother to see if he would be scolded too.

Nancy was angry at herself for the way her words had come out. She tried to smooth things over but this didn't help.

"Thank you for doing what you did," she said, but it sounded testy and cruel.

Walter said nothing but when he looked at her the hurt in his eyes almost brought tears to hers. The frustration of their situation, her situation, made her grit her teeth.

"To hell with it," she said, dropping her arms to her sides in defeat. "Do whatever the hell you want to do."

She stalked out of the room, leaving a stung Walter, a baffled daughter, and a frightened son. It was not what she had wanted to do, but as she tried to keep her emotions in check each time she spoke to him, everything she said or did turned out wrong. The result was she spoke as little as she could. She didn't want to hurt him. She just refused to let herself love him and this was unnatural for her, and therefore her conduct was unnatural.

Now, six weeks after it had all begun, his cast would be coming off. She'd overheard Walter setting a time for Jerry to pick him up and take him to the doctor's office the next day. When he left he would leave a vacuum she couldn't fill. The children would miss him and no babysitter could possibly fill his place. He'd become the father they never had. His abrupt departure would be like their father walking out of their home and their lives. But there was nothing she could do about it. Nothing, or accept his unspoken offer of love. But her fear of heartbreak was still stronger than her affection for him.

"They're taking your cast off tomorrow," she said, not looking at him.

"Yes," he half whispered, "finally."

Nancy wasn't sure what else she wanted to say. They'd left so much unsaid that it was impossible for her to begin an honest and open dialogue at this late date. She rose and started to go inside, stopping beside his half-prone lounge chair. "I'll put the kids to bed. They'll probably be back in your room before you know it."

"I don't mind."

She nodded. Her lips parted as though she were going to say more. Nothing came, the words held back. She turned and went inside.

Walter looked back to the western horizon. The lightning

had stopped. The last of the daily thunderstorms had ended. The sea-breeze brought ripples across the canal, lights from the houses on the other shore dancing in the dark water. He could hear Helen and Dixie complaining about having to stop watching television and having to go to bed. Little John was quiet so he must have fallen asleep. He smiled as he listened to their movements, his mind's eye seeing them pajama-clad and sleepy-eyed as they protested to their mother.

Nancy had given her bedroom to him after his first night on the cot in the living room. She moved much of her clothing into the adjoining bedroom and slept with the children, giving up her bed for his comfort. Helen had his cot, Little John and Dixie sharing one single bed and Nancy sleeping in the other. It was crowded and hot in that little bedroom without air conditioning.

This sacrifice of basic comfort to help a man she barely knew was beyond his comprehension. He never would have considered doing something like that. Nor, he was sure, would his wife, Laura. But Nancy was the most unusual woman he ever met.

His room was also warm even with a fan blowing. Being partially enclosed in a cast didn't help matters. By the third day the itching became unbearable. Sweating during the day and then continuing to be uncomfortably warm all night made the itching beneath the cast a nightmare of constantly needing to scratch at unreachable places. It became so bad that he overcame his shyness and asked Nancy if they could turn on the central air conditioning.

"It doesn't work," she told him. "It's old and worn out. I had it checked and it would cost as much to fix as it would to buy a new one. I don't have the money and even if I did I couldn't afford the electric bill."

"I'll pay for it," Walter offered. He had to do something or he would go crazy from the itching.

"I couldn't let you do that."

"I can afford it. You won't let me pay you for staying here so you can at least let me do this."

Nancy had refused to accept any payment from him. She was willing to share her home with someone who needed help for a few days but she wasn't going to have a renter living in her house.

"It's too much money," she told him. "I don't want to owe anybody that much."

"You won't owe me anything. This is for me, not for you."

When she refused to budge, he tried another tack. "Can I get a small unit then? One that fits in a window, just for my, er, your room? I'll pay for the electricity."

Nancy relented and that day he had an air conditioner installed in the bedroom. He had to bribe the local store owner in order to get him to come that day but it had been worth it. Having a cool room to sleep in and a place to go during the hottest part of the day helped with the nerve-wracking itching and it was comfortable sleeping at night.

His cool bedroom became the most attractive room in the house for the children, especially after Nancy moved their television set to Walter's room so that he could have something to watch without having to stay in the living room where the other TV was. His, Nancy's, double bed became their place during the hot afternoons as they watched cartoons in the cool, air conditioned room. He enjoyed the children's company, kept them in snacks and cold drinks with numerous crutch-aided trips to the kitchen, and quickly he and the children became friends and then family. He was doing what he regretted never having time to do with his own children.

Within days they were sleeping in his bedroom with him. It started with Little John shuffling in and crawling onto the bed in the middle of the night and immediately falling asleep. The next night Dixie also joined him and Little John in the coolness of his bedroom. Walter slept on the left side of the bed and the cast on his right leg and partially covered chest served as a bundling board, dividing the bed. Eventually Helen joined them, carrying her pillow with her and sleeping comfortably on the carpeted floor at the foot of the bed. Several times Nancy had come and checked on the children, Walter feigning sleep when he heard her quietly open the bedroom door and peer in, concerned about her children sleeping in a room with a man she hardly knew. But she said nothing and each night put the children to bed in her room and usually one if not all of them would be with him by morning.

Nancy's allowing him to pay the electric bill opened the door for him to at least pay part of the household expenses. He made it a point to get the mail each day, finding some excuse to be by the mailbox during those mornings when Nancy was home and accepting the mail from the postman at the roadside to be sure he received it and not her. She remained adamant about not accepting any money from him. He paid whatever bill came, electric, water, phone, her car insurance. She started receiving a women's monthly magazine after he paid for a two-year subscription on receiving an advertisement that looked like a bill.

His becoming the household cook started innocently enough. First it was cold cereal and milk or peanut butter and jelly sandwiches. Then it was soup or heating leftovers in the microwave for the children. Next he was preparing the simple meals they requested and cleaning up after himself in the kitchen as he hopped about, happy doing a chore that he hated until he arrived in this home. He couldn't drive, he never left the boundaries of Nancy's property, so as he used up available food or the children requested something that wasn't on the shelf he would make a list of things needed at the grocery store and leave it on the kitchen table for Nancy. The first two times he had left money with the list. Saying nothing, she took the list and left the money on the table. After his second attempt he stopped putting money with the list.

Now it was all coming to an end. When the doctor cut him free of the cast he would also be severing his excuse for remaining here. The time had come to depart and he had no idea what he would do next. *Windsong* waited, leaky and patient, but she wouldn't be leaving with the wind and squalls that were predicted for the next day. She would be staying here at Nancy's longer than he would. He took a final breath of the salty sea-air and let it out slowly. With a grunt, he pulled himself up and hopped to the rear door, opening and then closing it as quietly as possible and locked it. Nancy had left the kitchen and living room lights on. He turned on a small night light and flicked the switch to the overhead light. He hopped as quietly as he could into the living room and turned that light out also, the click of the switch sounding loud in the silent and darkened house. A thin strip of light from under his bedroom door guided him.

He lay in bed waiting for sleep to come, trying not to think, not to feel. The air conditioner hummed. Ribbons of light came through the blinds from a street lamp and fell across his feet, cast, and rumpled sheets. He looked at the wall separating his room from the one where Nancy and the children slept. On the other side was everything he had learned to care about. Each of the children had found a way around that wall and to his bed, but not Nancy. She had stayed behind the wall, unreachable, untouchable.

XVII
Eddie

He came out of the doctor's office walking with a strange gait. Shorts revealed an untanned, slightly thinner right leg which he lifted a little higher than normal and with every other step he seemed to be stepping over some invisible obstacle. The skin of the newly freed leg was white and scaly; a sharp contrast to his tanned left leg, arms and face. He carried the now unneeded crutches and shorts Nancy had altered to fit over the cast. He felt a hundred pounds lighter and slightly off balance.

Jerry waited in his pickup reading a newspaper and drinking coffee. He looked up when movement caught his eye. He grinned as he watched Walter walk with awkward freedom. Walter smiled back.

"Why didn't you wait in the office where it's air-conditioned?" Walter asked, as he climbed into the cab. Though Jerry had parked in the shade of a tree it was still hot and he was sweating heavily.

"I hate doctor's offices. And hospitals. Just the smell they all seem to have makes me nervous." Jerry laughed self-consciously. "Maybe it's childish, but I avoid those places."

"I know what you mean," Walter agreed.

Jerry finished his coffee and dropped the empty cup on the floorboard. The newspaper followed to join a growing pile of trash. He started the engine and began the drive from Merritt Island to Cocoa Beach.

"How's the leg?" he asked, glancing at Walter's mismatched legs.

"Fine. It just feels a little odd walking again."

"What are you going to do now?"

Walter was silent for a moment. "I don't know."

"You're not going to stay at Nancy's?"

"I can't." Walter whispered.

"I'm surprised nothing happened between you two after all this time," Jerry observed.

"Nothing happened." Walter spoke so softly it was almost inaudible.

"You like that lady a lot, don't you?" Jerry already knew the answer.

Walter took a deep breath. "Very much."

"Well, why don't you do something about it?"

"Like what?"

Jerry shrugged. "Hell, I don't know. At least tell her."

"I think she already knows. I know she does. It's just not there. Just because I care for her doesn't mean she has to care for me." He looked out the window, not seeing the passing traffic, stores and pedestrians. "I can understand that. I'm an old man and she's a beautiful young woman. I have nothing to offer and I know it."

"Bullshit," Jerry said forcefully. "Age doesn't have anything to do with it. If two people really love each other what difference should age make?" Jerry spoke with such emotion that Walter looked at him, eyebrows raised. Something was bothering Jerry. He hadn't been his usual happy-go-lucky self all morning.

"Are we talking about me and Nancy or you and Pokey?"

Jerry frowned, and then slowly began to smile. "Both, I guess."

"Are you two getting serious?"

"Serious?" Jerry repeated, as he weaved through traffic pondering the question. "I don't know what serious means. All I know is I'm beginning to feel that I need to do something about us one way or another." Jerry was quiet for a moment, driving slowly in the right lane instead of his usual breakneck speed. His jaw muscles worked as he thought and his facial expression changed as he considered what he might say next, first a frown, then pursed lips, and then a grimace, and finally a slight shrug and a resigned sigh.

"What I'm really talking about is Pokey going out last night. When I called her yesterday evening, her mother told me she had gone with her girlfriends for the evening." Jerry tightened his jaws and went on. "Maybe she went with some girlfriends and maybe she had a date. I don't know, but when I asked her about it she told me it was none of my damn business. She said we haven't made any commitment to each other and if she wanted to go out she damn well would. She's right of course, but I never thought she would do it. I have no real claim on her, but I thought, well, that it would only be the two of us." Jerry continued to drive slowly, his pickup becoming one of the slow moving obstacles he usually cursed as he sped from place to place.

Walter allowed a little time to pass before he spoke. "But you don't want her dating anyone else."

"Damn right I don't! I haven't fooled around with anyone else since we met. Hell, I don't have time what with the store and all the other stuff that keeps coming up. Anyway, I don't need anyone else. She's more than I can handle by herself."

Jerry chuckled, remembering how sexually demanding Pokey could be, and inventive, and totally shameless. The thought of her doing the things they did together with another man made him frown and his jaws tightened again. "I guess I'd better decide how important she is to me."

He mused for a moment, considering the possibilities. "Maybe we could live together for awhile. Marriage is out, definitely! I'm still hurting from that last bitch I married. I think I'd kill myself before I went through that shit again. But, if we live together for awhile, who the hell knows? Things might work out. You can never tell. And while I'm at it, I'll ask her to quit her job at the bank and come work with me at the store. Now the place is closed more than it's open and with her there I won't have to worry about it. She can take a salary, a piece of the profits, whatever the hell she wants." Jerry looked over at Walter. "How's that sound?"

"Sounds good to me. What do you think Pokey will say?"

Jerry shrugged his muscular shoulders, his usual answer to most questions, even his own. "Who the hell knows. Women are all crazy anyway, even the young ones. She might think it's the greatest thing since sliced bread, or she might tell me to drop dead. I never have figured out women and I doubt if I ever will. And Pokey's a full grown woman. You can bet your ass on that. She's full grown in every way that *I* can think of."

They drove along the causeway that connected Merritt Island and Cocoa Beach, strong gusts buffeting the pickup as they crossed the high bridge that passed over the Banana River. Whitecaps and wind-blown foam covered the shallow river and dark, low clouds swept by overhead. It wasn't raining but a heavy mist was in the air and Jerry kept turning squeaky wipers on and off, clearing the droplets from the windshield.

"I wonder what Eddie's doing," Walter said aloud, thinking of the tropical storm that was brewing somewhere out in the Atlantic.

"Let's try the radio," Jerry turned it on. "If there's anything happening they'll be announcing it. We're not supposed to get much, the last I heard."

Country music was playing and Jerry hummed along, tapping the steering wheel. He slammed his palm on the wheel and laughed. "That could be a pretty good idea, you know?"

"What's that?"

"Getting Pokey to move in with me. Just think of it. I'll get my laundry done, get help in the store, and have all the sex I can handle all for the same price." Jerry grinned at him. "And I'll make a hell of a lot more money at the store with Pokey there all the time. I lose half my sales because I'm gone as often as not. With her there I'll bet business will really pick up. Isn't that great? It's a win-win situation."

"And you'll know where she is all the time," Walter said, trying not to smile but not succeeding.

"Damn right I'll know. I'll keep her so busy she won't have time to go screwing around." Jerry slammed the steering wheel again. "I love it!"

It began to rain steadily as they turned south on A-1A and drove toward Nancy's house. Another country song came on the radio, the lyrics about a man and his eighteen wheeler and a lost love in the hills of West Virginia. Jerry wiped the condensation from the windshield with a dirty handkerchief as he hummed along.

"What about you?" Jerry asked. "Are you going to have to go back to work soon?"

"Not right away. I called my office and told them about the accident, breaking my leg and all, and about the fire on *Windsong*. Wrote them a letter and asked for an additional four weeks on my vacation. All the work should be done on *Windsong* by then. I sent a doctor's note along with the letter. They responded saying I was on a six week medical leave, the time the doctor said I would be in a cast, and this would not be deducted from my vacation. I don't know for sure what that means as far as the exact date I'm supposed to be back. It's up to me, I guess. They expect me to be responsible and do what's right."

"What about your family, your son and daughter?"

"They're fine. They both wanted to come down here when I told them about the broken leg, but I persuaded them I was okay and being well taken care of. I hardly ever see my son anyway, and my daughter calls every two or three days." Walter shook his head. "That phone at Nancy's never seems to stop ringing. That, and people constantly coming and going. I was beginning to feel like an answering service."

"Yeah, she's got a million friends. She's a nice lady."

"You know, I've stayed there for six weeks and I still don't know very much about her." Walter looked inquiringly at Jerry, hoping he would tell him more about Nancy and her life. Maybe if he knew more about her past he could break through the wall she had built between them.

Jerry was about to speak when a voice on the radio stopped him. "This is a special news bulletin," the newscaster announced in an ominous tone. "Tropical Storm Edward has been upgraded to a hurricane. It is now Hurricane Edward. The storm has changed direction and is no longer heading north but is now travelling north-north-west. The forecasters at the National Hurricane Center in Miami predict Hurricane Edward will continue to veer toward the west and hurricane warnings have been issued covering the area from Jupiter Inlet in Florida to Savannah, Georgia. Brevard and Volusia County residents are advised to take all precautions. Coastal residents are advised to evacuate immediately. Though Hurricane Edward is at present a Category One Hurricane, the storm could continue to build in strength and cause extensive damage and possible loss of life. Let me repeat again. This is a special news—"

"Holy shit!" Jerry exclaimed. "We're gonna get hit by that

storm." As if to confirm this, a sudden gust of wind shook the pickup and a curtain of heavy rain swept across the road. Again, Jerry wiped the fogged windshield, streaks remaining on the glass from the not too clean cloth. He turned onto Nancy's street and stopped in front of her house. "You'd better get that boat of your's tied down as good as you can."

"I will. What about you? What are you going to do?"

"I'm going back to the store and open up. Boat owners will be pouring in needing line and tarps and all kinds of stuff to protect their boats. It'll be a madhouse. They're probably lined up there now. If I don't open soon they might break the damn door down. I gotta get back and see what I can do to help."

"Aren't you going to evacuate?"

"Hell no. My job is to be there at the Port. I might not give a shit about keeping the store open very much but when it's important, I'll be where I'm supposed to be. You get the hell out of here though. It'd be stupid to stay on the beach. Some jerks do but they don't know the ocean. If that storm were to grow and a storm surge were to come this whole place would be under water. Grab Nancy and the kids and get the hell out of here."

Walter put out his hand and they shook. "Thanks for all of your help, Jerry," he said with feeling. "Not for just taking me to the doctor's office but for everything."

"Forget it. I didn't do anything special." Jerry put the pickup in gear and winked. "You damn Yankee landlubbers are always sailing down here getting into deep water and us ole dumb southern boys have to pull your asses out of the drink. Nothing new about that," he said, with an exaggerated southern drawl. "Now take another piece of advice from this old man of the sea and get the hell out of here."

"I will." Walter opened the door. A gust of wind almost pulled it out of his hand and jerked him partially off the seat. He climbed out into the blowing rain and pushed the door closed with both hands. Immediately, Jerry made a U-turn and began racing to his store at the port. Walter had forgotten the crutches which were propped against the rear window of the pickup. He walked through soggy grass to the backyard where *Windsong* was tied. He climbed aboard and started both engines, keeping the revolutions high enough for maximum charge to the batteries. He disconnected the extension cord from the dock and put the pumps on internal power. There was a good chance the electricity would be knocked out by the storm and the pumps would have to operate on battery power. There was enough juice in the two large batteries to last at least two or three days. If he couldn't get back to *Windsong* by then, due to Eddie causing so much damage, there probably wouldn't be anything to come back to anyway.

Oddly, it had stopped raining, the sun was shining and wind down to a normal sea-breeze. He turned on the Marine Weather Forecast Station and listened. Hurricane Edward was predicted to continue turning to the north-west and strike land somewhere fifty miles north or south of Cape Canaveral. The eye of the storm would probably reach land sometime after midnight. All mariners were being told to get into port as quickly as possible and stay there.

He secured *Windsong's* portholes, windows and doors as well as he could and began tying extra lines from *Windsong* to the small dock and two trees in the backyard. He used the heavy anchor line for the additional mooring, tying it to the base of the big oaks. These would hold no matter how high the wind rose. He walked around *Windsong's* deck, bringing in anything that could blow away and checked the hatches. Once he was sure he had done all he could top-side he went below and checked each of the cabins to see all was secure. The last thing he did was to gather the ship's log, ownership papers, insurance policy and a few personal items and put these in a cardboard box and carried it ashore. He turned and looked at *Windsong* once more before he entered the house. Lines crisscrossed the yard from deck to tree base and fenders protected *Windsong*'s hull from dock pilings. All hatches and latches had been double-checked. There was nothing more he could do. *Windsong* would either ride out the storm or not. He bit his lip and went in the back door of the house.

The children were with the babysitter across the street and Nancy was at work. He wondered how long it would be before she came home. They couldn't possibly keep the restaurant open with a hurricane approaching. A cloud suddenly obscured the sun and the empty house was dark and silent without the children and the ever-present noise surrounding them. Heavy raindrops struck windows and roof. He went from room to room making sure all the windows were closed and then went outside and began picking up lawn furniture and anything else loose, and piled it all in the shed alongside the house. His shorts, shirt, and sneakers were soaked. He ignored the rain as he cleared the property.

He was in the kitchen making sandwiches for the children when Nancy returned home. Her white uniform was rain-splattered and she shook the water from her hair. He watched her, a slice of bread in one hand, a butter knife with a glob of peanut butter held in the other.

"I thought you would have been home before now," he said. It was nearly four o'clock. They had been broadcasting the hurricane warning since noon.

"We had to tape the windows and get all the patio furniture in. Wouldn't you know, Beth called in sick this morning and there was only me, the cook, and the owner to do it all."

She took a towel out of a drawer and wiped her face and began rubbing her hair. He made the last peanut butter and jelly sandwich and stacked it on a plate.

"I'll go get the kids. We'll have to pack something for them," he said, wiping his hands with a dish towel.

"Pack?"

"We're leaving, aren't we? You're not planning on staying here with a hurricane coming?"

"We did last time. Hurricane Frederick passed right overhead. The eye of the storm came over the house. It was a minimal hurricane, too. It didn't cause very much damage. Only where a couple of tornadoes touched down south of here."

He couldn't believe she was considering staying. She was what they called a "Native Floridian," having been born here and living with the fierce thunderstorms, tropical storms and even the occasional hurricanes, but he couldn't understand her indifference. Hurricane Eddie might grow and become a truly destructive storm. The forecasters said it might grow into a killer.

"When was it Hurricane Fredrick came?" he asked, looking for an opening, some way to persuade her to leave.

"Oh," Nancy thought for a second. "About thirteen years ago."

He saw his opening. "Thirteen years ago. Did you have three children thirteen years ago? What about Helen and Dixie and Little John? What happens if there's a storm surge and this place goes under water?"

Nancy didn't answer immediately. Her eyes went from place to place in the small kitchen as if searching for something. She shook her head as if breaking off a thought. "Thirteen years ago, I was only fifteen years old. Living here with Momma. No, I didn't have three children thirteen years ago. I was only a kid."

She looked at him with dark eyes shielding thoughts and memories she would not speak to him about. He wanted to take her in his arms and hold her, comfort her, protect her, make love to her. There were times when her vulnerability showed, when her tough self-sufficiency cracked and the lonely woman, the frightened little girl, showed through.

"I think we ought to leave," he said flatly. "I think we ought to pack up a change of clothes or two for the kids and get out of here. Why stay? It's too dangerous, especially for the kids."

"But everything I own is here," Nancy spread her arms to encompass the house and everything in it.

"What the hell does that mean? If this place goes under water your being here sure as hell isn't going to stop it. Think of the kids. They could drown. It doesn't make any sense." He was pleading now. He used his last argument. If his blunt statement about the children didn't work, nothing would.

She lowered her head, turned and walked to the kitchen doorway. A plane's engines roared overhead followed quickly by another. They were evacuating nearby Patrick Air Force Base, the planes flying north, away from the storm and danger. He waited, Nancy still standing at the doorway, her back to him.

"I'll pack a few things," she said softly.

XVIII
Zephyr Hills

Little John dropped his sandwich, and jelly left a purple streak on his sister's dress before he could retrieve it. "Oooo," Helen said in disgust, wiping at the sticky stain with a napkin. "What a nasty, dirty little boy you are, Little John." She edged away and pressed closer to Dixie.

"Mook," was Little John's response, then biting into the peanut butter and jelly sandwich, jelly spreading on face and hands as he attacked.

"I forgot to bring anything to drink," Nancy said, reaching into the back seat and picking up Little John's empty baby bottle.

They had just left the house and were waiting for a traffic light to enter A1A and begin the trip toward Florida's interior. Traffic was heavy on A1A, the main highway along the beach, and moving slowly in a light rain and wind that alternated between near calm to moderately strong gusts. The eye of Hurricane Edward was still over one hundred fifty miles south-east and Cocoa Beach was only beginning to feel the effects of the storm.

A car pulled up behind the station wagon and there was no way he could turn. "Darn, we'll have to go back on another street."

"Don't bother. We'll get something at a store before we get on the Bee Line."

"You think the stores will be open?" he asked, surprised.

"Sure. People need things. The stores will stay open as long as they can. Most of them anyway."

"But what about the employees? Aren't they going to evacuate?"

"Maybe. But some will stay, managers, somebody. People need to buy gas, food. We might lose the water supply if the storm hits close by, according to the radio."

The traffic light changed and he turned onto A1A and joined the slow moving traffic. There were no pedestrians on the streets, but men and women were taping and boarding up windows. A police car pulled in front of them at the next intersection and turned on his lights, the officer getting out of the car wearing a bright yellow rain coat and holding up his hands to stop traffic. A city owned utility truck joined the officer at the intersection and a ladder mounted on the truck was slowly raised near the swaying traffic signal. A city worker quickly climbed the ladder and in less than a minute took down the light. The ladder came down and the truck pulled away. All else might be washed away but the City of Cocoa Beach would save its traffic lights. The police officer stayed and directed traffic.

"The mayor and the governor have ordered all the beaches evacuated. Won't everybody leave, except for a few real diehards?" he asked.

"Maybe." Her brow wrinkled as she thought. "Some will stay and some will leave. If it were a real big storm probably most people would go, but not for something like Eddie. The governor and mayor can order what they want. People are going to do what they're going to do. They aren't going to leave what they own," Nancy paused for a second, "and for some of them all they will ever own. They'll stay and try to protect it if they can."

He didn't pursue the conversation. He found it hard to understand why anyone would attempt to struggle against hundred-mile-an-hour winds and twenty-foot seas, if Eddie were to grow and the center of the storm strike here. What could anyone do against such tremendous forces? It didn't make any sense. But everything he owned wasn't sitting in one of these little houses on this spit of sand called Cocoa Beach. Perhaps if everything he'd worked for all of his life were here and threatened he would think differently. He doubted it, but he couldn't be sure. What was important to him was sitting in this car and he was doing his best to get them out of danger. If Nancy had insisted on staying in her home he knew he would have stayed also, no matter how big Hurricane Edward would become. He never would have deserted Nancy and the children to ride out a hurricane while he ran. So how different was he from those people who decided to stay? He wasn't different at all, when he thought about it.

"The Majik Market is open," Nancy pointed to the convenience store a little farther ahead.

He stopped behind a car at the gas pumps in front of the store. The wagon had more than half a tank of gas but it was as good a time as any to fill up. He had no idea how long they would be driving. A woman came out of the store carrying two gallon jugs of water and got in the car, pulling away. Walter pulled up to the pump and reached into his back pocket and took out his wallet. He offered it to Nancy.

"I'll fill it up. Pay for the gas and get something for the kids to drink. We'd better get moving. Traffic is getting worse."

She looked at the wallet but didn't take it. She was reaching for the door handle when he stopped her. "Nancy," he said, command in his voice. "Take the wallet."

Nancy looked back at him. She almost spoke but didn't. Slowly her hand came up and she took the wallet. "I'll get some snacks too. Stay in the car," she said to the children in the back seat. "I'll be right back."

He filled the tank and then moved the wagon away from the pump. Cars were lined up in each direction to get gas. The wind was picking up again and blowing sand from the beach pelted the windshield. It wasn't raining but dark, low clouds passed swiftly overhead. Nancy came out of the store carrying three plastic bags. She struggled to open the door against the wind.

"I got some snacks," she said, passing two of the bags to Helen. She handed Walter his wallet along with some loose change. She reached into the third bag and took out one of the two half-gallons of milk and a pack of cigarettes. She gave him the cigarettes and opened the milk and filled Little John's bottle.

Normally it would have taken little more than an hour to drive the sixty miles from Cocoa Beach to Orlando, but with the heavy traffic and occasional blinding rain it was two and a half hours before they reached the outskirts of the city. Accidents along the Bee Line were also a problem. Sudden downpours would occur and visibility instantly dropped to zero. Many of those leaving the beach area were elderly retirees and unaccustomed to driving in heavy traffic in nasty weather. Chain-reaction collisions of bumper-to-bumper cars were the result all along the sixty mile stretch of road. Half-jokingly Nancy wondered aloud which was more dangerous, being near the beach with Eddie coming or the probability of being crushed on the Bee Line trying to get out.

He exited on International Drive where a large number of major hotels and motels were located in Orlando. He pulled into the first motel he came to and realized there was no hope of finding rooms here. The parking lot was crammed with cars. He double parked near the entrance and left the engine running.

"I'll go check," he told Nancy before getting out. "This place looks full but maybe I can make some phone calls and find a place."

Nancy slid behind the wheel as he got out, nodding. "I'll pick you up near the door, if I have to move the car."

The lobby of the motel was full of milling people. An exasperated desk clerk tried to remain calm as she explained for the hundredth time to another group pressed against the counter that there were no vacancies here or at any motel in Orlando. The rooms had filled quickly once the hurricane warning was broadcast. Anyone could stay in the lounge, bar, or restaurant if they wished, here or at any of the other hotels or motels, but there just weren't any rooms to be had. He listened from the edge of the crowd as he glanced at filled couches and chairs and people trying to make themselves comfortable on the carpeted floor. The two public telephones were in use and a line of people waited patiently for their turn. He went back out to the parking lot. It was useless to try to find rooms in the Orlando area. Within hours, tens of thousands of people had poured in from the coast.

It was raining heavily again and Nancy had moved the station wagon from where he parked it. Cars were still trying to squeeze into the already jammed parking lot. He waited under the awning, looking in both directions for the wagon. He saw her driving slowly in a parade of cars coming from the back side of the building. She managed to work her way near the entrance. He made a dash for the car. She stopped the creeping wagon and slid over to the passenger side, relinquishing the driver's seat. He jumped in, dripping wet.

"You run pretty good," she said, smiling.

"That rain is cold." He shivered. His shirt, shorts, and sneakers were soaking wet. The sun was setting and night was coming quickly under a layer of black clouds.

"You know, I never asked how the leg was. By the way you were running, I guess it's okay now."

He looked at her and grinned. "Better than new. It looks a little weird, but it's fine. If the sun ever comes out and what with all of the exercise I've been getting," he chuckled, "I'll be back in shape in no time." He began working his way out of the parking lot. "There are no rooms here and none close by I'm sure."

"I figured that. What do you think we should do?"

"Go farther west. Keep heading toward Tampa. We might find a place along the way."

"I have to go to the bathroom," Dixie said.

"Me, too," Helen joined in.

Little John had fallen asleep and whatever bathroom business he had to take care of his diaper was seeing to. Walter pulled into a gas station. They used the restrooms and there was a resupply of candy and soda. The children had been exceptionally quiet during the trip. Neither he nor Nancy mentioned stopping for dinner. The sodas, sandwiches, and candy would have to do for the kids, and he and Nancy shared a bag of potato chips.

It was dark by the time they were back on the Bee Line, and the traffic thinned as they slowly moved west and further from the threatened east coast. They traveled at the same pace as Eddie and the squally weather changed little as they ran before the storm. This far inland there was little danger from the wind. Flooding from the expected heavy rains was the concern in the interior.

They had been driving for nearly an hour in silence before Walter spoke. Filled bellies and boredom had Helen and Dixie asleep along with their brother. The radio played Big Band Era music, intermittently interrupted with news and weather reports.

"We're about half way to Tampa. Do you think we should take the next exit and see if we can find something?"

"Might as well." Nancy looked over the seat at the children

sleeping peacefully, heads resting against brother or sister. "We could sleep in the car if we have to."

"We'll find something," he said, hoping it were true.

He took the next exit and followed the signs that pointed to lodging, gas, and food at Zephyr Hills. After three miles a neon sign announced they'd reached Zephyr Hills Inn. Walter stopped in front of the small office. All the parking places in front of the long, one-story motel were full. It was barely raining as he went into the tiny office. An elderly man sat behind the counter watching a small black and white television, volume high.

"Evening. Kind of messy out there," the man said, running his fingers through his few remaining strands of gray.

"I was hoping you would have some rooms." Walter replied, not sounding very positive after seeing the full parking lot.

"You all from the east coast?"

"Yes."

"Looks like you're gonna get hit pretty hard over there," he said, shaking his head in sympathy.

"It looks that way." Before Walter could ask about the rooms again the old man went on.

"Where you all from?"

"Cocoa Beach."

"They say the eye is gonna go north of there. Maybe you won't get it so bad."

"We hope so. About the rooms?"

"Ah, yes, of course," the old man reached for a pair of granny bifocals and perched them on the tip of his nose. He slowly ran his finger down a ledger, stopping at the last line.

"We've got one left, number twenty."

Walter pursed his lips. "I was hoping you would have two rooms."

"How many of there are you?" the old man asked, removing his glasses and squinting.

"Me, the mother and three children."

"That should work out all right. There's two double beds in number twenty. The cot and crib are in use but if the kids ain't too big they can use one bed and you and the missus can use the other." The old man saw Walter hesitating, and hoping to fill the last room, something that hadn't happened in years, added, "On a night like this, with the storm coming and all, you might not find anything else tonight."

Walter turned and was about to go to the car and ask Nancy but turned back. "We'll take it."

The old man took the last key from a peg board and handed it and a registration card to Walter. He took the key and wrote his name on the card and then stopped for a second. Under his name it asked for his address. Where was he from? Where was his home? He neatly printed the number and street of the house on Cocoa Beach. He signed the card and handed it and money to the ancient clerk.

"I'm sure y'all be comfortable," he said affably. "I turned the air-conditioning on awhile ago and the room should be nice and cool by now."

Walter nodded his thanks and went to the station wagon. He walked to the passenger side of the car, not knowing if Nancy was going to accept sharing a room. She rolled the window down.

"I got a room," he told her. "It has two double beds. It's their last room and with everything else full and all..." The last word hung in the air.

"Good," she said without hesitation. "At least we won't have to sleep in the car."

Relief, excitement, and fear all intermingled as he drove through the puddled lot and parked the wagon in the far corner. He wasn't sure what might happen, they did have the kids with them, but this might be his chance, probably his only chance, to... to what? To sleep with her? To make love to her? All he knew was he had the opportunity to be with her, and he was going to do or say *something* to let her know how he felt. He loved her. He had to *do* something.

They carried the sleeping children to the room, Helen coming sleepily awake for a moment and then her mother's soothing voice putting her back to sleep. They put all three on one of the double beds.

"You'd better get out of those wet clothes," Nancy said, going to the air conditioner and raising the temperature control. "It's cold in here."

"I forgot to bring a change of clothes." He rubbed his arms with his hands.

"Take a hot shower and put on a towel." Nancy began to change Little John's diaper. Her tone was the same as she would have used when speaking with the children. There was nothing to indicate she felt anything odd about sharing a motel room.

He took a hot shower. When he came out, a towel wrapped around his waist, she took his wet shorts and shirt and draped them over a chair to dry. Without saying anything she picked up a change of clothes for herself and went into the bathroom. A moment later he could hear the shower running.

One light was on in the room, the one over the empty double bed. Dixie and Little John were asleep on one side of the other bed. Nancy had taken the heavy covers from both beds and made a place for Helen on the floor. She had taken one of the pillows from his bed, and it was obviously *his* bed, and had turned down the sheet for him. The sheet by Dixie and Little John was turned back for herself. There was no doubt about sleeping arrangements. Walter sat on his bed, turned out the light on the headboard, pulled off the towel and slipped under the covers. The cotton sheets felt crisp and cold.

After awhile the sound of the shower stopped and light spilled into the room as Nancy opened the door. She left the light on and closed the door until a small seam of light shone on the far wall. She was leaving a night light on for the children. Her dark figure came toward him and then she sat on the bed with Dixie and Little John. In the dim light he could see she was wearing shorts and a halter. She had dressed before coming out of the bathroom. Nothing she was doing in any way indicated she wanted to be intimate.

His heart began to pound. He was frightened. He couldn't let this moment pass and yet he was afraid to speak, afraid of her response. But this was his last chance and he knew it. If he held back now he was lost. Without Nancy in his life he had nothing to look forward to except one dreary day only to be followed by another. He took a deep breath and prayed for courage.

"Nancy," he said, his throat tight.

"Yes?" she answered softly, almost invisible in the darkened room.

No words came to him. His body and soul were filled with the need for her, his love for her, his nothingness without her, but no words came. He tried to speak but all that came was, "Oh, Nancy." The agony he felt, the misery of an empty life, total love for her squeezed into these words which came as a cry of agony, a tearful groan for help, a plea.

For a few seconds she didn't move or say anything and then there was a squeak from the bed as she sat next to him. He could just see her profile, head lowered, hands folded in her lap, her breast a smooth, round mound rising and falling with each breath. He reached up and stroked her upper arm, slowly and tenderly, the soft, smooth skin like fire on his fingertips.

"I didn't sleep around," she said, not looking at him, sitting still and quiet under his touch.

"I know," he whispered.

"What I mean is..." She looked at him, barely able to make out his features. She liked this man, maybe even loved him, but she was afraid. She had been hurt before, more than once, and she didn't want the turmoil and pain that attachment to a man always seemed to bring. But Walter was a good man. And he loved her. She had known that after the first few days he stayed with them. But was that enough? Was she willing to give up her freedom and independence for the chance that this time it might work? She wasn't sure.

"What I mean is I don't know what I'm supposed to do."

He took her hands in his. "Do you know how I feel about you?"

Nancy nodded several times, confirming this to herself as much as to him. Her movement shook the bed. "I think so."

He closed his hand around hers and pulled her toward him, his other hand going to her back, shaking fingers bringing pressure to draw her closer. "Nancy," he said again. It wasn't just her name but a sound emitted from his heart. She didn't resist as her face came to his and their lips met.

The wind howled through the rigging of the gantries at Kennedy Space Center on Cape Canaveral. When NASA decided during the 1950s to build the Space Center in Florida, hurricanes had been considered and every building and launching site designed to withstand all but a super hurricane. Eddie was still a Category One Storm, with sustained winds of less than one hundred miles per hour, and would cause little damage to "America's Gateway To The Stars." Great seas crashed against the shore, seaspray and foam blown far onshore. Bright lights lit the towers and launch areas. Illuminated men struggled against wind and driving rain. Cables as thick as a man's arm laced the complex, securing equipment from damage. Within a week of Eddie's passing, no one would be able to tell that a hurricane had landed nearby.

The eye of the storm would come ashore at New Smyrna Beach, just south of Daytona and about thirty miles north of

Cocoa. Beach erosion and flooding would cause most of the damage to this area. Two people would be killed by the storm. A couple remained on their sail boat anchored in the Intercoastal Waterway and the boat capsized and they drowned. Many of the residents stayed in their homes and rode out the storm with no ill effect. It would take a bigger storm than Eddie to cause the loss of life that most experts expected to occur with the continued growth at the seaside. The day would come, this no one doubted, when a city would go under water and hundreds or perhaps thousands of men, women, and children would be swallowed by raging seas. But Eddie would not go down in the history books as the "Great Killer Storm." Eddie's effects were minor except to those few whose lives would be greatly changed by this natural event.

Distant thunder rumbled and raindrops sounding like small stones pounded the roof. Walter listened, hoping the thunder and lightning wouldn't come near. Little John would waken and have to be comforted and his cries would probably wake Dixie and Helen and the last thing he wanted to be doing was calming three cranky kids. Nancy was asleep beside him, her head in the crook of his arm, hair strands of silk on his shoulder and chest. He rolled toward her so he could look at her. He moved slowly, her leg, thigh, and hips warm against him.

There was enough light coming from the bathroom alcove so he could make out each detail of her lovely face. Long lashes rested on her cheeks, face relaxed and at peace in sleep, lips that he had kissed so hungrily only inches from his. The sheet had slipped and one breast was exposed. He looked at the round firmness of it, darker nipple available to his touch. His eyes followed the curve of her breast to shoulder and neck, small ear peeping from wavy hair. His eyes drank in her image, his mind still not sure he should believe this was real.

He couldn't be this lucky. This beautiful woman couldn't really be sleeping beside him. He couldn't have made love to her awhile ago. Her passion had grown with his, her urgency as fierce as his, her repressed feelings exploding and their lovemaking a wild thing, uncontrolled, rapid and beyond anything he ever experienced.

He needed to know this was all true, that he was real and she was real and somehow he wasn't dreaming or had become someone else, someone who deserved to have this woman love him. He was there, it had happened, but he still wondered if somehow a mistake hadn't been made. Nothing this good could really be happening. He could feel her soft warmth beside him. He put his face closer to hers. Her breath brushed his cheek. He could smell the scent of her hair. He brought his lips to her neck, lightly. Her heartbeat throbbed against his lips, her sweet body scent filling his senses. He moved his lips down, sliding on smooth skin between soft mounds, sheet pushed aside, to belly button and the soft fuzz beneath. He could taste her, salty and sweet, his lips returning to breast and nipple, caressing, tasting, absorbing her scent and feel and taste.

Her hand came to his head, stroking. His lips and tongue roamed her body and then he brought his lips to hers. He could taste her here also. Different parts of her body held different scents and tastes and yielded differently to his lips and touch and he wanted to do more, know more, absorb more. He wanted to become familiar with every inch of this woman, know her, have her part of him. They caressed unrushed this time, Nancy's hands stroking his back and shoulders, their breathing synchronized, breathing as one, heartbeats pulsing against each other, time slowing and then stopping as each brought passion and ecstasy to the other. Everything else was forgotten, everything beyond their combined bodies didn't exist. There was only them, as one, giving and receiving

exquisite pleasure, everyone and everything else excluded
from their world.

Windsong tugged at her lines, the wind shifting and
building as Eddie approached the coast. Lightning struck
nearby, thunder rolling constantly, booming roars crashing
from all directions. Rain swept over land and water, the great
wind holding raindrops nearly parallel to the earth. The
electricity was out, houses and street lamps now dark, but
Windsong's pumps continued to work, driven by battery
power. The strain on her mooring lines was tremendous, her
tall hull and superstructure acting as a giant sail as the wind
pressed tons of pressure against her.

The lines were strong enough to withstand this, ropes the
size of a man's wrist, but *Windsong*'s cleats began to work
loose. Wood softened by decades of exposure to sun and sea
began to give way as bolts under immense strain were slowly
pulled through. A ninety-mile-per-hour gust slammed into
Windsong and first one bolt and then the other tore out of her
deck. The cleat and lines fell into the water as *Windsong*'s
stern swung away from the pressure of the wind. This added
even greater strain on the forward cleat until it also pulled free.
Windsong swayed in the howling wind, the last line restrain-
ing her tied from the anchor winch on the forward deck to a
piling on the dock. The winch would hold. A steel plate was
bolted beneath and the whole deck would have to be torn free
before this would give.

A single piling on the dock now bore all the strain of
holding *Windsong*. A three-eighth-inch bolt and ten-penny
nails held for a moment or two, but *Windsong*'s twisting and
tugging in the shifting wind worked these loose and finally the
piling was pulled free of the other planks and yanked from the
canal's muddy bottom. *Windsong* drifted sideways across the
canal and slammed into the dock on the other shore. There was

a crunch as a protruding two-by-four pierced her hull and ribs cracked from the impact. All four bilge pumps came on as *Windsong* automatically tried to save herself from the water pouring in through parted hull planks. She began going down by the stern, her starboard side crushed and held by the wind against the neighbor's dock.

Pilings snagged hull planks as she began to fill, the added tons of water causing hull planks and deck to be ripped free as she settled to the bottom. All four bilge pumps continued to attempt to push the sea back out of the boat until the water level reached the electrical lines and a fuse blew. *Windsong* was dead. She slowly settled on the bottom of the canal on her port side, angled superstructure and torn starboard out of water, furniture and other things that could float finding their way out of her. She died without witness, the night black, wind roaring, rain striking and running off her broken shell.

Walter and Nancy slept in each other's arms. The thunder and lightning didn't wake the children.

XIX
Leslie

He had noticed the picture on the shelf but never really looked at it. He wasn't sure if he had been avoiding it, pushing it out of his mind. He told himself dozens of times that he didn't care and really didn't want to know. When he thought about it honestly he knew he did care, a lot, to his innermost being he cared, but he wasn't sure if he wanted to know about Leslie. Or the others. The picture of Leslie and Nancy was at eye level on a brass rack with three other shelves all containing photographs of Nancy and the children and family and friends. The newest addition was a picture of Walter, a snapshot in a brass frame, given prominence on the second shelf. He picked it up. He'd never become accustomed to seeing himself in a photo. The reflection returned from a mirror or in a photo didn't fit his self-image. He knew other people accepted him as he appeared in a photo, but somehow the body and face so recognizable to everyone else was a stranger to him. It was odd but it had always been that way.

Nancy had caught him off guard in the back yard. He held a hammer in one hand and a two-by-four in the other and a partially repaired dock in the background. He wore bib overalls and no shirt, chest, shoulders and arms glistening with sweat, a surprised and happy smile on his face. His muscle tone was good, he was in better shape than he'd been in many years, and the tan helped show off a healthy body. But it was in his face where he noticed the greatest change, especially the eyes. Nancy was inside the house and saw him coming and grabbed the camera on the spur of the moment and crept alongside the building to catch him in a candid shot. She had stepped from behind the house and yelled "Smile!" and caught his reaction to her. There was happiness in that face. The smile was genuine, not a "for the camera smile," and the eyes showed they were happy to be looking at what they were seeing, which was Nancy. He was an older man (God, how did it happen so fast?) but didn't look sixty. Maybe he wasn't forty anymore either, but still, he didn't look like a broken-down old man.

He thought about other pictures of himself that were on another shelf in Huntington. His wedding pictures, looking young and shy, with the children and more mature and assured, and the last picture taken with Laura and the children and the grandchildren, the photos being a fair representation of the changes that had taken place through the years. And now this picture. The man he saw here didn't belong in any of the photos taken in that other life. This was a different person. He didn't know how it happened but it had.

He put the picture back in its place and once again looked at the photo of Nancy and Leslie. Nancy was herself, a little heavier maybe, but the same shining smile and soft eyes and the golden brown hair. Leslie had his arm draped over her shoulder, the dark skin of his hand a sharp contrast against her fair skin. They were smiling, Leslie's a little lopsided and eyes sad even with the smile. Nancy had her hand around his waist and it was without doubt they were a couple. Him black and her white. He wasn't chocolate colored as many of the blacks were, but a deep, deep brown.

He wondered if Leslie's being black had anything to do with the way he felt. And he wasn't sure what he felt. As much as he hadn't taken a real look at the photo, he'd also refused to take an honest look at his feelings. This was Leslie, Dixie's father. Dixie, whom he was learning to love more each day. Leslie had made love to Nancy. She had loved him. Deep down Walter knew that. She wouldn't have been able to love a little. She slept with this man and loved him, completely, as Walter hoped and prayed that she loved him. But at one time it had been Leslie. And he was black. Did that mean anything? Maybe. And he had loved Nancy. This Walter could understand. Everybody loved Nancy. They just had to. She was beautiful. Was Walter jealous? Maybe. Yes, probably. But did he have a right to be jealous? Not really. He had been married too, and now Laura was dead and he was in love with Nancy. And Leslie was dead. And Nancy was in love with him. (Please, please God make that be true! I know it's true, but please make it true anyway.) So, what did he feel?

"You never asked about Leslie," Nancy said from behind him. Walter jumped and turned, not having heard her enter the room.

"I'm sorry if I startled you," she said, coming over and taking his hand. She stood on tip toe and kissed him lightly on the lips. He still found it hard to believe this beautiful young woman was his lover, and even more, his friend.

"I was looking at some of your pictures." He sounded like a boy caught with his hand in the cookie jar.

"So I noticed." She squeezed his hand and led him to the sofa to sit beside her. "I've been here for awhile and the way you were staring at that photo and not moving I thought you turned into a statue. You were a million miles away, that's for sure." She smiled and brushed a stray hair from his forehead with her finger tips.

"I was just thinking."

"About Leslie?"

He looked to the shelves of pictures and nodded. "Yeah. I guess so. That and a lot of other things. I'm so much older than you are." He hadn't expected to say that. It just came out. It was something that had bothered him right from the beginning and another thing he had set aside to be dealt with at a later time.

"I'm not so sure of that," she said, shaking her head. "Sometimes I feel pretty old." She paused for a moment and then smiled, eyes twinkling with merriment. "And sometimes you're pretty much a little boy." When he moved as though to protest she took his hand and kissed it, first on the back and then turning it over and kissing the palm. "But you're my little boy."

It was acts such as this, her kissing his hand, that would cause him to be completely helpless. No one ever kissed his hand. Oh, maybe one of his children when they were little, but not his wife or any other woman. For Nancy it was a simple act of love, spontaneous, and he was helpless.

"Would you like me to tell you about Leslie?" She cocked her head and looked at him with those liquid brown eyes.

Walter looked away and shrugged. "I don't know. That's more or less what I was thinking about. We don't owe each other explanations about our lives before we met, do we? You certainly don't have to tell me anything about your past. Not if you don't want to. And I'm not even sure I want to know." He sighed. "I'm not sure of anything, I don't guess. I'm kind of mixed up. The only thing I'm sure of is that I love you." He leaned over and kissed her forehead. "Of that I'm very sure." They sat quietly for a few moments before Nancy spoke again.

"I'll tell you about Leslie. If you want me to stop just say so. I don't have anything to hide, at least I don't think I do, and it's important we don't have anything hidden from each other.

I don't want to hurt you, but if you have questions on your mind I think they need to be answered."

She took his hand and kissed it again. It was as though the hand she held didn't belong to him and he was detached from himself as he watched. Sometimes he was only an observer in someone else's body. It was an eerie sensation. Her being with him, the reality of it.

When she began to speak it was softly and slowly, her eyes never wavering from the invisible spot on the wall.

"Leslie was a poet. He was the most sensitive person I've ever met. Too sensitive I think." Nancy nodded slightly, agreeing with her own conclusion. "He was a man who loved everything, life, people, a sunrise or sunset and children, especially children. He looked for beauty everywhere. He managed to see even the smallest of wildflowers among weeds. And he was kind and generous and caring and wouldn't hurt another person if it killed him. And I think that's what did kill him. He was too gentle for this world. He would hurt when other people hurt each other. He couldn't understand the harshness and the hate in this world. And his being black didn't help. People could be so cruel to him, to us sometimes, and they didn't even *know* him. He would share anything he had with anyone. The color of people's skin didn't mean anything to him and he could never understand people making such a big deal of it. It was like he had grown up with a man's body and a man's mind but still had the soul of a child. He was too easily hurt, too sensitive, too loving to live in this tough world. It's hard to explain. You had to know him. He just cared too damn much. And when someone would do or say something to hurt him he wouldn't strike back. He didn't know how. He couldn't hurt anyone or anything intentionally. But he hurt. Sometimes when he played his guitar and sang he would talk about it. He could sing about it. A little. And sometimes he would write poems. I've saved a few. I don't know if they're good enough to be in the books you read in school or anything like that, but to me they were beautiful. He saw things so clearly and no ugliness was there. And he loved me and Helen and Dixie. Poor Dixie. I see Leslie in her sometimes and it frightens me. My heart aches when I think about it.

"I'm afraid she's too loving and sensitive. But how can I stop that? I can't. No more than I could help Leslie." For the first time she looked at him. "Do you know how Leslie died?"

"A drug overdose."

She nodded slowly and once again her eyes went back to the spot on the wall. "Yes, he died of an overdose. And he didn't even use drugs. Not hard drugs. Oh, he would smoke a little pot if it were offered to him. And he drank at parties or picnics and maybe a beer or two in the afternoons if it were around. He even got drunk a couple of times."

She smiled at the recollection. Then her face dropped and the pain returned. "He became playful and happy those couple of times he did drink too much. He had terrible hangovers both times. No, he didn't abuse drinking, or drugs. He just wanted to be sociable. But he never was into heroin. He hated needles. One time Helen, I guess she was about three or four, fell and cut her elbow. We took her to the doctor for stitches and it was worse for Leslie than Helen. She was sniffling, scared more than hurt I think, and whimpered when the doctor put in a stitch. Leslie almost passed out. He had tears streaming down his cheeks as he watched. He was hurting for her. That's the way he was. Other people's pain became his pain. And just the thought of needles gave him the creeps. He wasn't hooked on heroin or anything else. I would have known. I can't image him sticking a needle in his arm. The courage that must have taken! I had no hint that he was going to kill himself. There were no signs, nothing unusual. I've gone over it a thousand times and I still don't know what happened. Maybe I should

have known. Maybe I could have helped if I had known
something like that was going on inside him. Maybe I could
have stopped him. I don't know. I just don't know. What I do
know is he wasn't on drugs. When he stuck that needle in his
arm he knew exactly what he was doing. The fool. That loving,
beautiful fool killed himself. I guess he couldn't take it
anymore. The world was too harsh for him. I don't know and
I guess I never will. It took me a long, long time to get over it.
I felt so guilty. I was a part of his life and somehow I must have
been a reason to be part of his death. But, it's over now. The
past is past and we must go on."

She took his hand and held it to her cheek. There were tears
glistening in her eyes and she blinked them back. "I'm so glad I met
you. You'll never know how much you've come to mean to me."

When he made as if to speak she held up her hand and
stopped him.

"I hope this will help you understand a little more. I've
never told anyone about this. They all think Les died of an OD.
What's the difference? Now he's just another statistic, another
junky dead of an overdose. It's not true, but so what? Is saying
he died of suicide better? Let him rest in peace. All I know is
that the world is a much poorer place without him. I don't think
people like him can survive in this world. It's too hard, too
uncaring. He didn't belong here and he knew it. When I think
about it now, I wonder how he lasted twenty-eight years. He
didn't know how to fight back."

Walter squeezed her hand. "I'm sorry."

Now he knew about Leslie, or at least enough about him
to make the little evil devils in his mind go away. Nancy had
loved Les. She would have loved him whatever color, white,
black, or green wouldn't have mattered. He was the kind of
man that a woman like her, a deeply caring woman, would
love. And Walter's feelings for her grew stronger the more he
got to know her.

"I'm glad you told me." His voice was husky with emotion.

"I might as well finish. Would you like to hear about the rest?" she asked, taking a tissue and blowing her nose.

Walter didn't know what "the rest" was but he knew he wanted to hear it. His fears had been totally misplaced. Instead of being harmed by knowing more about Nancy and her life, and her lovers, the more deeply he was falling in love with her. Jealously, what an ugly thief that could be, was buried by understanding.

She closed her eyes. He could see the strain it was for her to bring these memories back. She was in profile, a sun-filled window behind framing her face, her shaded cameo etching itself into his mind and heart.

"Sure. Tell me whatever you want. The more I know about you the more…" Walter's voice trailed off . The "I love you" was trapped inside him.

"It's funny when I think about Gary, and Gary and me, and how it was then. It's almost like it happened to someone else. I know it was me, but, it's almost as though it happened in another lifetime. Silly isn't it? I mean, it was only ten years ago when we were married, eight since he disappeared, and yet it's difficult for me to remember.

"Well, here goes. We met in high school. Gary was a year older and one grade ahead. He was a big man on campus, sports, football, all that stuff, and a catch for any girl. Or so I thought. Anyway, we started dating while I was a junior and he was a senior. It wasn't serious in the beginning. But that changed after he graduated and started working on the boats. It was a good season, and he would come back from sea with a pocket full of money and dreams of a new house for us and new cars and having this and having that and I believed him. I was young, just a kid, and so was he really, and it all sounded fine and grand and I wanted to be on my own and have my own things so we got engaged and married the summer after I graduated. It never dawned on me that he may have made a lot of money, a lot for us anyway, but he never saved a penny. And good fishing seasons don't last forever. He was always in debt and then we were always in debt, and I went to work right after we got married and continued to work except for a couple of months after Helen was born and we stayed broke no matter what I did. I know this sounds rushed but there isn't much to it and I just want to give you the highlights, if that's what you can call them, and say to hell with Gary Foch. God, what a stupid name, Foch."

Nancy paused, gathering her thoughts. She was looking at the pictures on the shelves. "Gary was, well, he wanted to do everything quickly, to have fun, to play and not to have to worry about tomorrow. After we were married it seemed as though it were a disappointment to him. I think all I was, and Helen after she was born, was a burden on him. His main interest was fast cars, partying, other women, the skunk, and having a good time. He was too young to be married. I was too young to be married, I know that now, but there we were trying to play house. I didn't see him much anyway. Most of the time he was fishing, and when he came in for a few days or a week, he wanted to play and not be stuck at home with a crying baby and a working wife who wasn't available when he wanted, and the bills were piling up when he needed money to put a new engine in his hot rod or to spend partying with his friends. I'm not mad at him anymore. We were just two dumb kids who got into something we shouldn't. But he really was a stinker. All he cared about were his toys, cars, and stereos and such, and ignored Helen and me. I didn't know what I was supposed to do. And then one day he came in and packed a few clothes and said he was going to Texas and fish out of some port or other. The fishing was good down there he said and he would make big money and everything was going to be all right. Well, that was the last time I saw him. The last anyone ever saw or heard from him. His mother didn't know where he disappeared to, she still doesn't, and I never heard from him again. Not a phone call, a post card, nothing. After a couple of months I must have called every State Police on the Gulf Coast *and* the East Coast and hospitals and I don't know what else. The phone bills were atrocious. He'd just disappeared. I didn't know if he was alive or dead.

"After a year of waiting I said to hell with it. Our marriage had been a wreck, if it ever was a marriage which I know now it wasn't, just two kids not knowing what they were doing, so I got a divorce for desertion. There wasn't much else I could think of to do. I was in limbo. I needed to make some kind of life for myself.

"I don't know if he's still alive somewhere or dead and it may be I never will. I only hope Helen isn't hurt too much when she gets older and this all may have meaning to her. Being deserted by her father I mean. What a creep. He didn't care about anyone but himself. Oh, I'm being too hard on him. He was just a kid and not ready for responsibility. We were too much for him. So, exit Gary Foch. I think during all of this is when I grew up. I mean, maybe that's why I can't associate what happened back then to me now. It all happened to a little girl who didn't know what was going on and just reacted to events as they came slamming into her life.

"Am I making any sense?" Nancy asked, cocking her head in the way she had.

Walter gently squeezed her hand. "All the sense in the world. It happens. Kids get married too young and there's no chance in the world it'll work. They're not ready yet. It was a fear I had for my own children." Once the words were out he wanted to bite his tongue. Why bring that up? Why mention the difference in their age?

"And then you know about my mother dying and me

getting this house." Nancy took a deep breath before continuing. "And then came Little John. It's not easy to talk about this and I may not be able to explain it very well."

"Don't talk about it if it's going to bother you."

"No, I want you to know, to understand. When I saw you standing there staring at those pictures looking so troubled I knew I had to explain some of these things. I'm not apologizing. I won't apologize for my life. I just want you to know a little about how it happened. Then you can judge. That's up to you."

He wanted to stop her, to tell her not to put herself through anymore pain. And yet he knew she needed to speak and he needed to hear it. He kept silent.

"Little John was a mistake." Nancy chuckled. "That sounds terrible! *He's* not a mistake. He's beautiful. How it all happened was a mistake. My mistake. When I think about it now I can see I was kind of set up. I don't think I was over Les' death yet and my mother had just died a couple of months before. I wasn't in the best of shape emotionally. One Friday night Billy Tillman came over and practically dragged me to go out on the town, as he put it, and 'get out of my own shit.' I hadn't been out of the house for months. Mom had just died, and before that Les—God, that was two years before!—and I don't know if I was in mourning or emotionally burned out or what. Billy brought one of his girlfriends over to babysit for me, and he and I went bar hopping. I met this guy Dean and had a few drinks and with a lot of encouragement from Billy I made a date with Dean for the following night. We went to the Sea Shore Lounge for a couple of cocktails and were supposed to go dancing after that. I don't know if we went dancing or not. I blacked out or passed out or something and the next thing I remember was I woke up naked in bed with this guy in a motel. He was asleep on the other side of the bed, or passed out drunk, I don't know, so I got up, got dressed, called a cab and came home.

"Dean was here on vacation and I guess he went back

home. I never heard from him again. I don't even know his last name. I kind of guessed what had happened that night but I couldn't be sure. My head hurt, I thought I was going to die it hurt so bad, and my whole body ached. I never had a hangover like that before. And I never blacked out or passed out before, or since, you can be sure, and I only remember having those two drinks at the Sea Shore. Liquor doesn't affect me like that, and besides, I never drink that much... I wonder if the guy gave me a micky or something. I hope not. I hope Little John's father isn't some kind of screwball. I take responsibility for what happened. It may have been me. So depressed and all. Anyway I missed my period and that was it. I thought about an abortion, a little bit, but couldn't go through with it. It didn't seem right. It wasn't the baby's fault. So I had Little John and I'm glad."

She paused and looked down at her hands in her lap. Her wavy hair hung loosely, framing her face. "So that's it. Not much of a life's story, is it?" She smiled weakly and shrugged. "I'm twenty-eight, twenty-nine next month, have three children, and I'm not sure how many of the things, the important things, in my life happened. I'm not a stupid person, and yet I never seem to be in control." She looked at him, head cocked again.

"Except recently. You came into my life and suddenly things calmed down. Did you know you're a stabilizing force, Mister Walter Marshall?" she asked, her face open and honest and beautiful, the look in her gentle eyes causing a tightening band to grip his chest.

He didn't know what to say. He knew he was in love with this young woman, this loving, sweet and beautiful girl. Compared to him she was just a kid. What did he have to offer her? How could she love him?

"Honey, I..." And no more came. His unfinished sentence hung in the air.

She lowered her head, face hidden by her draping hair. "Am I a disappointment to you?" she asked softly.

His heart almost burst. A disappointment to him! How could she think that? My God, she was the most caring, loving person he ever met. "Nancy, I... I love you... very much." His voice gurgled with emotion. The words had finally forced themselves out. Nancy's head snapped up. She questioned him with her eyes, the intensity of her gaze bringing a flush to his face.

He couldn't find the words to express himself. How could he tell her that he was too old for her? How could he say that at times when he looked at her he wanted to make love to her so badly that he had to look away. He wanted to keep her and Helen and Dixie and Little John near him always. They had become his life. He wanted to protect them, to watch the children grow, to feel their hugs in the evening.

He was dead before he met her. He understood that now. He had been walking through life the last few years doing what was expected of him, living, working, and sleeping in a routine that had no beginning and no end. And it had no meaning. He had been living just to be living. A lifetime of habits had taken over and each day was the same as the one before and the next day would be the same again with nothing to look forward to except death. And death had stopped being a threat. Death had started to look like an easy answer to a life of loneliness. But it wasn't that way now. Nancy was life, vibrant, exciting, loving. And he wanted to share that life with her. And he wasn't worthy.

Finally he spoke, the words that came not what he expected but the full meaning behind what he asked the total sum of how he felt. "Would you marry me?" he asked, and held his breath, fear gripping him. His life hung on her answer. Oh, he wouldn't drop dead on the spot. He would go on living. But there would be little purpose to the living. He needed her. He needed this family. He wanted to live, to love, and to be loved in return.

Her jaw dropped with his unexpected question. Her eyes searched his face, his love and anxiety clearly there. She had become greatly attached to this man. His obvious affection for the children, his gentle love for her, made their home a place of warmth and comfort. Sex had been a natural growth of their relationship. He had become a part of the family without fanfare. She had gotten to know him and then to love him. Her eyes filled with tears. She shook her head in disbelief, realizing she wanted to marry this man very, very much, and he'd just asked her. It was too wonderful.

He saw her shake her head and his breath came out in a rush. He sagged, deflated. "Oh," he said, the sound like a man being punched in the gut. He dropped his head, the color draining from his face. "I don't blame you. I'm not much of a catch. You're young and beautiful and I'm, well..." Walter turned his hands palms up, as if offering nothing.

"No! No!" Nancy cried, realizing that he mistook her shaking head to mean no to his question. She leaned across the sofa and hugged his neck, burying her face in his shoulder. "I mean YES! YES! Please, yes."

It took a second or two before he realized what she meant and then relief followed by exquisite joy pumped through his body with a rush. He felt light-headed. She was kissing him, her tears running onto his cheeks as she leaned over him, and his tears joined hers.

He hugged her, pressing her to him, feeling her softness yield to him, their bodies touching full length as she lay on top.

"Yes, I'll marry you." She whispered, her breath hot on his neck.

Thunder cracked, and then again, vibrating windows. Lightning struck close by and thunder rolled with the sound of a cannon shot fired in a valley.

"That's quite a kiss you've got." She chuckled, her body vibrating on top of him.

He took her face in his hands and kissed her salty cheeks, her forehead, her eyes, her nose, her lips. He wanted to touch her, all of her, to be filled with her.

"Oh God, I love you. I love you so very, very much," he said, the words coming out as forced air under pressure both from her weight on him and the emotion from within. She kissed him long and lovingly.

"And I love you," she said, slipping down and resting her head on his chest. Rain began, first a few heavy drops and then a downpour. Thunder was rolling continually, some booming close, others at a distance. Lightning struck and the windows flashed for a second, a crack and a "whumph" coming immediately after. The house shook with the roaring sound. Nancy stiffened and sat up quickly.

"Little John! He's going to be frightened silly. Lightning and thunder scare him to death. I left him and Dixie at Bertha's playing with her two." Nancy laughed, but concern was still there. "I'll bet he's under the bed right now, covered with dust and refusing to come out." She hurriedly kissed him. "I love you," she said, stroking his cheek, "but I have to get them. Little John will be howling."

She went to the kitchen and got a towel and threw it over her head and was out the front door at a run. He watched her through the window. The rain fell heavily, the wind swirling, and she was soaked before she reached the street. She dashed across, leaping over a foaming stream at the curb, breasts swaying and jiggling as she held the soggy towel over head and shoulders, strong legs carrying her across lawns.

Walter's breath fogged the window as he stood watching. How could such a young and beautiful woman truly love him? *And she was going to marry him!* He still couldn't believe it. He felt he were standing two feet off the floor. He was on a cloud and the world was lovely, and being alive was lovely, lovely. His chest swelled and his head felt light and he didn't know what to do.

Lightning struck on one side and then the other, thunder crashing and rolling in all directions. He took a deep breath and held it for a moment and then could hold it no more. As thunder rumbled over the houses and streets and across the water his voice joined the booming. Compressed air passed vocal cords and a sound much like that of a wolf merged with the roaring around him and years of suppressed emotions vented as the air was squeezed from his lungs with a howl. He wasn't a lawyer. He wasn't sixty years old. He wasn't an old man out of place in strange surroundings. He belonged. He was loved by an adorable woman and three wonderful children and he was needed and wanted. Tears gathered at the corners of his closed eyes and trickled slowly down his cheeks. He had cried only once before in his adult life. The day he buried his wife. Today, in the past ten minutes, he had cried twice. The ecstatic happiness he felt demanded an outlet and all he could do was stand there and let the tears flow. His lips moved slowly as he spoke.

"Thank you, God. Thank you for giving me this." He had never been a religious man but he needed to thank somebody. This was a gift, an exquisite, wonderful gift.

XX
Wildflower

He saw A.J. sitting on the grass in the backyard, knees drawn up to her chin, arms wrapped around her legs, a small, tight bundle motionlessly staring out over the water. She heard him coming through the thick grass and turned and smiled, her legs stretching down and arms going behind to prop her. Walter pushed a lawn mower, the mower not yet started.

"Hi," he said, returning her smile. He wiped his face with a large handkerchief. It was early September and the temperature was still over ninety degrees.

"Hi yourself," A.J. said, still smiling, face bright and happy.

It was impossible not to know her mood. A.J. radiated her inner feelings. Now, joy surrounded her. His smile broadened. Somehow she shared her happiness even without speaking. He pushed the mower out of the way and sat on a cushion of grass near her.

A.J. stared at the water, deep in thought. They were in the shade of a palm tree and a cool breeze ruffled the leaves. He leaned on one elbow and pulled a grass stem to chew on, enjoying the refreshing breeze. He was in no rush to mow in this stifling heat.

A.J. spoke slowly and softly, sometimes stopping between words. "I asked Sister Mary Louise—I don't know how I got the courage to do it—if they would take me. You know, to be a nun, to go into training or whatever it is I'll have to do. And you know what she said?" A.J. looked at him.

He shook his head, noticing the small butterflies tattooed over each breast above her halter. A *nun*?

"She said she's been waiting fifteen years for me to ask that question. She'd had a feeling ever since I was a little girl that it might be the life I would choose. I told her I wasn't worthy. My life had been a complete mess. I've done things..." A.J. spread her arms as if encompassing all the evils of the world. "And you know what she said?" A.J. didn't wait for an answer. "She said I'd had a path to follow, a journey to make. And now I can begin to live the life that was meant for me, if it was in my heart. She said if I were sure, and I know I am, she would see about making arrangements for me to start as a pre-novice." A.J. became silent again, looking out over the water, shaking her head. After a moment she said, almost to herself, "I can't believe it! They'll take me!"

Walter didn't know what to say. He wasn't a Catholic and had no idea what the requirements were for being a nun or priest or whatever else a Catholic might become. He'd always thought of those women in black, he recalled most of the nuns didn't wear habits anymore, were virgins and entered their orders while in their teens. Did it have to be that way? Apparently not. What other requirements could there be? He looked at A.J. She must have had ten years or more of wild living, at least by his upbringing and probably most other people's standards, and her tattoos, and drugs and booze, and men, he was sure of that, and could this be the background for a nun?

Walter felt he should say something but didn't know what.

He did know one thing. He had grown to like this girl—why was it that every female under thirty was a girl to him?—this young woman very much. He remembered the times—how many times? It must have been dozens—she came to the house while he was in his cast and cooked and cleaned and was loving with the children.

He felt a flash of shame. There were times when he resented her intrusions into *his* house, *his* domain, while she was trying to be helpful toward him and the children and Nancy. How could he not have seen it at the time. If being a loving woman was one of the requirements for being a nun, A.J. certainly met that one. About her previous lifestyle, who the hell was he to judge? Thinking back, he remembered A.J. spoke about the nuns before.

"You've been going there often, haven't you, visiting, ah, this Sister Mary Louise?" he asked, breaking the silence.

"Since grammar school. I went to Saint Martin's when I was in second grade. Just for one year. My family couldn't afford tuition after that. And we moved around a lot. Sister Mary Louise was my teacher. She was so young and beautiful then, she still is now, but then it was like being with an angel every day. I know it was a little girl thing, but that's the way I felt. I felt safe there. Sister Mary Louise was always so happy." A.J. stopped and thought for a moment. "No, not happy as we mean it. She was always so serene. Just being near her made me feel good. When I found out I wasn't going back to Saint Martin's for the third grade I cried and cried. It was silly in a way. I wouldn't have had Sister Mary Louise as my teacher anyway. She taught second grade, she still does, and I was going into the third. But I wanted to be near her. And the other nuns. They were all nice. So, I used to go visit her. It was quite a walk over there, four or five miles I guess, but when I felt lonely or there was trouble at home with Mom or Dad I would go and see her."

A.J. smiled at the recollection, eyes following a drifting cloud, thoughts going back to being an eight-year-old on her way to the convent. "She used to give me cold milk and cookies. Or fresh fruit. She always had time to chat with me, to show interest in what I talked about. She always made me feel what I had to say was important, that it mattered. That I mattered. I sure didn't get that at home. I usually felt I was just in the way.

"Anyway, when I think about it now, I sure must've been intrusive. I mean I would just walk up and knock on the door and ask for Sister Mary Louise, if she didn't answer the door, and she would come and spend a half hour or so with me. She must've had other things she wanted to do but that's not the feeling I got. It was like she was always there waiting for me. Even when I got older and didn't visit very often she was the same. When I was away, traveling, running around crazy, when I came back she would be there. And she still gives me cookies and milk." She laughed. "And those are still the best tasting cookies in the whole world."

He thought about A.J. and what she must have been like as a little girl. He could visualize her walking along traffic-clogged A1A, a skinny little kid strutting determinedly toward her goal, in heat and no doubt Florida's afternoon showers, arriving sweaty or rain soaked to see Sister. Year after year she had gone back. Even when she had been running with motorcycle gangs she had gone to see Sister and had cookies and milk and shared a piece of her life.

"Do you have any family?" he asked.

"I have a brother in the Air Force. He's in Germany now, I think. He's making a career of it. I haven't seen him in several years. And Mom is in Oklahoma. She's living with some guy. I stopped and visited her once. They're living in a trailer in the middle of nowhere. There aren't even any oil wells where they live. Only cornfields. And miles and miles of roads that go on forever. There's nothing there. I don't know how Mom can stand it. It's the loneliest place I've ever seen. Flat country with nothing to see from horizon to horizon. I didn't stay long. Only a couple of days. There was nothing to do and really nothing much for Mom and I to say to each other."

"And your father?" Walter asked. Maybe A.J. was becoming a nun because there was no where else to go. Did she have family or someone else to turn to?

"Pop's been dead for, oh, five years now. His liver finally gave out from all the drinking. He didn't care. I think he wanted to die. I don't think he felt life had given him a fair shake. Toward the end he just stayed drunk. He would sit in his chair or out in the backyard and sip on a bottle of vodka. He was killing himself and he knew it. He didn't bother anybody. He hardly ever said a word. He just slowly and quietly killed himself. What a waste. The man really had a brilliant mind. He just didn't do anything with it. Toward the end he got quiet at least. When I was a kid he used to beat the hell out of Mom and sometimes Bobby and me too. It was scary."

So, Walter thought, maybe that's it. She doesn't have any family really, no place to go, and becoming a nun is an answer. Is she running toward something, or is she running at all? How did I get into this conversation? Walter wondered. He looked at A.J. She was sitting placidly, staring off to the horizon, features relaxed, eyes clear and bright, the wind lifting and shifting her short hair.

"And now you want to be a nun for the rest of your life?"

Usually A.J. was extremely active, a body always in motion, never at rest. It was like something had been driving her, inner energy pushing her on, and then a pressure valve had been turned and that internal steam released. He had never seen her so calm.

"Oh God, yes. I couldn't think of anything better in the whole world. It's a dream I've had since I was little. I just thought I wasn't good enough. They're so kind and gentle."

"What made you decide, now, that you want to do this?"

She shrugged. "I don"t know. It's like there's nothing else for me to do. Nothing else makes sense. I'd rather be a nun, doing God's work, than the Queen of England. I've tried most everything, done everything I could think of to make my life have meaning, but in my heart I've always known that being a nun and working with the elderly was for me."

"You want to work with the elderly?"

A.J. nodded vigorously. "Always have. So many of them are just cast aside. It's like they've been used up and now they're not needed anymore and nobody knows what to do with them. And some of them are lonely, I can tell, and they've been made to feel they're useless and a burden. I've been made to feel that way and it's wrong. We're all God's children. We should care about each other."

Again, Walter had to search for a response. He could understand A.J. being a caregiver, for her it came naturally. But why a nun?

"It means you'll never marry, never have children," Walter said, knowing how much she loved children.

"I know. It's something I think I'll miss. But all children are beautiful. They don't have to be mine, come from my body, for me to love them. The world is full of beautiful things. I don't have to posses them. It's kind of hard to explain." A.J. thought for a moment. "Maybe it's something like you and your boat."

He thought about *Windsong*, spray flying from her bow as she cut through the water. She brought him here. She opened doors he didn't believe existed for him.

"You loved that boat. I've never been on it but I can imagine. You're out in the morning with the sun coming up and a breeze blowing and the sky clear and you're going somewhere you want to go. You didn't make the sun or the sky or the wind or the ocean, but you can enjoy them. They're yours, they're everybody else's too, but you're the one who wants to be there. You're the one who chose to be there. To someone else it might be torture on a boat, seasick or afraid of the water. But for you it's heaven. You're where you're supposed to be doing what you're supposed to be doing. It's kind of like that with me. Most people might not understand why I have to do what I have to do. When you feel it's right, when you know it's right, when everything comes together and finally makes sense, then nothing else matters."A.J. turned to him, her look open, expectant, seeking approval.

"Well, what do you think?" she asked.

He was uneasy. He didn't want to be put in the position of approving or disapproving someone else's life. "I don't know. Why would what I think make any difference?"

"Because you're my friend. Nancy's my best friend," A.J. stopped for a moment, lowering her eyes, chin on chest, bashful about going on, "You're educated and all. A lawyer. Nancy thinks you're the greatest thing that ever walked on earth. And you're honest. You may not say much, but when you do speak at least you're not trying to bullshit anyone." A.J. put her hand to her mouth and giggled. "Oh my, listen to my language. I'll have to watch that from now on. I may have lived like a motorcycle mama but I don't think I can talk like that anymore."

A.J. thinks I'm honest, Walter thought. Aren't I living, isn't everything I'm doing a sham? I have a family up North. Don't I belong in Huntington and aren't I supposed to be back working in Manhattan soon? Had he been honest with Nancy? With himself?

"To tell you the truth, A.J., I'm not sure of anything." At least *that* was honest. "Since I left New York and met Nancy, and the kids, and you and the others that are always popping in and out of this place, I find I don't really *know* anything.

How can I advise you on how to live your life when I don't even know what I'm supposed to be doing with mine? You seem to be happy now, much better than when you arrived. If doing what you're doing is going to make you happy, then do what you feel is right for you, good for *you*. If you live your life doing things just because of what other people think, you won't have much of a life."

Walter paused, then went on. "And it's taken me sixty years to get to this point. Knowing that I don't know. But I do know one thing. We have to live our own lives or we won't have a life. If you have to do something to make life worthwhile, then do it! What harm could you possibly be doing? And before I end what's become a speech, let me just say that those people you are going to are getting one fine young lady, and they ought to be grateful you chose to be with them."

Halfway through his voice had become louder and he spoke heatedly. Why was he so involved? Who was he speaking to? A.J. or himself? Would he be able to take his own advice? He had some choices he would have to be making himself soon. Not such little choices. Like what was he going to do with the rest of his life?

A.J. did the unexpected, but then, A.J. usually did the unexpected. She scooted closer and cradled his head in her arms and kissed him on the forehead. "Thank you, Walter," she said simply. He stiffened at the sound of Nancy's voice.

"Hey, what are you two up to?" Nancy called. She held the rear screen door as Little John waddled out, dragging his monster bottle behind him, holding the oversized toy by the large nipple. A.J. jumped up and ran and hugged her. Little John pushed at A.J.'s leg, trying to separate them. He didn't particularly like sharing his mother with anyone, even A.J.

"I'm so happy," A.J. said. There were tears in her voice.

"What's this all about?" Nancy asked, patting A.J.'s back. Seeing A.J. crying, Little John stopped pushing and was now rubbing her leg, making cooing sounds, as his mother did for him when he hurt himself and cried. Nancy looked to Walter as he approached. He said nothing. Nancy pushed A.J. from her, holding her at arms length. A.J. wiped the tears from her cheeks.

"Walter's wonderful and you're wonderful and I'm so happy," A.J. said, and hugged Nancy again.

Nancy looked to him for an explanation. He rocked from one foot to another scratching his head. He wasn't sure what she might be thinking, catching A.J. hugging and kissing him. He said, "A.J.'s going to be a nun," and left it at that.

A.J. stepped back and wiped her cheeks. "Isn't it wonderful?" she asked, the tears stopping. "I saw Sister Mary Louise this morning, and I finally asked if I could join them. And she said yes, I could try it. The training I mean. It's going to take a long time. Years I think. But that's okay. They actually let me in, at least to try to be like them. Sister Mary Louise is going to see about me getting started. I don't know where I'll have to go. It won't be here. I think they have a place in New Mexico. Gee, I've never been to New Mexico," A.J. laughed, all excited now, the words rushing out. Nancy listened, trying to follow what A.J. was saying with the words running together.

"You saw Sister Mary Louise," Nancy said, and A.J. nodded rapidly, happily. "And you're going into training to become a nun," Nancy repeated, making sure she understood. "And you're probably be leaving soon to go somewhere where you'll begin," she added, and looked to Walter for conformation. He shrugged slightly and also nodded. She looked back at A.J. who beamed jubilantly.

Little John stood between his mother and A.J., turning from one to the other, waiting for the next burst of emotion. Nancy put her hands on her hips, her face an ever-changing reflection of racing thoughts. She slowly shook her head, negatively and then positively and then a slow smile grew into a wide grin.

"Well, it's about time. All these years you've stayed in touch with the Sisters. I always wondered about that." Nancy ran her fingers through A.J.'s hair, as she habitually did with her children. "You used to come back from your visits to the Convent and moon about for hours, days sometimes. It all makes sense now. I'm glad you decided to do something with yourself. At least I won't have to worry about you getting yourself killed on one of those stupid motorcycles."

"I've gotta go tell Janie now." A.J. was bouncing on the balls of her feet, ready to spring off in new directions. "I wanted to tell you and Walter first." She scooped up Little John and gave him a hug and a kiss and swiftly put him back down. The sudden and unexpected elevator ride had Little John's eyes wide. A.J. trotted off waving. Janie, her roommate, would be the next to hear the good news.

"Do you kiss and roll in the hay with all the women who decide to become nuns?" Nancy asked him.

"Ah, I, ah," was all Walter could say. He blushed. She laughed.

"Just kidding. I don't *think* you were attacking A.J. She's so excitable. I hope this isn't one of her flights of fancy. I never thought of her being a nun, but why not? She's got more good in her than any person I've ever met. She's been abused often enough for it. People have always taken advantage of her good heart. She's so damn gullible! Maybe now she can be with people more like herself. She sure doesn't need to be with the bums she has hung around with."

"Yeah," was all Walter could think of to say. He walked over to the lawn mower and leaned on the handle.

"I've got a cake in the oven. Chocolate. The kind you like. Is there anything special you want for supper?" she asked, picking up Little John and preparing to return to the kitchen.

"Whatever you think."

"How about steak and home-fries?"

"That sounds good," Walter said with enthusiasm.

"Good," Nancy turned and walked toward the rear door, happy she was pleasing him.

He watched her, shorts revealing strong and shapely legs. Little John waved over his mother's back as the screen door closed and they disappeared. He returned the wave. He pulled at the starter cord on the mower. It started on the third try. The hot sun beat down as he pushed the mower through the thick grass, bare chest and back glistening with sweat. He thought about A.J. and the joy she radiated. She had finally found what she wanted to do. He still had some decisions to make. *Windsong* was gone but he felt as though he were still underway. He could see the coastline but he had yet to reach a protected port.

XXI

Home

The engines increased their whine and slowly the big jet began to roll. Walter looked out the plane's window, craving a cigarette. Flying always made him nervous. The airport terminal building was coming alongside as the aircraft gained speed and rotated nose up, wings angled for invisible air to pull them off the ground. he looked through the pressure resistant plexiglass to the tinted windows of the departure gate knowing Nancy was watching his plane leave. He wanted to take a taxi to the airport but Nancy insisted on driving him. She left the children with Bertha next door and drove him in silence to Orlando, instinctively knowing he needed time with his own thoughts. If she were nervous about his sudden decision to return to New York she hadn't shown it. He told her he needed to see after some unfinished business and the hundreds of questions on the tip of her tongue had been held back.

She asked only one question, "Is everything okay?" and when he told her everything was fine she probed no more. A.J. was the catalyst that brought about this trip. She had made a decision. Sooner or later he was going to have to make some decisions as to what he was going to do about his job, his family, his whole previous life. He was glad when Nancy didn't ask what he was going to do in New York. He wasn't sure himself. He hadn't told his son and daughter he was engaged to Nancy and this was first on his list of things to do. He couldn't bring himself to tell them over the phone. That was far too impersonal. He thought about bringing her with him to meet Lynda and Harold but decided against it. He wasn't sure of the reaction from either of them and didn't want Nancy hurt. It came as a shock when he realized how little he knew his own children. It seemed one day they were tots under his feet and the next thing he knew they were getting married. They had grown up and were gone before he noticed.

A.J.'s resolve to become a nun caused him to take a look at his life. He could never understand her previous life-style and couldn't imagine what the future held for her. When he thought about it, the same was true for himself. He felt torn between two lives. And now this Sunday afternoon flight from Orlando was bringing him to JFK International Airport and the other half of himself. His old self. He wasn't sure how he was going to bridge the old and the new.

Friday night, and into the early hours of Saturday morning, he had lain awake, his mind refusing to shut down, images surfacing to keep sleep at bay. He and Nancy made gentle love, each trying to please the other as pleasure was received in return. Afterwards, she fell asleep, her slow, regular breath his companion in the darkness. But sleep refused to come to him. A.J.'s glowing face, happy smile, and calm demeanor had affected him. She finally found what she had been looking for and she was at peace. He thought about what Nancy had called A.J. No, it had been Leslie who Nancy was speaking about. Leslie called A.J. a wildflower. He said she was a wildflower among the weeds. The man was a poet, Walter thought, but he was also a fool. Nancy had loved him. She bore him a beautiful daughter, Dixie. There was happiness in this house, and love. But Leslie chose death instead. That was something Walter would never be able to understand. He had come to terms with Leslie and any other men that may have been in Nancy's life. That was then and now was now and this beautiful woman who slept beside him loved him and wanted to be with him and that's all that mattered.

His life was irrevocably tied to Nancy and Dixie and Helen and Little John, but he still had a life in New York. He'd left a life unfinished there, a career, two grown children, grand-children. Could he put the two together or had one existence ended and another begun when *Windsong* pulled away from the dock in Northport just three months ago. Only three months? It seemed more like a lifetime. And in a way it was. He was living another life now, one completely different, and he didn't know how he was to connect one with the other. He stared out at blue sky and hazy blue-green nothingness below as the plane sped him at close to six hundred miles an hour above the sea toward the hustle and bustle of New York City.

He hadn't called anyone to tell them he was flying in, so when he arrived at JFK he had two choices on getting to his house. He could take a limousine that would drop him off at a town about ten miles from Huntington and get a taxi from there or he could take a taxi directly home. He thought about sharing the back of a crowded limo and decided on a taxi. The fare came close to what an average worker took home for a week's wage but he needed time to be alone and think. He carried no luggage, the jacket he carried on the plane in Orlando now buttoned against the chill of Long Island. He wondered if there were any truth to the saying that blood thinned out in a hot climate. He wasn't sure of the thickness of his blood, but the damp air penetrated his clothing as he sat huddled in the back seat of the taxi.

When the taxi stopped at his driveway, he noticed the manicured lawn, the lawn service doing a neater job than he would. The maple trees were just beginning to lose their deep green, a touch of yellow in the leaves as the taxi's headlights swept past. The roses under the large bay window were covered with late blooms. Winter was yet to strike its blow and strip the trees of their color and shock the shrubs into dormancy.

It was odd. The painting he had done on the house to kill the hours and the days of solitude still looked new. The big, comfortable house looked neat and trim. He spent many hours each week for the past two years working on the house and landscaping but he hadn't thought about it once he took *Windsong* on the trip south. He called the lawn service, and his daughter promised to stop by at least weekly and pick up the mail. The neighbors would also keep an eye on it. What had once been the center of so much of his attention had been completely forgotten. Now it waited for him, a house that could easily be on the cover of *Better Homes and Gardens.*

He dropped his keys in a crystal bowl on an antique stand near the door, as he had thousands of times before. He turned on the lights and went to the thermostat in the hall, turning on lights as he went. Something about the house being dark disturbed him. The thermostat was set on heat, the temperature setting an energy saving fifty-five degrees, his daughter's doing, and the actual room temperature a cool and damp sixty degrees. He turned the thermostat up to seventy-five and was rewarded with a click and a hum as the furnace came on. He shivered. The phone rang and he wondered who could be calling him. He had been gone for months.

"Hello?"

There was a pause on the other end for a second. "Oh, good, it's you Walter," Winfred Bascomb, his next door neighbor said. "I saw the lights and was wondering who might be in there. I didn't see your daughter's car and ah, just wanted to make sure everything was all right."

Walter could hear Winfred chewing on his pipe stem as he spoke. "Yes, Winny, it's me. Thanks for looking after the place."

"Well, of course I would." Winfred sounded wounded that anyone doubted his ability to notice a trespasser. Winnfred Bascomb was eighty-six years old and was sensitive about anyone thinking he had lost his abilities. "Are you back to stay?"

"No. Just a few days."

"You mean you haven't finished your vacation yet?" Winnfred asked, surprised.

Is that what I'm doing? Walter thought. Am I only on vacation, just doing something a little different for a change and then coming back to rejoin the real world?

"No, I just had to come up for a few days to get a couple of things settled."

"Wow, that must be some vacation. I never took more than one week a year in my entire life," Winfred said proudly.

Winfred Bascomb had made a small fortune buying and selling used airplanes. He spent most of his life traveling all over the world buying, selling, and trading aircraft. Walter doubted he was home more than two months out of the year with his wife and family. He stayed active in business well into his seventies and it was rumored he had a second family with a mistress in Minneapolis, his second base of operation, and had finally settled down when his mistress died and he stopped dashing off to the airport on one deal or another. Or so it was rumored. Walter tended to believe it. When would Winfred have had time for a vacation? He was seventy-nine when he sold his business. He still had a quick step and a twinkle in his eye. Walter liked him.

"Yeah, it has been awhile. How was your summer?"

Walter asked, being both polite and curious as to how his old friend was doing.

"Fine. Just fine," Winfred said, jovially. "But I'll bet not half as interesting as yours. There must be something or someone mighty interesting down in Florida to be keeping you so long."

How could Winfred know, or sense, or was he just fishing? Walter didn't take the bait. "Nothing spectacular. I've had some trouble with the boat and I've been stuck there trying to get things straightened out."

"Oh." Winfred sounded disappointed. Walter wasn't sure if he was disappointed because he was not more forthcoming or because he was living such a dull life. He smiled to himself. He was sure Winfred would love to hear the whole story. If Walter treated it lightly. If he treated the whole episode as a lark. But it wasn't a lark. It was his life, as confusing as it may be.

"Thanks again for looking after the place, Winny. Give my best to your wife."

"Sure. Glad to keep an eye on your place. Anytime. Not a whole lot to do around here anyway. Come on over if you can. I'd love to hear about your yachting trip."

"Okay, Winny. If I can."

The heat was coming through the vents and Walter took off his jacket. He looked at the familiar that had become unfamiliar. Nothing had changed except the house plants were gone. Lynda must have taken them home to care for them, and it seemed very large and very empty. He looked through the archway connecting the dining room and the living room with antique sofa and chairs, French tables and cabinets from one of the Louis' eras, crystal chandelier illuminating each piece of furniture set just so, a movie set waiting for the actor's arrival. After the time spent on Windsong and then Manatee Street, this place seemed immense. He wondered if Nancy's house would fit in the living room. No, it would probably be about as big as the living room *and* the dining room. The thick pile carpet had been freshly cleaned. Lynda must have had someone come in and do that for him. He thought about Nancy's house with toys constantly on the floor, him or her picking them up and putting the toys back in their box, only to be back out on the floor in ten minutes as Little John or Dixie or sometimes Helen would scatter their treasures again.

He tried to picture Nancy and the children living here. At least there would be enough room for everyone. With four bedrooms and three baths, each of the children would have his or her own bedroom. That would work. And he could put some swings and slides in the back yard, as when Harold and Lynda were children, and a pool, it would have to be heated if they were to get any use out of it, and anything else the kids might want or need. He thought of Dixie, Helen, and Little John tumbling in the snow, bundled and warm, playing in the yard. Or was it more natural for them to be where they are, barefoot most of the time, often only partially dressed, playing in the grass and sand, tan and healthy and happy.

And what about Nancy? Would she fit in here? She had so many friends near her now, it seemed to Walter she knew hundreds of people. How would it be for her to leave them and come here and be alone until she made new friends? Would he bring her here to be lonely? Then there was the question that was probably the main reason he returned to New York. Did *he* want to share his and Laura's home with Nancy and the children? Did they belong here? Did he belong here anymore?

He went from room to room switching on lights, walking into each room surveying the furniture, pictures, and then going to the next to do the same. He barely recalled what was in each room. His wife would mention she was going to get this or that piece of furniture and replace something or other and he would grunt and a month or a year later he would realize something was different. The house had been Laura's department, and he had little to do with its contents.

Lastly, he went into the master bedroom, his and Laura's room. The king-size bed was there along with the French antique dresser and chests. Embroidered drapes covered the windows and Tiffany lamps came on when he flipped the wall switch.

Lynda had taken her mother's clothing and other personal items from the house not long after Laura's death. It was supposed to help him heal, to forget. Only pictures of her remained on the dresser, and of him and her, and the children and grandchildren. Nothing of a living Laura was in the room, but he could feel her presence. She had slept beside him on that bed and wasted away to skin and bones. She had sat before that mirrored dressing table and cried as she brushed her hair and watched it pull free with each stroke, so that by the time she died there were more than twenty wigs in the closet to cover a bald skull.

He picked up a framed picture of Laura. It had been taken nearly twenty years before and it was probably the best photo she had ever taken. She was a lovely woman with smooth skin, naturally wavy brown hair, deep blue eyes, and an easy going manner. She had loved him and tried to be the kind of wife he wanted. She belonged to the garden club, and a bridge club, and the country club, and he didn't know how many charitable organizations, but she had always been there when he came home from work and on weekends. Her life revolved around him and his needs, and he never noticed until she was gone. She was dead now, what, two, no, two-and-a-half years and still he missed her and carried a sense of guilt. He wasn't sure what he was guilty of, but he felt he had failed her.

The thought struck him so hard it was almost like a physical blow. He rocked back on his heels and said aloud, "Two-and-a-half years! I've been in mourning for two-and-a-half years! My God!" He put the picture of his wife back on the dresser and went to the garage. He found an empty cardboard box and returned to the bedroom. He took one last, long look at Laura's face, the Laura that was a part of his innermost self, and then placed it in the box followed by the other photos in the room. He carried forty years of memories into his daughter's old room and placed it in an empty closet. He closed it, turned out the light, and shut the door. He went to each of the other bedrooms and turned the lights out, closing each door firmly. When he reached the master bedroom he stopped. He noticed there was a light film of dust on the dresser and darker patches where he removed the framed photos. He took his handkerchief and wiped the top. All traces of what had been there were gone. Tonight he would sleep in the guest bedroom.

He sat on the sofa and sneezed twice and blew his nose and wiped watery eyes. "Dust," he said aloud. He dialed her number not knowing what he was going to say. All he knew was he wanted to hear her voice, to know that she was there, to know she was real.

"Hello." Nancy's deep voice was a balm to his loneliness.

"Hi, Honey."

"Oh, good. I'm glad you called. I was worried about you."

"I'm glad you were worried," he said, and meant it. He needed to know she loved him. He needed to know she cared. He needed her.

"How was your trip? Where are you now?"

"The trip was okay. No problems. I'm home now."

"Home," Nancy repeated. It wasn't a question. It wasn't a statement. She only repeated that one word.

"No, I'm not home," Walter said, "I'm in New York at my old house. *You* are home."

"I'm not sure I understand. What are we talking about?"

He paused for a second. "We're talking about I love you very, very much. That's what we're talking about."

"And I love you, too." He could hear the television noise

in the background. The children would be on the floor in front of it, probably eating something that wasn't supposed to be good for them.

"You sound, ah, different. Are you sure you're all right?" She asked, concerned. He needed that concern. He had to be sure that this beautiful twenty-eight-year-old woman cared about a sixty-year-old man. Him. Why she did he would never understand. But if she did, then nothing else really mattered.

"I'm okay. I might be coming down with a cold or something though. I haven't felt warm since I got off the plane. I guess you've spoiled me with your Florida weather," he chuckled. It felt good just to be talking with her. It diminished the distance between them.

"How long are you going to be there?" She asked no questions before he left. Did he hear some doubt in her voice? This was the first time they had been separated.

"I think it'll take me a couple of days. I'm not sure yet. There are a few things I have to do. I'll be as quick as I can."

"Call me." It was a plea.

"I'll be calling. I miss you already. How are the kids?"

"The same," she said, slight exasperation coming through.

"What are they up to?" Walter wanted to know. He missed those kids.

"Oh, lets see. Dixie pushed Little John and now he has a knot on his head. Helen has been insisting for the past two hours that she *has* to have her ears pierced, like right now, and if not right now then tomorrow at the latest. And if she doesn't get her ears pierced by tomorrow she's going to lay down and die. Right here in front of me. That's what the little darlings are up to. Just driving me crazy as usual."

Walter laughed. He could picture it all in his mind. They were a lively bunch, those three. "I'll call you tomorrow."

"Good. I'm working till four, then I'll be home. Call me at work if you need to."

"I shouldn't need to. I'll call you tomorrow evening. I should know by then when I'll be able to come back, uh, home."

"Take care of yourself. Do you have plenty of warm clothes and coats and stuff?"

He smiled into the phone. "Yes, I have everything I need. I was a New Yorker before I became a Floridian, remember?"

"Well, dress warm."

"I will... I love you," he said softly.

"I love you, too. I'll be waiting for your call."

"Bye, Honey," he said, not really wanting to end the call.

"Bye, Darling." The phone went dead.

Two more calls and he would be able to relax. He called his son first, knowing Harold would have few questions, at least for now. He dialed his son's number and an answering machine came on informing him that the Marshalls were unavailable to come to the phone right now and his daughter-in-law's singsong voice asking the caller to please leave a message. He left a message that he was back in New York for a couple of days and would be calling again. He hung up and made a face. He hated talking to machines. Next he dialed his daughter's number and the phone was picked up before the second ring.

"Hello," Lynda said, sounding tired.

"Hello, beautiful. How's my girl?"

"Daddy!" Lynda exclaimed, not sounding like the mature mother that she was but once again his little girl.

"I'm in town and thought I'd give you a call."

"You're home? Why didn't you let us know? When did you get in?"

"A little while ago. I flew in. I'll just be here a day or two. There are a few things I need to do."

"But Dad, why didn't you let us know you were coming?" Lynda sounded hurt. "I would have come to the airport and met you. How did you get from the airport?"

"I took a cab. I wasn't sure about my flight so I didn't

trouble you," He said, telling a little lie. What he didn't want was his daughter's questions as soon as he got off the plane. He didn't have answers to many of those questions. That was why he was here.

"That must have been expensive."

"Oh, well. I don't do it very often." That was the truth. How often does a man change his whole life?

"You said something about only being here a day or so? When are we going to get to see you? When are you coming home? Don't you have to be back to work soon?"

These were some of the questions that he needed to answer for himself. "I'll tell you all about it tomorrow." He wasn't sure what he would be telling her, but he knew he was going to have to make his choices and then live with those choices.

"Can you come to dinner tomorrow?"

"I was hoping you'd ask. How does seven-thirty sound?"

"Perfect. There isn't time for me to fix your Long Island duck though. I'll have to make something else."

"That's fine. Anything will do. Don't go to any trouble."

"I almost forgot, Dad. How's your leg?"

"It's fine. Better than new." Walter rubbed his leg. The dampness and relative cold of Long Island had it aching.

"I was so worried about you. You and that boat!"

He laughed. "Don't kid yourself. Sometimes us old folks can do more than you think we can," he said, meaning more than he was saying. What would his daughter say and do when she found out he was going to marry a woman younger than she was?

"I'll bet," Lynda agreed. "We'll see you tomorrow at seven-thirty then."

"Right. Give my love to George and the kids."

"I will. Bye."

"Bye, Baby."

Strange, he hadn't even asked about George and the children. Normally he always did. He rubbed his temples. A headache was starting and he felt another chill. He blew his nose again. No doubt about it. He was coming down with a cold. Great. With a million things to do. He went to the bathroom in the master bedroom and took two aspirins, selected a suit, shirt, and underclothes and took them to the guest room. All he had eaten had been a light snack on the plane, but he wasn't hungry. He was tired and he ached all over. Rest would help. Turn the mind off and let tomorrow take care of itself. He pulled the covers back from the bed, stripped, and crawled in.

He took an earlier train than usual into New York City the next morning. There had been nothing in the house to make for breakfast and two cups of black instant coffee, aspirins and an antihistamine tablet started his day. His sniffles were not much worse than the night before, so whatever he was coming down with wouldn't be too bad. Taking an earlier train meant he knew few of his fellow passengers and he was able to be alone with his thoughts in the crowded car. He still wasn't sure what he was going to do. He kept trying to visualize Nancy and the children fitting into his life here on Long Island, the changes they would have to make, and the changes he would have to make, how good it would be to have them with him, the difficulties the family would have in making the adjustment to a new home, climate, and life-style.

The offices at Wheel, Kedder and Matthews were quiet as he got off the elevator and walked to his office down a silent corridor past closed doors with gilded names and titles. His was at the end, the largest on the floor, the prestigious corner with the extra window. There was no one at the secretaries' desks in his outer office. It was still early. He unlocked his inner office door and went in, closing the door and stopping to look around. Nothing had changed except his large, highly polished desk top was empty and waiting. He put his briefcase alongside it and walked to the double windows, not turning on any lights. Familiar tall, gray office buildings filled both windows. He stepped closer and looked down at the narrow street below. People scurried along sidewalks and darted through traffic as they rushed to work, disappearing into massive buildings to be spewed out again come evening. He was seeing himself multiplied by a thousand, ten thousand. How many times had he done what these people below were doing? His whole life, that's how many.

There was a light knock at the door. He turned and called, "Come."

Myra came in, first looking toward his desk, and then catching sight of him at the windows. "The receptionist at the front desk told me you had come in. I've been helping out at 'the pool.'" With Walter having been gone so long, Myra had been temporarily reassigned to the secretarial pool.

"Hello, Myra. How have you been?" he asked.

"Fine," she said, walking toward him, pen and pad in hand. "We missed you and everyone was worried when we heard about your accident. We..." Myra stopped in mid-sentence, staring at Walter in the window light. His tanned, relaxed features had stopped her. Years of worry lines had disappeared. His hair was cut shorter and sun-bleached, the gray at the temples less pronounced. He looked ten years younger. He even looked taller, shoulders back, head held high.

"You look wonderful!" Myra said in amazement.

"Thank you, Myra. You look wonderful, too." This wasn't exactly the truth. The natural light coming through the windows reflected off hair made brittle by too many trips to the beauty parlor, thick make-up covering palled, sagging skin, and a dress designed for a much slimmer, younger woman.

Myra tried not to stare at her boss but couldn't help herself. In less than three months, and she had counted every day waiting until he returned, there had been a total transformation in Walter Marshall. She couldn't take her eyes off his tranquil face. Somehow, one man left and another returned.

"I'm going to need a favor, Myra," Walter said. The mass of ants on the sidewalk below had helped him make up his mind. Seeing Myra struggling against age helped him make up his mind, and this dead office.

"Of course! Whatever I can do."

"I'll need you to be discreet," and when he noticed Myra stiffen he added, "I don't mean I'm worried about you being discreet. I mean I hope you'll be able to get this information from someone who will be discreet."

"What is it, Mister Marshall?" Myra asked, mollified.

"I'd like to know the specifics on my retirement account. How much do I have in it, when can I draw against it and how much will I receive. That sort of thing."

"You mean you're going to retire?" Myra was shocked, eyes wide, mouth agape. "Now?"

"I might." He turned away from Myra's shocked look and went to his desk, opened a drawer and took out a pen and paper. "I'm not really sure yet. I still have a little vacation time coming but I think I am."

Myra followed him and stood as she had so many times before. She looked as though she had just been told that the world was going to end today. "But—" was all she could say.

Walter knew how much his leaving the firm would mean to her. She would no longer be attached to a rising star. She would never be top secretary at Wheel, Kedder and Matthews with whatever pay and perks that might entail. She would now just be a senior secretary, not having to take any kind of pay cut of course, but never going any further in the secretarial chain of command either. The lawyers at Wheel, Kedder and Matthews kept their staffs intact, especially a lawyer on the rise. Myra would be a fifth wheel wherever she was assigned unless it was with one of the new attorneys just coming in.

She deserved an explanation. He sat at his desk looking up at her, sensing her shock, loss, and pain. "I met a woman," he said. Myra blinked, thick mascara holding her eyes closed an instant too long. "She's beautiful." There were several more blinks. "We're engaged." Now great, dark drops of tearing mascara began to make two black streaks slowly down her cheeks. Her lower lip trembled and she bit it, holding her lips compressed. Then she nodded and spoke, voice husky with emotion.

"I should have figured. You look so wonderful. She must be a very special woman." Myra gulped back more tears and went on. "I'm happy for you."

"Thank you, Myra," he said, feeling even more guilty knowing that she meant it. She was happy for him even though it would be a loss to herself.

Myra put her pen and pad on the desk and came around to where he sat. She took his face in her hands, her touch cold and clammy, and bent and kissed his forehead. Before backing away, she took a tissue out of her pocket and wiped the smudge of lipstick she had left. Then she went back to her side of the desk, blew her nose, wiped some of the black streaks from her cheeks and picked up pen and pad. "I know one of the girls in personnel. She's my cousin, actually. She'll know how to keep her mouth shut. Don't worry. Nobody will know anything about your inquiries."

"Thank you, Myra. You're a wonderful person. I'm going to miss you."

"I'll see that you get what you need, Walter." Myra had never called him by his first name before.

He smiled.

"I'm going to miss you, too," she added, holding back a sob.

He wrote something, tearing off the sheet and handing it to Myra. "This is my new address. From now on, please send any correspondence here."

Myra nodded. "Right," and left quickly.

He thought he heard a sob escape before she could get the door closed and then he was alone in his office again. He turned on the desk light and took a Rolodex out of a drawer. He made two calls, one to John Cramer, his stock broker, the other to his bank on Long Island where his paychecks were still being electronically deposited. He wanted a statement on his accounts at each, and to each gave his new home address in Cocoa Beach, Florida. Then he took the few personal items in his desk and put them in his briefcase and quickly and quietly left.

Saying good-bye to his daughter, Lynda, was going to be more difficult. He realized now that was why he had needed to return to New York. He needed to say good-bye to his home and its memories in Huntington, to Myra and an office where he had spent so much of his life, and to Lynda, his loving daughter. He never did reach his son on the phone. All he could do was leave a message that he would be writing Harold a letter to explain a few things.

A taxi brought him to his daughter's house at seven-thirty that evening. He carried two large valises and a small box tucked under one arm. His son-in-law, George, answered the chiming doorbell.

"Hello, Walter," George said, his smoldering pipe wiggling, stem clenched between teeth.

"Hello, George. Let's leave these here by the door." Walter put the valises down but held onto the decorative box. "The taxi will be back in less than an hour. I have to catch a flight out of JFK."

"So soon?" George asked, as they both walked toward the kitchen and the aroma of spaghetti cooking.

"Yeah. I just came to take care of a few things. I'll be telling you and Lynda about it. Where are the kids?"

"In the den with the TV blasting I would guess, or they

would have heard the bell and been here to greet you."

Walter realized he hadn't brought anything for his grand-children. This was the first time. They would be disappointed.

Lynda was stirring a large pot of spaghetti as George and Walter entered the kitchen. She came to her father and gave him a hug and a kiss on the cheek. "Supper will be ready in a minute," she said, stepping back and appraising him. "You look great, Dad. I didn't know what to expect what with all the problems you had down in Florida, breaking your leg, the boat sinking and all. But I shouldn't have worried. You look absolutely super!"

Lynda noticed the antique jewelry box he carried under his arm. She looked at him inquiringly.

"I'll tell you about it later," he said, and placed his wife's jewelry box on the counter.

That afternoon he had gone to the bank and taken every-thing out of his safety deposit box and turned in the key. Most of the contents were in one of the valises near the door. His dead wife's jewelry was in this jewelry box.

"Let's eat," Lynda said, giving the steaming pot one last stir. "Call the kids, will you, Honey?"

Dinner started off as it had so many times before. Walter was the center of attention answering dozens of questions about his trip, Hurricane Edward and the loss of *Windsong*, and of course, his broken leg. He mentioned Nancy and the children only in passing, not going into detail, waiting until the children left the table before announcing the news of his engagement to Nancy and his leaving New York. After dessert and the children returned to the den in the basement to watch a favorite program on TV, he broke the news to his daughter and son-in-law. First, he retrieved Laura's jewelry box from the kitchen and handed it to his daughter.

"Here, Honey. It's your mother's stuff. I know she would have wanted you to have it," he said, placing the inlaid box on the dining table in front of his daughter.

Lynda opened the lid and began taking rings, bracelets, necklaces, and earrings out of the case one at a time. She lifted each piece carefully, reverently, fingertips gliding over diamonds and gold and pearls. Memories of her mother came as she placed each one on the linen table cloth. Her eyes began to mist and Walter wanted to kick himself for being so thoughtless. He was going to tell his daughter about Nancy, at the same time he brought back all of the memories of her mother. It was too late. There was nothing he could do. The taxi would be coming soon.

He cleared his throat before he spoke, nervously rubbing his palms together. "I think I mentioned Nancy, the woman who took care of me when I broke my leg." He immediately got George's full attention, Lynda coming out of her reverie slowly.

"Yes, you did," George said, perceiving there would be more. His father-in-law had been behaving unnaturally all during dinner.

"She has three children, I think you said," George added.

"Yes, nice kids, very nice." Walter looked at his daughter. She was staring at him, face blank, waiting, her father's tone telling her something important was about to be said. She knew the way her father spoke when what he was saying was more important than usual. "And she's a fine woman," he went on, his eyes leaving his daughter's face, not wanting to see it if he hurt her, hoping he wouldn't. "We've become very attached."

"Attached?" Lynda asked, deep furrows forming between eyebrows.

"Yes. We're, er, we're engaged," Walter said, for some reason feeling foolish.

"Engaged?" Lynda repeated again. "You mean like engaged to be married?" Lynda's voice climbed an octave toward the end of the question.

"Yes." He looked at his hands, his son-in-law and then finally at his daughter's distraught face.

"But, but, how'd it happen?" Lynda asked, sounding as though she were asking about a car wreck.

"We fell in love," Walter said simply.

"That's wonderful news," George said, far more jovially than he felt. "Isn't that wonderful news, Lynda?"

His wife was staring at her father incredulously. "How long have you known her?" Lynda asked her father.

"I met her almost as soon as I got to Cocoa Beach, Port Canaveral actually." He reached across the table and covered his daughter's hand with his. She was still holding one of her mother's bracelets. "She's very nice, Lynda, really."

When Lynda didn't reply George tried to fill the gap. "I'll bet she is. She would have to be for you to fall for her. You haven't told us much about her. What's she like? How old are the children?" George asked.

"The children are young," Walter said, and paused. "Nancy's young too. She's twenty-eight."

"My God!" Lynda exclaimed. "She's younger than I am!"

"Well, I'll be," George said, looking at his father-in-law in surprise.

Without saying anything, Lynda rose from the table, her chair almost tipping over as she stood. She turned and left the room, going to her bedroom. She was going to cry. The tears were already streaming down her cheeks as she reached the bedroom door. Her father wanted her to be happy for him. She should be happy if he had found someone to love and share his life. She should be happy for him but all she could do was cry. She wanted to be glad for her father but tears came instead. She went into the bathroom and closed that door also, so her husband and father wouldn't hear the growing sobs she felt welling up.

"She'll be all right," George said to his father-in-law. "It all has come as a bit of a shock. She'll calm down in just a few minutes."

"I know she will. I should have done this differently. And I never should have brought Lynda her mother's jewelry to her now. It was stupid. I wasn't thinking. Too many memories. It's my fault. I could have handled this much better."

"Well, let's not make this into a tragedy. You bring good news, not bad. You look like a million dollars, better than you have in a long time. If this is what that woman can do for you, go to it. It's the best medicine I've seen in a long time." George meant it.

"Thanks, George." A horn tooted in the driveway. "That's my taxi."

George put out his hand. "Good luck. Everything will be all right at this end. Lynda will come around."

"Thanks. Tell Lynda I'm sorry I handled this so stupidly. You know what I mean." Walter picked up his bags and stepped out the front door.

"I will," George called as he walked to the waiting taxi. "It'll all be okay. Our congratulations to you and your fiancée."

He put his baggage into the back seat and waved to his son-in-law. Doctor George Evans watched as the taxi disappeared down the street, stroking his beard and nodding ever so slightly.

Nancy would be waiting for him at the airport in Orlando. He had tried to dissuade her from coming. He could just as easily have taken a taxi from the airport to Cocoa Beach, but she insisted. She would be waiting for him, Little John and Dixie and Helen asleep in the back seat of the station wagon, and she would slide over and let him drive after first giving him a kiss and a strong hug. Walter knew what to expect and he couldn't wait to get home.

XXII
Billy Tillman

Billy Tillman and Nancy Foch grew up together. His family lived five houses down, on Manatee Street, and they played as children, went to the first grade together, and throughout their school years were as often as not in the same class, had the same teachers, and shared the same friends. They knew each other and were friends as only life-long friends can be. They were as close as brother and sister and perhaps closer since they never had to struggle with sibling rivalry.

Billy had always been big. By the time they entered school he was a head taller than Nancy and twenty pounds heavier. They were equals in most things, Nancy stood her ground and saw to that, but Billy's size allowed him to play the role as her protector. Nancy was better at school work. As a matter of fact, everybody was better at school work than Billy. But he was big and strong and willing to listen to the coaches, probably the only adults he would listen to, and was a good athlete. He played on the football and baseball teams and was a local star on both. He turned down two athletic scholarships from small

Florida colleges and chose the Navy instead. The thought of going to another class made him shudder. He could barely read and had been promoted and graduated from high school strictly for his hard work on the playing fields. He refused to make himself a fool in any college.

Billy came back from the Navy covered with tattoos and gloom. He had been married and divorced while in the service and left a two-year-old son with his ex-wife in Virginia. He hadn't seen the boy since he walked out of the house after arriving home unexpectedly and catching his wife in bed with a petty officer who lived next door. His carefree boyishness was trampled by the events during the months it took to complete a bitter divorce.

He was discharged from the Navy and came home just three days before his father's third and final heart attack. Billy left the cemetery after burying his father and that day bought a Harley-Davidson motorcycle. He roared through the streets at night traveling from bar to bar, worked as a mechanic only long enough to keep in spending money, and refused to make plans any further than one day ahead. His mother cooked his meals, washed his clothes, and prayed for him each morning when she went to Mass.

Billy had been in the Navy and away during Nancy's marriage and divorce. They spoke little about their short marriages and the emotional turmoil of a divorce, but in a way it brought them even closer. Billy had a crush on Nancy during their teens and she was wise enough to avoid Billy's awkward advances and still keep their friendship intact.

Billy grew to six-foot-three while in high school and, after returning home, to two-hundred-eighty pounds while drinking pitcher after pitcher of beer in the bars along the beach. He was big and strong and even with his massive beer gut he was quick on his feet. He grew a beard and wore his hair in a pony-tail and had a deep tan from constantly being in the sun. He looked like a bear, a very ferocious and dangerous bear, and he could act that way if provoked. He would kill anyone who would try to hurt Nancy or her children. But normally he was easy going and mild mannered. He had a tendency to cry when he was drunk. He was one of those gentle giants who was still frightening.

Nancy wasn't frightened by him. Though she was little more than one third his size she had learned to stand up to him and hold her own when they had been kids and she still did. She could speak to him as no one else, scold him with shaking finger as she did often enough, and he would look at the ground, shuffle his feet and endure her harangue. He loved her.

When she stalked angrily to the back yard to speak to Billy about his teaching Helen how to roll marijuana cigarettes there was no question as to who was in command. She could have beaten him to death with a baseball bat and he would not have lifted one finger in defense. She was right and he was wrong and even if she had not been right he would have let her do whatever she wanted.

"You're a son-of-a-bitch, do you know that Billy? I ought to beat the pants off of you right here and now. One of these days I'm going to beat the tar out of you," she yelled, raising her hand.

Walter had followed Nancy and turned the corner of the house in time to see her swing at Billy. He fended her off with his forearms, blocking each blow easily.

"Wait. Wait," Billy pleaded. "What'd I do? What? What'd I do?" he asked plaintively. He sat on an old bench they used as a saw horse, the two-by-fours sagging under his weight, and though sitting, he was as tall as Nancy. She tried several times to punch him but he successfully blocked her small fists. Walter watched, at a loss as what to do.

"Ow, ow," Nancy cried, and backed away holding her hand. She hurt her knuckles hitting the bone of his elbow.

"I'm sorry. I'm sorry," Billy cried, getting up and trying to comfort her. "I didn't mean to hurt you." He weaved a little as he came to her, the warm wine and hot sun a poor combination for balance.

"Get away from me you big oaf. Don't touch me. I'm mad at you." She held her hurt hand and wiggled her fingers.

"I'm sorry," he said again, and tried to take her hand. "Can I get you some ice or something?"

"You can get me something. You can get me some brains for you. What the hell are you doing teaching a baby how to roll dope? Don't you have any sense at all?" The pain was easing and she felt her knuckles. Nothing was broken.

"I'm sorry, but you hit me," he said defensively.

"Never mind I hit you. What about Helen? What are you doing showing her how to roll joints? She's just a kid, for Christ's sake, a baby."

"She asked me to show her," Billy explained. "She asked me so I showed her," he said lamely.

"You're not supposed to be rolling dope in front of kids anyway. You know that. She's too young for that kind of stuff. What do you want to do, have her grow up to be a dope addict?" she asked angrily.

Billy hung his head dejectedly. "You're right, I'm sorry. I won't ever do it again," he said sincerely. He was the picture of remorse, and she couldn't hold on to her anger.

"Oh, I don't know what I'm going to do with you," she said, and stamped her foot. "I wish you'd grow up and stop being such a big jerk."

"I will." He wanted her to stop being angry with him. He would have agreed with anything she said. He was sorry he had shown Helen how to roll a joint. It was stupid. He hated himself when he did stupid things. And he was getting drunk again. A numbness worked its way from scalp to chin. "I mean I won't do that again. I promise."

"You'd better promise"

"I think I'm drunk. Maybe I better go home and get some sleep." Billy squeezed his cheek with thumb and forefinger. Three quarters of a gallon of warm grape Novocain had taken all feeling away.

"Go home, Billy. Get some sleep. Stay away from that wine for awhile. That stuff makes you crazy as hell. And don't bring any more dope over her, okay? The kids don't need to see that stuff all over the place."

"Okay. I won't." Billy started walking unsteadily when he stopped and turned back and spoke to Walter. "I'm sorry," he said softly, hanging his head. "I didn't mean to do nothing wrong. I love those kids. Nancy knows that. I wouldn't do anything to hurt them." He turned on his heels and left before Walter could respond. Walter looked at Nancy and she shook her head resignedly. She picked up the nearly empty gallon of wine and put the cap on it, placing it on a shelf in the shed.

"He didn't mean it," she said, half to Walter and half to herself. "He just had too much wine and too much sun. The jerk."

He took her hand, manipulating the fingers. "Are you hurt?"

"No. I can't hit that hard. And I sure couldn't hurt Billy. He's strong as an ox." He put her hand to his lips and kissed each knuckle. She smiled, and ran her fingers through his hair. "You're nice," she said gently.

"You're nice too." He kissed her palm. "Would you like me to speak to Helen, about drugs I mean? I don't know very much about it but…" He shrugged.

"Would you? I know it would be helpful. She listens to you more than she does me. I don't know what it is, but for some reason I can't seem to speak to her. Whenever we begin a conversation it ends up a battle."

"Perhaps you're both too much alike. Beautiful. Strong-willed. Independent."

"You mean thick-headed."

He laughed. "Your words, not mine."

Nancy laughed too. She leaned against him and kissed his cheek. He put his arms around her.

"What will the neighbors think?" He slowly rubbed her back, loving to touch and feel her against him.

"They'll think I'm a lucky woman, that's what." Her breath brushed the hairs on his chest.

"If we're going to do this, why don't we go inside?" He kissed her temple, the top of her head, hair silk to his lips.

"If we're going inside, why don't I bring the kids over to Bertha's?" Nancy stepped back, sparkling eyes mischievous.

"If we're going inside and if the kids are over at Bertha's why don't we...?" Walter's eyes were shining, alive with happiness and desire.

She took his hand and they began walking to the house. "I'll take the kids to Bertha's," she said, squeezing his hand.

"I'm going to jump in the shower." He felt sticky from the heat.

"Don't rush." Nancy opened the door for them. "I'll be right back and wash your back."

"And I'll wash yours," he said, the thought exciting him. He had never taken a shower with a woman. In sexual matters, and even nudity, his wife had been very shy. Since Laura was the only sexual partner he ever had, he was beginning to realize how unimaginative they had been together.

"Deal." Nancy said, and began rounding up the children to take them over to Bertha, friend and babysitter.

He was rinsing when she pulled back the shower curtain and stepped into the tub with him. There was little space to spare with both of them standing in the tub. Cool water beat on his chest and ran down his abdomen and legs, but it had little effect on the heat building within him.

"Hand me the soap," she said from behind him.

He took the bar of soap from the dish and handed it to her over his shoulder. She began washing his back and shoulders, her touch soft and gentle, his skin tingling. Her hands slid to buttocks, soapy hands sliding between his legs and then to thighs and calves. He stood with eyes closed, cold water running down the front of his body, Nancy's hands working in slow, circular motions behind him.

"Turn around," she said softly.

He hesitated, embarrassed by his pulsing erection standing stiff and hard. Slowly he turned, the confined space causing him to brush his arm against her breast, the back of his hand across her wet thigh and abdomen. He looked into her dark eyes, pools of black-brown liquid searching his face. Her hair was covered with tiny diamonds, spray caught in fine hair. Her firm breasts were erect, nipples taut, tips protruding points of pink flesh. She began washing his neck and shoulders and arms and armpits, chest and stomach. She took his swollen penis in her hands, one holding a small bar of soap, the other working a lather, and stroked him there. His breath caught in his throat.

She squatted before him and reached for the sack beneath, hands warm on his cool skin, fingers reaching all his hidden places. She washed his thighs and then down to his feet, his erection brushing her cheek and leaving a streak of suds. She worked her hands slowly back up, going over each part of his body a second time. He was completely and utterly sexually aroused, and yet what she was doing was more than a sexual act for his pleasure. She was humbling herself before him and cleansing him and caring for him. When she was standing again, her eyes rose to meet his, her face open, honest, beautiful. He put his arms around her and pulled her to him, bending to meet her lips, his hands sliding down her back and pressing her against him. Her lips responded, hands at his hips pulling him tightly to her.

Reluctantly, he released her, trying to keep his passion in check. "My turn," he said, voice tight.

They had to come together again as they pirouetted under the shower head and exchanged places in the small tub. Nancy had her back to him, water splashing down her front, and she reached over her shoulder and offered him the bar of aromatic soap. He began washing her back, soap pressed in the palm of one hand, the other following in slow circles. He knelt behind her, his feet jammed tight against the head of the tub, and washed her buttocks and then to thighs and calves and slowly back up again. When he was done he stood, his erection pressing against her hip. "Turn."

Nancy turned and he kissed her lightly on the lips, holding himself from taking her in his arms. He began washing her neck and then her arms, her limbs lose as he held them between his hands and stroked from fingertips to shoulders. He rubbed her breasts, nipples swollen and hard, eyes closed and lips slightly parted. He knelt before her and washed her belly and then down to the hair between her legs. He put his hand in this warm place and slowly worked up a lather in the soft, curly hair. He washed her legs and then the top of her feet and then back again to that warm place, hands and fingers moving slowly, searching each crevice, leaving no place untouched.

He stood and helped her rinse, four hands working together, spray splashing off both of them. Again they exchanged places and Nancy helped him rinse, neither saying anything, their hands a mutual language. He kissed her, long and tender this time, passion restrained so mutual love and caring could be shared.

"Let's go to the bedroom," he said, unable to restrain himself any longer.

She pulled back the shower curtain and stepped out of the tub. He turned the shower off and followed her. She took a bath towel and rubbed him dry. He was no longer embarrassed when she touched his private parts. They were beyond that now. There were no secret places each had not seen and touched. They knew each other and had cleansed each other and there was no need for shame. He dried her with a towel, her legs slightly apart to make it easier for him.

They held hands as they walked from the bathroom to the bedroom, each unwilling to let the other go. The air conditioner in the bedroom they now shared hummed, the cool air a sudden contrast from the warm house in the hot afternoon. The window blinds were closed, strips of sunlight between each blind lighting the room. They sat on the bed and kissed, his hand caressing her face and then moving down the smooth skin of her neck to breast, gently squeezing, fingertips caressing a nipple which responded, swelling and hardening. Her hand roamed his body, across his shoulders, down his side, along his thigh and back. Her touch was light, fingers barely touching his skin, but each fingertip a hot coal as her hand raked his body.

They leaned back on the bed and scooted toward the center, kissing as they wiggled along the sheet, always in contact. He held her face between his hands, fragrant, wavy hair framing her, beauty in his grasp. He kissed her forehead and nose and lips and neck and kept kissing to both breasts, taking nipple with lips, tongue manipulating. Her fingers stroked his hair as she breathed deeply. His lips moved to her belly, her heart pounding beneath his kisses. He kissed her belly button, tongue searching, and slid his lips down to soft fuzz to damp curly hair. His lips caressed, tongue searching, eyes closed. His mind was filled with her scent, his lips searching for taste, soft down causing a pleasurable tingling on his face.

She rolled over and straddled him, knees on each side of his head, offering herself to him. His lips and tongue searched for pleasure spots, his mind blank except for the pleasure he was receiving and trying to give. He felt her take him in her hand, stroking. Her lips caressed him as she gently and slowly stroked, tongue rubbing and soft moist mouth shutting out all else from his mind and senses. He pressed her hips to his face, the pleasure of her mouth and tongue and stroking hand agony. He shuddered, hips thrusting, a groan escaping as all the pleasure in the world focused and exploded where her lips held him, mouth warm and moist.

They lay there for a few moments, drained of passion, but not releasing each other. Slowly his breathing returned to normal and he stroked her buttocks and back as she lay above him. She slipped off and lay alongside, her face pressed against his chest.

"I love you very, very much," he whispered, putting his arms around her.

"I love you too," she said softly.

While they slept a shower passed, no thunder and lightning this time, only a light rain. The lawn mower in the back yard got wet and it would be a little more rusty by the time Walter mowed the back yard later that evening. Billy Tillman was also asleep. He had passed out in his room at his mother's house from too much wine and too much sun and brain cells that shut down so he wouldn't drink anymore that day or it might have killed him. His was not a restful sleep.

XXIII
The Wedding

The package from Myra arrived first. It contained the information Walter requested about his retirement account and the funds and income available to him. Myra added a personal note wishing him and his wife happiness. She asked for a picture of him and his bride if that were possible. He promised himself he would send photos of him and Nancy along with a letter trying to thank her for being such a good friend for so many years. Both a bank statement and a listing of his holdings with John Cramer arrived two days later. Walter went through it all, made a list of his possessions and probable income from the law firm, and that evening after the children had been put to bed he and Nancy sat at the kitchen table and talked about their future.

Walter went through his list quickly, giving values of stocks and bonds, cash on hand in his different bank accounts, and estimating the values of the house on Long Island and in Connecticut. He sounded much like he would at a meeting with a client in his law office going over a business account. Nancy interrupted only once. When he mentioned that his checking account at Cocoa Beach contained over one-hundred-thousand dollars she stopped him.

"You have over a hundred-thousand dollars in the bank here?" she asked, shocked. The figures Walter had been reading about money and property in New York or Connecticut was surprising to her but totally abstract. But the fact that he could walk three blocks to the bank and withdraw $112,000, in cash, any time he wanted struck her. This was real. Then when she realized the numbers he was speaking about, money he had and money he could get whenever he wanted, also became real.

"Why, yes," he said, stopping his accounting and looking up from the papers spread over the kitchen table. The astonished look on Nancy's face quickly reminded him she wasn't used to dealing with money in amounts this large. She was a waitress who lived on a small salary and tips. She lived from week to week and month to month and paid her bills and made do when money got tight and did what she could with what she had. And, she did a damn fine job of taking care of herself and three children by herself. He blushed.

"I put the money from the insurance company for the loss of *Windsong* and the other check from the fire in the Barnett account. I had also put some money in the account before *Windsong* sank to get her hauled and hull repaired."

Nancy's brow furrowed and her eyes squinted as she listened. She looked down at the papers. "You're rich," she said, a little bewildered.

Walter squirmed in his chair, scratched his head, and looked back at the table. He didn't consider himself rich, but to someone who had far less it might seem he were rich.

"I guess I accumulated things over time. No, I'm not rich. Not the way I think of rich, anyway. I guess I would say, with my income and all, that I'm comfortable."

He tried to smile and it faded when he saw Nancy still staring at him. He was embarrassed. They had never spoken about money. Maybe he was doing this all wrong.

Nancy's face began to relax and she smiled. "Comfortable," she said softly. Her smile widened and her dark eyes began to sparkle. "I think I like that, comfortable. I've never been comfortable. I think I'm going to enjoy comfortable."

She cocked her head, looking at him, white teeth showing behind her smile. "You're a comfortable man to be with. Why shouldn't you have comfortable money?"

Walter was relieved. "So, your not mad?"

"Mad? Why the hell should I be mad? The man I'm going to marry is rich. That's not supposed to make somebody mad."

She picked up a sheet of paper and looked at it with interest. There was a list of stocks held, number of shares and their estimated value per share, and bond amounts and maturity dates. It meant nothing to her. She put the paper back on the table. "Why didn't you tell me this before?"

He shrugged. When was he supposed to have told her and why and how?

"It didn't seem to matter much."

Nancy's head went back and she laughed with her deep, throaty laugh. She looked at him, eyes sparkling with merriment. "Having money only doesn't matter when you have it." She reached across the table and took his hands. "I'm glad you've got money. I'm glad *we've* got money. It'll make it easier for us and the kids. But you know, I'd have loved you even if you didn't have a dime. In fact, when I first met you, I didn't think you had a dime. I thought you were a boat bum without enough money to feed yourself."

"I know," he said, and squeezed her hands so hard it almost hurt. The love in his eyes said it all. She returned his grip.

That evening they set a wedding date. It would be in two and a half weeks. There was no reason to delay and that was the soonest Nancy thought they could have all of the arrangements made. She also agreed to quit her job at the restaurant.

She would leave as soon as a replacement could be found, which wouldn't be difficult. Walter stumbled for awhile before he brought up two other subjects that were important to him. He had a son and a daughter and he felt he should share with them some of what he had earned. He asked her if he could give them a portion of his possessions. Nancy told him to give whatever made him feel comfortable. She laughed when she said the word comfortable again.

The other thing he wanted to do was to adopt Nancy's children. Tears came to her eyes, and then she cried openly. What Walter wanted to do was not a gesture. He loved her children and they loved him. Not only was she getting a loving husband but they were getting a father, a true father, one who would love them as much as she did. She cried and he held her and that made her cry even harder. They were tears of happiness and gratefulness. Since Walter Marshall came into her life everything had changed for the better. She was a very, very lucky woman.

Walter was thinking back about that evening as he parked his new pickup in the parking lot of the Cocoa Beach Hilton. It was his wedding day and he was meeting Harold and Lynda and their spouses for brunch. He wouldn't be staying long. The wedding was at three that afternoon and he had to get back to Jerry's house to dress. He wasn't allowed to be in the house this morning. It belonged to Nancy and the other women who were attending the bride. He smiled to himself. He liked that. He had thought of it as *their* back yard. It was his and her house. And as soon as he could get the paper work completed and through the court system, Helen and Dixie and Little John would be their children. His children, whom he could love and care for and watch grow. But first he needed to complete an obligation he had with his other two children, his and Laura's children, whom he also loved.

They were sitting at a covered table near the pool, Harold and Winnifer and Lynda and George. George rose and shook his father's-in-law hand. "Congratulations, Dad," he said, giving a firm handshake and a smile. Walter looked at this bearded, and now graying man who had just called him Dad. He wasn't this man's Dad. He wasn't *that* old yet.

"Thank you, George. Hello everybody," Walter said, taking an empty seat. Quickly a waiter was at his side pouring coffee and prepared to take his order. He was sticking with just coffee this morning. His stomach had been doing flips since he woke up.

Good mornings and hellos went around the table. They had been talking about Walter, father and father-in-law, for over an hour before he arrived. The conversation had been strained. Each tried to be enthusiastic about the forthcoming marriage and it hadn't been easy. They had never met Nancy, knew nothing about her other than she had three children and was twenty-eight years old, and had helped Walter when he broke his leg. Each had reservations and doubts about an older man marrying such a young woman. But their doubts remained unspoken, with glances and overemphasized words occasionally escaping and expressing their true feelings.

George was the exception. His enthusiasm was real. He was glad to see his father-in-law looking so well and happy. It was beginning to annoy Lynda that her husband was so gleeful that a woman younger than she was would be taking her mother's place. She knew she was being resentful and was angry at herself for feeling that way. She was getting angry with her husband, and trying not to feel angry at this unknown Nancy Foch and her father. She was trying to be happy, kept a smile on her face, and held back from kicking her husband's shin under the table. That's exactly the way she felt. She wanted to give somebody, anybody, one good swift kick.

"You look good, Dad," Harold said, wiping his brow with

a handkerchief. He was wearing slacks, knitted shirt, and a sport jacket, too much clothing for Florida in October. Walter did look good. He was wearing a white short-sleeve polo shirt, white shorts, and white socks and tennis shoes. It set off his tan and good muscle tone. He'd had his hair cut the day before and it was so short it was almost a crew cut, the gray at the temples blending in with the sun-bleached hair that remained. He radiated health. "I feel good," he said, smiling. "If a little nervous."

Jokes were told about brides and grooms and wedding days, Harold and George giving anecdotes about their own weddings. They were all trying to keep it light, not knowing what else they should say, Harold and Lynda acting like teenagers with an adult parent whose behavior is embarrassing them in public. Walter could sense their feelings but there was little he could do about it now. Maybe after the wedding and he and Nancy were settled he would take a trip to New York and spend some time with Harold and Lynda and they could sort out years of accumulated emotions that they all held back. Maybe he would go to New York and do that, but he doubted it.

He reached into his back pocket and took out two long envelopes and handed one to Harold and one to Lynda. "There's been so little time that I haven't been able to speak with all of you as I would have liked." Walter paused for a second. "It's been like that most of our lives and I apologize."

When Harold and Lynda began to protest Walter held up his hand and stopped them. "No. It's true. I didn't spend as much time with you as I should have. I'm sorry about that now. I missed a lot by being so busy. Time goes by so quickly and before you know it kids have grown up and are adults and are off to school and then married and you can't go back and be the father that you should have. I don't know why I'm bringing this up. I didn't intend to. What I really want to say is that I love you all." He glanced around the table at each of them, "and I'm sorry if I haven't been as good a father to you as I could have been. That, and to say thank you for coming today. I know how hard it must have been to make arrangements so quickly and to have to leave the children and all. You could've brought them."

"No, Dad," Lynda said. "They would have been a distraction. It's your day and we wanted to be with you. The kids wouldn't have understood it anyway."

"What's this all about?" Harold asked, hefting the thick envelope his father had given him.

"Open it," Walter said.

Harold and Lynda tore open the envelopes. Each contained legal documents and Harold's also had a cashier's check in it. He looked at the check and let out a low whistle. Winnifer leaned over her husband's shoulder and quickly back to her father-in-law, eyebrows raised. The check was for fifty-thousand dollars and made out to her husband.

Lynda fumbled with the thick, legal documents she had taken out of her envelope. "What is all this?" she asked her father.

"It's the deed to the house in Huntington along with a limited power of attorney allowing you to transfer the title to whom you wish. There's an addendum there also for you to transfer or sell the cars and furniture and anything else on the property. It's yours. Keep it, sell it, do what you want."

Walter paused and looked at his son, a boy who had somehow grown into a man he barely knew. "If Harold wants something from the house, I hope you'll let him have what he wishes."

"But I don't understand," his daughter said, perplexed. "What are you trying to do, give us your house?"

"I'm not trying to, I've done it. The house is yours along with everything in it. There's a few things I'd like to keep, photos, my college diplomas, and such. It won't be much. I'll make a list and if you would you can ship it down to me."

Walter looked at his son and Winnifer. "I gave you the place in Connecticut. You seemed to like it there when you visited. I knew you wouldn't want to live in Huntington and have to commute every day. I must have heard you say that a hundred times. You have the same type of limited power of attorney as your sister. You can keep the place or sell it or do whatever you want. It's yours."

Harold still held the check from the envelope. Walter nodded to it. "I tried to be fair in balancing out the value of the two places. The house and property in Connecticut isn't worth what the house in Huntington is so I included the fifty-thousand to balance it all out. That should make it of equal value." Walter looked from his son to daughter. "I tried to be fair," he said again.

"But, but you can't do this, Dad. It's your home." Lynda said, her distress beginning to show.

He took her hand and squeezed it gently. "No, Honey, it's *your* house now. My home is here."

Harold had been shuffling through the papers, noticing the neat work and the meticulous care that had gone into the legal documents. "Jeez," he said, not thinking how his words might affect the others, the part of him that was a lawyer speaking. "I feel like I'm in a divorce settlement or reading a will."

Lynda's lower lip began to quiver and then she burst into tears, covering her face in her hands. Immediately, her husband put his arm around her and tried to comfort her.

"Damn," her brother said, wanting to bite his tongue. "I didn't mean it like that. I only meant... well..." and he was stuck for words.

The division of property *had* been much like a divorce or a death. Harold spread his arms, an apology written all over his face as he looked to his father. Walter smiled at him a little and nodded to show that he understood.

In a way his son was right. This wasn't a divorce; Walter

would do all he could to spend time with his children and grandchildren, but in a way it was much like a death. He had been dying there in Huntington, dying a slow death of boredom and uselessness. Here in Cocoa Beach he found a new life, a new beginning, and a new family. After returning to New York and thinking about it he knew there was no way he could mix the two. His life in New York had ended, a death in a way, and he was finishing the process that death brings with the division of property. He hadn't thought about it this way or planned it, but there was truth in his son's words.

"I'm sorry, Dad," Lynda said, blowing her nose with a handkerchief her husband gave her. "I didn't mean to become a cry-baby on your wedding day." She blew again and tried to smile, another tear escaping. "You know how I am at weddings. I always cry."

"I'm sorry too," Walter said. "I didn't mean to upset you. It's just that we all get to meet together so rarely that I thought this would be an opportune time to settle all of this. Maybe I should have waited till later."

"It's my fault. Dad. Me and my big mouth. I'm sorry, Lynda," Harold said. "I didn't mean anything by what I said." He patted his sister's hand. She kept a smile frozen on her face, wiping away the last tear.

Harold looked at Walter. "Thanks, Dad. This is very generous of you."

"Me too, Dad," Lynda said, sniffling once. "I feel kind of cheap. I brought you a silver tea service as a wedding gift and you give me a house full of... full of," and Lynda couldn't finish the sentence. She was going to cry again but stopped herself by locking a stiff smile back on her face. She felt as though she were losing her father forever, her last parent, and although she knew this wasn't really true she couldn't help feeling that way anyway.

Walter looked at his watch. It was getting late. He had to

get over to Jerry's and get dressed. Time was flying. He stood and went to his daughter and hugged her. "I love you," he whispered, patting her back. He could feel a tear on his cheek. His daughter didn't answer, words not coming. She patted his back and rubbed, her hands speaking for her.

He walked to his son and put his hand on Harold's shoulder and squeezed. His son looked up at him. "Good luck, Dad," he said, a little choked, in a rare show of emotion.

Walter patted his shoulder. He could feel tears coming to his own eyes. He looked around the table but said nothing, turned and left. All that needed to be said had been said.

The house on Manatee Street was ready. A large canopy covered much of the back yard. Tables and chairs were stacked nearby to be set up as soon as the ceremony was completed.

To one side stood a long table, its white table cloth flapping in the breeze, covered platters piled with food for the reception that was soon to follow. A flatbed truck was on the other side of the yard, its edges trimmed in white crepé and wedding decorations. Ice-covered kegs of beer lined one side of the flatbed and a band had set up instruments and amplifiers. Booms, screeches, and chords came blasting out of large speakers as the band adjusted the equipment and tuned their instruments. The beer kegs were already in use as a crowd of over two hundred waited for it all to begin. A make-shift bar serving mixed drinks was packed three deep as two volunteer bartenders poured as quickly as they could.

Lynda was feeling better now. Several stiff drinks helped settle her as she waited with her husband and Harold and Winnifer to watch her father be married. They stood in a small cluster sipping drinks and saying little as the other guests milled about greeting each other, talking and laughing. The crowd was the usual mix of Nancy's friends, and now some of them Walter's friends, and many were boisterous. Most were dressed semi-formally, there were a few gowns and a tuxedo here and there, but quite a few were dressed in shorts and shirts. There were even several in bathing suits, the last ones to get the word about the wedding, and they had come from the beach to join the celebration.

Lynda saw her father and another man approach the crowd from the street. Both were dressed in tuxedos and wearing boutonnieres. The man with her father was younger, taller, and huskier but there was no doubt as to who was better looking. Lynda had accepted as a matter of course that her father was good looking but on seeing him now she realized how truly handsome he was. Both men stopped at the edge of the crowd and looked around. It was obvious they didn't know what they were supposed to do next. Lynda waved and called. Eventually he spotted her, smiled, and he and his companion approached. He received handshakes and back slaps as he came through the throng.

"Hi," Walter said, kissing his daughter's cheek.

"Hi yourself. You look beautiful, Dad."

Winnifer stepped forward and also kissed her father-in-law cheek to cheek. She looked over at Lynda and winked. "Maybe I married the wrong Marshall," she said, eyeing Walter appreciatively. They all laughed.

Walter introduced Jerry to everyone and by the time he completed this there was a drum roll from the flatbed bandstand. After a squeak and a squeal a booming voice came over the large speakers.

"Ladies and gentlemen," the master of ceremonies said. It was the bar owner, Nancy's neighbor. "Please, let me have your attention. We're about to begin so please let's everybody settle down. First, we need the groom. Has anybody seen the groom? Did he bother to come today?" the M.C. joked.

There was some laughter and some people near Walter

pointed at him, whistling and yelling. He blushed. He hated attention.

"Oh, there you are," the M.C. said, pointing. "Would you please go under the tent? Your bride will be coming to you soon." The M.C. leered exaggeratedly. "If you know what I mean," he said to the crowd. There was some snickering and spotty laughter.

Walter and Jerry began working their way through the crowd toward the canopy. He received much back slapping and congratulations as he disappeared into the mass of people. Again there was a drum roll.

"Ladies and gentlemen," the M.C. intoned again, sounding much like an announcer at a prize fight. "Would you please open a path for the bridal party as they come down the, er, aisle so that the bride can get to her groom?"

The M.C. gave a signal and the drummer gave another roll, longer and louder this time.

"Are we ready?" the M.C. asked, looking toward the house. There were some yells from the crowd that they were ready. The drum continued to roll and then the M.C. saw a signal. He raised his hand and dropped it. The drum roll stopped.

A violinist picked up his violin and an accordionist ran his fingers silently over his keyboard. Two guitarists stood poised, fingers over strings. The drummer held his sticks high, watching the M.C.'s back, waiting for the signal. The M.C. raised his hand again. The band began to play the "Wedding March" and all eyes turned to where the M.C. had been looking. The band played for several seconds before anything happened and then two girls came from behind the building and began walking slowly alongside the house to the back yard.

Dixie was supposed to come first and Helen was to follow but on seeing the mob and the commotion Dixie had been too frightened to walk alone. Helen took her hand and she and her sister walked together, hand in hand, carrying their little bouquets. They wore knee-length white dresses covered with lace and veils hung from tiaras to waists. Cameras flashed and people elbowed their way to get a better view. Dixie's dark eyes wandered from face to face as an aisle opened for them to pass to the canopy. Small, black ringlets bobbed as Dixie strode stiff-legged beside her sister.

Helen walked beside Dixie smiling and proud. Helen liked being the center of attention and was enjoying this. She walked as slowly as she could and still be moving, looking right and left, granting those individuals she recognized an extra special smile and nod. A queen had never carried it off any better. Her blond hair framed her face and large curls swayed as she strutted through the path opening before her.

Next to appear was Bertha, Nancy's best friend and neighbor. She wore a powder blue gown that reached the grass. Bertha looked serious as she walked, slowly, eyes straight ahead, bouquet cradled in her arms. Lynda groaned when she saw her, thinking this was the bride. Bertha looked older than twenty-eight, and about eighty pounds overweight. Much of this was hidden under the flowing gown. She moved in the slow rhythm of the "Wedding March" as the band played.

Nancy appeared and stumbled, her heel catching a clump of grass. She regained her balance and composure and began walking. She wore a pale blue gown, so light it was almost white. A pearl tiara held a lace veil that reached the grass and trailed behind. The hairdresser had fixed her hair so it fell in golden locks to her shoulders. The graceful gown did nothing to hide her shapely figure. Though she felt nervous and awkward she walked gracefully, head high, eyes straight ahead, looking first at Bertha's back and then on seeing Walter waiting with a look of love, her eyes locked on his and she smiled and came slowly to him.

There was an audible intake of breath from Lynda when she saw Nancy for the first time.

"My God!" Winnifer whispered. "She's beautiful!"

The crowd was silent as Nancy passed, all eyes following. She had been pretty when she had been married the first time, and there were some present who had been there also, but now, ten years later, she had matured into a woman of beauty. Harold unconsciously let out a low whistle. He couldn't believe what he was seeing. Nancy, eyes sparkling with love, skin aglow with vitality and excitement, hair lovelier than the jewels and lace flowing from it, figure needing no gown to help her form, silently and unseeingly walked past Harold to his father. He glanced at his wife and Winnifer at him. It was all so unbelievable! His father's new wife was one of the most beautiful women Harold had ever seen.

Nancy reached Walter's side and they stood together, Jerry on Walter's right and Bertha and the two girls on Nancy's left. A woman with coiffured grey hair and wearing a business suit stepped up on a milk crate that had been covered with a white sheet. She tottered for a second, a little wobbly from the cocktails she had been drinking with her constituents this afternoon. Carol Hillman was the mayor of Cocoa Beach and a justice of the peace. She had gladly agreed to perform the marriage ceremony. This was an election year and election day was only a few weeks off. A great many Cocoa Beach residents were in the audience and this was a fine opportunity to do some politicking. The band stopped and the mayor cleared her throat and tried to focus on the booklet she held. She looked up at the audience, gave her best election year smile, and began the ceremony.

XXIV
Tom Watson

When Tom Watson saw Walter Marshall's office he almost laughed out loud. Walter's law office was located in a small mall. There were about a dozen one-story stores offering everything from used clothing to accounting. There was a large parking lot in front and for some reason, whether it was the raised sidewalk and the wooden facade of the stores or the hitching post in front of the leather crafts shop, it reminded Watson of the Wild West days. The mall would have fit perfectly in Tuscon. Fords, Chevys, and Toyotas were parked where horses and wagons would have been just as appropriate. It was a place where a young lawyer fresh out of law school might start but didn't seem a fitting place for a prominent New York attorney, sixty years old, would be setting up a new practice.

A wrought-iron arm extended from above Walter's office door and from it hung a hand-carved sign with his name and "Lawyer" beneath. The sign was swinging and squeaking as Watson stood on the sidewalk, admiring the careful workmanship and the intricate carving that could only be seen close up.

The sign was interesting but what really caught his eye was the large front window. WALTER MARSHALL, ATTORNEY-AT-LAW, was printed in bright gold lettering and then the eye was drawn to the delicately painted, transparent scene covering the rest of the window. Whoever did the lettering must have also been an artist, or an aspiring artist in any case, and Walter had let him or her use the office window as a canvas. The scene was of the ocean and the sky. The horizon was beneath the lettering, the ocean below and the sky above. The sea was filled with scores of marine life, from whales and shark to tiny, colorful tropical fish. Above the horizon were sky, cloud, sun, and dozens of vari-colored birds in flight. It took someone a great deal of time and effort. In its own way it was beautiful, but it was the oddest thing he had ever seen for an attorney to have as he presented himself to the public.

He entered the air conditioned waiting room. The cool air felt good. He left New York that morning, catching one of the earliest flights, and the temperature had been in the teens. Here the temperature was eighty degrees and expected to become warmer by afternoon. It was the kind of day the Florida Chamber of Commerce loved to advertise for early January. The reflected light coming through the multi-colored front window gave the waiting room a warm glow. Several people sat on each side of the office.

Watson walked to the reception desk, more like a round counter, and approached a large, very black woman. She wore a brightly colored dress wrapped around her body and great breasts, topped by a turban of matching cloth. Large, shiny jewelry hung from her ears and chains of costume necklaces and bracelets sparkled as she typed. Her attention was on her work, not seeing him enter. They were at eye level, though she was sitting. This was a very large woman with skin that was glossy ebony, a perfect background for her bright dress and sparkling jewelry.

When he stopped at the counter, she glanced up, immediately observing his expensive suit, age, and assured posture. He was not one of the usual clients. He obviously had money. Maybe Mister Marshall would get paid for a change. She gave this impressive gentleman her warmest smile, white teeth gleaming.

"Good morning," she said in a lilting accent that was unfamiliar to him.

"Good morning," Watson responded to this black Amazon. "I was hoping I could see Mister Marshall."

The receptionist nodded, noticing the gentleman's upper-class speech. "Do you have an appointment?" she asked, knowing he didn't. The appointment book was empty for the day. Their clients rarely called, usually just walking in when things had become a crisis, and as often as not they didn't return when an appointment was arranged. She sometimes wondered why she bothered trying to keep track. No one but her seemed to care.

"No. I don't," Watson said apologetically. "But I was hoping I might see him for just a moment. I'm Tom Watson. If you'll let him know I'm here, I'm sure he'll want to see me as soon as he can."

Janette Magando had no idea who Tom Watson was, but she was sure Mister Marshall would want to see him. The problem was that Mister Marshall had gone on some errand or other and she didn't know when he would be back. If he was a potential client she certainly didn't want him to get away. They needed someone who could pay his bill.

"I'm so sorry," Janette said softly. "But Mister Marshall had to leave the office for a moment. I expect him to be returning any second. Perhaps you can wait? I'm sure he'll see you as soon as he returns, which shouldn't be long at all."

Watson had known this might happen when he decided to come unannounced. He wanted to see what was really going on with his protegé and the best way to do that was to arrive unexpectedly. Watson was accustomed to lawyers making extensive preparations for a visit from him, although Walter never had to bother with that, and it annoyed him when he felt that things were being hidden from him.

"You say you expect Mister Marshall will be in shortly?" Watson asked, knowing he would wait. He'd made a special trip to Cocoa Beach to see if he couldn't talk Walter into returning to the firm. He wanted him back. He had planned on him being the next full partner and eventually to take his place as accepted leader of the firm. He still couldn't believe Walter was retiring. In fact, he insisted he stay on full salary until he, Tom Watson, could get all of this straightened out and Walter back at work where he belonged. But this couldn't go on forever. There was a Board Meeting next week and a decision would have to be made by then.

"I'm sure he'll be right back," Janette lied sweetly. "May I get you something cold to drink?"

He was thirsty now that the Amazon mentioned it. It had been a long morning and a lot of traveling. "Something cold will do."

"Coke?" Janette asked, rising from her seat. Watson watched her unfold until the top of her turban was almost two feet higher than his head. Where could Walter have found such a woman?

Watson usually preferred freshly squeezed juice. "A Coke would be fine."

He chose a seat by the door where there was a small table. Janette brought him a glass with some ice and a can of Coke. She placed the drink on the little corner table and returned to her typing. He took a sip of the drink. It was sweet and cold, better than he remembered. It was years since he drank canned soda.

Watson glanced at the wicker furniture, strange wall decorations, wooden carvings of brightly painted black peasants, and again to the giant, black receptionist. Something about it was vaguely familiar and he let his mind wander until he located its "file," as he called it. He prided himself in forgetting very little but it was taking longer than usual for him to recall the memory this room keyed. Then it came to him. It had been over forty years ago. That's why it had taken him so long. Port-au-Prince. That was the place. He had spent two days there on a business trip and had never been back since, thank God. A country that poor was not his cup of tea. Port-au-Prince, Haiti. It made him feel good that his memory was as keen as ever.

He observed the other people waiting. There was a middle-aged black couple sitting to the right, both dressed in clean but worn clothes. The woman held a package in her lap, the package wrapped in gift paper that was twisted at the top and a tiny bow attached. The man and woman sat silently and without movement, waiting patiently, eyes locked on the new, inexpensive carpeting.

To his left two men waited, an empty chair between. The younger of the two smoked nervously, hand going back and forth to an ash tray to flick , and back for another puff. His face showed why he was probably sitting in an attorney's office. His left eye was swollen and discolored and lower lip split and protruding. Scabs covered the knuckles of both hands. He wondered if he had won the fight or lost. Whether he had won or not, the outcome of the brawl was the man needed a lawyer.

The second man waiting to see Walter Marshall, Attorney at Law, was the type of person Watson saw only on television news. He was a street person and what he was doing in Walter's law office, Watson couldn't imagine. The man wore worn shower shoes, dirty toes protruding, a pair of soiled shorts that looked two sizes too large, and a dirty and torn short-sleeve shirt that may have been white at one time. He hadn't shaved for more than a week and Watson was glad he wasn't sitting near the man. He was sure the street bum would smell. Was this Walter Marshall's new client list? What in the world was he doing here?

The door opened and someone entered. It took him a moment to recognize Walter in tan shorts and a flowery shirt like tourists seemed to prefer. His bare feet were in scuffed tennis shoes. He certainly didn't look dressed for work. A strange thing happened when the others saw it was Walter who entered. They all stood, even the street bum managing to pull himself out of his chair. Watson had seen this happen automatically in only two other places. People stood out of respect when a presiding judge entered a court room and in the military subordinates stood when an officer entered a room. Watson remained seated, watching.

The middle-aged black woman stepped forward carrying her package. The man followed, staying a step behind. The woman offered the package to Walter.

"Thank you Mister Marshall for getting my Willie out of jail," the woman said, glancing over her shoulder to be sure Willie was close by.

"You're welcome." Walter winked at Willie. He answered with a big smile.

"He won't be gettin' in any more trouble. I promise. I'll make sure of that." She looked over her shoulder again, a stern expression showing her meaning. Willie's smile faded.

"I'm sure he won't. Willie's getting a little old for such foolishness, right?"

Willie shuffled his feet, looked down at the floor, and nodded.

"Darn right, Mister Marshall. And I'll see to it too." She wet her lips with a pink tongue before she went on. "I brung you some cookies I baked this morning special. We don't have no money to give you now, Mister Marshall, but as soon as Willie's back at work I'll come by and bring you what I can so's we pay up on our bill."

Walter held the package of cookies awkwardly. He placed it on the counter. The receptionist glanced at the home-made cookies and then at the couple, frowning. It was obvious this was not the payment she preferred. She saw the bills that came in every day.

The woman followed Walter to the counter and took his hand in both of hers. When she spoke it was softly and with sincerity. "I want to thank you, Mister Marshall, for all you done. I know you did more than you had to, takin' personal responsibility for Willie and all."

"That's okay, Mrs. Williams. Willie made a mistake," Walter said, and looked over at him, "but I'm sure nothing like this will happen again."

The woman still held Walter's hand, as if there were more she wanted to say. Then she released him and left, Willie trailing behind.

"Someone waiting to see you," the receptionist said to Walter. As Walter turned in his direction, he rose and walked toward him, hand extended.

"I'm sorry to come unannounced," Watson said, shaking Walter's hand heartily. Walter's look of surprise changed to a grin.

"Hello, Tom. What a surprise! What are you doing here?"

"Oh," Watson said, nonchalantly, "I had to come down to Orlando to see someone and I thought since I was in the neighborhood I'd drop by and see how you were doing." The only reason Watson had taken the trip to Florida was to get Walter Marshall back at work with the firm, but he wasn't going to tell him that. Not as an opening. He would wait for the right moment and then use his considerable powers of persuasion.

"Good! I'm glad to see you. I hope you haven't been waiting to long."

"Not at all. It gave me time to admire your office decor."

Walter gave the room a quick glance. Janette Magando said she wanted to decorate the waiting room and he let her. It had taken him a while to get used to it, but he had grown to like this unusual room. Each carving or decorative wall piece was a minor work of art that its creator had spent much time on.

"I can thank Janette for all of this. She's the one who did it. Janette, I'd like you to meet Tom Watson. He's my old boss and good friend from New York."

Watson bowed courteously to Janette. "How do you do?" he said formally. He couldn't remember ever having been introduced to a receptionist before. An office worker's status was so low that no attorney ever bothered.

Janette Magando nodded to Watson, her intelligent, dark eyes observing him. "It's a pleasure, Mister Watson," she said, her song-like accent very pronounced.

"Come to my office," Walter said, leading the way toward the back of the remodeled store. They walked a few steps down a narrow hall and turned into his office. He left the door open.

Walter sat behind a desk littered with stacked files and papers. It was obvious he had more work than he could handle. Watson sat on a simple wooden chair. There was no soft, heavily padded leather seats in this office. It was also about one-fifth the size that Walter had waiting for him in New York.

"You're looking very well, Tom," Walter said, his pleasure at seeing his old friend and mentor obvious.

"And so do you," Watson said, and added, "Extraordinarily well."

There was no doubt about it. Walter had changed considerably, and Watson had to admit, physically at least, it was a change for the better. Besides his tan and shorter hair cut, and the casual clothes, he looked different. He looked younger. The deep lines on his forehead and around his eyes were mostly gone and those that remained had become laugh wrinkles rather than worry lines. His face was relaxed, open, eyes clear and active. There was an energy now, a lightness of step. It had been only eight months since he had last seen Walter but in that time there had been a transformation.

"I feel good, Tom. Ever since I arrived here," Walter thought for a second, scratching at the short hair at the top of his head, "there've been a lot of changes in my life. All for the better, I might add."

"Sometimes change is good for people," Watson agreed. "But that doesn't mean you have to give up everything you've worked for your whole life."

"I'm not sure I understand what you mean, Tom," Walter said, although he did. Tom Watson was talking about Wheel, Kedder and Matthews. The firm was the center of Tom's existence and everything he did or said would have the firm as its reference point.

"I'm talking about your place with us." Watson leaned forward on the hard chair. "You're needed there. I know we never talked about it openly, but I thought it was understood between us that you would soon be a partner. It's guaranteed. There's a board meeting next week and I can bring it up then."

What Walter had been working toward all of his life was being offered to him on a silver platter, more a gold platter. His income would soar if he accepted what his old friend was offering. He had to look away from a friend so earnestly trying to persuade him.

"Thank you, Tom. That's a wonderful offer but you see, my place is here."

"Here?" Watson looked left and right at the cramped, unadorned office and back at the man he planned on taking over as leader of the firm. "But I don't understand. Maybe I'm not making myself clear. I've never talked to you about this and maybe I should have. You know I never had children, never had a son, and I always felt that you, in a way—" Watson stopped and pressed his lips together. It was hard for him to speak about his personal life and feelings. "You know what I mean. I felt sure you would be there when it was time for me to step aside. Do you know what I'm saying? Do you know how much wealth and even a certain amount of power there is? You'll be in a position where you can help make decisions that affect the whole country. Think of the good you could do."

Before Walter could answer, and the only answer he could think of was "No thank you," Janette called from the front office.

"There's a call for you. Judge Lipscomb," Janette yelled through the open door. To explain her interruption of an important meeting she added, "He says it's important."

Walter was relieved by the interruption. He hated having to turn down Tom when the man was offering what he considered the greatest of all gifts. He had hoped to avoid this when he wrote the letter of resignation and mailed in all the retirement forms.

"We've been waiting for weeks for the man to come and install our intercom," he told Watson. "Nothing happens very fast here. I have to keep reminding myself that I'm still in the South. Excuse me. This shouldn't take very long."

Walter picked up the phone. Watson stepped away from his desk, giving him as much privacy as he could in the tiny office.

Watson's eyes wandered over the framed pictures and certificates on the walls. Walter's college diplomas were there along with his membership certificate in the Florida Bar Association. When Walter was still a young attorney with the firm he had represented a client who needed an attorney to represent him in Florida on occasion. He had been assigned the task and he joined the Florida Bar to do so. For all these years Wheel, Kedder and Matthews payed his annual dues and he'd remained a member in good standing. He'd had to come here rarely but it certainly made it easy for him to set up practice. All he needed to do was hang out his shingle. That, and give up millions of dollars in future earnings. Watson half listened to Walter's one-sided phone conversation. It seemed a judge had called to confer about whether or not to release a young man from jail. Odd that a judge would call a defense attorney about a case. Odder still since Walter had been in practice locally for such a short period. He was an effective attorney. There was no doubt about that. Watson had known that right from the start, years ago. He'd been excellent at business law. Why wouldn't he be just as good at criminal law? In a way he envied Walter. Watson enjoyed the times he'd spent doing battle in a courtroom. It was good to use one's wits and knowledge of the law against another attorney who was trying to defeat you. He was sorry he hadn't been able to do more of it. But there was no money in it. No real money. And more often than not while defending a client in a criminal case, the defense lost. And Watson did not like to lose.

He looked at the pictures Walter selected to place on one wall. There were photos of his son and daughter and their families. Watson had met the son and daughter a couple of times at dinners given by the firm. The years passed quickly and the young man and woman were now mature adults with children of their own. Laura's picture was there also. She had been about thirty-five years old when this was taken. She was a good-looking woman and as far as he knew she had been a good wife to him.

Next to the photos of his family was a large frame containing a collage of snap-shots. There were pictures of three children, two girls and a boy, one of the girls dark-skinned, the others fair. There was a photo taken of Walter and his bride on their wedding day, the bride young and beautiful in her wedding gown. He peered more closely. She was very pretty, and young. How could they have met? What kind of relationship would they have with such a wide age difference? Would it all come apart once the strains of living together put pressure on the marriage? Could it all end in six months and Walter's future thrown to the winds for no reason? Only time would tell and Watson was running out of time.

There were two other things mounted on the wall, both a little unusual. A shelf had been built and on it sat a large bell polished to a high gloss and Watson could see his reflection clearly. Inscribed was the word *Windsong* and the year 1926 below. Next to this was a plaque about one foot wide and three feet long. A parchment-like paper sealed in a thick coat of plastic held a proclamation followed by scores of signatures. He read the proclamation written in old English script. It stated that Walter Marshall was a deacon of the Universal Church of God. There were two rows of signatures beneath.

"I'm sorry I took so long," Walter said.

"It's lunchtime," Janette announced, filling the open door. She was looking at Walter meaningfully. If she didn't get him out of his office he would continue to work and miss lunch, and in a little while Nancy would be calling, worried about him. Janette made it her duty to get her boss home for lunch even if she had to pick him up and put him outside the building, which she was very capable of doing. Her expression showed her determination. As far as Janette was concerned, no client was more important than Nancy having her husband home when he was expected.

Walter gave Watson a lopsided grin. "I guess it's time for lunch. You'll join me won't you? I'd love for you to meet Nancy."

"I don't want to impose."

"It's no imposition, I assure you. Nancy would love to have you." Walter stood, and on seeing her boss was actually going to leave, Janette disappeared.

"I didn't mean to disrupt anything," Watson said.

Walter chuckled. "You won't be disrupting anything, that's for sure. The house is a mess. We're having an addition put on and Nancy's feeding half the construction workers in Cocoa Beach anyway. I assure you, one more won't mean a thing. Besides, I'd like you two to meet."

"I'd like to meet her, too." Tom Watson definitely wanted to meet the woman who had caused him to end a career with what he felt was the greatest law firm in America and, therefore, the world.

"Let's go out the back way," Walter said at the door. "There's always a crowd in the waiting room. I'll get to them as soon as I can."

They turned left at the door and in a few steps Walter opened a door to a storage room. Boxes filled with hymnals and Bibles were stacked in the stuffy room along with three pews and a partially completed stained-glass window. He unlocked the back door and they stepped out into bright sunshine.

"I forgot. I usually walk to work. Did you want to take your car?" Walter asked.

"Is it far?" Watson could feel the sun beating down on his skin.

"About three blocks. We'll drive if you like."

"Let's walk. I can use the exercise."

By the time they reached the house Watson had removed his jacket and loosened his tie. Perspiration dotted his forehead and he dabbed at it with a monogrammed silk handkerchief. Walter was unaffected by the warm January sun. He strode along easily, keeping his pace slow so Watson could keep up.

There was a great deal of activity going on at the house. Men stood on scaffolds laying the last row of concrete block on the addition that would double the size of the house. Others were on the roof stacking lumber or hammering. Walter didn't go to the front door, instead he walked past the new construction, admiring the neat work of the masons.

"Hey, Deacon," one of the men on the roof called and waved. Others joined in and he waved to each, smiling.

He led Watson to the back yard where under a large water oak two tables had been set for lunch. Walter walked to the picnic table where a little girl sat watching the men work. Her eyes shifted to Walter and his friend as they approached. Watson recognized her as the dark-skinned girl in the photo in the office. When Walter neared she raised her arms and he picked her up and hugged her, giving her a noisy kiss. "Where's your mother?" he asked.

"She's making lunch. We get potato chips today," Dixie said happily.

Walter sat her on the bench. "This is Dixie," he said. "Dixie, this is my friend Mister Watson."

Dixie nodded gravely. "Hello," she said softly.

"How do you do?"

A screen door slammed and Nancy came out carrying pitchers of ice and lemonade.

Little John waddled behind dragging his giant toy bottle.

She put one of the pitchers on a make-shift table on saw horses that had been set up for the construction workers and brought the other to the picnic table. She came to Walter and stood on her tip toes and kissed his cheek.

"Good. You're home," she said. "Everything's ready."

"I brought a friend. This is Tom Watson." Watson put his jacket on and straightened his tie. He bowed to the new Mrs. Marshall. "How do you do?"

"Tom Watson from New York?" she asked.

"The same," Watson said, smiling. "It's nice meeting you. Walter has talked a lot about you."

"All good I hope." Nancy looked at Walter, her eyes sparkling.

"Oh, yes. All good."

"Is it lunch time yet?" Someone called from the roof.

Nancy waved for the men to come down. "Come and get it!" There were hoops and yells as men scrambled down ladders and scaffolds.

"I'm sorry, Mister Watson." Nancy said, making a place for him at the table. "I didn't make anything special. Just sandwiches and snacks."

"This will be fine," Watson said, sitting on the bench. "I'm sorry to intrude like this."

Nancy laughed, her deep, throaty laugh. "It's no intrusion. This place is a mad house. I can't wait until all the work is done."

Walter sat opposite Watson. As soon as he took a seat Dixie climbed onto his lap. Seeing this, Little John climbed onto Walter's other leg. He hugged them both and kissed the top of each head. If Helen hadn't been at school, she too would be trying to get her share of attention.

Nancy lifted Little John off his lap. "Dixie, let your father eat." Reluctantly, Dixie wiggled off. She spotted a bowl of potato chips and dug in. Walter passed a platter of sandwiches to Watson.

"Georgia Schmidt called," Nancy said. She was still standing near Walter, watching him enjoy his sandwich.

"Oh? What about?" he asked, chewing a sandwich and taking a handful of potato chips.

"They asked a favor." Nancy poured iced lemonade for everyone. "You know they got married a couple of weeks ago," Nancy said, smoothing the table cloth around Walter's plate. "It was at the courthouse. She and Wendell were wondering, well, if you would bless their marriage."

"Me?" Walter asked, pointing to himself.

"You're their Deacon now."

"But I don't know anything about blessing people. What am I supposed to do? I only became a deacon because they said they needed someone to sign for their mail."

Walter looked over at Watson. "Some people started a little church in a store down the mall from my office," he said, explaining what he and Nancy were talking about. "Since my office is always open, a church member asked if I would accept their mail and I agreed." He shrugged. "It was no big deal. And then they needed someone to sign for stuff they ordered. I was willing to go along with that, too. They have no pastor or church officers, so when they needed a church representative they asked me if I would be a deacon so I could represent them and sign for the church to open accounts at various places so they could order things by mail or phone. I never expected it to become such a big deal."

He looked at Nancy. "Aren't they supposed to have a visiting pastor come and preach this Sunday? Can't he do it?"

"They don't want him. They want you."

"But I'm not a minister. What am I supposed to do?"

Nancy ran her fingers through Walter's hair, stroking him. "Just be yourself," she said, softly. "They've written a ceremony and all you'll have to do is read it. It'll be nice. They want to have a candlelight ceremony this Friday night, if you're willing. It would mean a lot to them."

Walter sighed, a signal of surrender. He shook his head slowly in wonder. "What time?"

"They thought nine o'clock would be good."

He took a bite of his sandwich and slowly chewed, staring at the rippling water of the canal, deep in thought. He nodded slightly, saying yes to whatever he was thinking. Nancy still stroked his head, looking down at him, her eyes filled with love. Unconsciously, he put his arm around her legs, his hand resting on her thigh beneath her shorts. The men at the other table were loudly talking and joking, but the noise didn't penetrate the peace at the picnic table. The mutual affection, the intimacy, that Walter and Nancy were sharing made Watson look away.

Nancy didn't sit and eat but went from table to table making sure everyone had what they needed. Watson watched her, admiring her figure and the energetic, happy way she moved. While she was at his table, he noticed the bulge of her abdomen and hips that were beginning to swell. The top button of her shorts was threatening to pull free from the strain of an expanding midsection. He glanced over at Walter who had been watching him. Walter blushed deeply. Watson almost choked on his sandwich. He took a sip of cold lemonade. Nancy Marshall was pregnant with Walter's baby! How about that!

Walter and Tom Watson walked back to his office in silence. They reached his rental car when Watson put out his hand and they shook. "I'm going to have to take you off payroll."

"I couldn't understand why I was still drawing my salary. I sent my papers in months ago. I even called payroll to see if there were a mistake."

"There was no mistake," Watson said. "I never believed you would leave us. I'm still not sure I believe it. Can't you take your family back with you? Why can't you continue your career?"

"My place is here now," Walter said with finality.

Watson got in his car and rolled down the window and started the engine to get the air conditioning going. The sun made the interior of the car an oven. "I'll stay in touch."

"Please, Tom, do that. And... thanks for everything."

"You don't have to thank me for anything, Walter. I didn't even get you a wedding gift. Good luck. I'll be in touch with you soon."

Watson began the long drive back to Orlando Airport. He couldn't put Walter out of his mind. He thought about his oddball office and the Amazonian receptionist who so obviously cared about him. He thought about Walter's new clients, too poor to afford an attorney or another attorney's rejects. He thought about those two children who fought for a place in his lap so they could get hugs. And he thought about Nancy—a beautiful woman that Nancy—and the love that was there and a baby on the way.

He laughed out loud. "He's a Goddamn deacon," he said, laughing again. He'd begun talking to himself more and more lately when he was alone. "He's a deacon and he doesn't even know what a deacon is! Blessing people. That's something."

He thought about Walter's law practice again. He didn't want to lose him completely. He would put him on a retainer and Walter could represent Wheel, Kedder and Matthews in Florida. That would work and he wouldn't have any trouble getting it approved by the board. Walter had a lot of friends on the board, and besides that, he was a damn fine attorney. The retainer fee would be more than enough to cover the cost of the oddball practice he had started. Between the retainer fee and what he'll draw on retirement he ought to live comfortably. He'd never get rich. By God, he was getting paid in cookies! No, he would never get rich but Tom Watson could see to it that he would at least live comfortably.

Watson laughed aloud again. "He did it! By God, the man did it! He's got a second shot at it. He's starting all over again. That lucky son-of-a-bitch!" Watson laughed so hard that his sides began to hurt. He hadn't laughed like that in a long, long time. He caught his breath before he spoke again. "I wonder how he pulled it off?"

Watson thought for a moment. "He went on vacation." Watson thought some more. "He bought a boat. That was it. He bought that boat and that started it all. What was the name of the boat again?" Watson asked himself. He smiled. He remembered. He was proud of the fact that he could recall even minor details when he wanted to.

"*Windsong*. That was it. *Windsong!*"